It's the end of civilization, but the show must go on.

The Loyale Traveling Circus and Menagerie is in turmoil. During their ocean voyage from British India to Boston, someone murdered their ringmaster. The killer must be one of their own. Unfortunately, that is the least of their problems.

While they were at sea, an aetheric calamity sent a wave of death rolling across the world. In post-Civil War America, a third of the population died outright, and many of the survivors suffer strange nervous symptoms that are steadily increasing in severity. Basic technology is also rendered dangerously unstable by the disaster. The circus members find themselves traveling through the collapse of civilization. In such desperate times, what use is a circus?

If they can defend themselves against the starving populace, if they can outwit and outperform the political factions that have seized power, if they can fight off the ravening monstrosities born of the aether storm ... they just might find the answer.

A Circus of Brass and Bone

~* * *~

Abra SW

Bimulous Books | Minneapolis

~ * ~

A Circus of Brass and Bone

Bimulous Books, Minneapolis, MN

Cover art by Jared Tuttle.

Publisher's Cataloging-in-Publication Data

SW, Abra.
  A Circus of brass and bone / Abra SW.
  p. cm.
  ISBN 978-0986377501
1. Circus --Fiction. 2. Reconstruction (U.S. history, 1865-1877) -- Fiction. 3. Alternative histories (Fiction). 4. Steampunk fiction. 5. Science fiction. 6. Mystery fiction. I. Title.
PS3619.W .C57 2015
813.6 --dc23   2014922758

Table of Contents

Extras

Author's Note

The setting of this story is roughly the late 1800s America, but it is an alternate history, and so events, landmarks, city/state boundaries, and notable personages may be different. Perhaps you wonder which of these changes are deliberate and which are unintentional. You may continue to wonder at your leisure.

Chapter 1

~* * *~

Everyone Dies

On the day the ringmaster died, so did civilization.

Knowing nothing of what was to come, we complained of boredom as the ship steamed from Bombay to Boston. There was little to do except rehearse, drink, and gamble over cards. Everything tasted of salt, and bathing in seawater anointed us all with the perfume of dead fish. A plague of short temper spread through the troupe. I had no friends among them, so I took pleasure at seeing them snarl at each other like fighting dogs.

A three-day bout of seasickness soured the ringmaster's disposition further. Though Mr. Loyale's health seemed to recover, his temper didn't. When Miss Miller declared her intention to begin her dress rehearsal without him, her expression was promising.

Promising that if Mr. Loyale berated her for not waiting, he'd better hope a gelding knife wasn't to hand.

Promising a fine show for us.

~ * ~

Lacey Miller, the Fabulous Lady Equestrienne Who Defies the Fiery Rings of Death!
On the Ship, Aether's Bounty, the Atlantic Ocean

"If anyone sees Mr. Loyale," Lacey Miller said to the group playing poker by the rail, "please inform him that I'm rehearsing." She walked away, her polished riding boots clicking across the deck.

The ringmaster had said they'd meet at sixth bell. She'd warmed her horses up before she went through the ship asking about the absent ringmaster. She wouldn't let them suffer, waiting with their saddles on, simply because he wasn't going to show.

Mr. Loyale didn't appreciate her skills; it would surprise nobody that he disrespected her by showing up late. Why, when she wished to buy a new pair of matched Arabian yearlings to train, he'd as good as said that her style of equestrian show had lost its novelty and the future of the circus lay elsewhere. A hot ball of anger flared up inside her. A lady never loses her temper, she heard her mother say, in memory. Lacey kept her back straight and her walk smooth. The heavy skirts of her riding habit swirled around her ankles. She raised her chin slightly, balancing the weight of the heavy chignon she'd swept her blonde hair up in. She brushed her fingers across her riding hat, checking that it tipped forward to precisely the right angle and that the hatpin still anchored it securely. Always check your appearance before a show.

Behind her, she heard the flutter of cards being shuffled back into the pack. A low whistle alerted other performers that something was going on. The whistle repeated along the length of the ship. The monkeys out for their daily promenade chattered excitedly when their handler changed their routine, heading after her. The shuffle of feet on the deck told her that others followed. Let them. She didn't mind an audience, she told herself, though her stomach knotted.

She'd been raised to be a proper lady, but that didn't mean she would back down to a bully.

Lacey climbed down into the hold, where the poor animals huddled in their cages. The monkeys were among the lucky ones: small and nimble enough to be taken out, tame enough to be trusted on deck. And when the aerialists allowed the monkeys to play among their ropes, the creatures made a delightful spectacle.

The lion snarled half-heartedly at Lacey as she passed, more a complaint about his circumstances than anything personal, and then rested his chin back on his paws.

The camels felt well enough to be mean about it, smelly, ill-tempered beasts that they were. One worked his jaw preparatory to spitting; Lacey darted past. By a muffled curse behind her, she guessed the camel had found another target among those who'd followed her down. She smothered a grin.

The new aether-powered elephant they'd acquired in India loomed in the darkness of the hold. Brass capped the ends of the monstrous elephant bones and linked to shining ball-and-socket joints. In place of muscle and tendon, it had rod and piston. Metal pipes drilled into bone and conducted the aether to glass storage tubes. The elephant golem fueled itself. Lacey had to admire the efficiency, though the use of bone aether to golem dead creatures caused her to shudder.

Bad enough that the living might be strapped into golem harnesses and forced to labor with strength granted from the consumption of their vital energies. That even death was no escape ...

Lacey hastened past the elephant golem to her horses, stabled together near the edge of the makeshift ring. She expected the tardy ringmaster to be waiting for her there, but she kept her eyes on her horses, caressing their heads and feeding them a couple of sugar cubes, strengthening herself for what was to come.

She heard discontented whispers from the people who had followed her down into the hold. Time for the show.

Lacey paced forward to the darkened ring. Brass piping connected aether lamps spaced around the perimeter of the ring. Lacey bent and flipped a toggle to release fire aether into the pipe, and then struck a match to light the source lamp. The aether conducted the fire from the source, dividing its heat and lumina among the outer lamps. Around the ring, they flared to pale light.

The ring was empty. The crowd behind Lacey grumbled with dissatisfaction. Maybe they'd also been anticipating Mr. Loyale— expecting him to be waiting to admonish her for being late, when *she'd* been looking for *him*. After a moment of readjusting her expectations, Lacey squared her shoulders and went to the side of the hold. Ropes snaked down from the shadows above and looped around a heavy iron ring that served as an anchor, keeping aerial props and equipment high in the shadows above until needed. Mr. Loyale had booked passage on a steamship with a hold nearly as deep as the circus' main tent was high, to allow for practice inside.

Lacey unwound the jeff to lower the *Fiery Rings of Death!* They wouldn't be fiery until her actual performance. None of them were so foolish as to have uncontained fire in the hold of a ship.

The loop of rope slithered up and snapped taut against its new limit. Behind Lacey, the hoops plummeted down. Somebody screamed. Lacey whirled to look at the group of onlookers. One of the albino twins pressed his hand to his mouth as if to call back the scream, his pink eyes wide. The aerialists tensed, rising to their toes. The Indian *mahout* cast a quick glance around the hold and returned to staring at her—no, past her—along with the rest. The acrobats looked ready to flip backward. The snake charmer stood statue-still, the only motion the slow movement of Samson, the baby boa draped across her shoulders.

The fortune teller slowly raised one ring-heavy finger to point at the hoops. A prickling sensation ran along Lacey's spine, and she pivoted to look.

A dark figure swayed between the shining hoops. Their ropes crisscrossed around his neck, suspending Mr. Loyale above the rink he'd ruled in life. A macabre boutonniere of blood flowered from his chest, and liquid of uncertain provenance oozed drop by drop from the tips of his boots.

"I suppose Mr. Loyale will not be joining me for my rehearsal after all," Lacey said faintly, stunned by the gruesome puppet dangling above the ring.

A scuffling noise came from the crowd as a short man of middling years with a plain face and a calm demeanor pushed through to the front. "The ringmaster said he wanted to discuss my act. He wanted to meet at the fourth bell." He hesitated. "It seemed urgent, but he never showed."

"Thank you, Ginger," Lacey told the man, whose nickname came not from his current unremarkable coif, but from the fiery orange wig he wore while clowning. Ginger nodded and faded back into the crowd. He seemed to only come alive in the ring, as if he folded up his personality and tucked it away along with the wig and face paint.

Lacey looked at the other performers. They stared back.

"We'll get Doc," a voice piped up from the back of the crowd.

Lacey squinted into the shadows. One of the conjoined sisters had spoken. She wasn't sure which one. The sisters seemed to be waiting for something. Lacey jerked her head in an awkward nod. The sisters left, running in lockstep, their arms wrapped around each other's waists.

A midget stepped forward and crossed his arms over his chest. "It ain't right to just leave him there." He frowned up at Lacey as if he expected *her* to do something about it.

"That's so," his wife said, a matching scowl on her small face.

Goaded, Lacey said, "He's hanging about a foot too high for me to untangle him!" She scanned the crowd. "Bradley, can you get him down?"

The enormous black strongman stepped into the ring and cocked his head. "Yes. Push up on his legs. Too much weight on the ropes."

Bradley Roberts' massive frame dwarfed Lacey when he stood beside her. She wrapped her arms around the corpse's knees and lifted. Foul liquid oozed over her arms. She breathed through her mouth to avoid the smells of death. It was no worse than mucking out stalls, she told herself. No worse, and just as necessary.

Bradley unwound the ropes from around Mr. Loyale's puffed-up neck. He caught the weight of the body as it fell. When he flexed his muscles, the black tattoos covering his skin writhed. Lacey released her hold and staggered backwards. Cradling the corpse as gently as if it were his own baby, Bradley stood.

The conjoined sisters trotted back into the hold, pulling Doc behind them. He took one look and shook his head. "Too dark. Bring him up."

Above decks, the blood seeping through Mr. Loyale's shirt showed clearly in the afternoon sunlight. Doc bent over the body. What began as a quick exam slowed once he'd removed the shirt and bared the corpse's torso to the light. He inspected Mr. Loyale's mouth, surveyed his arms, ankles, and calves, felt under his chin, and pressed his fingers into Mr. Loyale's armpits.

As word spread through the ship, it drew others to the little tableau. The ring of watchers grew two, three, four deep, and kept growing until all the members of the circus crowded onto the deck: freaks and geeks, aerialists and clowns, canvasmen and hostlers, blacksmiths and carpenters, costumers and cooks, musicians and games riggers, contortionists and fortune tellers, tumblers and gymnasts, museum keepers and ticket takers, food butchers and roustabouts.

"Did anyone see him recently?" Doc asked.

"He stopped by the card game and watched for a bit," a candy butcher said.

"When was that?"

"When I had a full house, aces high, and the damn albino beat me with four of a kind—twos! Who holds onto twos!?"

Lacey narrowed her eyes, giving him her best "boss stallion" look.

"I don't know when! All the damn days are the same at sea!" He squinted. "It was a couple of hands before the elephant keeper came up from the engine room. That hand I won with two pair."

The Indian *mahout* said, speaking carefully in his heavily accented English, "I am coming up after I hear the fourth bell."

"Probably you saw Mr. Loyale right before he died," Doc told the candy seller. "How did he look?"

"Kinda sleepy looking, I guess. Pale. Tired. I figured he was still recovering from the seasickness. He seemed in good enough spirits. Winked at me to wish me luck before he left."

"Hmph," Doc muttered. "Well, what killed him was being stabbed." He spread his fingers over the wound on the corpse's chest. "I'd have to cut him open to see what kind of knife did it. Since I don't want to get arrested—" a wry smile twisted up the edges of his lips, "—again, it'll have to wait for the coroner."

"Who would do that?" said Bradley, the strongman. "He helped many of us when we needed it most."

Nobody else spoke up to defend the dead man. They shuffled back a bit, looking at their neighbors to see what they'd say—and then, really *looking* at their neighbors as it sank in that the murderer was one of their own.

Doc looked up at Bradley. "He helped some of us, yes. And he fought with us, and tampered with our acts, and pushed us to do things we would rather not, and generally made himself unpleasant. He was, in short, the ringmaster. I don't know what we'll do without him. Or without the circus."

Most circusfolk couldn't make it as townies. A freak worth paying to see in a sideshow would fare poorly without the protective air of the exotic granted by the circus. A performer who'd trained for years to master his art would wither if forced to unskilled labor. Others had their own reasons to keep moving.

Lacey saw the moment the fear took them, as she would see a skittish horse tense before bolting. Instinctively she moved to intervene.

"Everyone dies sometime," she said, "but it doesn't mean the end!" She cast about. "The backers! We'll telegraph them once we reach Boston. Surely they won't want to waste their investment. They'll hire another ringmaster, and the circus will go on!"

The crowd paused, still prepared to bolt but willing to listen.

"What about the coppers?" the skeleton man called, looking ready to fade back behind the chimney stack he leaned against.

"That must depend on what the investors demand," she temporized.

Doubt lingered on a few faces, but they drifted apart instead of bolting.

"What will you do with Mister—with the body?" Lacey asked Doc, once the crowd dispersed. She felt an odd reluctance to leave him alone with the corpse—or, perhaps, to leave the corpse alone with him.

"We're docking at Boston sometime tonight?"

She nodded.

"I'll take him down to the engine room, then, and put him in the aether containment chamber. The influence of the flux bottle will stir his bone aether to greater vitality. It will keep his flesh from degrading, at least until we dock."

"Is that safe?" she asked, astonished.

He smiled a crooked smile. "For a living man, certainly not. After a factory explosion, I once—. Ah, but that tale isn't fit for ladylike ears. Suffice it to say that for a dead man, secondhand exposure for a few hours should cause no troubles."

"Once we arrive in Boston, we can telegraph the investors. They will know what we ought to do," Lacey said. It was almost a prayer.

~ * ~

The Mountains of East Tennessee

It began with an imperfection in a handblown glass tube. The join of the stopcock made the small air bubble nigh-invisible. The new assistant assigned to maintain the lab didn't notice a thing. Likely, he was regretting having agreed to take a position in the remote mountains of East Tennessee. The town nearby wasn't what anyone would call lively. Most of the young girls had moved to the cities for paying jobs in factories. The ones who remained weren't the brightest or the most beautiful, and they all had relatives with shotguns.

The imperfection hardly mattered, but it had gone unnoticed for a month, allowing the slow leak of fire aether to form an invisible bubble that floated and danced in the assistant's wake, now behind him, now ahead.

The assistant opened the exterior door to the aether enrichment chamber, and then hesitated. Beyond the interior door, the enriched aether was stored. He could not resist the urge to peek.

And even that would not have caused serious harm, except to any potential progeny of the assistant, if he had not squinted at the interior, decided it needed a closer look, and struck a match to light his lamp—too close to the invisible bubble of fire aether.

~ * ~

Nearby

Mina trudged home. It was the last year her parents could afford to send her to school. She planned to treasure every bit of it, even the long walk back. At the Culhane farm, she stopped to pet the farm cats that lingered near the fence.

After one last scratch behind the ears of a raggedy tom, she straightened and looked up—as the sky exploded in spreading whiteness. Mina clapped her hands over her eyes. Tears streamed down her cheeks. Then sound like a thunderclap picked her up and threw her off the path to tumble down the mountain. She came to rest in a trickle of water in a shallow gorge. Blackness took her. She never felt the rocks bouncing down the scree and striking her body.

~ * ~

40 Miles West of Topeka, Kansas

Gerhardt Yoder straightened from cutting hay and wiped the sweat from his forehead with the back of his arm. Only a few more hours to sundown, and then he could enjoy a beer cooled in the spring. He looked across his field with pride. He and his sons had worked hard: his cattle would not go hungry this winter. Life in the new country was good.

Light flashed in the East, bright as if another sun was rising. He squinted and shielded his eyes with his hand. The brilliant whiteness rolled closer. He couldn't bear to look at it directly for more than a few seconds. When his sons were small, he'd bought a circle of smoked glass from a peddler so that the family could watch the eclipse. He wished for it now.

Closer.

It moved faster than any cloud. The storm grew at an uneven rate, suddenly expanding forward or to one side as if it had hit a pocket of accelerant. Streaks of lightning crossed the sky, and where they led, the brilliant whiteness followed.

Gerhardt sensed that the others had stopped working as well, but he didn't scold them. In snatched glances before his eyes burned and watered, he saw tornado funnels of whiteness reaching down. In the distance, smoke.

"Fire!" he shouted. "I think the Johansen farm. Come! We hitch the horses and go. Wilhelm, get shovels. Johan, axes."

"Wait!" Johan said, pointing. "There are more!"

Other columns of smoke rose where the twisters touched down. The leading edge of the white storm approached Gerhardt's farm. Even the crickets in the field grew silent. A sizzle and snap made the hairs on Gerhardt's arms stand on end. When he looked up, lightning arched across the sky over his field like a cathedral dome. A vortex of fire reached down.

"Run!" Gerhardt shouted.

Mercifully, the intense heat from the fire killed him before he realized that he did not die alone.

~ * ~

Denver, Colorado

Mrs. Du Voix (Marcella Simmons, according to her identification papers) surveyed her "guests" with lidded eyes. Half her gift was timing. Three women and one man sat around the table. They held hands to form a circle, their eyes closed, their expressions anticipatory. Almost ready, Mrs. Du Voix thought. The drapes shrouding the windows provided the perfect atmosphere— though more light seeped through than she expected.

She made a mental note to order heavier drapes from the seamstress, though she kept her outer expression tranquil. "Oh, Sister Lucia Magdalene," she intoned, "come to me. Aid us to communicate with our dearly departed. Share with us the wisdom of those beyond the veil!"

Really, the light *was* too bright.

"I feel Sister Lucia entering me!" she cried. The hands holding hers jerked satisfactorily in surprise. This would be a good session, she thought—and then she *did* feel something.

Her eyes sprang open. Brilliant light streamed through the heavy drapes. Her back arched. Her mouth gasped in a paroxysm of pain. She felt her bones expand, radiance pouring out of them and into her flesh at an unbearable rate.

Around her, her clients thrashed, caught in spasms of their own.

"Have mercy!" she croaked, fearing that a powerful spirit had taken offense at her deceptions. She hoped it would release her.

Instead, she felt her heart rate accelerate like a runaway horse. Blood vessels burst beneath her skin. Trails of blood oozed from her nose, mouth, ears, and eyes. And then the almost-famous spiritualist Mrs. Du Voix achieved her final, permanent communion with the departed.

~ * ~

On the Outskirts of Augusta, Georgia

The sun beat down on Jacob's neck as he bent and heaved a massive boulder out of the ground. Sweat beaded on his dark skin and trickled across the brass and leather aether harness he wore. He hated the thing with all his heart. After the war, when he got his freedom, he'd sworn he'd never put it on again.

The night his master said he had to work for another year, he and his wife—and the two of their children who hadn't been sold away yet—bundled up what little they had and stole away in the night. They hid in the woods until they stumbled across a group of freed slaves building their own town.

In Freeville, they scratched a living out of soil so poor that no whites contested them for it. They built themselves a one-room house, ate what they could grow and raise and trade for, and dressed in cast-offs, but they had very little money. When they could, they went to Augusta to buy or barter for necessities.

Life got harder when Augusta passed Black Codes. Only the ex-slaves with work papers from a white master were allowed in town. Jacob still wouldn't put the aether harness back on.

It wasn't worth it, he argued to the other free blacks who thought it was the only way. The harness stole the aether from their bones to provide extra vitality to their muscles—at the cost of years of their life, and weakness in their old age. And the harness could control them. They might as well be slaves again!

But when Jacob and his wife's new baby was born, it was weak and fitful and in need of proper doctoring, doctoring that cost money.

Jacob carried the boulder over to the cart, tumbled it in, and walked, at his own pace, to the next large rock. The overseer gave him a dirty look but made no threat. Jacob smiled to himself. At least that had changed.

The overseer's expression grew confused, then fearful. Jacob looked over his shoulder. A vast white cloud expanded toward them from three sides, glittering like mica in the sunlight.

"Boss, what—" he began. He stopped. The overseer was plainly as pig-ignorant as he.

When had an overseer provided help anyway? Jacob touched his charm bag, squared his shoulders, and prepared to take it, whatever "it" might be.

The sky went white. His aether harness tightened around his chest as if it were a living thing. Jacob felt a tug on his bones that he recognized as the harness spindling bone aether out to power his muscles. He gasped and tensed. The power flooded his body. Then the flow reversed. Energy poured *into* him, until his whole body vibrated with it. He threw back his head and howled. The cascade of energy didn't stop. The harness tried to store all that power—and failed. It funneled the excess into his flesh. His muscles all convulsed simultaneously. Pain radiated through him where the overload fired his muscles so strongly that they tore away from bone and ligament. His face locked into a rictus, his eyes wide and staring at the sky. He fell to the ground. Shuddering gasps and groans provided the accompaniment to his pain. Some of them came from his throat, and some, not.

Thrashing like a fish drowning in air, he flopped onto his side. The overseer had crumpled to the ground, dead or unconscious. Convulsions like Jacob's wracked one of the other harnessed freedmen. The second had died in his traces, withered down to half his size in only a few minutes. If Jacob had had control over his muscles, he would have flinched. Instead, he writhed on the ground and prayed for the pain to end.

~ * ~

William McCormack
Boston, Massachusetts

William McCormack's legs ached and his feet throbbed. He'd walked all day looking for a place that might hire him. His father had died in the last sickness that spread through the slums, but William wasn't big enough to take his place canal-building. When he'd tried to get a job as a newspaper hawker, the other boys chased him away with cries of, "Stinking Paddy!"

Across the street, he saw a sign in the window of a butcher shop saying "Help Wanted." He trotted over, lured by the scent of sausages on the breeze. If he worked there, maybe the butcher would let him take scraps home sometimes. He was at the door, hand raised to knock, when he saw the smaller sign in the window: "No Irishmen or Dogs Allowed."

Shoulders slumped, he plodded away, his dreams of sausages evaporating.

His mam's shift in the crystal workshop at Peacock Chandeliers ended soon. The supervisor, Mr. Roger, wasn't a bad man. He'd let William sit at the edge of the shop floor and wait for his mam, so long as William kept quiet and didn't get in the way. Mr. Roger kept candy in his pocket, and he gave a piece to each child worker at the end of their shift. Sometimes William would get a wrapped molasses taffy or a piece of horehound candy at shift change, too.

The waiting list for jobs in the crystal workshop grew longer each time a new shipful of immigrants docked. Conditions were much better than at some of the other factories. Twenty minutes for lunch, a row of thick glass blocks near the ceiling letting in plenty of light, a fan to keep the heat bearable. Mr. Roger wasn't the kind to take personal liberties with the workers, either.

William slipped inside the noisy factory and found his way to the crystal workshop. His mam glanced across at him and smiled, but her fingers never stopped flying as she fished a crystal prism from the basket on her table, hooked it onto a short chain, and draped the chain over a hook on the slow-moving conveyor that snaked its way past the work tables. At the end of the conveyor, children plucked the hanging prisms and attached them to loops on child-high chandelier skeletons. They spun the chandeliers this way and that, to make sure no crystals were missing—and perhaps to send rainbows cavorting across the workshop.

Mr. Roger looked down from his glass-windowed office up above the shop floor, where he could watch all that went on. Though he didn't come out and chase William away, he didn't smile either. No candy today, William thought. That was okay. All he really wanted was to rest.

William sat near the door, his back to the wall. He drew up his knees, pillowed his head on his arms, and closed his eyes.

He woke slowly from a dream in which person after person turned him down for a job as his face grew hotter and hotter. Awake, the heat was real enough. White light blazed through the glass blocks above, illuminating the factory floor with unbearable clarity and bleaching the crystal-cast rainbows to invisibility.

White-hot brightness flashed like lightning inside his eyes, blotting out everything else. Pain swept through him with prickling heat. He fell to the ground, screaming. Around him, he heard other people crying out and sharp cracking sounds that he couldn't identify. Something sharp cut his cheek. He struggled against the pain and pushed himself up to his knees. A *bang!* rattled the workshop and hurled him to the ground.

The horrible, painful brightness faded, leaving blindness in its wake. William pushed himself up to hands and knees. He swayed. Standing seemed impossible. If he had to crawl, he would.

His vision seeped back, though he stared at the world through a heavy veil. Everything was black and shades of gray. Slowly, he understood what he looked at. A hole gaped where a wall had stood. Rubble was strewn across the workshop. The workers lay like tantrum-tossed dolls. Only a handful struggled to push themselves up.

Across the room, the heavy worktable his mother sat behind had crashed to the side. He couldn't see her. Glimmering crystal shards were strewn across the floor, their beauty promising only pain. He crawled toward his mother's table, picking his way around the fallen, careful where he placed his hands and knees. He tried not to look at the dead workers, but he could not keep himself from studying their faces. Blood ran from their eyes, their nose, their ears, but he stared at each one until he knew: not his mam.

Halfway there, he saw her. She huddled in a crumpled heap under the heavy weight of the worktable. He pushed himself to his feet to run to her, but on the first step, his muscles gave way. He fell and hit the ground with bruising force.

He crawled faster, no longer choosing his way but simply plowing through. The crystal shards cut into his palms and his knees. It hurt, but the anticipatory, waiting-to-unfold pain in his heart overwhelmed it.

"Mam!" he said, when he reached her. "Mam, it's William! Mam, look at me!" He cradled her head with bloody hands.

When she opened her eyes to look at him and managed a faint smile, he knew everything could still be all right. "Hello—." A frown crossed her face. "Can't—breathe." She gasped for air. "Too—heavy."

William pushed against the worktable, but he couldn't budge it.

He crawled to the doorway of the factory and pulled himself up to stand. Bodies sprawled in the street, but nobody moved.

"Hello, can somebody help?" he called. "Please, my mother is trapped! Please help! Is anybody there?"

He held his breath, but all he heard were the soft whimpers and moans coming from the factory behind him.

~ * ~

Meanwhile, the igniting aetheric wave swept past Boston and over the Atlantic Ocean, where a steamship called *Aether's Bounty* traveled unknowingly into it.

Chapter 2

~* * *~

The Great Boston Pyre, Part I

The first wave of death rolled across America. The chain reaction of supercharged air and fire aether agitated any other aether it passed close to. Steam power stopped working when the containment chambers blew out. Factories exploded. Munitions depots with the new fire aether tanks were wiped from the face of the earth, along with any nearby buildings. All the lights went out. Water ceased to flow from spigots, or in some cases, erupted out with force enough to demolish anything in its path. Such commotion and turmoil! I wish I could have seen it.

Bone aether did not remain unaffected. Whether vital force was thrust into bone, or drawn out from it, pity the mortal flesh caught between. Death was not stingy with her favors.

Seawater absorbed the roil of aether, weakening it and slowing its spread. Those bathing at the seaside were unaffected, though their holidays turned grim when they saw the devastation that awaited them on shore. America's neighbors across the sea survived the first wave better.

Except England and France. They both had their own secret aether enrichment projects. When the wave of charged aether—reduced in strength, but still much more powerful than in its natural state—activated the enriched aether, the chain reaction regained its original vigor.

Death poured out.

*Countries without enrichment projects were less affected.
Perhaps only two out of every five people died in the first wave,
compared to the four in five who died in North America.*

*The circus survived because we were surrounded by salt
water. We got off practically scot-free, although our aetheric
devices were affected. The steam engine that powered the ship
surged, rocketing us forward through the waves. The engineers
talked knowledgeably about "natural aether fluctuations" in an
attempt to hide their bafflement. The Indian elephant of bone and
brass acted odd afterward, as if the vast wave of aetheric power
had reminded it of being a living creature. We kept it, for it was a
lovely showpiece. But we began to treat it cautiously, as if it truly
were a vast creature of uncertain temperament. I say we, though
I didn't interact with it until much later. At this time, I was still
silenced and smothered in layers of cloth, my arm bound to my
side.*

~ * ~

*Jonathan Matzke, the Man So Thin He Wears a Wedding Ring As
a Belt!*
On the Ship, Aether's Bounty, the Atlantic Ocean.

The skeleton man *hungered.*

Breakfast seemed so long ago, though he'd gobbled biscuits
and tea until his stomach hurt. His precious stash of tasties was
buried in his wagon for their grand entrance into Boston, along
with everything else he had to his name. He had so little—he
thought self-pityingly—that his kit was packed and loaded while
others still dallied in their quarters, packing away the wondrous
sprawl of their belongings. And so Jonathan Matzke, *The Man So
Thin He Wears a Wedding Ring as a Belt!*, went without. His
stomach clenched tight in rebellion.

Though the hardtack and cheese and dried apples he'd packed
didn't appeal to him, anyway. Jonathan *ravened,* but not for that.
For something else. He didn't know what yet.

He'd know it when he saw it, by the salivating of his mouth.
Maybe one of the others might have something that would fill the
aching pit in his stomach. Maybe they'd give him some if he asked
nicely. Or—in the upset of packing, they wouldn't notice or care if
a little bit here or there went missing. Mice. Ships always had
mice.

Slip and slide around the corners, he could. Nobody noticed the Skeleton Man, because there was a quarter as much man to notice!

He drifted out and down the corridor, pausing at each door like a hungry ghost.

The snake charmer sang to her charges as she coiled them into large woven baskets. The sheets on her bunk writhed of their own accord as serpentine bodies slithered beneath them. One of the closed baskets rattled angrily at her. When the circus made its grand processional, she'd sit in her special glass-sided wagon and let the snakes weave around her.

Jonathan didn't like snakes. He knew how many unexpected places he could fit because of his size, and most of her snakes were even smaller. He hadn't known she let them loose in her cabin, or he'd have slept worse of a night. He shuddered and passed on.

Little whirlwinds of gaudy fabrics and spangles swirled between the aerialists.

"The green and silver one is mine!" Leah Eads exclaimed.

"No, it's mine, for the act with the sea green banners!" Pamela Dyer-Bennet said.

"You always steal my clothes! Where is my silver bracelet?" Leah asked.

"I didn't take that. You were wearing it last. You lost it yourself!" Pamela answered with exasperated patience.

Grace and strength intrinsic in their tightly muscled bodies even when they were fighting over their costumes, the aerialists gave a good show, on- or off-stage. But no food. Jonathan pocketed an ivory ribbon that had blown out into the corridor and kept going.

The Indian *mahout*'s cabin smelled of incense and curry. Jonathan's nose twitched. During their time in India, he'd eaten curry and found it good. And if it didn't sit well afterward, it tasted much the same on the way up as it had on the way down, which could only be an advantage, what with his delicate stomach. *My Johnny can't eat like normal boys*, his mother had always said.

The Indian sat on his steam trunk and twirled an oddly curved knife with a fancy enamel-and-brass hilt. A pink-petaled plant with spiky green leaves sat beside him. Teak traveling boxes, a tiffin carrier, and a rolled-up carpet lay at his feet. Jonathan looked longingly at the tiffin the curry scent was wafting from, took a longer look at the blade in the Indian's hand, and shuffled away.

The contortionist's room was empty except for a number of closed boxes and trunks. Jonathan eyed them suspiciously and kept going.

Ginger the whitefaced clown juggled his belongings above barrels and boxes spilling over with wigs and costumes and hoops and mallets. Jonathan crept closer, his eye on a sausage that *might* be a prop—or might just be real. A board creaked ever so slightly under his foot. Other ship noises should have drowned it out, but the clown whipped around fast, his hand on a mallet that Jonathan suddenly doubted was a cotton-stuffed prop. The clown's hand relaxed when he saw Jonathan, but his eyes narrowed. Jonathan laughed awkwardly and backed away down the corridor. Out of sight, he stopped and wiped cold sweat from the back of his neck.

The equestrienne's door was closed. Didn't want the world to see her packing her underthings. Always trying to be a lady of Quality no matter the circumstances, Jonathan thought, half-jeeringly, half-respectfully. He looked longingly at her closed door. She was just the type to keep a tin of cookies out for tea, too. He bent to peer in the keyhole.

The soldierlike stride of the approaching Indian *mahout* sent Jonathan skittering further on down the corridor, where he leaned against the wall and attempted to look like he hadn't just been spying.

The *mahout* knocked. A murmured inquiry came from inside, the Indian answered, and then the equestrienne opened the door. She wouldn't have opened the door to *him*, Jonathan thought enviously. Though she did leave the door ajar to maintain propriety. He crept to the door jamb and peeked through the crack.

"When I am packing, I am seeing this," the *mahout* said clumsily in his heavily accented English. "I am not needing it for the elephant, but I am thinking that you might use." He extended the knife he'd been fiddling with earlier.

"A hoof pick!" the equestrienne said, surprise shaking her usual composure. "Ah, what an unusual gift. Thank you."

The *mahout* gave an odd, short little bow with his hands pressed together.

An unusual gift indeed, Jonathan thought. Orientals had weird ideas about women, if they thought that sort of thing to be a grand idea. Chocolates were much more the thing.

Chocolates! Remembering where he'd seen chocolate recently, Jonathan hurried off. Before they embarked, an admirer had brought chocolates to Ms. Selena, the fat lady.

He never had admirers who brought him chocolate, Jonathan thought morosely. Ms. Selena might complain that some of them looked at her "like they'd eat me right up, toes to nose!" but he thought he wouldn't mind if they brought him chocolate.

Ms. Selena's wide back was to the door of her cabin when Jonathan walked past all casual-like. She moved slowly, with the ponderous grace of a hippopotamus in the water. The cabin shrank by comparison. She hummed to herself as she folded tent-sized dresses.

Near the door, the open chocolate tin balanced atop a higgledy-piggledy stack of shawls and fans and silk flowers and other tokens of affection. She'd only consumed a third of the chocolate pieces. She wouldn't notice one missing, surely? Jonathan sidled into her quarters, keeping a wary eye on her back, and snatched a chocolate. He backed out the door rapidly, clutching his treasure.

The excitement of a close escape jolted through him as he retreated to the ringmaster's uninhabited quarters to enjoy the chocolate in privacy.

He lifted up the chocolate and stared at it for a long while, treasuring the moment. The ship whistle blew, signaling that they were making their approach to Boston Harbor. Jonathan popped the chocolate into his mouth. Age and India's heat had turned the chocolate chalky and fragile, but he rolled it around on his tongue in ecstasy.

The last trace of sugary deliciousness dissolved too soon. He still *hungered*. Ms. Selena might count her chocolates, he thought morosely. He couldn't risk taking another one. They were all such misers, hoarding everything away as if they could take it with them to heaven.

But if one of them had already *gone* to heaven (or hell— Jonathan wasn't partial), they couldn't object to him making sure nothing would go to waste, now could they? Nobody had thought to pack up the ringmaster's things. Jonathan stood among shadow-shrouded mounds of clothes and books and the odds and ends that sum up a life. A grin spread across his face as he closed the cabin door and kindled the ship lamp. Parcels and pockets and bags and boxes and chests and oh! the wonderful things he might find.

The mother lode was inside a burlap bag slumped beside the bunk. *Real* sausage, and hard cheese finer than what he'd packed away, toffees, pickled vegetables in jars, a half-full bottle of port, pickled eggs, and a dozen clove-studded oranges. He sighed happily, and set to with a will.

His mouth stuffed full of pickled egg and sausage, a wedge of cheese in one hand and the bottle of port in the other, Jonathan poked and pried. He didn't have long before everyone would go up on deck. It was possible that they'd miss him and somebody might come looking—and they might not understand the importance of making sure nothing was wasted.

A flamboyant but rarely worn scarf and a pair of cufflinks found their way into Jonathan's pockets. His stomach bulged, but his mouth still watered. He felt compelled to *keep eating*. He stopped in front of a chest with a padlock. Locked chests hid the loveliest things.

He darted back and pressed his ear to the cabin door. Silence. Most of the others must be on deck. He picked up a paperweight and slammed it down on the padlock. Once. Twice. Third time was the charm. He struck the padlock off. His stomach churned with excitement as he pushed the lid up.

No food, he thought first, but he didn't regret that at the moment. His stomach sloshed in rhythm with the waves hitting the ship. A King James bible sat on top, which surprised Jonathan. He'd never thought the ringmaster was the religious type. Underneath it, papers. He scowled and riffled through them quickly. Numbers and names, but most made no sense. One sheet of paper had a list of names and places that he recognized as towns along the circus route, but the rest were a mystery. He began to smile as he pulled the papers out and tucked them under his shirt. A secret was almost as filling as food.

The whistle blew again.

Jonathan went to the cabin door and listened to the silence to make sure he could leave unseen. On the other side of the door, silence listened to Jonathan.

He eased out of the cabin and trotted off down the corridor. The motion agitated his overstuffed stomach something terrible. By the time he burst out onto the deck, it was swishing and see-sawing so much that he couldn't think of anything but lurching to the rail. He bent over and heaved his guts out in a long acidic stream that splashed into the waves below. (*Such a delicate boy, my Johnny.*) A waste of the sausage and cheese and toffee, he thought mournfully. Fin and scale churned the water. He hoped the fish enjoyed their feast.

He straightened, wiping his mouth sheepishly. He hated it when people saw him being sick. But—nobody was looking in his direction! They stood still, gazing toward Boston Harbor like silent ranks of brightly painted dolls. The breeze off the ocean ruffled their grand entrance finery.

Ahead of them, a thick pillar of dark smoke billowed up from Boston. Rivulets of smoke straggled into the sky from smaller fires, but the monstrous column was the star of the show.

"That fire's the North End," Jonathan whispered. "*All* the North End."

The *mahout* climbed up onto the deck, returning from one last visit to the engine room. He stopped and stared. "What happened to Boston?" he said, the words clear despite his shock.

"What should we do now?" the equestrienne asked, her usually excellent diction broken and soft. "Where do we go?"

Jonathan watched the circus members look at each other, each hoping another held the answer. None of them looked at *him*, of course. Why would—.

His head went up.

Jonathan hated giving up his treasures, but it wasn't like he was obsessed with them. He could give them up if he needed to. If the circus really needed them. He could. He told himself that, but his hand stayed pressed flat against the wad of papers he'd jammed under his shirt.

He closed his eyes and pulled out the sheet with the names and towns. With a wrench that was almost physically painful, he waved the sheet in the air. "Here!" he shouted. "Mr. Loyale had this page with names on it! It says, 'Mr. Roderick White' beside Boston."

The fortune teller narrowed her eyes at Jonathan, but she didn't scold him for having the paper—yet. "Mr. White is the assistant to the mayor of Boston," she said. Nobody wanted to ask her how she knew.

"But—why would Mr. Loyale have his name?" the equestrienne asked.

"Let's ask him," the fortune teller said cannily.

"Yes," the equestrienne agreed. "Maybe he'll be able to tell us what *happened* here."

They stared out across the city and watched it burn.

~ * ~

William McCormick
Boston, Massachusetts

The previous day.

"Hello, can somebody help?" William called. "Please, my mother is trapped! Is anybody there?"

He held his breath. Soft whimpers and moans came from the wounded in the factory behind him. As if in answer, he heard a man shouting, "Help! Help me!" He sounded nearby.

A man grown might be strong enough to move the table pinning William's mother. He was strong enough to shout; maybe he wasn't hurt too bad. If William helped him, he could help William's mother.

William let go of the door frame and stood on his own. He swayed a bit, but didn't fall. He took a step. So far, so good. If he had to, he would crawl to get help for his mother—but he'd rather walk.

By taking it slow and stopping often to lean against a light post or a doorway, William made it two blocks. "Oh, bless you! May the sun shine upon you!" he heard.

William peered around the corner. One man lay trapped beneath the wreckage of a cart and the mound of coal it had carried. The dead carthorse lay beside him. A group of about ten rough-looking men worked together to free him, under the direction of a large man with a jaunty hat that sat oddly with his stained workman's clothes. They were hard men, William's da would have said, but then, his da looked a hard man himself, when he came back from building canals. He only softened up when he'd spent some time around William's mam.

Two of the men pulled out the splintered planks that used to be a cart. The rest shifted the mound of coal. Some carried it away in their hands or their hats. Others used pieces of wreckage to clear a large swathe away. They were *helping*.

William lurked near the corner, watching, as he tried to figure out the best way to introduce himself. When the rough-looking men pulled a particularly large piece of wreckage out, the fallen man gasped and winced. The man with the hat squatted beside him.

"Are you alright there?" asked the man with the hat. "It'll be over soon. Tell me, stranger, what's your name?"

"Conrad Zero," the trapped man gasped.

"Zero? What kind of name is that for a man?"

"At immigration, they asked my name. When I hesitated too long—not sure if I wanted to give my full name, you see, in case trouble tried to follow me here—the official shrugged and wrote, 'Zero'. Suits me well enough. A new life, a new start, a new name." He looked down at the debris covering him. "If I get out of here."

"I'm Chad Valentine," the man with the hat said, "and we'll be getting you out."

"Call him Valentine," chorused the other men.

"It's 'cause he's such a sweetheart of a slave driver," one of the men added.

"It's not like we'll be going back to canal-building, Tommy-boy," Valentine said. "Not after this."

"No," Tommy-boy agreed, looking around. "It'll be building the factories back up for us."

"Maybe. Then again, maybe not." A smile William didn't understand crossed Valentine's lips. He looked back over his shoulder at where William lurked. "And what's your name, boy? Come on out, don't be shy."

William eased around the corner. Nerves made him want to fiddle with something, so he stuck his hands in his pockets.

"William McCormick, sir. My mam's hurt. Will you help her, please?"

Valentine puffed up his chest. "Sure and we will! Where is she?"

"The crystal factory, sir."

"A factory full of womenfolk needing help, you say? How about it, lads?"

A chorus of approval came from the group.

William smiled, glad they'd help but a little uncomfortable.

"Let's just get Conrad out, and then we'll be along to help your mam." Valentine studied the reduced weight of the coal on top of the man. "Conrad, we'll grab your arms and pull you out. Holler if you feel something shifting in a real bad way."

Valentine and Tommy each took an arm and heaved. Conrad yelped and hissed between his teeth, but he didn't tell them to stop. He popped out like a chimney sweep from a smokestack, his clothing rags, covered in coal dust from neck to toe.

"Much obliged!" he said.

"Now, a prosperous businessman like yourself will be wanting to repay those who helped you, surely?" Valentine asked. His gang stepped closer.

"Oh, aye," Conrad agreed sourly, "and I just happen to have the monies from the coal I've sold so far here in my pocket."

"Would never have occurred to me," Valentine said blandly.

Conrad winced. "Agh, but I feel like I've got ants biting all over me!" He bent and swatted at his trousers, sending a cloud of black dust up into the air. When he straightened, he swayed. He grabbed ahold of Tommy to steady himself.

Tommy tensed and his hand knotted. As quickly, he relaxed, but not before William saw.

William edged back a bit. "Mr. Valentine, sir, can you help my mam?"

"Lead the way, kid!" Valentine said, counting the coins Conrad had handed him and passing a few along to his friends.

The men laughed and patted each other on the back, their spirits raised by the successful rescue. Conrad shrugged and followed along. When William led them along and they passed those lying in the street, dead or struggling to push themselves up, the men grew quieter. When they entered the factory, they were utterly silent as they took in what had happened in the crystal workshop.

William's vision had recovered from the blinding effect of the flash of light. He could see clearly now. He wished he couldn't. Most of the women and children laboring in the workshop looked like they'd died painfully, if quickly. Their bodies had contorted beyond the tolerance of muscle and bone. Blood congealed in their eyes. He'd seen it before, when he'd crawled to his mam, but not—not all at once, like. Some hadn't died from the storm. Flying bricks from the wall had done for two more. Crystal shards pincushioned half-a-dozen others. Children lay in pools of their life's blood, their faces cut beyond recognition by crystal prisms that had exploded at precisely child-height.

"They were just kids," said Patrick Sullivan, one of the younger men in Valentine's mob.

One of the small bleeding bodies stirred. Patrick jumped forward to help. "Here now, we'll get you to a doctor—"

The child gave a last convulsive shudder and then—stopped. A fly straggled in from outside and landed on the body. It scuttled around, its suckered tongue tasting dried sweat and blood.

Patrick turned to the side, braced himself against the wall, and vomited a chunky spew that splashed when it struck the ground. It looked like he'd eaten stew, William thought. He felt shaky and cold. His mam cooked up a good stew.

Sensing richer reward, the fly buzzed up and flew over to investigate. That made William wonder: why weren't there more flies? It was a terrible thought, but it nagged at him.

"William ..."

The whispery voice of his mam fetched him across the room so fast he didn't remember anything between here and there.

"Praise be, one still lives," Valentine said in a subdued voice. Louder: "Come along, lads!"

Even the new rescuee, Conrad, charged forward and helped to lift the heavy worktable away. He winced a couple of times, but he didn't slack and he didn't complain.

William danced impatiently from foot to foot. As soon as the men heaved the worktable to the side, he darted in and clutched his mam's hand.

"How do you feel?" he asked.

"Better. I can breathe. But—ah!—it still hurts."

"William," Valentine said, "I know a doc who'll fix your mam up. The doc lives not too far from here, near the edge of the rich district." He didn't add, *If he's still alive*, but he didn't have to. "We can go and bring the doctor back to your mam."

Fear of being left alone with the dead and dying gripped William. What if they didn't come back? Something of the same feeling must have touched his mam, for she said, "I can walk, I think. With help."

Valentine said, "Could be I saw something that might help."

He left and returned with a wooden pole cut down to the right size for a walking staff. A minute's quick work with his knife rounded the top into a knob that wouldn't hurt to rest weight on.

"And why would a man like you happen to have noticed a fine *shillelagh* like that?" William's mam asked, a touch of humor in her voice despite everything.

A blush tinged Valentine's ears. For a moment, he looked much less like a hard man.

They levered William's mam to her feet and braced her when she swayed. With the staff under her hand, Valentine holding her elbow, and William hovering nearby, she hobbled unsteadily to the door. Patrick went ahead of them, clearing obstructions away so she wouldn't trip and fall. Some obstructions he moved more gently than others.

Out on the street, William looked around with newly clear eyes. The few folk who had been struggling to push themselves up now swayed on their feet. One man clutched his arm to his side; it hung at an unnatural angle.

William tugged at Valentine's sleeve. "Can he come, too?"

"Very well," Valentine said magnanimously. He paused near the injured man. "We're going along to the doctor. You may have a walk with us, if you like."

Desperate gratitude filled the man's face. "Aye, I will! Blessings on you." He fell into line behind them.

The others swayed in place, their eyes still shocked and dazed. William remembered the horrible clutch of fear he'd felt at the idea of being left alone. He shouted, "You lot can keep company with us."

Valentine looked down on him, a peculiar expression on his face. "Can they, then? Well." He raised his voice and added, "*If* you help along those with trouble."

Most roused and stumbled along, helping each other when it was needed.

One man remained. "I—I have to find my wife," he said.

William looked down at his feet to avoid seeing the man's desperate, hoping expression.

A dead fly curled on the ground. Two feet away, there was another one. A cluster of sparrows sprawled on their backs near a wall, feathers ruffled in death, twiglike legs bent and twisted.

They walked on.

Corpses salted the streets: men, women, children, horses, dogs, cats, rats, birds, and even insects. No living thing that moved upon the earth had been spared.

Survivors sat on stoops or clung to the doorways of shops and factories. William wondered what awaited inside. He didn't go look. None of Valentine's mob did; they clung close together and stuck to the center of the street. They called out to the other survivors, though, offering help and inviting them along.

The survivors would look up, staring at them with haunted eyes.

Did you see—? those eyes would ask.

Yes, yes, I did, their eyes answered.

Some of them would follow. The mob doubled and then tripled in size. A carthorse that had outlived its master trotted alongside them, and skittish dogs trailed in their shadow.

Valentine looked down at William with a wry twist to his mouth, as if to say, "See what you started?"

William lifted his chin. His mam watched. What else could he have done?

When they reached the doctor's house, on the outskirts of Beacon Hill, Valentine waved the crowd to silence and knocked on the door. After a wait long enough to be worrying, William heard the snick of a lock being turned.

A disheveled lady opened the door, got one look at the small mob following in Valentine's wake, and slammed it shut again. Patrick started forward with an angry look on his face, but Valentine waved him back.

Making his case to the door, he wheedled, "Ach, Elizabeth, it's your old friend Valentine. You wouldna turn away a friend on such a grim day? And the boy beside me with his injured mother?"

The door creaked open. The lady had taken the opportunity to twist her black hair up into a bun, perch spectacles on her nose, and cover her dress with an apron starched stiff enough to repel a sea of blood. She glared at Valentine over her spectacles, her dark brows set in an unyielding line. "I only have room for the wounded inside. The rest of your ducklings can wait. And to you, my name is Dr. Fallon."

Dead silence greeted her. "What—?" Patrick began, with an expression like a stunned ox. A sharp elbow to the ribs from Valentine silenced him.

Relenting somewhat, Dr. Fallon added, "Your lads can put the kettle on the hob and make tea for the rest of the lot. With sugar, whether they like it or not. Might have to wait their turn for a teacup."

She strode back into the house, not looking back to see if any followed.

In an undertone, Valentine hissed to Patrick, "Keep yer gob shut! Did you think a high-and-mighty doctor with his choice of patients would tend to Irish rabble? Lizzie's worked harder to prove herself than any man among us. She's a mighty fine doctor, too. Don't call her Lizzie, though, or she'll tear a strip out of your hide. Now go on and make tea!"

Valentine assisted William's mam into the house. She made little noises that might, William worried, be a sign of pain—but sounded more like a suppressed case of the giggles.

Dr. Fallon's parlor had been converted into a patient examination room. Valentine and William got her into the room and settled according to the doctor's instructions.

"Valentine—" Dr. Fallon began.

"Ah, it fair gladdened my heart to see you standing there when we opened the door!" he interrupted. "So many dead, I feared you'd be among them."

Dr. Fallon seemed immune to Valentine's heart-gladdening. "I was down in the cellar, preparing solutions, when the storm hit.

My lights went out. I heard the most terrible sound, like hundreds of voices screaming. Then a convulsive fit struck me. I had just recovered when you arrived. Now, Valentine, go on out—I have a patient to see to, and I think she'd like her privacy for the exam."

The tips of Valentine's ears turned red, and he bowed himself out. William stayed.

William helped Dr. Fallon move his mother. The doctor listened to her breathing, had her spit in a cup, asked questions, and gently probed to find where the pain was.

"Your chances are good," Dr. Fallon said, finally. "That worktable broke some ribs, but there's no blood in your spit, and I don't hear any fluid gurgling when you breathe. That means the ribs didn't puncture your lungs. Your abdomen isn't stiff, so you may be lucky enough to not have internal bleeding. I'd give you a shot of bone aether to speed healing, but all my vials shattered when that—that ungodly whatever-it-was struck. Keep breathing normally, stay abed for a week and then go very slow for the next five. Wrap your ribs before you go about your day. Your boy here can help you with that. And don't lift anything!"

William's mam smiled weakly. "I'm not even a bit tempted."

Dr. Fallon barked a laugh. "You're more sensible than most of my male patients!"

William helped his mother to sit in an overstuffed chair in the entranceway and then came back in to watch. His sense of propriety no longer threatened, Valentine did as well. Dr. Fallon was less gentle with her next patient.

"There's nothing wrong with you that a good scrubbing won't take care of," Dr. Fallon told Conrad. "Bathe with soap, until you're clean all over, or those cuts and scrapes will get infected. With all this commotion," she said disapprovingly, "the bath houses are probably closed. Bathe in a barrel of water if you have to, but get the coal dust and filth off. Then apply this liniment and bandages."

"Barrel it is," Conrad said gloomily. "Not like I have a fancy bathtub like those highfalutin rich folk with their indoor running water and all."

Valentine leaned forward, and his eyes gleamed. "Says who? Think on it, man. How many died? Did you think the rich were spared? If we go knocking on doors, we'll find one where nobody answers. And then—" He laughed, leaning back. "Then you'll have your bath!"

Dr. Fallon didn't look shocked, and she didn't tell Valentine that what he was thinking was wrong, William noticed. Maybe she wasn't too fond of her neighbors, either.

"Ten blocks up, there's a fine blue and white mansion with hydrangeas growing in front. The owner rushes to the physician when any member of his family so much as sneezes. I'm only a poor substitute when his regular physician isn't available, of course—" she cut a length of bandage off the roll with a vicious snip, "—but under the circumstances, I doubt he would have been able to reach his regular physician. I haven't heard from him, which makes me think that neither he nor his household is up to repelling visitors."

"Bless you, doctor!"

She snorted. "Get those who need medical care organized before you leave, with able-bodied men to help them."

"I will that!"

"Leave?" William asked, but nobody answered him.

William trailed after Valentine as he left the doctor's parlor. Valentine was as good as his word. He got volunteers to help the injured, checked to see that they'd all had sweet tea, shook hands, and patted backs.

William followed. He saw how heads turned after them, how dull, stunned faces regained a semblance of life when they passed.

William stayed hot on Valentine's heels as he rounded the corner of the house. His work gang loitered there, waiting. "Come on, lads!" he said.

"You can't just leave them!" William burst out.

"I'm not one of the saints, lad, to be watching out for all in need!" William felt his face fall. Valentine hastily added, "But that's not what I'm doing at all! Just—looking about a bit. You should go and tend to your mam."

"She's resting here as well as she can. Where could I take her? Back to the North End? You think she'll get better care there? You think maybe this only hurt the rich folk? I'm coming along with you, I am."

Or you might not come back.

A trace of a scowl lingering on his lips, Valentine led the others off at a pace brisk enough that William had to trot to keep up.

When he saw the house Dr. Fallon had recommended, however, Valentine seemed to forget his irritation. "Now, lads, isn't that there better than living all crowded together in a one-room apartment with your friends who fart in their sleep and never wash their socks?"

A roar of agreement went up from the half-dozen men following him. William couldn't help but shout along. He and his mam shared an apartment with another family, and the youngest boy had a digestion that cabbage disagreed with. William himself, of course, never offended.

He tilted his head back and stared up at the big house. Blue and white, yes, but that was like describing a castle as "greyish." Gingerbread trim curlicued around the house. Turrets jutted from the roof. Perfect for a boy to guard over the house from, he couldn't help thinking. Large bay windows opened up onto the lawn, and he imagined curling up in the sunlight with a schoolbook, as he thought a boy who lived in this house would. *That* boy would still be in school, not trudging all over town trying to find any job that would take him.

Envy spiked through William.

Valentine jerked the bell pull. A bell rang inside the house, but no footsteps answered it. They waited long enough for a maid to reach the door. They waited long enough for the mistress of the house to rouse herself and answer the door if the maid could not. They waited even a bit longer than that.

Valentine opened the door a crack. No irate butler appeared to chase them out. Valentine pushed the door open wider and strode inside.

William timidly followed. Over the threshold, he stopped and gaped. Only the grumbled curses of the men piling up behind him propelled him into the house. Polished wood gleamed, oak and mahogany carved so artfully that William thought they belonged in a museum. He wouldn't dare sit on one of the fancy chairs in case he messed it up, even though his legs still ached. They looked awful inviting, though, all overstuffed plush and brocade.

A hunting landscape papered the hall, dogs baying happily after a fox while figures on horseback watched from a distant hill. Birds flew through blue skies near the ceiling. The poppies and daisies painted at the bottom stood out sharp and vivid, as if they sprouted from the baseboards; William felt an impulse to stoop and pick one. A grand open staircase swept up from the entryway to the second floor.

It seemed so fantastic, like something from a dream or a storybook. They could live here now, he and his mam, if they wanted to. William tilted back his head, a huge smile on his face, and saw—a gas-lit chandelier. It hung above their heads like the

Sword of Damocles. Sunlight glittered on brass. Broken rainbows danced across their faces.

Fragments of memory. Flesh cut to ribbons. Small bodies. The cries of the dying.

William bolted outside and vomited in the hydrangeas. Valentine followed him out and patted him awkwardly on the shoulder. "It's all right, boy. Bad things take some men like that. They'll be strong as long as they need to be, and then ... Everything will be fine now."

William looked up at him and didn't believe a word he said. But he went back in, though he avoided looking at the chandelier, afraid of what he might see reflected in its prisms.

Valentine's men spread out to explore their new domain.

Two rampaged upstairs. "I'm sleeping on a feather bed tonight!" Tommy hollered.

Patrick said, "I'm going to eat like a rich man!" The others scoffed and asked him if he'd be cooking up this rich food himself, but that didn't stop him from going in search of the kitchen.

The joyful shouts upstairs stopped abruptly, and the men came back to stand above the staircase, grim-faced. "We found the nursery," Tommy said. "And the master's study," the other added.

Patrick returned from the kitchen looking as if he'd lost his appetite. "The butler, the maid, the footman, and the cook were all in the kitchen when the storm hit. I think the cook would have lived if she hadn't collapsed onto the range."

Valentine winced. "That's not pork for dinner I was smelling, then." He pointed at William. "You stay here. We'll need to haul them out."

"Bury them, you mean?" William asked.

Valentine hesitated. "Of course, of course. In the garden. That'll be nice for them, won't it? Like sleeping under flowers."

"I know they're dead," William told him. "I'm not a baby."

"That you're not," Valentine said dryly. "More like a bird chirping in my ear."

William stayed.

Valentine's gang went up the curving staircase. There was thumping, and some cursing, and then they came down the stairs with carefully sheet-wrapped bundles, some pitifully small. They went out back. The *thunk* of shovel hitting dirt carried into the entryway, but William stayed where he was. More cursing. When silence fell, William went out into the back garden.

The men stood, hats in hand, around a large, churned-up patch of ground. Seven new mounds lay at the foot of the rose bushes, but what had been planted would not blossom into life next spring. Valentine mumbled the Lord's prayer and they all trouped back inside.

"Rich folk like these will have their own indoor water closet," Patrick said. "Did anyone see it? I'd like to wash the grave dirt from under my fingernails." One of the others pointed him in the right direction. After a few moments, he came back looking disgusted. "I thought I'd like using one of those fancy water closets, but the water wasn't running at all! I used a pitcher and basin to wash my hands, just like usual."

"Was there a bathtub?" Conrad asked.

"Aye and there was, but likely it won't be working!"

"I'll just be seeing about that!" Conrad said. "Even if I still need to haul the water, I'll be having a bath in a proper bathtub! Just like *I* was a rich man!"

He darted off, and after a moment, the sound of trickling water came to their ears. "I left the tap open, and there came a few drops. Now it's a proper stream, it is!" he shouted down.

Patrick scowled.

Valentine laughed. "Lads, I found something a mite more important than water: the liquor cabinet. It'll be a proper wake!"

That roused the spirits of the men and they happily followed Valentine. William trailed along, though his mam didn't let him drink anything stronger than short beer.

"Here's to the man of the house and his generous stock of liquor!" Valentine said, lifting a glass of whiskey.

William thought of the folk lying under a thin blanket of dirt in the garden, and he couldn't smile.

Valentine looked William's way, and his smile faded a bit. "May God and the angels welcome him and his family, and Mary intercede—"

A horrible gurgling scream interrupted the toast.

Chapter 3

~* * *~

The Great Boston Pyre, Part II

William McCormack
Beacon Hill, Boston, Massachusetts

Glasses shattered on the floor as the men dashed out.

"Conrad!" Valentine shouted.

No answer came.

They ran to the bathroom. Steam filled the room. Water overflowed the clawfoot tub and turned the carpet into a bubbling marsh. Conrad slumped back in the tub, his head lolling. A torrent of boiling-hot water jetted from the broken pipe at the foot of the bath and buffeted Conrad's unresponsive body.

Conrad wouldn't be enjoying a bath "like a rich man" ever again. The spout of the bath jutted out from his neck. A foamy mix of blood and air dripped onto his chest. He must have settled into the tub and leaned his head back, putting his throat on a direct-line trajectory from the faucet.

His skin hung strangely loose. The water was boiling it away from his body, William realized. The sight made him feel cold and empty and like he'd never enjoy soup again.

Even as they watched, the water sputtered, surged forward again, and then dwindled to a normal stream.

Valentine squished over to the bathtub. As carefully as if he handled a live firecracker, he reached behind the bathtub and turned the valve to shut off the water. "Luck is with you that you didn't try the tap longer, Patrick," he said quietly.

Patrick turned pale. "What happened?"

Grimly, Valentine said, "Something bollixed the flow. I wonder if it's happening everywhere?"

"We should warn people!" William said.

"Because rich people want help from the likes of us?"

William frowned. "Because my mam says we're supposed to help people."

Valentine found that impossible to refute. "All right, boys, you heard the lad. We've folk to help." More matter-of-factly, he added, "Besides, if the rich folk next door are beyond needing help, they'll start to smell soon. Can't have them dragging down the tone of the neighborhood."

On the way out, Valentine paused in the entrance hall. "I wonder." He waved them out of the house, pressed the chandelier's push-button switch, and ducked outside. Nothing happened for a moment, and then a slow glow brightened the windows. He shrugged. "Worth checking."

A tinkling crash sounded as the chandelier *exploded*, sending a sideways rain of crystal prisms through the air. The window cracked from side to side.

After a thoughtful pause, Valentine said, "Today is not a good day to be a rich man."

The next house over, the only survivors were the butler and the cook, an Irish woman who said she and the butler were perfectly fine, thanks much for the warning. She insisted on feeding them cheese and biscuits before they left.

At the house after, the owner still lived. Beyond that, they found out nothing. The owner seemed to agree that it wasn't a good day to be a rich man, but being a rich man, he took it as a personal slight. He answered Valentine's knock at the door with a rifle in his hands and a cornered-rat look in his eyes.

"Good day," Valentine said. "We're looking to see if there's any as need help. Are there wounded here?"

"I don't need help from any damned paddies!" The owner waved his rifle. "Get off my property! Your kind isn't welcome here."

William pushed forward. "Sir," he said, "we just—"

"Off!" the man bellowed. The boom of the rifle near-deafened William. A cloud of dirt kicked up in front of his feet.

Panicked, he bolted. Valentine's men skedaddled after him, but their legs were longer than his. They rounded the gate first.

The rifle boomed again, splintering the gatepost beside him. Pain shredded William's shoulder. He stumbled and fell, clutching his arm.

Valentine looked over his shoulder, saw the fallen boy, and ran back. He pulled William up and along to safety. They stopped when they were out of sight.

"Let me see your arm, little man," Valentine said, with a gentleness that worried William.

William bit his lip. He let Valentine pull back his shirt to look.

Valentine blew out his breath and smiled. "You're all right. A large splinter hit your arm, but it's right under your skin. It'll only be a minute to get it out."

After the impromptu operation—William was very brave and didn't complain, even though it hurt—Valentine sat back, a jagged four-inch splinter of gatepost in his hand and a dark look on his face.

"Shooting at a wee lad! That motherless son! Fine. If that lot don't want our help, we won't try. Let's go back to *our* mansion."

William pressed his palm against his injured arm. A slow, stubborn anger rose in him, fed by days of walking, looking for any job that would have him. Fed by the way the rich ladies pulled back their skirts when he came by, as if he were an animal. Fed by how tired his mother looked when she came back from the factory job that she was so grateful to have. Fed by endless meals of soup that his mother "stretched" with more water when they had nothing else to put in the stew pot.

Why help the rich?

The question echoed through William. He looked up to find Valentine watching him with an odd expression.

"What's wrong?" William asked.

"This is usually where you chime in and insist we help someone."

William looked away. He tried to shake off his anger. His mam had told him time and again that anger and bitterness weren't the way to a better life. "Accept what is, and work for what will be," she'd say, "and a brighter tomorrow will come along."

A brighter tomorrow didn't seem likely, though surely it couldn't be worse than today. He hoped. After the terrible topsy-turvy day, he could rely on nothing. The world pressed down on him, and he was about as much use as a pebble underfoot.

"Come along, lad."

William trailed after Valentine, his insides knotting more with every step.

He wished he could make his mam feel better, like she always did for him when he sickened. She'd get out the nice wool shawl she'd brought over from Ireland, wrap it around his shoulders, and sing him to sleep. Maybe she'd like to have the shawl now? He could bring it back for her. And the precious tintype photo of his mam and his da when they first arrived off the boat, all wide eyes and bright hopes, himself a bundle in his mam's arms. And their papers and letters, and his mam's church dress, and the two patchwork quilts they huddled together under when it grew cold, and his mam's best ladle, and—it wasn't much, but it was more than one small boy could carry.

"Valentine, would you help me get a few of my mam's belongings, to make her feel better?"

"Sure and I would! But not tonight."

William thought of the people who shared the one-room apartment with him and his mam: the Tienkens, a newly arrived German family. Mr. Tienken had died on the boat, leaving Mrs. Tienken with four children to tend to. The youngest's nightly cabbage-inspired symphony might irritate William, but the girls were okay, for girls. They helped William's mam with mending and such.

The oldest boy, Robert, was better than okay. Robert had been able to get a job as a newspaper boy, because everyone knew that Germans were hard-working and trustworthy, but Robert said the other newspaper boys were boring. William and Robert stood up for each other when anybody tried to bully one of them. When Robert found a starveling puppy, he brought it home and—with many tears and even more promises that it wouldn't be a burden, that it could live off rats and the scraps of scraps—persuaded the mothers to let him keep it. Robert's puppy grew into a fine spaniel who made the children laugh and their mothers smile and kept their feet warm in the winter.

William hoped they were still alive.

As he thought these things, William followed after Valentine and his gang. By the time he reached the mansion, he'd come to a conclusion. He stopped in front of the porch steps. The men kept going into the house. Valentine only noticed the boy when he turned around to close the door and found William still outside.

"Going back to see to your mam?" Valentine asked kindly.

"We should go to the slums and help the people there," William said. "*They* won't turn away our help."

Valentine blinked. "Ah, that's a fine idea, but—" he looked at the sky, "—it's coming on sunset. Tonight is not the night for small boys to be out in the street. And we've a nasty job to do here. I brought Conrad into this house, so I owe him a decent burial." He patted William's shoulder. "You should not see it. Your mam must miss you by now."

William stuck out his chin. "We have to help them! Nobody else will, you know that! *You* have to help them!" He stared at Valentine and Tommy and Patrick and the other men accusingly.

"They'll be fine 'til tomorrow or they'll die anyway," Valentine said. "You go on back to your mam."

Unhappy, William bit his lip. He couldn't help on his own, and he suspected his mam would agree about boys staying in tonight.

Seeing his distress, Valentine softened. "Tomorrow morning we'll go down to the North End, all right? But now you should be going along to Dr. Fallon's house. You and your mam will be fine there, with that great lot of people you gathered."

Valentine had the same *stretched* look William's mam got when he'd pestered her past bearing, so William reluctantly agreed.

He walked down the hill with many reproachful looks over his shoulder. But Valentine had closed the door, and if anybody watched him from the windows, William couldn't tell.

He reached Dr. Fallon's home safely, but the night was not made for sleeping. He curled up in a chair beside his mam and listened to her breathing. Dr. Fallon's laudanum let her sleep through the night, but not him. William would drift off easily enough, but then he would wake with a start, convinced his mam had stopped breathing. He had to hold his breath and wait until his heart stopped racing before he could hear her soft exhalations. He lost track of how many times he woke in the night.

The people camped on Dr. Fallon's lawn also slept poorly. Some woke screaming from their sleep, which set all the babies crying. Farther away, shouting and the sound of breaking glass and screams bore out Valentine's warning. William hoped that none of the troublemakers would bother the men who'd rescued his mam.

~ * ~

William rose when the first fingers of dawn stretched under the door. His mam slept on, her breathing even and undisturbed. He kissed her on the forehead and slipped outside.

Most of the people outside had fallen into a restless sleep. Here and there, a person or a pair sat and watched the sun rise.

The forgiving golden light of earliest morning washed across the survivors on the lawn. It erased worry lines and cleansed grime-coated skin. The red-gold sun rose, promising new hope and new beginnings.

Except.

Thin rivulets of dark smoke trickled up into the sky across the city, putting the lie to sunrise's promise. Fires had broken out overnight—though they did not seem to be spreading.

William gathered his courage and walked back to the mansion that Valentine and his lads had taken over. The streets were quiet, but it was a *listening-for-danger* quiet. Windows had been smashed out in many of the mansions that lined the street. A dead body lay on the lawn in front of the house that they had been rebuffed from the evening before. It wasn't the owner. Gas lights flickered and flared and died behind windows. Water oozed out from under one door and streamed down the hill. William crossed the street to avoid walking in it.

When William entered the blue and white mansion, he noticed a hodgepodge of precious things that hadn't been there the previous day. They didn't seem to match the furnishings of the house, but he supposed they might have been found in the attic.

The men who were awake greeted him with cries of "Ho there!" and "Hey!" and "There's our little man!"

Valentine sprawled across the parlor sofa. The shouting roused him. His eyes opened. He yawned and scratched his balls and waved his hand in greeting.

Tommy walked down the stairs wearing a very satisfied expression. A woman with disheveled hair and a shawl wrapped around her bare torso leaned over the balcony and called, "Mind ye be careful out there, Tom!" Seeing William, she added, "I beg your pardon, I didn't see the lad," and retreated back to the bedroom.

Patrick ambled out of the kitchen with a napkin full of biscuits. He offered one to William. William would have politely refused, but his stomach answered before he could. Noisily. Patrick laughed and gave him *two* biscuits.

A black eye bloomed gloriously on Patrick's face. Tommy and Valentine both had split knuckles. Yet they all seemed to be in a fine humor.

"Can we go now?" William asked, as soon as he'd devoured the biscuits. "To help the people in the North End?"

"If there are any *left* in the North End," Patrick mumbled.

"Patrick speaks true, lad," Valentine said. "Most of the North End has left for finer surroundings."

"All the more reason that we should help the ones who are still there!" William looked up at the men. "And I'd like to take a few things to my mam, but there's too much for me to carry on my own, and—"

"Of course we'll be helping you!" Tommy said. "You've brought us our good luck!"

"But first we've to empty our bladders and fill our stomachs," Valentine added.

They all avoided the water closet. The men went into the back garden and pissed over the fence, making sport of a grim situation. It embarrassed William. His mam had always insisted he wait to use the outhouse, though there was only the one for the whole building, and filth crusted its floor. The other boys pissed in the alley, "like the animals they call us," his mother said. "My son will not."

Before leaving, Valentine and his gang—and William, too—breakfasted well on smoked ham and the last of the cornbread the cook had made before her final encounter with the stove.

Walking through Beacon Hill, the men strode down the street six abreast, as if they owned it. Even the bruises added a certain flair.

When they reached the warren of tenement houses in the North End, however, they slowed down and bunched together. Valentine hefted the *shillelagh* that he'd acquired overnight.

In the slum, the evidence of disturbances was more—disturbing. Windows had been broken from the inside. People's belongings were strewn out into the street like rubbish. Somewhere, a baby cried weakly.

Mounds of bodies lurked in the alleys, waiting to catch an unwary glance. Most had the arched bodies and bloodied faces of those who had died in the storm, but a few bore wounds from knives, guns, or fists. A few wore clothing too fine for the North End. William saw one young man whose arms were extended, his fingers curved into claws, as if he'd been trying to pull himself out of the pile when he died. Stains patched the street. Dead animals lay in the gutter, cats and dogs and rats forming a peaceful kingdom in death.

The rats who survived ate well.

"This way." It came out in a whisper. William cleared his throat and tried again. "This way!" He led them into the tenement house he and his mam lived in.

Once, it had been a fine house for a family. Then their landlord bought it and divided it up into rooms-to-rent with partitions that preserved the *appearance* of privacy, but nothing else. Everybody heard the fights between couples, and the making-up after. One colicky baby could ruin everyone's rest, though the residents learned to sleep through the tromping of feet up the stairs as workers returned from the night shift. Everybody smelled everybody else's cooking. (All the residents agreed that Mrs. MacDougal was the best cook.)

Mrs. MacDougal's closet-sized room was on the first floor. Her door was ajar, and the smell of burnt scones hung in the hallway.

The hinges squealed as William pushed the door open.

The room appeared to be empty. William let out a pent-up breath—and then he saw the foot. A single, naked foot poked out from under the mound of Mrs. MacDougal's bedding. He stepped closer.

Patrick put out a hand to stop him. "Here now, lad, there's no need for you to see this. We can—"

The bed exploded with a screech. A tangle of blankets flew through the air and resolved into a sullen-mouthed girl wrapped in one of Mrs. MacDougal's quilts. She pressed a fitful babe to her chest.

"Get out!" she yelled.

"Where's Mrs. MacDougal?" William asked.

A little sympathy came into the girl's expression. "She's dead now, isn't she? Died in the storm."

"And you just moved into her room?"

"She wasn't using it, was she? And the baby fussed so much that my brothers threatened to throw me out in the street if I couldn't quiet him." She shuddered. "'Twasn't a good night to be in the street."

"Where's her—" William swallowed. "Where's her body?"

The girl jerked her head to the window that looked out over the alley..

"You tossed her out like trash!?" William sputtered.

The girl stared at him, open-mouthed. "What else can we do? We're not the ones in charge." Her baby started squalling, and she put him to her breast.

"Come along, lad. Let's leave the colleen be." Valentine pulled William into the hallway and gently closed the door on the girl nursing her babe.

"It's not how it *ought* to be!"

"No, that it's not. But she had the right of it when she said we're not the ones in charge. We can hardly bury all the North End's dead. There's not enough stones in the city to make a cairn big enough."

William looked at the narrow, dark hallway and the small, unlit rooms. "It's a cairn already."

"The bodies will cause disease if they're not taken care of proper," Patrick said unexpectedly. "When they rot."

Valentine raised an eyebrow.

"That's what Dr. Fallon said. Fire or earth, that's what it takes to keep disease from rising among us and killing even more." Patrick's face did a funny thing, as if it were trying very hard not to allow a smile to escape. "She's awful clever."

William only remembered bits and pieces from when the disease swept through the slum and killed his da, but he knew how tight his mam's face grew when it was talked of, and how memory shadowed her eyes.

He remembered other things, too. How tired his mam was when she got back from the factory. The few times she'd come home without her basket or with a new tear in her sleeve, though she'd shrugged it off as, "Rowdies too drunk to know what they're doing." How the noise and the heat and the smells of the tenement house wore on her.

"The whole city's rotting," he said. His arm ached.

He looked at the narrow warren of rooms that had suffocated the dreams of so many. "Burn it."

"Burn the bodies?" asked Patrick. "They're too close to the walls. The buildings would catch fire."

"The slums?" Valentine said wonderingly. "Well, now, I think the lad has a most *interesting* idea. They cannot force us back here if there's no *here* to force us to. And it's not like there's much here worth, ah, retrieving."

"It's no proper burial," Tommy protested.

"The Church makes allowances," Valentine said. "And since when have you worried about your every action being right with God?"

The other men looked uneasy, too.

"Would you let them sit out and rot like meat gone bad?" Valentine demanded.

Their faces went from uneasy to queasy.

"There are corpses in the better part of town to see to, too," Patrick said.

Why help the rich?

"Not near so many. And the rich will take care of their own."

Why should the rich be spared what the poor suffer?

"Not just the slums. Burn it *all*," William said, his eyes sharp and glittering with unshed tears.

Valentine frowned. "That's a harsh thing to say, lad. And think of all the fine houses and all the fine things in them."

"Fewer fine things than there used to be," Tommy said, residual guilt lingering in his tone.

Valentine pulled William aside a bit, and squatted down to talk to him face-to-face. "William, we've fallen into hard times. My lads believe you've brought us luck. You, ah, *persuaded* us to help those folk yesterday, and last night, well, we fared far better than most others on the street. Casting bread upon the waters, like. Your presence was why Dr. Fallon agreed to help us, and she's the one who told us of our fine new house. You couldn't bear to look at the chandelier, so I told the lads not to light it up. If we had, it would have sliced us to bloody ribbons. Since surviving that storm of death, we're all a mite more superstitious. If you say we should burn the city, they'll give it a serious try."

William glared, his face hot and hard. "You think the rich deserve better?"

"Dr. Fallon's in a rich part of town. She's tending to your mam. Would you burn her house, too?"

"I—"

"Mind you, I think burning the slums is a *fine* idea. We live packed in here, and any who stay here now will be cheek-to-jowl with their neighbors' corpses. That's not a healthy thing for a body. Think on it, though, before you goad the lads on."

William reluctantly nodded.

"Good lad." Valentine patted William's shoulder. "Don't fret. We have plenty to do here—helping people, right?"

Valentine stood and walked back to the others, with William at his side. "Right, then, lads! We're going to help William gather his mam's things—and then we're going to burn the North End to the ground!"

The men cheered. How could they resist the appeal of burning something right down to the ground?

"We'll need to go through each tenement house room by room to make sure all the survivors are out before we burn it."

"What will we do with them?" Patrick asked. "Dr. Fallon's home is full."

Valentine cut his eyes at William. "Let's ask our luck. Where will they be safe from burning, William?"

William's stomach tightened and his skin heated, but he kept his voice level when he said, "The Common." Boston's central park was large enough for everyone to have a patch of ground to spread their blanket out on.

"A good choice. Patrick, go back to Dr. Fallon's house and see if you can get volunteers to help us: some to herd survivors away, and some to aid the injured. And don't spend overmuch time chatting up the *clever* doctor," Valentine added dryly.

Patrick nearly tripped over his own feet in his haste to escape.

Valentine, Tommy, and the other lads went down the hallway of the tenement house. William walked ahead, shouting, "Fire!" It was the one thing that slum-dwellers feared even above rent-collecting bullyboys.

Some might have hesitated if a harsh-sounding man tried to get them out of their rooms, but nobody suspected a child of lying. And he wasn't, not precisely.

The few surviving inhabitants fled their rooms clutching whatever was most precious to them. Facing hard men who still bore the marks of recent battle, they chose not to argue about leaving.

At first, Valentine and the lads checked every room carefully, making sure that no survivors hid inside. Despite the mounds of dead outside, corpses yet lay concealed behind flimsy doors: a man face-down in his bowl of soup; a woman sprawled across her mending; an old man who'd been abed with his liquor bottle when he was stricken; a half-clothed child whose dead mother still held its dress; a couple entwined together whose lovemaking had ended in death spasms; and other, more pedestrian corpses.

Some few they found injured or unconscious. It didn't take close inspection to tell the difference between the softly crumpled insensate and the rigor-locked dead.

As with the corpses on the street, not all had died on the fire.

William looked in the first room they found that had a kicked-in door. He gulped. He hadn't liked the woman who lived there much—she'd been able to afford a whole room to herself, for one thing, which seemed terribly greedy—but nobody should die like that. She'd survived the storm, but not the other survivors.

After that, he didn't look.

No man among them was hardened enough to remain unaffected. They went from careful searches to glancing looks that could catch the essentials—dead or alive—without absorbing the details.

In that way, they worked through the tenement house until William stood in front of the door to the room he shared with his mam and the Tienken family. He cleared his throat.

"Fire," he tried to say, but it came out a squeak.

"Do you want me to go ahead and check?" Valentine asked.

William shook his head, his throat too tight to speak.

The men broke down the locked door as gently as possible.

Best get it over fast, William thought. He charged into the room—and halted. Another boy had charged forward at the same time and stopped as abruptly. Now he stood, staring, the knife in his hand hanging down by his side.

"William?" Robert Tienken said. His spaniel dodged past him and jumped up to lick William's hands. "You're alive!" Robert sat down abruptly. The knife fell from his grasp. "I didn't know what was going on, and there were the most terrible noises."

"How—how are the others?" William asked.

Robert pressed the heels of his hands hard against his eyes. "It's just me and Lena now." His sister crept out from her hiding place in the corner and curled up beside him. The spaniel wagged his tail and licked her tear-stained face.

William swallowed hard. He had guessed Mrs. Tienken dead when he saw Robert alone, with a knife in hand. That he'd lost one sister and his little brother too—

William felt about two feet tall when he remembered how much he'd teased Robert's brother about his unfortunate reaction to cabbage.

"They're in the bed," Robert said, pointing. A green quilt ("the color of Irish grass," his mam had called it) covered three mounds.

"Come with me," William said. "My mam will be happy to see you and Lena. Choose what you want to take and these men will help us."

"This is home." Robert hugged his sister closer to him.

"We'll burn it down once the people are out. Too many died here."

"Mam has to be buried proper in consecrated ground!"

Valentine stepped into the room. "The church gives dispensation for special circumstances. A priest will say a blessing over the ashes, and the ground will all be consecrated. Lad, you must look out for your sister, and the way to do that is to go to William's mam. Choose what you wish to take."

They took the little money they had and the things that held good memories or family history, but little else. The grass-green quilt they left.

They were last out of the house. A handful of survivors huddled together in a clutch. Others began walking to the Common, their belongings knotted up in quilts and slung over their backs.

Grinning, Tommy sloshed the contents of an unmarked brown bottle onto the wall. The reek of cheap alcohol filled the air. He struck a lucifer and poised it on his fingertips, ready to flick into the puddle of alcohol at the base of the wall.

"Not yet, you daft fool!" Valentine seized Tommy's arm. "It'll catch the other houses on fire before we can clear them!"

Too late.

His sudden movement sent the match flying. The world seemed to stop, holding its breath, as the match turned end over end. It struck the puddle with a hiss and a fizzle—and then the fire flared to life, crackling like the flames of hell.

The shoddy wood made excellent tinder. The fire ate the alcohol-soaked wood hungrily and climbed higher, seeking more food. The survivors stared at the flames licking their way up the building. One woman screamed. They started to run.

William grabbed Robert's hand. Robert grabbed little Lena's hand. "This way!" William shouted, tugging them toward Beacon Hill.

"Wait!" Valentine said. He stared at the fire. "I've burned—ah, that is, I've *seen* a fair number of fires, and something about this isn't right."

He picked up a wooden spoon dropped in the scuffle, narrowed his eyes, and strode forward to stand as close as he could get to the burning building. Heat burnished his skin a cherry red. He threw up one arm to protect his face, but he held the wooden spoon out until it nearly touched the fire.

And stood there.

"Madness," Tommy muttered, but he waited to see what would happen, as did William.

The answer was—nothing. The fire didn't lick out to swallow the spoon.

Valentine backed away. "The fire is sticking close to what it burns." He brandished the unscorched wooden spoon. "It will not be jumping to other houses unless they actually *touch*."

The men laughed with relief. Tommy ruffled William's hair— as if *he'd* had anything to do with their narrow escape from becoming mass murderers.

William tried to recall his science lessons. "As if there's not enough fire aether to let it spread?" He vividly remembered one demonstration. His teacher had lit a match, and a stack of kindling a foot away had exploded into flame. Only the tube of aether between them made the transmission of fire possible.

Patrick spoke up. "It's all aether-related things that the storm damaged, Dr. Fallon says."

Valentine nodded slowly. "If the aether surged, it could explain the torrent of water that killed Conrad, and the exploding chandelier."

"Dr. Fallon thinks the dead might have been killed by their own bone aether, too." Patrick cleared his throat. "Er, she hoped we'd bring her a body to examine."

Valentine raised his eyebrows. "Oh, she did, did she? There are enough dead on Beacon Hill that if your ladylove wants a special gift, you can get it and wrap it up for her closer to home."

"I didn't—. She's not—. It's not—." Patrick stuttered until Valentine laughed hugely and relieved him of the need to answer.

"What about the bodies in the alley?" William asked. "Will they still burn?"

"Most of them touch the wall. As far as the others," Valentine grinned, "we'll set every tenement house in this cursed slum afire! Burning timbers, stones, falling embers ... the bodies *will* burn." Valentine narrowed his eyes. "When you strike a match, things burn. While you're back up on Beacon Hill with your mam, you be thinking about that before you say something to my lads that will start a fire you won't be able to put out."

~ * ~

Jonathan Matzke, the Man So Thin He Wears a Wedding Ring As a Belt!
Boston Harbor, Boston, Massachusetts

The circus members stared out across the city and watched it burn. A thick pillar of dark smoke billowed up from Boston's North End, and thin rivulets straggled up into the sky from elsewhere in the city.

The skeleton man swallowed hard against the lingering bite of acid in his throat. Jonathan hadn't looked forward to returning to Boston, but he'd never imagined anything like this!

Lacey Miller, the equestrienne, squared her shoulders and touched her hat quickly, as if to be sure it sat at the perfect angle. A fine time for her to be concerned with fashion! "The situation calls for us to keep level heads. Perhaps this Mr. Roderick White can advise us as to our best course. There must be a reason his name was on the ringmaster's list."

In that moment, her unshakable upper-class composure made Jonathan hate her a little. Stiff upper lip and *noblesse oblige* be damned, the situation seemed to him to call for some old-fashioned screaming and running around waving your arms in the air.

Lacey turned to the fortune teller. "Mrs. Wershow, who do you think we should send to speak with him?"

Good choice, Jonathan admitted. The old witch always had a suggestion or six ready for anyone who asked. Uncanny accurate they were, too, based on things she had no business knowing.

"So kind of you to ask an old woman, dearie!"

Jonathan carefully didn't snort. Her ears were far too sharp, her movements far too quick (when she wanted them to be), and her eyes were far too keen for her to be *that* old. He rubbed his arm, remembering The Fried Chicken Incident. His elbow had been a reliable barometer of bad weather for six months after. She might act old if she pleased, but nobody could tell what she really looked like under all her scarves and shawls and paste jewels, and her veil concealed her face.

"You should go, for one," the fortune teller told Lacey.

Lacey's eyes widened. "I? Surely we should send someone with authority in the circus!"

"Hmm, yes. Dear, you're so *achingly* genteel that sometimes you make my back teeth hurt. Isn't that what we need to speak with someone close to the mayor?"

"I—I shall do my best."

Jonathan coughed to conceal a laugh.

"And for the second person—" the fortune teller's eyes gleamed through her veil, "Jonathan Matzke, the skeleton man."

Jonathan tried to swallow his laugh, but it went down the wrong way and wound up as an all-too-genuine coughing fit.

"Not me!"

"You were raised in Boston, and you still keep contact with some of your old friends. You'll have a much better idea of what's really going on."

Jonathan glared, but the fortune teller's veil foiled his attempt to stare her down. He'd never told anyone that he grew up in Boston, much less that he still wrote letters home. What *else* did she know?

"There's another important question that we must consider," the fortune teller added. "Who will act as ringmaster now that Mr. Loyale is dead?"

Chapter 4

~* * *~

Who's Running the Show?

Jonathan Matzke, the Man So Thin He Wears a Wedding Ring As a Belt!
Boston, Massachusetts

When Jonathan and Lacey disembarked from the ship, they descended into chaos. Children and women climbed aboard ships or held up their arms, pleading to be taken away. Sailors' wives and favored dockside tarts got equal treatment. In at least one case, the same sailor pulled both aboard. Even the chickens and geese stacked in crates on the wharf squawked hysterically, as if begging for passage.

Men wheeled handcarts back to their ships, the contents piled high and hidden with tarp or sheet or tablecloth. Jonathan's eyes gleamed. It was a lovely opportunity for a little look-see around the cargo to be loaded. If only he weren't with the equestrienne.

No hackney cabs waited near the docks

"We shall have to walk," Lacey said, her tone slightly dismayed. "Fortunately, I decided that walking dress would be the most appropriate attire, since we didn't know what we'd find."

"Oh, aye, couldn't have you wearing the wrong dress," Jonathan agreed.

"We shall need an escort. I would bring the strongman, but the appearance of a free black might cause trouble with things so unsettled." She gave Jonathan an assessing once-over.

"I may not be the strongest—" Jonathan began, but he spoke to empty air.

Lacey walked up to a burly man heading back into Boston proper. "Excuse me, kind sir," she said.

Jonathan edged closer, fascinated by the bemused expression on the sailor's face. A strong smell of saltwater and fish came off the man, but the long voyage back from India had left them all well-acquainted with the scent of seafarers.

"Um, yes, miss?" the sailor said hesitantly, after a glance around to make certain he was the one being so addressed.

"My companion and I find ourselves in need of an escort to City Hall. On School Street?" she added hopefully.

"I know where it is," the sailor admitted.

"Thank you so much! You are a true gentleman." Lacey leaned in and placed a gloved hand delicately on the sailor's arm. "I shall feel so safe in your company."

Still somewhat confused, the sailor puffed up his chest nonetheless.

"And of course, we will compensate you for your trouble," she added.

The presence of a lady and the promise of compensation seemed to reconcile the sailor to being shanghaied.

Jonathan soon grew glad of the larger man's presence. A prickling feeling along his back warned him that not-so-friendly eyes watched their progress. Men roamed the streets in packs, eying each other like dogs deciding whether to fight.

Jonathan could handle himself in a situation that called for a quick escape or a quicker stick with a knife, but the sailor's size kept such situations from even arising.

Flies buzzed around dead animals in the gutters. Jonathan caught glimpses of human bodies in alleys and closed shops. He did not look more closely. Broken glass crunched underfoot. Stores, factories, and homes all stared down at the street with darkened eyes, though furtive shadows moved behind some of those windows.

From Lacey's demeanor, a body would think that nothing out of the ordinary occurred around them. Jonathan found himself grateful for that pretense of normality.

When they reached School Street, they found that someone had made an effort. The street was clear of corpses and refuse. Oil lamps burned behind windows. A dozen coppers walked back and forth along the street, clearly on guard, and just as clearly not guarding other places: groceries and confectioneries and butcher shops and dry goods stores and bakeries.

At Jonathan's sigh, Lacey looked back over her shoulder at him. "We're nearly there. See?" She pointed along the street to a building whose granite exterior gleamed in the sun. The massive doors stood open, revealing a darkened maw inside. Jonathan shuffled his feet, staying behind Lacey and their fishy escort.

As they walked up the path to those huge doors, the statue of Benjamin Franklin gazed down upon them from his pedestal with serious, considering eyes. All very well for him, Jonathan thought. *He* was safely dead. *They* still needed to avoid joining him prematurely.

The sailor coughed. "I'll wait outside, ma'am." He nodded toward a bench under a tree.

"Thank you," Lacey said, nothing in voice or deed betraying any awareness that the sailor might abandon them to make their own way back through the haunted streets.

Inside City Hall, Lacey paused. Jonathan stopped just in time to keep from barreling into her. Squares of sunlight fell from the tall windows and illuminated the entrance. Gentlemen hurried through the halls. It seemed a hive of activity.

A young man clutching a sheaf of papers stopped when he saw them. "I'm terribly sorry," he said, "but City Hall is closed to regular petitioners today." He pointed. "If you see that gentleman, he'll record your name and information, so that we may contact you once—once the current crisis is past."

"Oh, we're not petitioners!" Lacey said. "We're from the Loyale Traveling Circus and Museum of Educational Novelties. Our ringmaster had an appointment with the mayor's assistant, a Mr. Roderick White?"

An appointment? Perhaps Lacey wasn't so propriety-bound as to be useless after all. Jonathan wouldn't queer her pitch.

"Circus?" The young man blinked. For a moment, the weariness in his face gave way to an echo of childhood delight. "Perhaps this will lift the mayor's spirits. Please wait here."

"We have no need to inconvenience the mayor. We only wish—" Lacey began, but the clickety-clack of the man's boots faded before she could complete her sentence. "—to see Mr. White," she concluded feebly.

"Looks like we'll have an appointment with the mayor," Jonathan said.

She visibly rearranged her expectations. "If that is so, it will be an honor. But I'm certain such an important man will have other responsibilities, in this—current crisis."

It appeared not, however. When the young man returned, he radiated expectant pleasure. "This way, please. The mayor will see you now."

The mayor's well-appointed office held books that spoke of learning, paintings that spoke of wealth, and a tall stack of paperwork that spoke of importance. The mayor paid attention to none of it. When they entered, they found him standing beside the window, his back to the door, rubbing his right arm absentmindedly as he stared at the thick pillar of smoke they'd seen from the *Aether's Bounty*.

"My city is burning," he said quietly. He faced them. His patrician bone structure may have been bred to hold the hopes of millions, but his pale blue eyes were shadowed and sad.

"Mr. Mayor," said the young man, "these are the personages from the, uh, Loyal Circus and Museum, Miss—." He floundered.

"Miss Lacey Miller and Mr. Jonathan Matzke," Lacey rescued him, "from the Loyale Traveling Circus and Museum of Educational Novelties."

The young man cleared his throat and repeated their names. "And this is Mayor Arthur Padgett."

Mayor Padgett nodded and the young man disappeared as quickly as he could.

"Forgive him," Mayor Padgett said, "he's not my regular assistant."

"We did not mean to intrude," Lacey said. "In truth, we'd hoped to see Mr. White. Our circus ringmaster had a list, and Mr. White's name was written beside Boston."

"Had?" Mayor Padgett raised a finely carved brow.

"Mr. Loyale died at sea before we docked."

Jonathan admired Lacey's careful omissions, but not so much that he didn't notice a precariously balanced dip pen beside the inkwell on the mayor's desk. The pen had a lovely feather design etched into the handle. He edged closer to it.

"I'm sorry for your loss," Mayor Padgett said gravely.

Lacey nodded acknowledgment.

"Alas, Mr. White was among those taken from us by this crisis."

Lacey sagged. Jonathan shifted a little closer to the dip pen. His fingers itched to caress those curving lines.

"Forgive me, but—what has happened?" Lacey asked. "We have been at sea and only docked this morning."

"You must thank Providence for that. Yesterday, a terrible and uncanny storm struck our fair city. Uncounted numbers died. I fear their corpses still line our streets."

Jonathan fumbled and the pen fell to the carpet. He froze.

The mayor bent, quite naturally. He picked up the pen, and set it back beside the inkwell.

"Animals and even humble plants died in equal proportions." He pointed out the window. "Vandals have looted homes and set fires all over the city. With police numbers so reduced by the storm, my ability to maintain order is negligible. The whole city is a powder keg."

While Lacey and Mayor Padgett gazed out the window, Jonathan deftly slipped the pen into his pocket and eased farther back from the desk. Satisfaction thrilled through him as he ran his finger along the lines of the engraving.

"I thought I could do nothing to draw the city together. But now—you come."

"We come?" Lacey echoed.

"Something wonderful and joyful and wholesome. Something that will remind Boston's citizens of happier times."

Wholesome. Mr. Loyale would have loved to hear that. He had added "Museum of Educational" to "Novelties" to give that impression, along with introducing Biblical tableaus to the menagerie: The Garden of Eden, The Lion and the Child, that sort of thing. His measures had prevented small-town ministers from preaching against the immorality of the circus, but they'd never actually been called wholesome by anybody but sign-painters before.

"I fear you lend us more importance than we have," Lacy said. "Yet, if you believe our presence can provide hope in a dark time, we shall do our humble best."

"Can you get the circus set up by this evening? I fear that another lawless night will rip this city apart."

"I—it usually takes us a full day to set the circus up!" Lacey protested. "But, yes, I suppose. If we must. As I recall, the last time we were here we set up in Boston Common. Does that still suit?"

"Refugees from the North End—that's where the big fire is— have taken up residence in the Common." Mayor Padgett paused. "All the better for my purpose, I suppose. Yes, the Common is an excellent choice. You have my personal gratitude and the gratitude of the City of Boston for your assistance."

Jonathan shifted uneasily, feeling the weight of the pen in his pocket.

"We're honored," Lacey murmured. "I hesitate to impose, but would it be possible to use your telegraph machine? Under the circumstances, I fear the telegraph office is closed."

"My dear, I'm sorry. All our aetheric devices failed or exploded. As you value your health, stay away from all such things. The telegraph's demise was less dramatic than most, but it is impossible to send or receive any messages. I've sent a messenger to the mayor of New York to beg for assistance, but it will take him more than four days to reach the city, and longer for any aid to return."

"No telegraph."

Mayor Padgett patted her gloved hands, momentarily resembling the benevolent patriarch Boston had elected.

Lacey withdrew her hands coolly. "No matter. Thank you for the information. And I do hope you can make it to our opening performance."

"I am so sorry I cannot help more. Please allow me to show you to my assistant's desk. Perhaps Mr. White left some message for your ringmaster."

Lacey thanked him, and they proceeded into the adjoining room. Mr. White's desk was more modest than the mayor's, but the stacks of paper were even higher. Lacey, with a quick apologetic look directed at Mayor Padgett, began sifting through the papers.

Jonathan rifled the drawers. The contents bored him: nothing shiny or colorful or edible, not so much as a tin of mints. He sat back on his haunches and scowled at it. Above him, Lacey continued reading the documents sitting on top of the desk, but he knew better. Nothing *really* interesting would be left out in plain sight.

He flopped down on his back, ignoring Lacey's startled exclamation, and wormed his way under the desk to stare up at the middle drawer. A cobweb clung to his face, but he brushed it aside. Something jutted out from the back of the drawer.

Using a delicate touch, he felt around until he found a spot that gave slightly under his fingertips, pressed it, and caught the hidden drawer as it fell into his hands. He emerged from under the desk triumphant, if with a low opinion of the maid's cleaning skills.

The hidden drawer held a Bible and a small parcel with 'Loyale' written across it.

"That's Mr. White's handwriting," Mayor Padgett said, leaning forward with interest.

Lacey reached out her hand for the parcel. Jonathan clutched it closer.

"Open it, then," she said.

Reluctant to lose the savor of the moment, he unwrapped the parcel as slowly as he dared. His eyebrows raised. He looked up at Lacey and Mayor Padgett to find that their expressions of blank amazement mirrored his own.

In his hands, he cradled a bundle of hundred-dollar treasury notes, more money than he'd ever seen in one place before. The urge to tighten his grip and bolt past Lacey and Major Padgett swept over him. He resisted until it faded, leaving him sweating. With all the coppers in front of City Hall, it would only take one shout from Mayor Padgett to have him arrested. And even if by some miracle he escaped the coppers, the state of the city didn't seem friendly to a thin, feeble-looking man on his own, especially one carrying anything valuable.

Lacey kept her composure. "Ah, he must have been passing along monies from one of the investors to the circus. Is there anything else?"

Jonathan shook his head.

Lacey smiled at Mayor Padgett. "Thank you so much for your assistance, Mayor. I'd best get back to the steamship so that the circus can prepare."

"It was a pleasure meeting you, Miss Miller." The mayor rubbed his arm again.

Lacey tilted her head slightly. "Likewise, I'm sure. Are you feeling well, sir?"

"As well as any." He laughed mirthlessly. "My arm still throbs sometimes. It's nothing."

They departed the mayor's office and reached the *Aether's Bounty* in safety. Lacey gave a few coins to the burly sailor who had escorted them, along with her thanks and two tickets to the circus. Still looking a bit bewildered by the whole affair, the sailor gave his cap a respectful tug and struck off along the dock.

In their absence, the crew of the *Aether's Bounty* had organized a watch to stand guard. A sailor walked the length of the ship, rifle in hand. When Lacey waved to him, he hurried over and let down the gangplank.

Jonathan tried to follow Lacey to see where she would hide the ringmaster's bounty. After only a few minutes, though, he stepped on a creaky board. Without looking over her shoulder, she called, "Go back and get ready for the grand entrance, skeleton man! I'll tell the others."

Discouraged, he went back to his room and sulked—until he remembered that he still had secret papers from the ringmaster's locked chest, and better than that, nobody cared what happened to the ringmaster's sausage. What was left of it. Jonathan had just nipped into the ringmaster's cabin and hid the bag of tasties under his tailcoat, along with a few other small items, when he heard the fortune teller and the whiteface clown coming down the passageway talking about packing up the ringmaster's belongings.

Jonathan dodged out the door and scuttled down the passageway in the opposite direction. Around a bend, he stopped, pressed his back to the wall, and listened. No outcry sounded. He breathed a sigh of relief. There was just enough time for a quick snack before he went to take his place in the grand entry procession.

He passed the animal trainer's assistant leading one of his new charges, a red-bearded langur monkey.

"Come along, Mr. Doom," the assistant said.

Jonathan stopped. "The monkey's name is *Doom*?"

"Ben Doom." The assistant shrugged sheepishly. "It seemed like a funny idea at the time."

"Our audience isn't in the best mood today. They might take it the wrong way."

They might take anything the wrong way. Jonathan pressed his hand to his waistcoat and felt the reassuring outline of the knife he'd taken the opportunity to secrete in his clothing, just in case.

The assistant sighed. "Come along, *Ben*."

Jonathan nodded and continued on to the circus wagon line-up.

In the depths of the ship, he heard the steam calliope start. It traditionally traveled last in the procession, but its music carried for blocks and blocks, summoning people to see the parade.

The sparkling silvery trim on the white circus wagon Jonathan shared with the fat lady always reminded him of sugar sprinkled onto a cake. He sat on the high carriage seat, while she sat in the back. They contrasted each other nicely and, he supposed, his slight weight helped keep the specially reinforced carriage from buckling under her poundage. He counted them lucky that the black Clydesdale that pulled their wagon was among the horses they'd taken with them to India. Not long after their return, Lacey had stalked by fuming about how impossible it was to buy or hire the necessary horses to haul the wagons.

The circus folk were arrayed in all their gaudy finery, the mud tarps pulled from gilded circus wagons, and the menagerie staring out from behind the bars of their cages (or, in the case of the snake charmer and her charges, the glass walls).They jockeyed into order for the grand processional, and then—the ship's crew lowered the gangplank. Jonathan found himself holding his breath as butterflies danced in his stomach.

The aether-powered elephant led the way. Brass chimed and clanked as its weight swung from side to side. The planks shook beneath its ponderous steps, but the mahout rode atop the massive animated elephant skeleton with rajah-like indifference.

Behind the elephant came the snake charmer's wagon. She dressed in green silks with an Egyptianish tiara on her forehead, and snakes twined around her arms and legs. They coiled against the glass sides of the wagon, pressing against it as if they tried to break free and spill out into the street. Jonathan shuddered.

Next came the ostrich cage. Their plumage gleamed in the sun. Improbably long necks stretched up above the top of the wagon, curving and bending as the ostriches bobbed their tiny heads. They eyed their surroundings, looking for something interesting to gobble up.

Jonathan and the fat lady's wagon followed, and after them, the lion cage. Whenever the procession rounded a corner, Jonathan glanced over his shoulder, just to make sure the lion still sat majestically in his cage.

Silence fell across the dock as the circus passed. The only sound was the whistle of wind and the strains of the calliope organ. Sailors and their women, tarts and wives alike, stared as if at the ghost of a former time. Jonathan smiled and waved and doffed his stovepipe hat to anything remotely female.

When the circus proceeded into Boston, the difference from the normal welcome they received was marked. Curtains twitched in darkened windows. Faces appeared, wraithlike, in shadowed alleys. People who dared the street stopped to watch when the parade went by, but they didn't cheer and they didn't smile.

Ginger the clown, in full whiteface makeup and fiery orange wig, strode alongside the wagons. "Come one, come all, see the greatest circus of them all!" he called. "The Loyale Traveling Menagerie, Hippodrome, Circus, and Museum of Educational Novelties! Witness amazements and wonders unlike any you've seen before!"

A grimy child of indeterminate gender peered around a lamppost as Ginger passed.

Ginger stopped and bowed so deeply his hat fell off. "Dear Mr. Lamppost," he said. "How good it is to see you again! How is Mrs. Lamppost keeping?"

The child stared, but didn't flee.

Ginger did a double-take. "Goodness, there's a child! Is it a young lamppost?"

Solemn-faced, the child shook its head.

"Let me see—." Ginger reached into his hat. "Could you taste this for me?" He handed a horehound candy to the child.

Eyes wide, the child stuck the candy in its mouth. The clown tilted his head. "Now, was that candy or a marble I gave you?" he asked, sounding very concerned.

"S'candy," the urchin admitted.

"That's such a relief!" The clown clapped his floppy-gloved hands to his chest and appeared to trip over his own feet. He took a pratfall, flipped up out of it to land on his feet, and kept going. Behind him, the child broke into a surprisingly white-toothed grin as it gurgled with laughter.

When the first circus wagons reached the Boston Common, they halted abruptly. The circus parade disintegrated into milling confusion. Jonathan craned his neck to see around the ostriches in front of him. Instead of a wide expanse of green, a patchwork of quilts and tarps and blankets sprouted across the Common. Fallen tree branches fueled cooking fires. Living trees formed the center beams for makeshift tents.

Lacey trotted up, riding the white mare she favored. She reined in when she saw the spectacle presented. "I see the mayor was not exaggerating." She ran her fingers along the brim of her hat, checking its straightness, and then pointed at a wide swath of green inhabited by only a couple of squatters. "That will do nicely. I'm sure they can be persuaded to move in exchange for free tickets." She glanced at the sky. "We had better hurry. There's not much time to get everything set up before sundown."

That there wasn't. As soon as the roustabouts raised the tent he shared with the other human oddities, Jonathan unfurled the canvas poster painting of "The Skeleton Man"—a flattering likeness, despite the attenuation of his waistline—and hooked it onto the rings at the top of the tent wall. He arranged his extra-wide chair (the better to appear narrow next to, my dear), and set his fife on the footstool beside it. A little pipe music helped to lure in the townies, and the long narrow instrument contributed nicely to the skeleton man act, just as his tall stovepipe hat did.

Then Jonathan made himself scarce, lest he be drafted into the war against the setting sun. Tent men unloaded the big top's center pole, attached ropes to it, and pulled. Once they'd raised the king pole, they hitched draft horses to the smaller poles and levered them up into alignment while stake men pegged down the base of the tent and canvas men laced together the pieces of canvas to form the walls. Too much was going on, in too short of a time, for any available hand *not* to be drafted, so Jonathan took himself and his hands off to lurk in the shadows among the animal cages. The animal handlers had eyes only for their charges as they soothed them, fed them, and prepared them for their acts. Jonathan found a darkened corner between the hippopotamus and the alligator wagons and settled down on a straw bale to wait.

When he heard voices on the other side of the hippopotamus, he peered around the corner. The hippopotamus flicked an ear as if to shoo away a fly, but didn't give him away.

The fortune teller and Ginger the clown had buttonholed the equestrienne. Behind them, the snake charmer lifted her giant boa from the glass-sided wagon and draped him over her shoulders. "There, there, Goliath," she cooed, as she stroked the snake's head.

"Who do you think the new ringmaster should be?" the clown asked Lacey.

"I don't know," she said. "Shouldn't we vote on it?"

"There's hardly time, dearie," the fortune teller said.

The snake charmer turned from stroking her boa, clearly interested in the conversation. "Why not you?" she asked Lacey. "You have authority in the ring."

"A woman? Don't be absurd. They would boo me out," Lacey said briskly.

"Somebody has to be first."

"Not today. Today has to be the show as usual. We need a man."

"With a fine suit," the fortune teller said. "And some authority in his presence."

Jonathan drew himself up, fluffed out his frock coat, and straightened his cravat. He was about to step forth from the shadows when Lacey said, "The doctor!"

He deflated.

"An excellent idea! I'll ask him directly."

Jonathan sulked away.

Miraculously, the circus came together just as the sun lowered to the horizon. The tents were raised, the posters hung, the freaks in their positions, the menagerie arranged, the acts prepared, the performers in costume, the lemonade seller fully juiced, and the barkers poised to unleash their spiel.

The circus was ready to awaken wonder and delight—and now, oddly enough, a sense of normality.

~ * ~

William McCormick
Beacon Hill, Boston, Massachusetts

Earlier that morning.

When William's mam saw that he'd brought Robert and Lena back to Dr. Fallon's house, she opened her arms and said, "Oh, poor children! Come here!"

Lena ran to her and burrowed under her arm like a rabbit. Robert took stiff, jerky steps until he stood beside her. When she wrapped an arm around him, he bowed his head and his shoulders shook with sobs that he didn't let himself voice. If hugging them hurt her ribs, William's mam didn't show it.

William wanted to curl up in his mam's arms. He wanted to tell her about all the awful things he'd seen and let her kiss it better. But the words couldn't fit past the lump of indigestible anger in his throat. It choked out his happiness at finding his mam doing better, and his relief that Robert and his sister still lived, and his gratitude to Dr. Fallon for tending to his mam.

So he didn't say anything. He just went and sat on the floor beside his mam's chair, leaned his head against her knee, and closed his eyes. The gentle rise and fall of her voice washed over William.

After the other two children were all cried out, she took them into the dining room. Robert and Lena fell upon the boiled potatoes, cold meat, and rolls. By the time the pace of their eating slowed, their eyes were closing. William's mam led them into a servant's bedroom, empty for reasons that none of them asked, and tucked the two into bed. It was barely afternoon, but Robert fell asleep between one breath and the next. He must have been exhausted from standing guard over his little sister all night, knife in hand.

William's mam sat in a chair beside the bed. William lay down on the carpet but kept his eyes open. He feared the dreams that sleep would bring. Eventually, he heard his mam's breathing slow and deepen. He stared at the ceiling and tried to think of nothing. His body ached with tiredness, but he didn't close his eyes. When he found his mind drifting and his eyes shut, he opened them again as fast as he could.

After an eternity or two, William's mam woke. She stood and moved around the room, straightening a picture frame here or dusting a shelf there. When the rustling of her skirts woke Robert and Lena, she led them back to the kitchen. William trailed wordlessly after. She washed their hands and faces with a pitcher and basin, she brewed another pot of hot tea, and she began cooking soup. Robert and Lena kept close to her skirts. William sat in the corner. Once or twice, his mam looked at him with a concerned furrow between her brows. When Lena burst into a storm of tears, however, all his mam's attention went to the current catastrophe and William was able to exit unnoticed.

He flitted from one room to another and another. He couldn't settle. He picked up Dr. Fallon's knickknacks and set them down again. He sat on the couch, but only on the edge and only for a moment. He climbed the stairs, leaving a trail of squeaks behind him. On the landing, he stopped and gazed out over the lawn.

His not-sleep had *felt* like eternity. From the position of the sun, it had actually taken most of the afternoon.

The majority of the refugees camped out on Dr. Fallon's lawn had vanished. A steady trickle of those who remained were shouldering their burdens and marching off, like ants forging a trail to a new nest. Soon, only the injured would remain.

"Where are they going?"

William jumped. Robert had come up behind him and caught him unaware. "Where'd you come from?"

"I followed the noise," Robert said mildly. "You Irish can't do anything quietly."

An urge to laugh bubbled up inside William, but it didn't seem right, not looking out over the dying city. He smothered it. "They're going to the Common. Plenty of room for everyone, and it's safe."

"They're as safe here as anywhere—Beacon Hill isn't burning."

"It might." Any urge to laugh died. "And how safe do you think our kind really is, anywhere? The Irish are dogs for everyone else to kick."

Robert looked at him, eyes distressed. "I'm not Irish. And I don't kick dogs."

"I—no, of course not." William swallowed hard. "Do you want to go see how they're doing in the Common? It'll be safe, I know the men who are—who are helping them."

"Could we?"

William's relief at hearing that *we* kept him from thinking too much about fire—and who should burn—until they'd walked far enough to see the Common. The trees' gold-green autumn finery glowed as the sun sank. Refugees littered the grass. Some huddled together under quilts. Others just sat and stared into nothingness. William averted his gaze hastily, lest he remember the horrors that danced in front of their unseeing eyes. *His* eyes felt grainy from lack of sleep. The feeling got worse when he looked at the refugees. So he didn't.

Around them, the sun's last rays struck the city. Where they touched, they created the illusion of fire. That, William could watch unflinching.

Robert gasped.

His eyes still on the city, William said, "Aye, it looks like fire."

"No! It looks like a *circus!*"

William blinked. Robert pointed at one of the dark tents, and just like that, William's understanding of it shifted. Instead of being nearby, it had been raised on the other side of the Common. Instead of being small, it was *huge*. And it was not alone.

A *circus*?! Zebras and elephants and candy and clowns stampeded through William's head. The memory of a tent filled with wondrously fabulous creatures—and animals, too—drew him down and into the Common before his fears could catch up with his feet.

"William! Little man!" Patrick waved at them.

"Who's that?" Robert asked.

"A—friend," William said, watching Patrick bend down and speak earnestly to two little girls with their arms wrapped around each other.

Patrick pointed to a scarlet blanket hanging from a tree branch and shooed the little girls in that direction. To one side of the blanket, Dr. Fallon scowled at a redheaded man holding his arm. On the other side, a woman round enough to withstand a minor famine stirred a huge steaming cauldron. She was the Irish cook from the mansion next door to the one Valentine's gang had taken over. When she saw the little girls walking timidly toward her, she beamed and dug out a couple of metal bowls as she waved them closer. Even Dr. Fallon attempted a smile, though it would have scared the little girls off if they'd had eyes for anything but that soup cauldron.

"Hallo, boys!" Patrick said when they drew near. "Are you going to the circus, then?"

"Yes!" Robert said.

"No," William said glumly, as he realized the truth of it. "We can't spare the money."

"Now, it would be a shame if that stopped you," Patrick said, frowning. "You just wait here, and I'll be back along in a minute. Happens I know some people who'd be delighted to help you lads out."

Patrick loped off to begin a circuit of the Common. Now and again, he'd stop and chat for a minute with one or another of the men from Valentine's gang. When he came back to the boys, his hands overflowed with fractional currency, little scraps of wartime money printed with "3 cents" or "2 cents" or "5 cents."

"Here you go," Patrick said, grinning broadly. "Enough to buy you both tickets to the circus and the menagerie—and peanuts and lemonade besides. It's twenty-five cents to see the circus, and five for the animals, and the lads came up with almost thirty-five cents for each of you. Hold out your hands!"

The whispery paper money didn't feel real in William's hands, it was so light. But the clink of coin was real, and the weight of it, when Patrick added a scattering of half-pennies and even a couple of shiny nickels.

William looked around and found newly sharpened eyes looking back.

"Could you walk us to the circus?" William asked Patrick.

"Sure and I can! You could ask a lot more of me than that!"

William didn't. Yet.

At the ticket booth, William and Robert waved goodbye to Patrick. A wizened old man took their sweat-dampened, scrunched-up notes, gave them tickets to the big top, and warned them that the show would not start until full dark. Trumpets would sound to warn the crowds.

William and Robert wandered past the candy seller, and the ring-toss game, and a man selling brightly colored fish in jars, and the fortune-teller's tent—there was an awfully long line in front of it—and a little girl telling a story while she cut shapes out of newspaper, and all kinds of interesting things. William didn't want to waste his money, but he did buy a lemonade that still had a tiny bit of lemon floating on top and only tasted mostly like water.

Shadows pooled at the base of the tents as twilight settled over the circus. The last sliver of sun dropped below the horizon. For a few minutes, the only illumination came from the oil lamps carried by roustabouts and the torches the fire-eater juggled.

Then the tents bloomed Chinese-lantern bright. A heartbeat later, circles of aether lamps ringing the tents glowed to life. For a moment, all William thought was how magically the pale flickering lights lit the circus.

A man screamed.

William remembered the sideways rain of crystal shards when the chandelier exploded, and he yanked Robert away by the arm. "We have to run!"

"What?"

"All the aether is messed up! Those lights will blow up!"

The crowd around them stirred, restive. "What?" an improbably redheaded woman said. "What did that boy say?"

"He said the lamps would explode!"

"What?"

"Dear folk," a deep voice said, "do not be afraid. I have been personally assured that the aether lights the circus has were *unaffected* by the freak aether storm we have been so devastated by."

Robert stopped letting William pull him away. "That's the *mayor.*"

William paused, unconvinced.

"My daughter is with me," the mayor continued. "Would I have brought my only surviving child here if it was dangerous?" A wide-eyed, brown-haired child clutched his hand.

"Doesn't he have two sons, too?" William whispered to Robert.

"They must have died in the storm."

"Oh. Yes, I guess maybe they did."

The mayor rubbed his arm. "None of us have escaped unhurt, but there's nothing to fear from these aether lamps. Enjoy the circus while it's here!"

The crowd still muttered and eyed the lights suspiciously, but nobody left.

William and Robert bought menagerie tickets and went inside the tent to see the animals. A giant hippopotamus whorrfled at them as they entered, and they backed away until their backs hit bars. Something behind them yawned. A huge gust of hot breath washed over William's neck. When he looked over his shoulder, a lion grinned at him. William yelped and jerked Robert into the center of the tent. They admired the zebras, even if the stripes were so similar from one to the other that Robert said they must have been painted on. They made faces at the monkeys, who made faces back. They whistled at the birds-of-paradise, who didn't whistle back. They dared each other to touch the glass wall that kept the snakes from pouring out of their cage into the tent, and they were pretty happy that the snakes didn't touch them back.

Even if they'd missed the trumpet announcing that the big show would start soon, they would have heard the ostriches hissing like angry cats in response. *Giant* angry cats. William and Robert edged past the cage, keeping careful watch on the ostriches' bobbing heads and beady eyes.

"Don't mind them," the carnie sitting on a stool next to the cage said, smiling. "They just don't like that trumpet. Go on!"

They left the tent in a hurry but slowed down when they reached a small crowd clustered around a wagon whose sides were painted with advertisements for the Great Doctor Panjandrum's miracle remedy. Doctor Panjandrum himself stood on the high seat, holding aloft a bottle filled with green-gleaming liquid.

"Excellent for toothache, neuralgia, and sore chests! It will make women's hair more lustrous and prevent men from losing theirs! A sure-fire cure for rheumatism and inflammation! Good for muscle aches and nervousness or weakness of the constitution!"

"How about—um—too much energy? Tremors?" a burly man at the back of the crowd called.

"Absolutely!" Doctor Panjandrum adapted. "It's soothing and strengthening. It balances the humors! Regular internal application—along with a strengthening routine," he riffled through the stack of pamphlets beside him, "that is described in this pamphlet—will decrease the severity and frequency of tremors."

A female dressed in a scandalously short, bright blue riding habit that barely reached below her knees interrupted him. "Doctor," she said. "We need you elsewhere."

"I'm sorry, good people," the doctor said, handing out bottles to the last people with their money out, "but I must depart. Tell your friends of the Great Doctor Panjandrum's amazing remedy!"

William trotted after the doctor, hoping to ask if he could buy just a little of the remedy with his remaining coin. If it was as good as that, then surely it would be a grand help for his mam?

"I'm glad to see you," the doctor told the lady in the riding habit. "At least I don't need to put on an act just to escape these people." He looked over his shoulder at the dispersing crowd but paid no attention to the small boy dogging his heels. "They're so desperate for any doctoring, even this worthless snake oil, that I almost sold out. I'll need to get more gin and herbs before tomorrow."

William frowned and dropped back, but not so far that he didn't hear the lady's reply. "We may not have time for that."

"You don't understand. Normally, I sell twice as much the second night, after my—patients—tell their friends that they like my tonic. If I've sold out, they get upset." He lowered his voice, and William could barely hear his next words. "I don't want to see what they'd do if they got upset now. Did you notice the bodies as we rode into town?"

"Yes, of course."

"Did you notice the *fresher* bodies?" the doctor asked as they walked out of earshot.

William didn't want to hear more about bodies, so he waited for Robert to catch up and then they went inside the main tent and sat. The aether lights inside still made him nervous—with so many people jammed together, it would be a slaughterhouse if the lamps exploded.

"Do you think they'll have an elephant?" Robert whispered. "I heard they had one, but it wasn't in the menagerie."

The answer was: not exactly. A monstrously elephantine bone and brass creature marched into the ring with two passengers, a dark-skinned man with a turban and a white man wearing a frock coat and top hat. The elephant's long, ivory tusks gleamed menacingly, and glass tubes filled with bone aether lined its ribcage. William gasped and heard his reaction echoed by the crowd around him. If the mayor of Boston hadn't already assured them that the circus aether devices were fine—if that mayor weren't sitting right at the edge of the ring with his daughter—.

The turbaned man raised a long stick and tapped the elephant's skull. The elephant bent bone knees and lowered itself to the ground with a clatter of bone and metal. The befrocked man slid down the side of the elephant and bowed deeply to the crowd, doffing his hat as he did so.

William squinted, but it wasn't until the man spoke that he was sure it was the Great Doctor Panjandrum.

"Welcome to the Loyale Traveling Menagerie, Hippodrome, Circus, and Museum of Educational Novelties," Doctor Panjandrum said pompously. He still sounded like he was selling something. "Our aether-powered elephant, which you have seen, returned with us from India, along with—"

He spoke a bit too fast and not quite loudly enough, and he kept looking off at one corner of the tent, until William looked in that direction too. There wasn't anything interesting there, though. Doctor Panjandrum talked on. William fidgeted and glanced around the crowd. Most of them weren't paying attention to the ring, either. William looked at the mayor. He expected to find him drumming his fingers, ostentatiously consulting his fob watch, or using one of the hundred other tricks the rich had for letting you know you weren't worth their time.

Instead, the mayor was simply watching his daughter. Seeing the mix of thankfulness and sorrow in his expression made William feel raw inside. The little girl laughed then, pointing at the ring. The mayor's face rearranged itself into a mask of benevolent approval as his gaze followed her pointing finger.

As Doctor Panjandrum pontificated, a clown had crept out of the shadows of the tent and snuck up behind him, placing each oversized shoe with excessive care. He put his finger to his lips to ask for silence, but a wave of laughter answered. Doctor Panjandrum halted, startled, and then continued his awkward and overlong introduction of the first act. Behind him, the clown pantomimed broad exaggerations of the doctor's mannerisms.

The clown was mid-strut, his fingers hooked under his suspenders, his chest puffed out, when Doctor Panjandrum whirled around and caught him in the act.

The crowd held its breath as the two stared at each other.

Finally, Doctor Panjandrum invited the clown into the center of the ring with a broad sweep of his arm. The clown shrugged his shoulders and wrung his hands until Doctor Panjandrum repeated the gesture. Then the clown stepped forward, struck a pose, opened his mouth to speak—and nothing came out. He stepped back, thumped his chest a few times, cleared his throat, and tried again. Nothing. He made a sad face and turned to Doctor Panjandrum, shooing him forward.

Doctor Panjandrum started to speak and then stopped, startled, when the clown bent down and tugged at his feet. He shifted position until the clown was satisfied, opened his mouth— and stopped when the clown took hold of one of the doctor's arms and rested it on the doctor's hip, then raised his other arm in an oratory pose. The clown gripped the doctor's shoulders and pulled up until the doctor straightened, then pushed his shoulders back a bit more.

The doctor waited. When no further adjustments were made to his person, he began to speak. The clown reached out and pushed his palm hard against the doctor's diaphragm, sending his voice booming out into the tent. Once the crowd's laughter died, the improvement in the doctor's voice was noticeable.

And so the performance went, with Doctor Panjandrum announcing the acts and the clown correcting him to properly ringmasterly behavior. The doctor's face reddened a few times, but maybe it was just from being in front of the hot lights.

The aether elephant did tricks. The lady in the blue riding habit came out standing on the back of two horses, with one foot on each as they galloped around the ring, and then she rode through hoops of fire. A man stuck his head inside a lion's mouth. Acrobats flipped and rolled and twisted in ways that made William wonder if they had any bones at all.

During the grand finale, three trapeze artists swooped down on swings suspended from the tent poles. The girl in the green costume smiled hugely as she dove down out of the dark. William caught his breath. Their fragile limbs flashed through the air as they circled and dove and performed acrobatic twists high above the hard ground, with no net to save them if they fell.

The girl in green flipped up into a one-armed handstand that had her audience cheering. Then her hand slipped.

She plummeted. As one, the crowd gasped.

William wanted to close his eyes. She would die. She would hit the ground and her back would break and she'd die in front of them, all twisted up with blood streaming from her eyes and her ears and her nose and her mouth and—the other trapeze artist swung down out of the shadows and caught her. He hung upside-down, anchored only by his feet, and he caught her arm as she fell past. He grimaced at the weight, but he didn't let go. He drew her up until she could grasp the trapeze swing and pull herself up to stand on it, and then he hauled himself up to stand beside her—no fancy acrobatics this time!

William gulped in air. He'd forgotten to breathe. His eyes smarted, and his cheeks were wet. He wiped the moisture away with the back of his hand, sneaking a glance at Robert to see if he'd noticed. Robert's face was buried in his hands, and his back shook as if he were learning how to breathe again, and doing a poor job of it.

William looked across the shadowed crowd. The mayor was also doubled-over, his face in his hands.

As if he'd suffered like the poor!

The mayor's daughter patted his back. His only child, now.

Well, and maybe he had.

Robert chattered away as they left the circus tent, but William stayed quiet until they were outside, walking across the Common, and he saw Valentine leaning against a tree as if he'd been waiting for them. Valentine's gang didn't accompany him, but he held his *shillelagh* by his side.

"Hello, Valentine."

"Hello, little man," Valentine said, falling into step with them. "Did you see much that was interesting at the circus?"

"Oh, all kinds of things!" Robert burst in. "There was a *huge* bone elephant, and they had the best clown!"

William only nodded.

"Did you have something you wanted to talk to the lads about, William?" Valentine asked.

William shook his head. "Robert and I are just going back up Beacon Hill to stay with my mam and Dr. Fallon."

"That's a good thing, that is," Valentine said. "Being together is the only way we'll all get through this."

~ * ~

Jonathan Matzke, the Man So Thin He Wears a Wedding Ring As a Belt!
Boston, Massachusetts

The next morning, the circus sat on benches and dug into a hearty breakfast. As a sort of celebration of their first breakfast on dry land again, the cook had fried up a mess of sausages and eggs to go along with their porridge, and the delicious smells made the day seem promising. The sky was bright and blue, and the trails of smoke above the city thinned as the fires died.

Jonathan eschewed the porridge entirely in favor of a mound of eggs and so many sausages that the cook gave him a dirty look and muttered about 'wasting good food'. Jonathan took his breakfast and sat on the bench near the equestrienne, the doctor, the fortune teller, and Ginger the clown.

"I'm sorry, doctor," Lacey said, "but I think you're better off as our doctor than as our new ringmaster."

Jonathan stifled a laugh at the understatement. He'd snuck out of the freak tent to watch part of the show, and the doctor was *terrible*. The ostriches would have done a better job.

"To be honest, that's a relief," the doctor said. "I don't know what I would have done without Ginger."

"Yes, Ginger, you did a very nice job getting the doctor to act as a proper ringmaster ought," the fortune teller said. "Though I suppose that makes sense."

"You really saved the show," Lacey said thoughtfully. "I'm sure we could find a fine suit that would fit you."

"Oh, no!" Ginger said. "You won't get me up there with a naked face in front of all those wit—those people."

"You may be our best option."

"Oh no, I'm not!"

"Then perhaps you're the best one to find our new ringmaster and train him properly," the fortune teller said, squinting at her sausages.

"Divining from your sausages?" Ginger asked.

"Just picking the best one." She speared a fat sausage and bit into it with relish.

A boy barely old enough to shave approached them hesitantly, a wrapped box in his hands. "Miss, are you the equestrienne?" he asked Lacey. "The mayor wanted you to have this." He handed the box and a card to her and then retreated.

"With thanks for your circus' fine performance," Lacey read. She opened the box and frowned. "A pen holder?"

Jonathan fingered the mayor's pen in his pocket and eyed the pen holder. It would be his as soon as nobody was looking at it.

The doctor spooned up his last bite of porridge and stood. "If I'm not going to be the ringmaster—thank God—then I'd best practice my profession. And there's one task I have to do that shouldn't wait any longer."

"What's that?" the fortune teller asked.

"An autopsy." The doctor walked away, leaving the circus members sitting in a spreading silence.

Chapter 5

~* * *~

The Harvest

Connecticut, Midway Between Boston and New York

The second wave of death swept across the nation before we even knew it existed. It was subtle, made of all the little individual deaths that would have been prevented only a few weeks earlier. The child who fell down a well because his father and mother and oldest sister had all died, and his brother wasn't used to looking out for him. The executed prisoner whose reprieve would have been telegraphed in time, if the telegraphs still worked. The baker whose burned arm became infected, who died of blood poisoning because there was no doctor to insist on amputating before the infection spread. The sailor who started the steam engine on a boat that had been dry docked for repairs when the aether storm struck. The woman who went back into the fields too soon after childbirth because the family ox had died, who bled out among the furrows. The bystanders caught in the crossfire between rival bandit gangs who came to town and found there was no sheriff to stop them. The maid who switched on a gas light. The baby who starved in its own crib.

Many people starved, or were so weakened by malnutrition that they died of common ailments.

The cityfolk starved because few farmers hauled vegetables in by cart to sell in the market. The railroad let farmers ship their produce to the big cities. Cowboys herded thousands of cattle to the railheads, where they were transported East. But the aether wave ruptured all the locomotives' steam engines. In one afternoon, the trains went from being the power that pushed civilization out to the frontier, to being very expensive sheds of scrap metal, filled with rotting produce and starving cattle.

Food grew dear while we were in Boston, though our supply master saw the way it was going soon enough and bought all the non-perishables he could get his hands on. One night, the men went out and came back carrying barrels of flour and salt pork. I do not think they paid for them.

The farmers were in hardly better shape. The railroads had allowed them to specialize—they could reach enough customers to justify growing only high-profit crops like strawberries, or grapes, or asparagus. Before the storm, it was an excellent way to prosper. After the storm—well, a body could try to survive on a diet of strawberries, but they'd find themselves shivering, weak, and afflicted with constant bouts of diarrhea. That was if enough of their crop could be harvested.

In their frenzy to butcher and preserve the meat of the animals the aether storm killed, it took the countryfolk a while to notice that the storm had killed more than animals. Some trees bore withered fruit, while gobbets of exploded fruit flesh draped the limbs of others. One wheat stalk might be strong and firm, and its neighbor disintegrate to dust at a touch. Root vegetables fared better than aboveground plants, but without digging up the crop, it was hard to tell what amount would be edible. In farms across the (Rapidly-Less-)United States of America, the same amount of work gave a smaller yield.

Ravenous insects attacked the harvest. Every bird in the air when the storm struck had died instantly. The insects survived in greater numbers, and they bred faster. Without enough birds to keep them in check, the insects ate and ate and ate.

The humans tried not to starve, using a variety of tactics.

We left Boston a couple of days after the Mayor instituted a rationing system. Surprisingly, no riots impeded our exit.

We'd been on the road for a week and were halfway to New York. I was enjoying the brief freedom—my arm was free and my face turned up to the sun, though I was still mostly concealed. From my position, facing backwards in the second-to-last wagon, I looked out over the land. Only the trailing supply wagon, far behind us, marred the pretty picture made by Connecticut in autumn, and even that blemish would vanish from sight as we followed the curve of the road.

Those riding ahead in the caravan could stare at horse butts and circus wagons covered with muddy canvas. I preferred my view of rolling hills. White oaks and red maples glowed dark red and scarlet in the sun. Even the pinkish-red clumps of sumac were lovely.

In the distance, a flock of sparrows launched into the air. A small miracle. I find the world so precious and amazing that I sometimes think you all should be blinded and bound until you learn to appreciate it properly.

A breeze played across my sun-warmed arm. I knew I'd be blistered with sunburn if I left my mushroom-pale skin uncovered for too long, but I didn't care. The only sounds were the jingle of harnesses, the creak of our wagon wheels, and the occasional swear word or grunted comment from farther up in the wagon train. It might have been an uncomfortable silence to them, but I liked the absence of chatter that I wasn't welcome to join. And I felt none of their discomfort at the idea that there was a murderer among us. I welcomed my companion-in-infamy, whoever he or she might be.

I was watching the trees, and so I saw them first. Four men eased out of the woods behind us just as we rounded the bend that would hide them and the supply wagon from sight. I heard faint sounds of a scuffle, though if I hadn't been listening for something, I wouldn't have noticed it over the clop of the horses' hooves.

My silence was a habit of such long-standing that it took me precious moments to realize I should scream.

"Bandits!" I shrieked, my voice rusty and horrible-sounding from disuse. "The supply wagon!"

A clanking cacophony answered me as the Indian charged past us on that monstrous, beautiful bone elephant. He glanced in my direction. He had not known of my existence until that moment, but he did not flinch when he saw me. Our eyes locked— and then he was galloping away down the road.

~ * ~

Dr. Christopher Janzen, the Great Doctor Panjandrum and His Amazing Panacea That Cures All Ills!
Connecticut, Midway Between Boston and New York

Dr. Christopher Janzen sat on his bunk, which rocked back and forth with the movement of the wagon. Sleep helped pass the tedious travel time, but since performing the ringmaster's autopsy, dark thoughts circled around him whenever he lay down. He tilted a small glass bottle carefully as he measured out a few drops of laudanum to help him sleep.

"Bandits!" a woman screamed.

The scream startled him, and his hand shook, spilling the laudanum on the floor. He looked at the wet drops seeping into the planks of the wagon. "Damnation," he said mildly. His wagon lurched as the caravan halted.

But—bandits? It was as well he hadn't taken his sleeping medicine yet. He reached into his steamer trunk and brought out the black leather doctor's bag he kept there. It would have been a useful prop for his Doctor Panjandrum act, but he never used it for that. He couldn't bring himself to disrespect the memory of young Dr. Christopher Janzen, just out of medical school, filled with fresh-scrubbed pride and as shiny as his new patent-leather doctor's bag.

The bag Dr. Janzen took out of the bottom of his trunk now might be worn down, but it still held all the tools a proper doctor would need in a hurry. He might no longer be licensed to practice, but if he stayed out of the big cities, his patients didn't care. As long as he had his tools, he was still a doctor.

He stuck his head out the door of his wagon and into chaos. The caravan boiled with activity. The equestrienne slid a derringer into her pocket and mounted her white mare. The fat lady loaded a shotgun. The skeleton man jumped down from his wagon and ran off into the underbrush, a burlap sack in hand. A trapeze artist furiously unharnessed the horse from his wagon. The hostlers tried to lead balking horses around to circle the wagons—a move they hadn't practiced recently, not expecting to need it this far East. A dozen men (mostly roustabouts) set off. They rode whatever nag hadn't been harnessed or ran afoot. They carried mallets and crowbars or other weapons. The knife thrower wore a full bandolier of shining blades.

Dr. Janzen scowled. Whatever lay around the curve of the hill, he would definitely be needed.

In the distance, the Indian *mahout* sprinted along the road on his elephant. For something so large and gangly, it moved with frightening speed. That the *mahout* stayed on its back said something for his tenacity, his skill, and his disregard for his own mortality.

Dr. Janzen picked up his sturdy walking stick and his black bag, and he set off after the rest. He was nearly to the curve in the road when he heard the sharp bark of a gun. He broke into a run.

When he rounded the hill, breathing hard, the first thing he saw was the equestrienne struggling to control her rearing mare. She leaned forward against its neck, both her hands wrapped in its mane. A strange man lay dead in front of her, a rifle in his hand. Her derringer lay between the mare's dancing hooves.

Dr. Janzen needed only to glance at the dead man to see the cause of death: a red-black tunnel into his skull where his eye should be.

"I didn't know you were a sharpshooter, Miss," he said, looking up at the equestrienne.

She laughed shakily as she succeeded in getting the mare to settle with all four feet on the ground. "Not I. When I wouldn't dismount at riflepoint, he grabbed my stirrup and tried to pull me down. My derringer nearly touched him when I pulled the trigger."

Many of the boys who'd fought in the War would have hesitated to shoot a man so close, Dr. Janzen thought. Shock must be insulating her from her natural feminine reaction.

"How many were there?"

"Three others. They fled into the woods when I fired. The men went after them, except for him." She nodded at the Indian *mahout*.

The *mahout* rested on top of his elephant, his face inscrutable but his eyes flickering back and forth along the road and the woods. With him standing lookout, Dr. Janzen went to the supply wagon.

The wagon master was just coming to. He grumbled as he tried to push himself up from the wagon bed. "Young ne'er-do-wells. They weren't even good at being ne'er-do-wells! They hit me on the head, but not near as hard as I've been hit before!"

"Maybe they weren't trying to kill you," Dr. Janzen said, helping the older man to sit up. "Whoa!" he added, as the supply master tried to stand. "Let me take a look at you."

"I need to see what the bastards got," the supply master protested.

"In a minute." Dr. Janzen took a candle out of his bag, lit it, and held it close to one of the supply master's eyes, and then the other. "Your pupils aren't reacting equally. Don't drink hard liquor or lift anything heavy until after breakfast tomorrow."

"I don't drink hard liquor until at least noon, anyway." The supply master tried to stand again. "Can you tell me what the bastards got?"

"I can tell you that you'll probably live," Dr. Janzen said acerbically, "since you're so concerned. Come find me if you feel yourself falling asleep in the middle of the day. That could mean you've got bleeding on your brain. And avoid any further trauma."

"What's that?" The supply master stared at him suspiciously.

"Try not to get hit on the head again!"

With a grunt of acknowledgment, the supply master pushed himself up and began taking inventory. He tended to repeat himself and to wobble slightly, but at least he wasn't trying to lift anything heavy. *Yet.* With a sigh, Dr. Janzen climbed back out of the wagon.

The roustabouts returned empty-handed from their pursuit, though they bore the bruises and cuts of combat. "Come along to my wagon," Dr. Janzen told them sternly. "You need to clean those with boiling water and lye soap."

The tallest one scoffed. "It's just a couple of scrapes. We're big strong men; we'll be fine without a nurse.

We got the strangers, too. One has a broken arm, and another has a knife stuck in his shoulder." He nodded respectfully to the knife-thrower.

The attackers weren't alone in their injuries. The tally on the circus' side stood at one sprained wrist, two head injuries, three broken toes (one of the roustabouts had dropped his mallet on his own foot in the heat of the moment), and a plethora of scrapes and bruises.

The less-damaged men helped the injured back to the caravan, and at Dr. Janzen's request, the *mahout* slung the stranger's corpse across the back of the elephant and took it with them.

The caravan's defenders lowered their rifles and leaned them against the wagons as soon as they saw that the return was a victorious one. Dr. Janzen observed hands that shook and eyes that showed a little too much white around the edges. The midget and his wife began to quarrel over who bore the responsibility for cleaning their child-sized .22 rifle. The two female aerialists yawned in unison. The skeleton man sat in the grass beside his wagon, eating a chunk of bread that he held with both hands as if he were afraid it would be snatched away from him. All signs of stress that might lead to nervous disorders if not ameliorated.

Usually, the ringmaster enforced a rest day—or two, if needed—every five days or so, as soon as they found a good place to camp. They were past due. Dr. Janzen edged closer to the equestrienne. "Do the horses need a break?"

She frowned as she studied the horses hitched up to the wagons. "Yes, if we want to keep them healthy. And given how expensive these were to get, we *want* to keep them healthy. I'll speak to the head hostler, though he's probably already keeping an eye out for good places to camp." She looked around. "This isn't a bad spot. There's space enough between the trees over there, and I think I see a creek—."

"The horses might not care, but the *people* would probably prefer if we camped a bit further away from where we were attacked."

"Ah, yes." She nodded. "I daresay you're right."

Dr. Janzen studied her and wondered. Shock, or nerves of steel?

"Thank you, Doctor," she said, before striding off in search of the head hostler.

The midget fight had grown to include the maintenance of their wagon, how she didn't mend his costumes fast enough, and how he had been ogling female townies of the tall persuasion. The rifle waved in the air. Dr. Janzen sighed.

Unearthing the root of their stress can only help.

"The attackers have been driven off," he said. "We are safe now."

Or not.

They both glared at him.

"Sure we are!" the midget scoffed. "It's not like there's a *murderer* among us, oh no!"

"Yes," his wife added, with a glower that was small, but fierce. "Don't you have something to add to that, *Doctor*?"

Those nearby left off their other activities to watch with interest. Their expressions gave Dr. Janzen little hope of escape, despite his attacker's small stature.

"You *took* the ringmaster's body," she accused him. "You kept the lamp in your wagon burning the night long, and we all heard sawing and squishing noises coming from under your door."

He winced. *I must try blocking the door with a feed sack to mute the sound.*

"So who killed him?" the midget asked, in as close to a non-combative tone as Dr. Janzen had ever heard him use.

The only sound was the rustling of leaves and the *shush* of the horses shifting their hooves.

"I—think that would be best told to someone in authority," Dr. Janzen tried.

"In case you hadn't noticed, the 'authority' is dead!"

"Of course I noticed!" Dr. Janzen said. "I meant—." He gave up. "Very well. I'll tell you what I found once everyone's gathered. Everybody should hear this at once."

They gathered with remarkable speed, faster even than when Cook made his famous Dutch oven apple pie.

He did it quick, like an amputation. "You all saw he'd been stabbed. What you didn't see was that he'd been poisoned."

Gasps. A rising murmur that he raised his voice to speak above.

"More than once, if—as I suspect—his seasickness was no such thing. The sweats, vomit—I wager if I'd looked in his chamber pot, I'd have found bloody feces."

He pointed to the candy seller. "You were playing cards and saw him right before he died. He looked tired. You thought he winked at you to wish you luck. He wasn't tired, and that was no wink. Those were poisoning symptoms. His eyelids drooped, his skin had a pallor, and his lymph nodes were swollen when he died."

"He was poisoned?" the equestrienne asked, her eyes wide and astonished.

"Yes. The murderer probably stabbed him to death because the first two attempts failed."

"What kind of a knife did he use?" the knife-thrower asked, his tone uneasy as he fingered the blade on his belt. The crowd drew back from him.

"A thin knife with an unusual curve at the end," Dr. Janzen said.

The knife-thrower relaxed. "None of mine are curved," he explained to his neighbors. "Makes the balance more difficult."

"There!" Dr. Janzen told the midget. "Now you know. Do you feel better?"

"Not—especially."

"Poison," the fortune teller mused.

An unnatural silence descended over the crowd, broken only when the railer returned from scouting up the road. The railer's job was to ride ahead and find the best road for the circus to take. When the road forked, he found the roads that dead-ended in a muddy bog or led away from the caravan's destination, and he took a rail from a farmer's fence and used it to block off those paths. He *shouldn't* have been back in the middle of the day.

"Why are you back so soon?" Dr. Janzen asked him, hoping to distract the others from their dark thoughts. Distraction was a good technique for coping with pain, whether the pain be physical or mental.

"The head hostler told me to keep an eye out for a good spot to camp for a day or two," the railer said. "There's a small town in the valley up ahead that has the space and seems friendly. A nice lady offered me dinner and a place to sleep in her boarding house, for free, but I thought I should report back. Mrs. Margaret Della Rocca, her name is. She seems to be the local welcoming committee. Came right out to greet me when I rode into Seppanen Town. Won't she be surprised to see all of us!"

"How long of a ride is it?" the equestrienne asked. "The horses are already tired."

"We could make it by sunset if we pushed the pace. The horses would be able to rest for a couple of days afterward."

"You seem eager to get back."

The railer sighed. "She had buttermilk biscuits baking. They smelled delicious."

"A rest would do us good," Dr. Janzen observed.

"The horses won't make it all the way to New York," the equestrienne added.

"And where better to stop than in a nice, *friendly* town," the fortune teller concluded.

~ * ~

It did look like a nice town, Dr. Janzen thought approvingly as they approached the outskirts. A wooden sign welcomed them to Seppanen Town, Population—blank. The number had been scraped off, though the welcome hadn't.

Through maple trees glowing golden-red in the light of the setting sun, he saw a fresh-cleared space with dozens of grave mounds in it. No church sat nearby, so the grave site must have been made in a hurry, but it was well-away from the town's water supply. Each grave had a proper wooden cross at its head and a mound of rocks on top of it to keep animals from unearthing the dead. Good planning and good hygiene.

The circus caravan rolled past a long field of dark green chicory. A scattering of summer's flowers still shone the cobalt blue of bachelor's buttons and Union hospital medicine bottles.

Men and women walked the rows, pulling the plants and tossing them in wide woven baskets. Children worked alongside them. A heavily pregnant woman sat on a stump at the edge of the field, keeping guard with a shotgun resting on her knees. They must have had bandit trouble, too.

One of the men working the rows straightened and stared at the circus as it passed. A youngish fellow with an open, honest sort of face, he wore clothes of a cut and cloth too fine for his labor. *Everyone must work in a community this small, if they wish to survive the winter. Perhaps he was a shop assistant, before the storm.*

The young man stared after the circus with a focus Dr. Janzen found alarming. It was not the reaction of amused interest or mild disdain they usually received. That intensity put him in mind of a few of the inmates in the mental asylum he'd toured as part of his medical education. Perhaps the young man was one of those individuals who became unbalanced on the subject of moral corruption and saw the circus as the Whore of Babylon. *I should warn* ... The thought trailed off. He *would* have warned the ringmaster, but that individual was beyond warning now.

The warmth of the town's welcome reassured him. A little girl from the chicory field darted in front of the circus and sprinted ahead to beat them into town, her sandals flapping and her pigtails bobbing as she ran. As the lead circus wagon turned onto Main Street, the little girl trotted back out of the general goods store with a lolly in her hand and a burly, balding man in a shopkeeper's apron following behind her.

The shopkeeper blanched a bit as wagons kept rolling down Main Street, but he recovered quickly and stepped out to greet them. "Welcome to Seppanen Town, strangers!" he called. "Just passing through?"

At the front of the procession, the equestrienne reined her white mare to a halt. "We're the Loyale Traveling Circus. We need to camp and rest the horses for a couple of days before proceeding on to New York. When was the last time your town had a circus visit?"

"Ah, quite some time!" the shopkeeper managed.

"Where would the best place for us to camp be?"

"Why don't you, um, fine folks come see Mrs. Della Rocca? She runs our boarding house. She likes welcoming visitors personally." His gaze fell on the rather battered-looking roustabouts walking beside the wagons. "She was a nurse in the War, too, and she does pretty well patching us up."

The equestrienne looked questioningly over her shoulder at the rest of the circus folk. Nobody said aye or nay. She shrugged and then dismounted gracefully, letting the reins fall from her hand to hang loose. Her mare stood stock-still, as if she'd been anchored in the middle of the street. "Thank you. I'd be delighted."

Dr. Janzen got down from his wagon to follow her, as did a handful of other circus folk, including the railer, the strongman, the conjoined sisters, and the roustabouts who'd been a little banged up fighting off bandits. The rest stayed close to the circus wagons, a wise practice in a strange town, even an ostensibly friendly one.

Ginger the clown, however, walked down the block to an establishment graced by an ornately carved sign advertising "Sally's Saloon." Dr. Janzen shook his head disapprovingly. Every town they stopped in, the first thing the clown did was head to the saloon. If he didn't take better care of himself, he'd die with pebbles of scar tissue scaling his alcohol-soaked liver.

Mrs. Della Rocca seemed much more wholesome. She opened her door wearing an apron lightly dusted in flour and adorned by promisingly food-like stains.

"Welcome!" she said. "You must be new to town! My, what an awful *lot* of you there are!" She tossed a questioning glance in the storekeeper's direction.

"A whole circus came to town," he said quickly. "This is just a couple of them."

"We were hoping to find a place to camp, where we could break from traveling for a few days. Of course, we'll perform while we're here," the equestrienne interjected.

"How wonderful," Mrs. Della Rocca said. "Where are you headed?"

"New York."

"Lovely." She caught the storekeeper's eye. "And then they'll all be going on to New York City," she repeated absently. "Shouldn't you be getting back to your store?"

"Oh. Yes'm." He bobbed his head and ducked out.

"Come on in," she invited the circus folk. The equestrienne stepped over the threshold. The railer followed eagerly (no doubt hoping for buttermilk biscuits), and the others straggled after.

Inside, Dr. Janzen sniffed. The air smelt of flour and cinnamon and cloves and—smoke?

Mrs. Della Rocca's eyes widened when she noticed the bruises and scrapes the roustabouts had acquired. "Oh dear, you're hurt!

Come into the kitchen where I keep my supplies. I was a nurse in the War, you know."

The same big strong men who'd resisted Dr. Janzen's ministrations followed her as meekly as kittens.

A faint scent of burning lingered in the kitchen, and a pan of scorched buttermilk biscuits sat on top of the stove beside a pan of bloody water.

Following Dr. Janzen's gaze, Mrs. Della Rocca laughed, though it sounded forced. "Those biscuits might go to feed the hogs, I'm afraid. The beef fared better. I don't know how it was where *you* were when that unnatural storm hit, but we lost half our herds, between the ones that died outright and the ones that sickened after. We hung and cured what meat we could, but it's still steak for breakfast, lunch, and dinner!"

She gestured to an unbaked pumpkin pie sitting on her kitchen table, next to a roll of bandages. "But the pumpkins are ripe now, though we're short hands to pick them. I am so looking forward to seeing that pumpkin pie at breakfast tomorrow. But listen to me ramble on!"

"Pumpkin pie," a girl's voice murmured longingly. Dr. Janzen thought it was one of the conjoined sisters.

He had to agree with her sentiment. He wished for more variety, too. Their dinners were getting awfully repetitive, though Cook grumbled so much about the lack of supplies that nobody dared complain—which was no doubt the point.

~ * ~

Ginger, the Whitefaced Clown
Seppanen Town, Connecticut

"I'll have a blackstrap, please," Ginger said, leaning against the bar. Behind him, the door swung open and the burly storekeeper who'd welcomed the circus into town came in and sat down in a corner. Odd. The sun wasn't down yet; there was still business to be done.

The curly-haired woman behind the bar lifted down a bottle of rum and a jar of molasses and began mixing the drink. "Military man, are you? Sailor?"

"Why do you ask that?"

"Some men get a taste for the rum."

Ginger smiled pleasantly. "I just have a taste for molasses. So, are you Sally?"

The bartender chuckled. "There is no Sally. The saloon's owned by Miss Lindsay Kleinman. She decided folks would think it sounded more welcoming than 'Lindsay's Liquors.' My name's Cathy Williamson. I'm watching the place for her while she's otherwise occupied."

Miss Williamson didn't specify what the owner was occupied with, Ginger noted but did not comment on. "What do I owe you?" he asked.

"Don't worry about it!" Miss Williamson said jovially. "Strangers drink free." She smiled. "This town couldn't make it without you."

"Don't bother," the storekeeper spoke up, from his table in the corner. "He's with the circus. They'll all be leaving town soon enough."

At that news, Miss Williamson lost some of her cheer and all of her loquaciousness. When Ginger ordered another drink, she said gruffly, "That'll be twenty-five cents."

Ginger tried asking general questions about Seppanen Town, but all he could finagle out of her were monosyllabic answers.

He swiveled on the bar stool, looking over the few men in the saloon. "Next round's on me!" he said.

They all avoided his eye, even the two playing a game of poker. That was truly odd. A man buying drinks should be everybody's friend, and he'd never known a poker game that didn't welcome a stranger who was free with his money.

Ginger decided he didn't want to have his back to the crowd *or* the bartender, so he smiled pleasantly, took his drink, and sat down at a table near the door. He put his hand in his right pocket. He had slit the pocket's bottom open long ago, to allow easy access to the hideaway pistol he kept strapped to his thigh. He kept his back to the wall and finished his drink by the simple expedient of spilling most of it on the floor when nobody was watching.

Despite his sense that something was amiss, he finished his drink and left in peace. He returned to the circus caravan a few minutes before the other explorers came back from their meeting with the town greeter. The railer looked unhappy: no buttermilk biscuits had been forthcoming, then.

"We have directions to a camp site," the equestrienne announced. She led them through town and took the left-hand fork after they passed an apple orchard on the outskirts. They reached an empty field just as the sun set. "This field is fallow and the farmer is dead," she said, "so we don't need to worry about trampling any crops."

Oil lamps were lit, horses unharnessed and tethered to graze, and Cook had started a huge pot of pork and beans cooking, when their settling-in was interrupted.

A young man stepped out of the shadows. His clothes had once been good quality, but his trousers were covered with mud and his shirt was stained. His eyes had a set, fixed look to them that had Ginger slipping a hand into his right pocket.

The young man looked around desperately. "Please, you have to hide me from them!"

Chapter 6

~* * *~

How to Be a Clown

Christopher Knall
Seppanen Town, Connecticut

One week ago.

"Welcome to Seppanen Town," the wooden sign read.

Customers! Christopher Knall thought. He stopped to beat the travel dust out of his clothes and straighten his hat before he walked on. As he approached a farm on the outskirts, the little boy sitting on the farmhouse steps sprang to his feet and ran ahead. Christopher smiled. He wished he could make a more stylish entry into town, but his horse had died in the giant freak storm that struck the area a week ago. He'd been traveling by foot ever since. The one-horse towns he'd passed through recently were reluctant to lose a valuable animal, and he couldn't sell enough merchandise to afford their price. This town looked big enough that he might have better luck.

As Christopher entered Main Street, the little boy trotted back out of the general goods store with a peppermint stick in his hand and a burly, balding man in a shopkeeper's apron following him.

"Welcome to Seppanen Town, stranger!" the shopkeeper greeted Christopher. "I run the general goods store. Just passing through, are you?"

"After a fashion," Christopher said. "I'm a traveling purveyor of fine ladies' hair combs and men's shaving sets. Just the thing your customers would appreciate. I can arrange a discounted rate." He winked. "But I won't tell anyone you paid less."

The storekeeper wrinkled his forehead. After a moment, he said awkwardly, "Come with me to lunch at Margaret Della Rocca's and we can discuss it. Mrs. Della Rocca runs our boarding house. Her buttermilk biscuits are famous around these parts."

It was a bit of an odd invitation, but Christopher wouldn't miss the first real opportunity he'd gotten since that hell-storm.

When they knocked, Mrs. Della Rocca opened her door wearing an apron lightly dusted with flour. The aroma of biscuits drifted out to greet them.

"Welcome!" she said. "You must be new to town!" She tossed a questioning glance in the storekeeper's direction.

"This is Mr. Knall," the storekeeper told her. "He's a traveling salesman, selling ladies combs. I told him how good your biscuits were."

"Marvelous. Come on in! Lunch is still cooking, but I'll get you some biscuits and tea."

As soon as they sat at the table, Christopher opened his salesman's suitcase. "Let me show you—"

"Wait." The storekeeper put up his hand. "First, let's enjoy the biscuits."

Mrs. Della Rocca came out of the kitchen with a plate in each hand, and a biscuit on each plate. She set the biscuits in front of the men and beamed. "Go on then!"

Obediently, Christopher picked up his biscuit and bit in. The biscuit was hot and fluffy on the inside, but he noticed a slight bitter aftertaste he didn't like. Too much baking soda in the recipe, perhaps.

Not wanting to alienate his host, however, he finished the biscuit, smiled, took a sip of tea—and slid sideways as the world tilted and darkened around him. He barely felt the impact when he hit the floor.

Today.

Christopher Knall straightened from his labor in the chicory field, pressed his hand to the small of his back, and leaned into a stretch. Dried sweat made his shirt crackle under his hand. Mud coated his pants. He was hardly the fine sight he'd been when he walked into town with a suitcase full of ladies' hair combs and men's shaving sets to sell.

Something moved along the road in the distance. He squinted. Wagons, traveling their way. *Poor bastards don't know what they're getting into. Can I warn them somehow?*

When the caravan got closer, the thought vanished. He gaped.

It must be a hallucination. He'd finally cracked. The procession was led by a woman standing on top of her saddle as if that was a perfectly ordinary way to ride a horse. A freakishly thin and elongated man rode in one of the wagons behind her. A pair of miniature humans perched atop another. And the giant bone and brass *thing* that flanked them could only have ridden out of a nightmare.

"Impossible," Christopher breathed. Beside him, Francis straightened.

Seppanen Town had caught Francis on his way to a promised job in Boston, he'd told Christopher. A stranger in town, he'd gratefully agreed to stay the night in Mrs. Della Rocca's boarding house. He'd woken up to chains, a strict lecture on how things were going to be during the harvest, and a nourishing breakfast of steak and buttermilk biscuits. Francis wasn't a stranger to hard labor, as his dark tan and rough hands attested. He'd showed Christopher the ropes.

"It's not break time yet," Francis said now, with a quick glance at the heavily pregnant woman sitting with a shotgun across her knees. "We'd best get back to work soon, or Clara will feel she has to do something."

"We have a few more minutes," Christopher said. Clara, the woman on guard duty, was not unsympathetic. She let them rest when they needed it, and she saw to it that they had enough water. She seemed almost embarrassed by the situation.

"Although I reckon she'll understand us stopping to look at *that*," Francis continued, staring in the same direction as Christopher.

"You can see it, too?" Christopher asked. "I thought I was hallucinating."

Francis laughed. "I couldn't dream up those—those whatever-they-are!" He pointed.

"Ostriches." Christopher studied them as they passed. *An equestrienne, a thin man, midgets, exotic animals ... it's a circus. That's a lot of strangers.* He stared after them with eyes that felt scorched dry, and he began to plan.

Slowly-slowly, he worked his way over, a row at a time, until he was in the row right beside the woods. Francis drifted after him. "What are you up to?"

"I'm going to run away and join the circus."

"You're cracked!" Francis hissed. "Do you know what they'll do to you when they catch you?"

Christopher tensed his shoulders. "Well enough. I won't get caught. I know where I'm going. Come with me! We can both escape."

"Clara will get in trouble."

Christopher stared at Francis. "She'll be fine. She's one of their own."

"And if the circus won't hide you?"

"Come with me!"

Francis shook his head. "No. This isn't so bad for me, really." He turned up work-calloused palms. "I'm used to it. And winter's coming on. Here at least I know I'll get food and a place to stay. Out there—what if it's the same everywhere? You think they'll treat us better?"

Christopher hissed through his teeth in frustration. "I'll come back for you if it's safe. Don't tell them where I went."

Francis nodded and eased back away through the rows, so that by the time twilight let down her hair to hide the forest in deepening shadow, he was working quite far away from Christopher. Christopher braced to bolt into the woods. Soon, Clara would push herself awkwardly up from her seat on the tree stump and say—

"That's it for the day," she called. "Take your baskets and move to the road."

Christopher sprinted into the woods. He made no attempt at sneaking away. *Speed and darkness are my only allies.* He blundered through the woods like a wounded boar. *And maybe Clara's soft heart.* He paused and listened, his back muscles tensing in anticipation of pain, but she didn't fire the shotgun after him. Branches snapped underfoot and snagged and tore his clothes. Clara wouldn't chase after him, not burdened as she was. Since she hadn't shot him already, he figured he had until she got back to town to get a head start. Then they'd send serious men with dogs and lanterns after him.

Dogs. He veered to run in the direction of the stream that was the town's water supply. They might expect that, but it could still help hide his scent. Cold air stung his skin. His breath rasped in and out of his lungs.

The townsfolk would expect him to go upstream, away from the town, so he'd go down instead. That was his best shot for finding the circus, too. It was dark. They would need to camp. They'd want to get through town first, to make sure they wouldn't have an unfriendly welcome. Always check out your surroundings before you camp for the night, that was a basic rule of traveling folk. He guessed he'd failed that one.

He crested a hill. Through the trees, he saw the glimmer of water in the moonlight. He ran in that direction.

Something heavy smacked him across the face so hard that he fell down, stunned. He lay there expecting to be seized, but nothing happened. The only sound was the rustle of leaves in the breeze and the faint gurgle of water. A branch. He'd run into a tree branch. He pushed himself up and ran again. No time to go more carefully.

He plunged into the stream. Water rose over his shoes and soaked his socks. He splashed downstream with no care for the noise. His foot slipped on a slimy river rock. He lurched off-balance for a moment, tottered, then straightened and waded on. He spared a moment to thank God that his captors were too inexperienced to take away his shoes.

When he saw lantern light ahead, he slowed, placing his feet with care and trying not to splash too loudly. Seppanen Town's lit windows glowed yellow against the gloaming twilight. That glow promised warmth and comfort and safety, and he hated it for the lie.

The cold water numbed his feet and made him clumsy. Exhaustion slowed his reactions. The adrenaline was fading, leaving his thoughts slow as treacle.

But he knew these things, and so he could account for them. He was clumsy? He would test each chancy step. He was slow? It didn't matter. All he had to do was reach the circus before dawn, and he could guess where they'd camp. His pursuers wouldn't think to hunt downriver, not for a long time. He had trouble thinking? He didn't need to think, just follow his plan.

He splashed downstream as quietly as any fugitive could. He was halfway through the town when he heard a shout go up. Dogs barked and men swore. He froze, swaying. He couldn't make himself take another frigid step until he heard them heading to the chicory field.

He plunged onward.

By the time he made it past the edge of town, his feet and lower legs were insensate, sodden logs that he dragged with him.

He followed the stream because that was the plan. His world narrowed to the cold and the dark and the plan.

It came as a shock when he reached the fallow field on the far side of town and saw bobbing oil lamps. He'd been right in his crazy, last-chance guess of where the circus would go. If they'd hide him—no, they *must* hide him, he had to believe that—then safety was so close, just across the river and up the bank. He had to ford the river. He could have climbed up the bank on his side and crossed the bridge, but to his cold-addled brain, that seemed a huge risk to take when he was so close.

He waded into the river. At its deepest point, it rose to his waist. The current tugged at his clothes and tried to pull him away. He was nearly halfway across when he slipped on something his numb feet couldn't feel, and fell. The river almost won, but he found his footing and kept going. Just a few more steps.

Something heavy smashed into his side and buffeted his back. He grabbed his attacker and felt bark beneath his hand. The current had sent a long, broken-off branch twice as thick as his arm careening into him.

The trees really have it in for me, he thought muzzily. That seemed almost normal. Men were after him, and dogs—why not trees, too?

A thought moved sludgily through his brain. *Dogs. Who will smell where I climbed up the bank.* The dogs would sniff along the base of the bank to find where somebody had climbed out of the water. Christopher looked at the branch he'd caught and laughed. It hurt, so he stopped quickly, but he dragged the branch through the river with him. It fought like a granddaddy catfish. Half the time, it seemed that one or the other of them would be lost to the river before they reached the other side.

Each step became easier, until he stood in ankle-deep water. He hoisted up that branch and leaned it up against the riverbank, and then he climbed up it. The dogs would only catch his scent on what he touched. When he got to the top of the riverbank, he threw the branch back in the river and watched the current take it.

He stumbled forward across the fallow field. The wind sent icy little spears stabbing through his clothing. When he tripped over an exposed root and measured his length in the dirt, it seemed so inevitable that he merely pushed himself up and staggered on, without even bothering to scrape the dirt-rapidly-becoming-mud from his trousers.

He passed picketed horses. Their soft whickers and ruminations—and the warm, solid windbreak their large bodies made—were so comforting that he might have lingered if the smell of cooking pork and beans hadn't drawn him on.

He approached the circus wagons, trying to ignore the leaden fear that they would turn him back over to the townsfolk. A man so perfectly ordinary-looking that Christopher worried he *wasn't* with the circus stood beside the nearest wagon, talking with a shawl-swathed, bejeweled, heavily veiled woman.

Christopher stepped out of the shadows, his eyes fixed on them. When the excessively ordinary man saw Christopher, he tensed and slipped his hand into his pocket.

"Please, you have to hide me from them!" Christopher pleaded. "Please, help me!"

He tried to step closer, but his feet were frozen weights. He lurched and would have fallen, except the veiled lady darted forward—with a quickness surprising in one so encumbered—and slipped her shoulder under his arm. She gasped. "You're soaked through! And so cold!"

As if her words reminded him, he began to shiver convulsively.

"Careful, Mrs. Wershow," the ordinary man said. His eyes narrowed as he stared at Christopher. "Hide you from who, stranger? And what did you do to get them after you?"

"Ginger, we have to get him warmed up before he'll even be able to understand questions, much less answer them," Mrs. Wershow said sharply. She cleared her throat, seeming to remember herself. "Come along, then, young man," she said to Christopher.

She carried most of his weight all the way to the campfire. The ordinary man—Ginger—followed behind, his hand still in his pocket. Now and then Christopher stumbled, but Mrs. Wershow kept him on his feet until she could sit him down on a log beside the fire. Tutting, she unwound one of her shawls, shrinking in the process. She wrapped it around his shoulders. "I'll beg a plate of food for you," she said, and left.

Ginger squatted in front of him. The fire cast Ginger's face in shadow, but his eyes still gleamed. "I saw you in the field when we rode into town," he said.

Christopher nodded, or perhaps he just shivered so furiously his head bobbed. He himself wasn't sure.

"Who are you hiding from?"

"Seppanen Town," Christopher managed to get out from between chattering teeth.

"Who in Seppanen Town?"

"All of them."

Ginger rocked back on his heels. "*All* of them?" There was something almost like admiration in his voice. "That takes talent. What did you do?"

"Ran away."

Mrs. Wershow returned from her conversation with the cook holding a tin plate filled with steaming pork and beans. At the smell, Christopher's mouth watered and his stomach cramped painfully.

She set the plate on his knees. "Hold it there for a bit," she said. "It'll help warm you up. Don't eat too fast or you'll be sick. I *will not have* somebody being sick on my second-best shawl."

"No, ma'am," Christopher managed. His brain began to thaw. At first he'd thought she wasn't old enough to call him 'young man', but now she sounded just like his grandmother.

A huge black man approached the fire. Swirling tattoos covered his skin and writhed over bulging muscles. The way he frowned made Christopher particularly notice those muscles. "Who's this?" he asked.

Christopher spooned up the pork and beans, chewed conscientiously, and swallowed. He felt the hot, savory beans warming him all the way down to his toes. He closed his eyes for a moment in sheer happiness.

"That's what I'm trying to find out, Bradley," Ginger said, mildly. "If I wasn't being constantly interrupted, I'd already know." He faced Christopher. "Who are you, where did you come from, and why did you need to run away?"

Christopher spilled the metaphorical beans in hopes of being allowed to eat the real ones in peace. He explained his trade, and how he came to be in Seppanen Town, how he'd fallen asleep in Mrs. Della Rocca's boarding house and woken up in chains, and how he'd escaped.

When he'd finished, he shoveled in more pork and beans as they digested the news.

"They'll be suspicious unless they find him again," the veiled lady, Mrs. Wershow, said thoughtfully. "It could be dangerous for us."

Christopher looked up, startled. He would have felt betrayed if his standards for betrayal weren't quite high after his recent experiences. She'd seemed so kind.

"We are *not* turning anyone over to slave-catchers!" the strongman rumbled. The gathering dark seemed to swell his size.

Ginger and Mrs. Wershow exchanged a look. Or Christopher thought they did. It was hard to tell, what with the veil.

Other circusfolk drifted closer, curious about what was going on—or hungry for pork and beans. *Maybe a little of both. The beans are good enough to draw a crowd.* Christopher's spoon scraped the bottom of his bowl.

"It's a pleasure to see someone properly enjoy my food," the cook said deliberately, ladling out another scoop that Christopher hadn't been presumptuous enough to ask for, "but what will he do? With things the way they're going, can we afford to feed an extra roustabout?"

"Well," Ginger said slowly, "we do need a ringmaster."

The others stared at him as if he were insane. Christopher was inclined to agree.

"He's a total rube!" a midget protested. "And you want him to be ringmaster?"

"You all thought that I should be ringmaster, after that performance in Boston!"

"Yeah, so?"

"So I declined the honor. Firmly. But I can teach him to be a ringmaster. At least, I can teach him to be a really good clown, and if you're a really good clown, you can *be* the ringmaster if you need to."

"A clown?" Christopher asked faintly. Despite the warm plate of beans in his hands, this whole scene was taking on the surreal aspect of a dream. *Please don't let me wake up and find myself in that damned shed.*

"He doesn't know anything about being ... a clown," Mrs. Wershow said.

"Average height, hair that some will call brown and others blond, a nice, friendly, open face—he's perfect."

"He don't look funny to *me*!" the midget complained.

"None of this is funny," Christopher muttered. *Peculiar, yes.*

Ginger spun to face him. "You don't think this is funny? Laugh anyway. Laugh like your life depended on it!"

Christopher stared, his stomach tightening, the beans suddenly sitting uneasily. Ginger didn't seem to be joking.

The notion that his life depended on a laugh was worth an uneasy chuckle, the kind a man gives when he's not sure if there's a joke or not.

The midget made a disgusted sound. "Call that a laugh?"

Christopher's bowels tightened in instinctive anticipation of bad things. The beans suddenly seemed like a terrible idea.

In the firelight, Ginger's face became a thing of sharp edges and shadows.

Christopher forced a chuckle, a harsh and crackling thing that the midget winced away from.

"Look—" Christopher leaned forward to plead his case, but he was interrupted by a traitor within.

A long, sonorous fart rolled out. The combination of beans, nervous bowels, and a sudden shift in position was too much.

Ginger's face twitched oddly. The midget's eyes bulged. Silence hung in the redolent air.

And suddenly, it *was* funny.

Christopher burst out laughing. He had to set his plate of beans to the side because his body was shaking so much he would have spilled it otherwise. It felt like he hadn't laughed in weeks, and maybe he hadn't. He laughed at Ginger's sudden silence and the midget's bulging eyes. He laughed at his own rebellious bodily gasses. He'd escaped; why shouldn't they? He laughed at himself for running away to join the circus. He laughed at the idea of his life depending on a laugh.

He laughed until he cried, and then he laughed some more.

And somewhere in there, they started laughing too.

"Oh, you'll do!" Ginger said. "You'll do just fine."

The black strongman frowned. "They'll send dogs after him."

Ginger looked at the crowd. "We've all been on the road a while. I've always liked taking care of dirty laundry in the moonlight." He paused. "I suppose the horses should all be walked down to the stream and watered. After that—it's a lovely night to take the lion for a walk."

A swarthy man with furrowed claw marks scarring his forearms grinned. "Those dogs won't know *what* they smelled, but they'll sure react to it! They won't care about a boring old human when there's lion scent around."

"Good," the strongman said. He gave Christopher a nod and a gap-toothed smile. "They're mostly good people here. You don't need to be afraid." With that reassurance, matters were apparently settled to his satisfaction. He lifted a tin plate of beans and headed off into the shadows.

"I—thank you," Christopher managed, looking around him. "Thank you so much."

The cook smiled. "Finish your beans."

Ginger answered more seriously. "You'll have to work to earn this. Being a clown is more difficult than it looks from the outside."

"I will!"

"Then the first thing to learn is Rule Number 1: Know when to disappear."

Christopher didn't answer because his mouth was full, but he cocked his head. *What does that have to do with being a clown?*

"When you want to surprise your audience, you'd better make sure they don't see you," Ginger explained. "Tonight, that means hiding. Rule Number 2 is always know how your audience will react. You ran away right when strangers came to town? If the hunters don't find you right away, they'll come here for sure."

Ginger raised his voice, addressing the dispersing crowd. "Put the word out that *anybody* who says *anything* to the townies about our newest member will answer to me. The kid might be wet behind the ears, but he's one of ours now. Don't even gossip about him to each other until we're out of here."

"Where should I hide?" Christopher asked, still bewildered.

Ginger smiled. "This isn't the first time we've needed to hide somebody. The old ringmaster set up something special. Now, most of the circusfolk don't need to know about this. Some of the animal handlers know, and the fortune teller—that's Mrs. Wershow—and I. Bradley—the strongman—knows because he once had to hide in there for a week."

"A week?"

"We'll just hide you tonight. You're a lot less *noticeable* than Bradley. Also, about half his size. He managed it, so you'll be just fine. Follow me." Ginger walked in the direction of the animal cages, extinguishing his lantern as he went. The only light was from the sliver of a moon rising above the trees. Over his shoulder, Ginger said, "Tomorrow, I have other plans for you."

"I've got a plan of my own! I need to go back and rescue my friend."

"A woman?" Ginger asked, with a sigh.

"No—just a fellow captive. He helped me out a lot when I started in the fields. I owe him."

Ginger paused to let the hostlers lead the horses past, down to the river. "But he didn't escape with you."

"He didn't believe it was safe. And he didn't want to get the woman watching us in trouble."

"You don't say. Well, tomorrow's soon enough to discuss such things. Tonight, it's time to hide." Ginger stopped beside the ostrich wagon. The giant birds inside shifted, their feathers rustling as they settled down for the night. Ginger pulled aside the canvas protecting the wagon's carved wooden side panel and its gilt and mirror adornments. "What was it again?" he muttered to himself. "Oh, yes."

He pushed down on two mirrored spots simultaneously, reached up and turned a carved piece at the very top of the wagon, and then hooked his finger into a hip-high crevice and pulled.

The side panel of the wagon came away. A heavy cloth hung behind it. Ginger swept the cloth to the side, revealing a dark space about three feet deep and as wide as the wagon.

"There's a blanket in there, some hardtack if you get hungry again—sorry about the quality of the food, but this place doesn't get used too much and it has to stay stocked—and two jugs. One jug is for drinking water, and one jug is," Ginger coughed, "empty until you make it not. Don't get the two mixed up! There's an oil lantern with matches. Don't use it unless you have to. The cloth should block light from escaping, but there's no sense in taking risks. Try to sleep. I'll get you out tomorrow morning."

~ * ~

Dr. Christopher Janzen, the Great Doctor Panjandrum and His Amazing Panacea That Cures All Ills!
Seppanen Town, Connecticut

Dr. Janzen surveyed his wagon and considered his plans for the evening.

He remembered the midget's complaint about hearing "squishing and sawing" during the ringmaster's autopsy, and so he blocked the gap under his door with his pillow and a half-full sack of feed grain he'd borrowed when the head hostler wasn't looking. He hung one blanket in front of the door and another over his window. As he did so, he glanced outside. Other circus members headed to the campfire for dinner. He pushed aside the urge to join them. He *was* a bit hungry, but he worked best with an empty stomach. The hunger would vanish soon.

He pulled on a stiff butcher's apron. He unrolled the cloth holding his medical instruments. He laid them out on the bench. He lit all four of the oil lamps he owned. Only then did he unwrap the gift the Indian *mahout* had carried back for him after they were attacked: the body of one of the bandits. Dr. Janzen had wrapped it in canvas and stored it in his bunk until they were safely through Seppanen Town.

Now he unwrapped the canvas, folding the edges up fastidiously to prevent any bodily fluids from escaping. The dead man glared up at him with one remaining eye. The equestrienne's pistol shot had turned the other eye into a crusted red-black ruin. The bullet's track passed through the eye and into the cranium. Once in, the lightweight bullet would have ricocheted inside the skull case, slashing through the brain until that organ was an uninformative hash.

The cause of death was too obvious to interest Dr. Janzen, though he noted in passing that the gunpowder stippling around the wound implied that the equestrienne had shot from a very close distance indeed. What he *wished* to learn was the nature of the dead man's life and the condition of his health. Knowing the effects of the aether storm on its survivors could be crucial scientific knowledge, but the uneducated rarely offered up their relatives' bodies for dissection.

"*Hic locus est ubi mors gaudet succurrere vitae,*" he said before he began. *This is the place where death delights to help the living.*

The gross examination of the corpse showed that the man had lost weight recently but maintained acceptable health. He was in good physical shape, though one of his arms was notably more muscular. He had probably not been a bandit long, since he still had callouses from handling farm tools and dirt under his fingernails. And his clothes were freshly laundered, implying the care of a female.

Dr. Janzen felt the usual anticipation at the first cut of his scalpel. What might he learn?

He made a Y-shaped incision from the shoulders to mid-chest and then straight down to the public bone. Carrying the incisions across allowed him to gently peel back flaps of flesh to reveal the ribcage and glistening organs.

He followed the modern Virchow autopsy procedure, which dictated removing each organ individually, carefully examining it for abnormalities, and preserving what was necessary before proceeding. He felt pride that he followed techniques still taught in the premier medical schools of Berlin. Never mind that he wasn't licensed and that his patient was quite dead. He would not let his standards slip. And the circus' Museum of Educational Novelties provided a good source of formaldehyde for specimens.

At some point, the sound of men talking loudly outside and the barking of dogs disturbed him. He pushed aside the blanket covering his window. Lanterns bobbed around the animal wagons. He listened, but he heard no shots, and none of the circus raised an alarm, so he kept working.

The corpse's over-muscled arm drew his attention. He cut a flap along the forearm and peeled the skin fascia back. He found the lesions he'd feared.

Hoping to disprove his theory, he pulled out sections of muscle and ligament so he could study them more closely beside the lamp. Signs of sudden growth were apparent. The main veins were scaled by fresh scarring, and he noted blood extravasation. The blood leakage into surrounding tissues could have been caused by an allergic reaction or a burn, but there were no other indicators of such a thing. When Dr. Janzen flensed the arm down to the bone, he noted bone deformities, nodules of improper growth that would cause trauma to the area. The man must have been in great discomfort, though he couldn't have known the cause.

Dr. Janzen had only seen such symptoms during the War. He'd hoped never to see them again.

Long after the corpse was once more bundled up in canvas, the implications kept Dr. Janzen from his rest. Dark thoughts spiraled like buzzards above the dying. Finally, he rose and measured out laudanum sufficient to let him sleep through to sunrise.

Chapter 7

~* * *~

A Stranger Comes To Town

Christopher Knall
Seppanen Town, Connecticut

Christopher was hungry enough that the hardtack crackers were starting to look good. Morning light filtered through chinks in the wall. He heard people and animals moving around. But Ginger hadn't come back yet.

He pressed his mouth to a crack and hissed, "Hey, Ginger! Could somebody get—"

The secret panel unlocked with a click. He pulled back barely in time to get out of the way before it opened. Ginger stood there, glowering.

"Sorry," Christopher said. "I—I thought you were going to let me out earlier. I thought you'd forgotten me or been caught." He climbed out of the dark hidey-hole and stretched. The bright blue morning sky arched above him. A brisk autumn wind ruffled dark red maple leaves. The smoky smell of the cook's fire wafted on the breeze to him. It all seemed new and precious.

"Fugitives in hiding tend to come out for breakfast," Ginger told him. "A smart hunter always checks back in the morning."

Christopher tensed. "They're here?"

Ginger shrugged. "They aren't smart hunters. I didn't think they would be."

"So you kept me locked up for *nothing*?"

"Ah!" Ginger raised three fingers. "Rule Number 3: Never underestimate your audience. If they *had* come back, they wouldn't have found you. Now you're going back in your hiding place until I'm absolutely certain it's safe. Be quiet in there. No calling my name." He paused. "I'll bring you a plate of eggs later."

"Sorry," Christopher mumbled.

"What are you planning to do today?"

"I need to rescue my friend."

"And after that? Will you two hide until we're out of town?"

Christopher frowned. "I can't just walk away, knowing that they'll keep doing this to other people. That's not right."

"Oh, I have a *plan* for that." Ginger smiled a smile with sharper edges than Christopher would expect from such a mild-mannered man.

"What plan?"

"Can you shoot? —Well, never mind, I have explosive charges that will do the job. Rule Number 4: Keep extra explosives on hand. You never know when they'll be useful."

~ * ~

Dr. Christopher Janzen, the Great Doctor Panjandrum and His Amazing Panacea That Cures All Ills!
Seppanen Town, Connecticut

Dr. Janzen found the other circus members to be strangely quiet over breakfast. He didn't mind. When in his circus persona, The Great Doctor Panjandrum, he unreeled an amazing spiel. The rest of the time, Dr. Janzen enjoyed silence and the ability to observe but say nothing.

This morning, he observed that several people's appetites were diminished. The group lacked the conviviality typical of a rest day. Only Ginger the clown seemed unaffected.

At least nobody complained about odd noises coming from his wagon the night before, Dr. Janzen thought. The pillow and feed sack must have provided adequate insulation. Or perhaps the circusfolk were distracted by the men who'd visited during the night.

"Did everyone sleep well?" he asked. *He* certainly hadn't, but what was their excuse? They remained in blessed ignorance.

They stared at him as if an ostrich had talked.

"Quite well, thank you!" Ginger said cheerily.

"Excellent. Won't a couple of days rest be welcome? Seeing new faces?"

"They're just ordinary folks, and we'll be treating them as such," Ginger said firmly.

"Certainly, but—"

"I can't stomach this," the knife-thrower interrupted harshly, standing up and stalking away.

Dr. Janzen made a mental note to keep an eye on the knife-thrower. His reaction must be due to delayed shock from the attack yesterday. If it persisted, it might be a cause for concern.

"Is anyone going into Seppanen Town?" the midget's wife asked. "I need a couple of things from the dry goods store, but I don't trust myself to act all nice."

Female troubles, Dr. Janzen diagnosed but didn't say. Women were touchy about such things. "I'd be happy to make your purchases for you," he said. "I'm planning on walking into town to consult with Mrs. Della Rocca, as a fellow medicine practitioner." He hoped nobody would ask about *what*; he didn't wish to alarm them unnecessarily.

Her lip curled. "Voluntarily? You doctors are cold-blooded."

Dr. Janzen looked around and found disapprobation on every face except for Ginger's.

"Did you skip supper?" Ginger asked.

Dr. Janzen blinked at the non sequitur. "Why, yes. I was— working."

Understanding dawned on the faces around him.

"I thought that must be it, since you're eating your eggs so heartily!" Ginger said. "Cook's pork and beans didn't ruin your appetite. You sure missed something."

"I'm sorry for snarling," the female midget said. "I—" She cast about for the right words.

Dr. Janzen held his hand out before she resorted to indelicacy. "Don't worry about it, dear lady. I understand your condition entirely." He lowered his voice and murmured, "If it's particularly bad, I may be able to prescribe a dose of laudanum."

Her eyebrows went up. "Thank you," she said in a constricted voice.

"Come to think of it, Doctor," Ginger said, "you may be the best man to discuss trading for supplies with Mrs. Della Rocca. Nothing in Seppanen Town happens without her say-so, and since you hope to speak with her anyway ..."

"But I've never—"

"The supply master's still recovering from being hit in the head," Ginger said. "He's subject to spells of confusion."

"Well, yes, but—"

"You'll have more of a friendly relationship with her than the rest of us could. Collegial. And you won't actually be trading, just finding out who's willing to trade what and for how much."

~ * ~

Dr. Janzen found himself in front of Mrs. Della Rocca's boarding house still not entirely sure exactly when he'd agreed to act as the circus' emissary. Still, he *did* need to speak with her. It made sense to talk trade at the same time.

Mrs. Della Rocca answered his knock wearing a fresh apron and a harried smile. "Good morning!" She squinted. "Are you with the circus?"

"Yes, ma'am. I'm the circus doctor, actually, and I was hoping that—"

"You must have come to retrieve your sleepwalker! Sleepwalkers. I confess I was afraid that my little flock was going to grow even larger!"

"Your flock? Sleepwalkers? I don't—"

A child's shout interrupted him. "It's bubbling over!"

"Oh, dear!" Mrs. Della Rocca said. "Come in, come in—I have to take care of this!" She dashed kitchenward.

Dr. Janzen followed at a more dignified pace. When he entered the kitchen, he found her lifting a massive pot of bubbling porridge off the stove, her apron skirt wrapped around the hot handle. *Pop!* went the porridge, and an oatmeal splat landed on her pristine apron.

"Drat," she said, looking down. The children giggled.

The children. Almost a dozen children perched in her kitchen, sitting on stools, leaning against the counter, or sitting on the floor. Dr. Janzen studied Mrs. Della Rocca's "flock." They ranged in age from toddlers to youths almost old enough to strike out on their own. Their faces glowed with fresh-scrubbed health and their eyes were bright. Some of their clothing was thin to the point of translucency, but hand-stitched patches covered any holes. A couple of the children were on the scrawny side, but their faces weren't hollow with need.

Every child held a thin sliver of pumpkin pie. He noticed that Mrs. Della Rocca was not having a piece of pie herself; it was all for the children. A treat. A row of porridge bowls on the kitchen table would hold the main course. The bandages and medical supplies had vanished overnight.

A familiar light laugh brought his attention to the corner of the room. A redheaded boy of about thirteen, who must be in the middle of a growth spurt, blocked his view. Dr. Janzen leaned forward. Two familiar faces smiled back at him: the conjoined sisters, Roxane and Betty Murray. One was blonde, the other brunette. Both were pretty enough, setting aside the jointure that left the freak show as their best option for supporting themselves in life. They gave their age as sixteen, but their small stature made them seem closer to twelve. Their act played that up, and so they wore the ruffles and braids of younger girls. He understood why Mrs. Della Rocca thought them children.

Roxane Murray ate her piece of pie daintily but with every evidence of pleasure. Betty took a bite and then set hers down on the counter she leaned against. The redheaded boy eyed the pie and sidled a bit closer.

"Sleepwalkers?" Dr. Janzen asked Mrs. Della Rocca.

She shrugged. "I came downstairs this morning to find them in my kitchen. Both of them were genuinely asleep. I'm certain of that."

"Thank you for finding them, but I came here to discuss—" he glanced around, "—medical matters not for tender ears. And to gain your advice on acquiring supplies," he added, as an afterthought.

"Hey!" the redheaded boy complained. "Where did that piece of pie go?"

Roxane turned to him. "It wasn't *your* pie!"

In the lull that followed, the only sound was the happy smacking of lips.

"And no, they're not all my children," Mrs. Della Rocca said. "I'm sure you were wondering. Some of their parents were townsfolk who died in the storm. Some of them wandered in on the road. They were half-starved! They stay in my boarding house now, and I take care of them. We *must* protect the children and make sure they have enough food," she said fiercely. "No matter what it takes. Without the children, we have no future."

"Commendable. Er, the circus has children to take care of, too. Who would you recommend we talk to about buying food supplies?" Dr. Janzen asked awkwardly. "We have money enough."

"Paper money? You might as well use it like the Sears catalog. Some farmers might sell you supplies in exchange for hard coin.

Try Farmer Johnson. He's got a lot of good windfall apples but not enough hands to gather them." She shook her head. "Food is tight, though. We need enough to last us through the winter and to feed our children. But we don't have hands enough to bring in the harvest." She sighed. "If there even *is* a crop to harvest."

"What do you mean?"

"Our crops are dying. Unpredictably. We just started harvesting potatoes, but many of the plants are hardly edible. They're shriveled, twisted things. We can't tell which are ruined until we dig them all up. Sometimes just the leaves are shriveled, sometimes the whole plant."

"And some are normal," Dr. Janzen continued. "And some— are some unusually large?"

"Yes!" She smiled. "They don't make up for the bad ones, but they help."

He glanced around. "That's what I wanted to speak with you about. Not in front of the children, though." He gave her a meaningful look.

"Once they've had their breakfast, I'll send them out. As far as buying food goes," she shook her head, "you're on your own. The dry goods store doesn't have much. Mostly we barter food with each other. A bushel of apples for six pumpkins. Like that. I make sure that even those who don't have anything worth bartering still get a little food. Nobody in Seppanen Town will starve if I can help it." She squared her shoulders. "But the circus isn't part of Seppanen Town."

"The children must come first," Dr. Janzen murmured. The town was lucky to have such a determined champion. That didn't get food in the bellies of circusfolk, though. "More food than you can harvest," he said musingly. "Wasting food in these times is a sin. Can we harvest what would otherwise go to waste?"

Her eyes sharpened with interest. "That doesn't benefit us if you keep everything you gather. We might yet be able to bring in the harvest ourselves, if we can get more labor from travelers passing through."

"So we only keep part of our take. What's a fair percentage?"

A tow-headed little boy tugged on Mrs. Della Rocca's skirt, holding up an empty bowl. "Please, ma'am, may I have some more?"

"Just a little bit, Oliver. We have to share." She dolloped out another ladle of porridge. Then she tilted her head, considering Dr. Janzen. "I understand that sharecroppers would usually keep half," she said dubiously.

"Done!"

She looked a bit regretful, as if she should have named a lower amount. To distract her, Dr. Janzen said, "Not much sharecropping up here. Have you lived in the South?"

"I worked as a nurse in Fredericksburg, during the War and a bit after. I met my husband there." Her eyes softened. "But it wasn't to be. And you? Where were you during the war?"

"Chattanooga."

"Did you know Dr. Mary Walker? An eccentric, to be sure, but also a fine doctor and a gallant lady."

"I—mostly dealt with the dead," he temporized, remembering the terrible softening of the limbs that occurred as the dead settled into their new state. It was worse, somehow, when he didn't have to fight to strip the corpses of their soiled clothes. The yielding flesh was too lifelike, so that he almost believed he bathed and wrapped and boarded living men into coffins. When he had nightmares of the dead, he woke with the imprint of that feeling still lingering on his fingertips.

"Can our people start harvesting today?" he asked, pushing away the memory. "We'll trade for what we can, but from what you say, I doubt that will be enough."

She answered with a quickness that hinted she had nightmares of her own to banish. "Yes. We need more hands in the potato field to bring the crop in. You can start there."

He waited in silence while the children finished scraping the last bit of porridge out of their bowls. As soon as they were done, Mrs. Della Rocca shooed them outside to go help in the fields.

Dr. Janzen tilted his head to indicate that the conjoined sisters should wait outside too. Betty blinked at him, but Roxane nodded and whispered in her sister's ear. As they passed, Dr. Janzen noticed a smear of pumpkin pie on the back of their dress, but it didn't seem to be the moment to comment.

"I apologize for making you wait," Mrs. Della Rocca said to him, once the last child had stacked its bowl in her washing basin and left, "but a few of these children went hungry for so long that, if I don't watch them, they'll bolt their food and then get sick later."

"Your concern is admirable."

"I do what I can, and the devil take the hindmost." She drew in a deep breath and let it out again. "What did you want to talk to me about that couldn't be discussed in front of the children?" she asked, as she began to tidy up the kitchen.

"We were attacked before we reached your town."

"Oh?" She moved over to the stove.

"One of the men died during the attack. When I performed the autopsy, I discovered some disturbing signs that may explain why they attacked us."

She lifted a heavy cast iron skillet from the stove top and walked toward him. "Did you tell anyone else about it before you came here?"

He shook his head. "No. I didn't want to alarm them unnecessarily. But you have a medical background, and even more importantly, you were on the front lines during the War."

She stopped in front of him. "What does that have to do with it?" she asked, running one hand over the curve of the frying pan.

"Did you ever treat any of the Confederacy's Grey Steel regiment? The ones who had been taking bone aether for too long, or in too high of a dose?"

She paled. "Yes. But that can't have anything to do with the— bandits. The Union banned the military use of bone aether and destroyed the war harnesses."

"Surely they missed a few. Something so valuable, so dangerous—people would keep it in case of need. Bury it in the back yard. Or maybe a clever person could jury-rig something similar up from an old slave harness. Those are still legal, even if slavery isn't."

"I don't think it would be that simple."

"Are you certain you didn't bring home a souvenir from your time in the South? Something you thought you'd never use, but now, with everything so unsettled and a town to protect—"

"I would never! Those things are *abominations*." Her chest heaved as she glared at him. Her knuckles whitened on the skillet handle.

Dr. Janzen looked at her with grave eyes. "I wish you had. When I performed the autopsy, I found symptoms of an overabundance of bone aether that, given time, would have led to full manifestation."

"But a war harness—"

"I don't think he had access to a war harness. I suspect the freak storm excited his bone aether." He paused. "I've observed early symptoms in other people. Muscle aches, nervous energy in one or more limbs, spasms."

The cast iron skillet slipped from numb fingers and crashed to the floor. "Oh, merciful God," she whispered.

~ * ~

"Good day, Doctor-*sahib*. And Missies," the Indian *mahout* greeted them as they returned. He sat cross-legged on the ground at the edge of camp. "Missies are going for walk? I did not see you leave."

"They sleepwalked," Dr. Janzen answered. "Fortunately, they ended up safely in Mrs. Della Rocca's kitchen."

"For the pumpkin pie, yes?"

"How did you know?"

"I hear one of them say, 'Pie' when we visit Mrs. Della Rocca's kitchen. They are dreaming of it, yes?"

"Er, yes, I suppose." Dr. Janzen vaguely recalled seeing the *mahout* in the kitchen. He must have been standing way in the back.

"And now missy has her pie." The *mahout* smiled to himself. "Everybody dreams."

Dr. Janzen nodded, though his dreams were not ones he cared for.

Roxane Murray said, "Goodbye, Doctor. We want to go rest in our wagon."

Betty added, "We're tired after we sleepwalk."

"Do you sleepwalk often?" Dr. Janzen asked, concerned.

"Hardly ever," Roxane answered. "It won't happen again."

"Not soon," Betty said.

"Are you alright?" Dr. Janzen asked.

They nodded in unison, but they wouldn't meet his eyes. He let them go.

When Dr. Janzen knocked on the door of the supply wagon, the supply master poked his head out and blinked over his spectacles at him. "Yes? Why are you back so soon? I knew I should have gone to negotiate! How much money will it take for us to get supplied?"

Dr. Janzen shook his head. "They won't take fractional currency. How much do we have in coin?"

The supply master scowled. "Enough. Barely."

"I heard that the equestrienne brought back money from her visit to the mayor of Boston. Was it all paper money?"

"I think so. You'd have to ask her—she squirreled it away somewhere. To keep any of us from getting ideas, I suppose. Only gave me a count." He scowled. "Heaven only knows if it's right. Oh, I'm not saying she'd steal any! But untrained people ..."

"I'm not sure it's a good idea to spend all our money here—"

"Of course it's not," Madame Wershow interrupted, as she emerged from the shadows of the wagon.

Dr. Janzen started, but controlled his reaction quickly. He should be used to the fortune teller's habit of appearing out of thin air by now, though how she managed it with all her rings and brooches and necklaces was beyond him.

"This is a small farming town that will survive the winter well if they can get the harvest in," she said. "It will be worse in New York, much worse. You're sure they won't take paper?"

Dr. Janzen shook his head. "According to Mrs. Della Rocca, only if they need paper for the outhouse. They're short-handed, however, and so—"

The supply master snorted with disgust. "I bet they are, those lousy—"

"Let him finish," Madame Wershow interrupted.

Dr. Janzen cleared his throat. "Ah, because they're short-handed, they're willing to trade food for labor. Mrs. Della Rocca said that food would go unharvested, so I asked if we could gather the gleanings. Any hands we can spare are welcome, and they'll let us keep half of what we reap from their fields."

"An excellent idea," Madame Wershow said. "I'll pass the word—and make sure everyone know that any food they bring home had better go directly to the supply master and not to their own wagon."

"They must be desperate!" the supply master said. "What if we talk to the folks they've kidnapped?"

Dr. Janzen stopped cold. "What?"

Madame Wershow sighed. "I suppose you won't need to deal with Mrs. Della Rocca again, so there's no need to keep you in ignorance. Seppanen Town has been kidnapping travelers and forcing them to work in the fields. One escaped last night and fled here."

"The men and the dogs," Dr. Janzen said. "Last night. That's what they were looking for. But—"

"Mrs. Della Rocca welcomes visitors. Then she drugs them, and they wake up enslaved."

"She's a good woman!" he protested. "She wouldn't do that! She's providing for a dozen orphans, herself ..." He trailed off as he recalled her speech. "A dozen orphans she'd do anything to protect."

Madame Wershow nodded. He fancied he detected sympathy in the set of her shoulders, but the veil made it impossible to tell.

"The bandages on her table," he said slowly. "Those were there on our first visit, but not this morning. It doesn't make sense to keep your medical supplies out like that. And—that basin of bloody water. That wasn't from cleaning meat. She'd been seeing to the wounded. Those men who attacked the supply wagon, they weren't bandits at all!"

"Only as much as the whole town is," Madame Wershow said. "And now you understand. Make sure the ticket taker knows not to accept fractional currency. If it's worthless to them, it's worthless to us. I'll tell the rest of the circus that now we're farmers, too."

Dr. Janzen nodded and left. When he found the wizened old ticket taker, he told him, "Don't accept paper money. The people in this town think it's worthless—and they might be right, soon enough. Coin or food only."

"Food?" the old man squawked. "How do I know what a potato's worth? How much 'change' do I give back for a chicken? Half an egg!?"

"Er, um." Dr. Janzen floundered. "Charge one meal's worth of food."

The old man squinted at him. "Is it a meal for somebody who's really hungry, or for somebody who's not so hungry?"

"Use your best judgment!"

~ * ~

Lindsay Kleinman
Sally's Saloon, Seppanen Town, Connecticut

Lindsay Kleinman wiped down her bar top with a wet rag. Her dark hair fell forward and she pushed it back with a wince. The motion sent an ache through her arms. She'd worked a dawn-to-dusk shift in the fields for the last five days straight, and now she had a half-day off. A sane woman would be sleeping, but here she was, opening her saloon even though it was too early for most anyone to be drinking. She'd worked hard to open her own saloon, and she'd be damned if a minor inconvenience like the end of the world was going to make her give it up. Cathy helped out when she could, but it was Lindsay's saloon and Lindsay knew better than to rely on anyone else doing her work for her. At least she had one customer. One of the circusfolk had stopped in, a bland-looking man who sat at the edge of the bar.

She looked up when the saloon doors swung open. Another stranger walked in, his long duster billowing around him. He wore his hat pulled down low, but she saw a long puckered scar running down his cheek.

"I'm looking for a friend of mine," the stranger said in a low, gravelly voice. He sat down at the bar and fixed her with an unnervingly cold gaze. "A young man, average tall, brown hair, easygoing. He would have said he was a salesman."

"Wh—what do you mean, he would have *said* he was a salesman?" She was so intent on the stranger that she ignored the bland-looking man—one of the circus people—who struck a match to light his cigarette and then leaned across the bar and turned one of the bottles to read the label.

The stranger didn't answer. "Our boss expected him back two weeks ago. Have you seen him?"

Lindsay cleared her throat. "No, no, I haven't. Sorry I can't help you, sir, but here—have a drink on the house! Strangers drink free."

"I don't like alcohol." The stranger stood to go.

She drew a breath in relief when he reached the door. Then the stranger paused and looked over his shoulder. "And I don't like the color blue."

He pushed back his duster. When the stranger's coat opened, Lindsay glimpsed the shine of a badge she recognized. The stranger pulled his pistol in a move so fast and smooth that Lindsay knew if this man wanted to kill her, she was a goner. He was a Pinkerton, and nobody stood against them—at least not for long. She ducked behind the bar with no thought of going after her own gun.

Bang! An alcohol bottle exploded. She flattened herself to the ground and threw her arms over her head. Another bottle. Then another. Glass shards rained down behind the bar. Lindsay kept her head covered and hoped she wasn't whimpering aloud.

The *bang!*, the sharp crack of breaking bottles, the tinkling glass. The sounds echoed in her ears long after the shots stopped. When she uncovered her head and gingerly pushed herself up, she saw she was surrounded by a sea of blue glass shards. She looked up at the rack of booze behind the bar. Every shot had shattered a blue bottle, and every blue bottle had been shot. Nothing else was touched.

"Oh, God, we have Pinkertons in town," she whispered.

~ * ~

Christopher Knall

Seppanen Town, Connecticut

Two houses away, Christopher braced his back against the outhouse wall, his hands on his knees as he breathed deeply.

"What did I tell you?" Ginger said. "Show them a pistol apparently shooting, and bottles exploding, and they fill in the rest. Last night, I even added spent bullets to the explosive squibs. When they look through the wreckage, they'll find bullets."

"And the fuse?"

"Burned so fast it would barely scorch the wood. Even if they notice a little mark they won't know what it is."

"I thought I would fumble the pistol for sure!" Christopher gasped.

Ginger clapped him on the shoulder. "Not after all that practice. You had it four out of five times."

"And the fifth time didn't worry you?"

"I needed to see how you handle yourself under stress. Some people cave. Other people sharpen. You sharpened." Ginger smiled. "Always know how the person you're working with will react."

"Let me guess, that's Rule Number 6 of being a clown?"

"Rule Number 5, actually. Rule Number 6 is to keep track of your numbers."

Christopher laughed. Adrenaline made it shaky. "I'm surprised she didn't just shoot me."

"You flashed the badge. Townies don't want to shoot a Pinkerton. All killing a Pinkerton gets you is another, angrier Pinkerton. They won't risk that. They're civilians."

"And we're not?"

"Us? Why, we're clowns!" He clapped Christopher on the shoulder. "You're circus now, and we watch out for our own! If anybody had made a move in your direction, I would have taken care of it."

Christopher shrugged it off with a laugh, but he couldn't help feeling a little warmth. After so long on his own, being part of something was—well, it was really something, that's what.

~ * ~

I'm back to being slave labor, Christopher thought, two hours later. Sweat beaded on his forehead from the exertion of digging up potato mounds. He prayed the sweat wouldn't loosen his magnificent false mustache or wash off the walnut stain that darkened his skin.

He sank his spading fork under a potato mound and heaved the plant up. He shook the dirt from it. This time, all the potatoes were good. A monstrous beetle buzzed up from the field, landed on a potato, and *chomp! chomp! chomp!* Half the potato disappeared. Christopher struck the beetle, knocking it off. It buzzed angrily, but retreated.

"Insects grow big around here," he muttered.

Without farm animals, the harvesting went slow. At least he wasn't alone. Around him, circusfolk and townsfolk alike worked the field. A skinny circus roustabout worked on one side of Christopher, and Dr. Janzen on the other. Mrs. Della Rocca herself worked, though Christopher tried not to look at her. He didn't want her to sense the hostility in his gaze. Even the town's captives worked, though somehow there were always townsfolk between them and the circus people. Clara sat on a rock at the edge of the field, her shotgun across her knees. The circus people had been told she was there to protect them from bandits, or wild animals. They'd all nodded like they believed it.

Even the children worked, depending on their age and inclination. One small boy picked a wildflower from the edge of the field and ran to Mrs. Della Rocca. He held the flower up. She took it with a smile and bent to hug him and plant a kiss on his forehead.

Christopher noticed Dr. Janzen watching with a smile on his face.

"He's not her child," Christopher told him. "His mother was a refugee from New York. She made it all the way here on her own, but when she reached Seppanen Town, a nice woman gave her soup and a bed and she woke up indentured. Field labor didn't suit her. She died soon after."

Dr. Janzen's smile vanished. Christopher moved on to the next potato mound. And he watched.

He watched as his captive friend Francis left the field for the third time to bring Clara a cup of cold spring water. She smiled appreciatively and set aside her shotgun as she took the cup. After she finished the water, she handed the cup back to Francis and their fingers touched. When she grimaced and pressed her hand against her belly, bending forward, Francis—hovered. There was no other word for it. When Clara relaxed again, he took her arm and led her to a fallen log at the base of a tree. She sat and leaned back against the tree trunk with a sigh. Then he went back and brought her her shotgun.

Christopher had seen enough. Time for the second part of his job here—or the third part, if he counted actually harvesting potatoes.

"Who's that?" he shouted. "There! I saw a man in the woods!" He pointed to a perfectly innocuous section of trees.

The other harvesters stopped working. Clara pushed herself up laboriously and swung the shotgun around to point in the direction he'd indicated.

"I don't see anything," a buxom woman with her hair tied back in a kerchief grumbled.

From behind them came the distinctive sound of a lever-action rifle chambering a round.

They swung around. On the edge of the field stood a stranger with greasy, shoulder-length black hair and his hat pulled low. He shifted, and a stray beam of sunlight gleamed off the badge pinned to his long duster.

"Pinkerton," Mrs. Della Rocca said damningly.

"We're looking for our man," the stranger called. "He would have passed through as a traveling salesman. If he came to misfortune in this town, you will *all* regret it. Your best bet is to release him unharmed."

"I wish I could," Mrs. Della Rocca muttered. Christopher thought she didn't realize she'd said it aloud.

The stranger backed away, stepped behind a particularly large oak tree—and vanished.

Everyone waited. He didn't reappear.

"Where did he go?" Mrs. Della Rocca asked. "Find him!"

The townsfolk scattered into the woods. Christopher scooped his share of the potatoes he'd harvested into a burlap sack and returned to the circus campground.

He headed across camp toward the supply wagon, carrying his quarter-full sack of potatoes. Were the potatoes all he'd gained, it would have been a poor reward for several hours' work.

He passed the snake charmer as she hung out her laundry on a line stretched between her wagon and a nearby tree. Lots of filmy, silky things, including her unmentionables. She saw him looking and winked. He sighed inwardly, regretting his lost career as a traveling salesman. She was just the type he could have persuaded to buy the expensive mother-of-pearl brush and comb set.

The equestrienne trotted by, exercising her horse. Now, *she* didn't seem to be the type for fancy brushes, unless they were horse brushes. Not much interest in the feminine fripperies or in gussying-up for a man. Christopher was respectful in his manner and nice-enough looking that he usually got a second glance from ladies. Not her.

The cook boiled dirty dishes in a cauldron of water. As he scraped food off with a long wooden paddle, he muttered about the ingratitude of the people who could have been helping him do this. Christopher hurried past.

The Indian *mahout* sat on the steps of his wagon, watering his glossy-leaved oleander plant and turning it to face the sun. Then he reclined with a slim volume in his hand. When the *mahout* saw Christopher approaching, he set the book to the side and folded his limbs into an unnatural position. He pressed his palms together and closed his eyes. Christopher had seen pictures of Indian *fakirs* in that same pose. Something to do with their religion, he thought. He glanced at the *mahout's* book as he passed. *Aetheric Engineering, Volume I.* He noticed the *mahout* hadn't felt compelled to volunteer for harvesting duty, unlike most able-bodied folks who weren't busy at another job.

Ginger waited for him in front of the supply wagon. Hat, duster, and black wig gone, Ginger appeared once more to be his unremarkable self.

"How did you disappear like that?" he asked Ginger, as he deposited his meager haul of potatoes inside the supply wagon.

Ginger grinned. "Rule Number 7 of how to be a clown: Nobody ever looks up."

"You climbed a tree? How is that a rule for being a clown?"

Ginger smiled slyly. "Why, being a ... clown is all about knowing how to distract people. Part of that's being the big, shiny thing in the center of the ring. And part of that's knowing where people don't usually look."

"So what's next?"

"Did you watch your friend?"

"Yes."

"And?"

"He won't want to leave," Christopher admitted. "He's sparking Clara, though she hasn't figured it out yet."

"And so?"

"You can only make a person do what they're willing to do," Christopher said slowly. "And he's not willing to leave."

"Rule Number 2: Always—"

"—know how your audience will react," Christopher finished. He shrugged his shoulders uncomfortably. "He's happier here. So what now?"

"One of the most important parts of being a clown is entertaining the children," Ginger said.

"Oh, yes?" Christopher asked suspiciously. This sounded like it actually pertained to being a clown. He didn't trust it.

"Rule Number 8 of being a clown: Win children's trust." Ginger smiled. "You need to practice."

"I do?"

"Oh, yes. Why don't you go to Mrs. Della Rocca's boarding house this afternoon and—collect—the younger children. Bring them here. At a small stop like this, the circus will only set up the freaks, the menagerie, and the Museum of Educational Novelties. No acts or performances, but it's still more than this town's ever seen. The children will love it, and you'll get good practice."

"Do you think Mrs. Della Rocca will give her permission?"

"I happen to know that she's planning on touring all the fields this afternoon. Following up on those mysterious sightings of strange men in the woods, I daresay."

"Should I leave a note?"

"Of course! Something along the lines of, 'Return our man,' would be appropriate."

"You don't want me wearing a clown costume when I take the children, I'm guessing?"

"Now you're catching on!" Ginger snapped his fingers. "The Pinkerton with the scar should do nicely—unless you think we need another stranger. Probably not. We've already got them jumping at shadows in the fields. Take the children, entertain them out of sight for about an hour, and then bring them to the circus. Let Mrs. Della Rocca start to fret. Then I'll tell her where her children are."

"Wait—you don't want them as hostages to get her to stop kidnapping people?"

Ginger waved a hand. "Hostages are so much trouble. Far better to take your enemy's mind hostage. Let their fears do all the work."

~ * ~

Ginger, the Whitefaced Clown
Seppanen Town, Connecticut

Dressed as just another circus roustabout who'd been working in the fields all day, Ginger headed to the saloon, burlap sack in hand. He bellied up to the bar and reached into the sack, a move that made the dark-haired saloon keeper tense up. She reached a hand under the bar. Concealed shotgun, he guessed. Yes, he and the new kid had made the townies plenty nervous. He let the smile show as he pulled out a potato and plunked it down.

"Can I trade that for a whiskey?" he asked.

"Two potatoes," she answered matter-of-factly.

Ginger nodded and pulled out another one. When he got his drink, he retired to a table by the window with a good view of Mrs. Della Rocca's boarding house.

He'd sipped his way through half his whiskey by the time she came back from the fields. She went into the house. Lamps flared to life. Minutes later she dashed back out, looking around frantically. She shouted, waited, and shouted again. She stormed off down the street.

Ginger sipped. A quarter of a whiskey glass later, she returned, shoulders sagging. She sat on the steps and buried her face in her hands. Almost there, Ginger judged. Eventually, she pushed herself to her feet and plodded back into the house.

Ginger sipped the rest of his drink at the same slow pace and then got up and left. In a dark alley, he pulled the wig, the duster, and the badge out of his burlap sack. He tucked the empty sack into a corner and walked across to Mrs. Della Rocca's boarding house. He knocked politely and smiled when she answered the door.

She stared at him. Her knuckles whitened around the door edge. "Where—are—they?" she hissed.

"I *am* sorry about that misunderstanding, ma'am," he said. "The children are fine. My partner returned them to a safe place before he left. Our missing man was sighted in New York—the messenger found us just a little bit ago. My partner's tracking the lead. I'm to head West."

"So nobody's expecting you?"

"Not for months."

She glued a smile on. "Please, come in. Sit down. Have some biscuits and tea and we can talk."

She busied herself in the kitchen and then returned with a mug of tea and a biscuit for him. She sat down opposite. He noticed she didn't get refreshments for herself.

"Where are the children?" she asked, in a controlled voice.

"The circus," he told her. "My partner wanted to avoid a confrontation. He figured they'd be safe there and they'd enjoy themselves. He bought the tickets."

"So now you'll go and leave our little town in peace." She stretched her smile. "You haven't tried your biscuit yet."

He picked it up. "Well, *I'll* leave you in peace. Of course, since we've got an operation nearby, our men—and women—will be passing through right regular-like. Mostly in disguise as ordinary travelers. I'll check in with our operation headquarters before I go, to make sure they know everything's fine here now."

She lunged across the table and batted the biscuit out of his hand. It hit the floor and rolled into a corner. "I'm terribly sorry," she babbled. "I just remembered that one fell on the floor earlier. I set it on the counter, but somehow—let me get you another one!"

~ * ~

Christopher Knall
Seppanen Town, Connecticut

Christopher hovered near the edge of the circus encampment. He wore the rough clothes of the laborer disguise. The circus tents had been set up on the other side of the field. The music and lights would attract the townsfolk. When he saw Ginger approaching, burlap sack over his shoulder, he hurried out to meet him.

"How did it go?" he demanded.

"Her understanding of the situation has been—altered." Ginger gave Christopher an up-and-down assessment. "You look strained."

"Have you ever tried wrangling that many kids? I was happy as heck to turn them loose. With all the townsfolk heading out for the circus, though, I'm worried somebody will recognize me."

"Recognize you as what?"

Christopher struggled for words. "Recognize me as any of the things I've been!"

Ginger smiled. "I'll put you into clown makeup and a costume. Nobody will look at a clown and see a Pinkerton, or an escaped laborer."

"Is that what being a clown is about?" Christopher asked. "Hiding who you really are?"

"Oh, it's nothing that simple," Ginger said. His voice was grave, but his eyes were merry. "Being a clown is about becoming whoever is needed, whenever they're needed."

~ * ~

*Dr. Christopher Janzen, the Great Doctor Panjandrum and His
Amazing Panacea That Cures All Ills!*
Seppanen Town, Connecticut

Dr. Janzen, as the Great Doctor Panjandrum, gave his spiel
and sold his snake oil and noted down the names of those who
complained of muscle aches and weakness, or nervous energy. He
would give the names to Mrs. Della Rocca. She could keep her eye
on them, though that might not do much good. It was a long list.

After the townies returned home, he retired to his wagon. He
stared glumly at the bed. He didn't see himself sleeping well for a
long time to come.

A knock on the door shook him from his reverie. "Hello," the
fortune teller said, when he opened the door. "I was wondering if
we could leave the body of the 'bandit' here so Seppanen Town can
give him a decent burial."

He coughed. "Ah, that might not be a good idea. He's a bit—
cut up."

Behind her veil, the fortune teller's lips moved in an
unexpected smile. "Now, would that tendency be why you lost your
license? Did you pay the grave robbers for their harvest?"

"A knowledge of the human body is indispensable for a
practicing doctor," he said stiffly. "The education given in most
medical schools is wholly inadequate. If the knowledge I have was
gained by unconventional means, it has still saved many lives."

She sighed happily. "I do love it when the pieces fall together.
But, ah, you should bury the body before it starts to smell. No
keeping it in formaldehyde." She paused. "Nobody will complain
about the ringmaster, though. He'll make a nice addition to the
Museum of Educational Novelties. And after all, his body might be
evidence in a murder trial. The police tend to get cranky when you
dispose of evidence."

He stared at her. "Who *are* you?"

Chapter 8

~* * *~

The Peculiar Case of the Fortune Teller's Veil, Part I

Rajesh, the Hindoo Mystic, and His Fearsome Aether-Powered
Bone-and-Brass Elephant!
A Few Miles From New York City

***T**urban, or no turban?* The bloody thing made Martin Smythe's head itch, but it was part of the disguise. He'd worn it for three weeks straight when he first joined the circus, until the circus members all accepted him as Rajesh, the Indian *mahout*. Anyone who'd ever read a penny-dreadful recognized the Indian mystic type. Give them a turban, a few cryptic statements, and a yoga pose or two, and they'd fill in the rest.

Most of the disguise he liked. He enjoyed practicing yoga again—it hadn't been quite the thing at Cambridge, though he would have appreciated a good revitalizing stretch after some of those cricket matches. And though his thick Indian accent might be a bit over the top, it made a change from having to disguise all hint of his mother tongue. That dratted turban was another matter.

He sighed. When the Maharana of Udaipur gave you a mission, you did a pukka job of it. You tried not to doubt whether there was still a Maharana, or an Udaipur, or a British India. You tried not to wonder if your widowed mother still lived, if she still brought her *dupatta* up to cover her mouth when she laughed, if she still made *chapatis* for the neighborhood kids.

Martin reined his thoughts in with an effort.

At least the bloody turban was so conspicuous that nobody seeing it would ever suspect he had anything sneaky in mind. He squared the turban on his head, slid his Gurkha knife inside his embroidered waistcoat, and slipped out of his wagon.

Against the rich blue of the sky before dawn, trees stretched their skeletal limbs up to the heavens. The circus wagons were dark, quiet lumps. The morning air carried the shifting of the horses, the yawns and grumbles of the menagerie animals, and the first chirpings of the dawn chorus. In the distance, the skyline of New York City loomed like a distant mountain range.

Martin felt a cold foreboding in the pit of his stomach as he stared at the darkened city. What awaited them there? What awaited *him* there?

He shrugged it off and wound his way through the maze of circus wagons. Pre-mission jitters, that was all it was. Collywobbles. He should have taken care of this earlier. As soon as he saw the skeleton man produce that coded page with the name of the ringmaster's Boston contact, he'd guessed that there were other pages that the skeleton man kept to himself. He could have interrogated the skeleton man during those early, hectic days, but the man's disappearance would seem more natural now. In Boston, people might have wondered where the skeleton man could go, but here—well, New York was still a fine, large city to disappear in. It made more sense to do it here. *Besides*, Martin admitted to himself, *I was shaken by the catastrophe. Thrown off my game. Who wouldn't be? It was like the lord of death himself had come to earth.*

Martin passed under the shadow of his mechanical elephant and knocked on the door of the wagon beside it. Last night, he'd been careful to position the beast beside this particular wagon.

No sound came from inside. He knocked again. He heard muffled grumbling and the creak of the floorboards. A match hissed, and light seeped from under the crack in the door. The door swung open, and the skeleton man squinted out. "What do you want, Rajesh?" he asked, shining the lantern into Martin's eyes. "It's hardly the time for a social call."

Martin waggled his head in that yes-no Indian gesture he knew foreigners found so annoying. "I am having these sausages," he said, "but my religion is forbidding me from the eating of cows, and I am wondering—"

"Come in, come in!" the skeleton man said, all smiles at the mention of sausages, even though Martin's hands were empty.

He'd taken the lure. It even happened to be true. After years of eating beef in England, Martin felt a sudden rush of freedom at being able to say so. Trying to persuade himself that only Indian cows were sacred hadn't helped much. He'd made such sacrifices for his country—and he didn't mean England.

As Martin stepped up into the wagon, he thought he heard a rustle nearby. But when he scanned his surroundings, he saw only the dark blotches of wagons.

The inside of the skeleton man's wagon appeared to be half the size of the outside because of the jumble it held. Stacks of books and newspaper broadsheets and candy tins rose to the ceiling. Bric-a-brac nestled in the nooks and crannies. Silk flowers and ribbons dangled from the ceiling and spilled across the floor. Martin took a step further inside, closed the door, and had to duck as the movement sent a ham dangling from the ceiling to swinging in a hazardous arc.

"Sausages?" the skeleton man asked, holding out his hands. Those long, thin fingers trembled slightly.

"Not yet," Martin said. "I am wanting a trade, yes? You are finding papers in the ringmaster's cabin?" His accent slipped a little, but it hardly mattered.

"Yeeesss," the skeleton man said warily, backing away. "I gave them to the fortune teller and the equestrienne when we reached Boston."

"I am trading the sausages for the other papers."

The skeleton man shook his head quickly. "There were no other papers. And where are these sausages anyways?"

Martin ignored the question. "You are lying." He let the last traces of his thick Indian accent slip away as he backed the skeleton man into the corner. He slid his Gurkha knife out of his waistcoat, angling it so the lantern light ran along its blade.

The skeleton man kept shaking his head, his eyes riveted on that sharp gleam of light. From the direction of the wagon window, Martin heard a faint scratching sound, as if a short person were trying to pull themself up to peer in the window. He spun and dashed to the door.

When he threw open the door and leapt out, knife in hand and ready for an ambush, he found—nothing. The person, if person there had been, was gone.

The scuffle of footsteps inside the wagon behind him gave him enough warning to dive forward and seize the door before the skeleton man could slam it shut and throw the bar. The door still slammed, but on Martin's hand instead. Red pain seared through him, but he bit back both the pain and the urge to scream or swear aloud.

He reached around with his other hand and muscled the door open despite the skeleton man's attempt to hold it shut. It wasn't difficult. The skeleton man, well, he was thin and stringy and mostly made of brittle bones.

Once inside, Martin shut the door quietly and slid the bar across it. The skeleton man's eyes widened. "Where are the papers?" Martin asked.

The skeleton man shook his head, backing away. Martin felt a bit sorry for him, but he didn't let it show in his face as he closed the distance, knife in hand. "Where are they?" he asked again.

The skeleton man's eyes flickered to the corner his bed was wedged into. A chocolate tin lay beside the bed. Martin crab-walked sideways, scooped the tin up, and shook it. They both heard the hissing sound of sliding paper. Careful to keep an eye on the skeleton man, Martin braced the tin against his hip and pried the lid off. He smiled when he saw the papers scribbled with code. "Did you take anything else?" he asked.

The skeleton man shook his head.

"Think, man! Was there anything else with these?"

"Just a King James bible."

Martin felt a rush of excitement go through him. "Thank you. Sorry for the scare I must have given you. Here, sit down." He gestured to the bed.

The skeleton man perched on the edge and smiled back at him tentatively. Martin picked up the blanket from the bed and wrapped it around the skeleton man's shoulders. Then he took one quick step closer and rammed his knife between his ribs. The skeleton man's face whitened. He pressed a hand to his chest. "You."

"Sorry, old chap." *If 'twere done, 'twere best done quickly, and all that rot.* Martin jerked the knife out and brought it up in a smooth stroke across the skeleton man's throat. He pulled the blanket up as he did so. The thick wool soaked up all the blood. A gurgle, a gasp, and then Martin was the only living person in the wagon.

Into a burlap sack went—as best he could judge—the skeleton man's most prized possessions, the ones that would be obvious in their absence or conspicuous in their presence. In these uncertain times, surely it was reasonable to think that a performer or two might run away to join the city? He avoided looking at the tintype photographs as he swept them into the sack.

Finished, he blew out the lantern and opened the wagon door a crack. He listened. Nothing. He peered out. Nobody.

He slipped out the door and went to the bone elephant. A sequence of taps with his *mahout's* stick along the brass keys arrayed between the elephant's ribs, and the elephant reached up with its snakelike leather trunk and pulled off the extra rug he'd thrown across its back last night. He wrapped the skeleton man's body up in the rug, tied the ends up with rope, and hustled the parcel outside. Then he climbed up to sit on the elephant's back, had the elephant lift the body, and breathed a deep sigh of relief. The riskiest part was past.

He'd always practiced the elephant's act with a toss-tool of a rug wrapped around a log, to prepare for just this eventuality. The first time people saw something body-shaped wrapped in a rug, they'd look close at it. The dozenth time, they wouldn't even spare it a glance. Martin had hoped never to need the ruse, but he supposed that after the ringmaster grew suspicious, it was only a matter of time.

He tapped his stick, and the elephant twirled the body, tossed it high in the air, and caught it. Another signal, and the elephant lurched forward, its ponderous dinner plate-sized feet crunching over the thin crust of snow. The rug-wrapped body twirled, swooped up into the air, and fell again, caught at the last moment by the elephant's trunk. After the first mile, Martin stopped the show. Two miles farther away, he stopped in a copse of trees and dumped the skeleton man's body and the bag of his precious possessions in a hollow. He covered the body with stones and fallen branches and then covered it with frozen leaves. He made a thorough job of it, despite his injured hand slowing him down. When he was done, nobody would have suspected a body lay there. The area still looked disturbed, but the next snow would cover that. He squinted at the grey-streaked sky. Perhaps even today.

After he'd finished disposing of the body, he returned to the skeleton man's wagon. He knelt and studied the ground next to the wagon window. He thought he saw something, but it was hard to be sure in the cool blue light of early dawn. He took a chance and lit the lantern.

"Bloody hell," he swore.

There were boot prints under the window, small, neat ones with square heels. He studied them for a moment, imprinting the image into his mind, and then he blew out the lamp.

Chapter 9

~* * *~

The Peculiar Case of the Fortune Teller's Veil, Part II

Madame Tonya Wershow, Fortune Teller Extraordinaire
The Loyale Traveling Circus Campground, Some Distance From
New York City

Tonya lay rigid in her wagon bunk. She waited to hear the sounds of the camp stirring to life around her. Then and only then would she allow herself to rise, light her lantern, and move about the wagon. She would join the others around the cooking fire. She would eat a hearty breakfast, and not in haste. Then she would walk out into the woods, as a modest woman might when she felt the call of nature.

She would never come back. Last night, she'd overheard enough to initiate Operation White Rabbit. Madame Tonya Wershow, fortune teller extraordinaire, would cease to exist.

Her eyes stared unseeing into the lightening dark. She heard the crackle of logs in the fire pit and the clank of Cook's porridge cauldron being hoisted onto the spit. Not yet. She lay still and breathed deeply, in and out.

The skeleton man had stolen the ringmaster's secret files. Someone else—a new player—feared what was in those files, feared it enough to menace the skeleton man until he handed them over. This new player had a British accent, but she could have sworn she'd never heard his voice before. Had it been one of the hostlers they picked up on the docks of Bombay? The British card sharp who had been in deep to the wrong people until he slipped out of town with their caravan? A sleeper agent who had been in their caravan as long as she? If only she'd managed to see his face!

Alas, when she had tried to pull herself up to peer in the skeleton man's window, her foot had slipped, scraping the side of the wagon. She'd frozen. The *thump* of sudden movement inside the wagon had sent her bolting into the shadows. She didn't try to linger to see who it was or—ha!—to ambush and capture them. That wasn't her job.

Today she must leave the circus, but it wasn't as if she hadn't known this day was coming.

Tonya foresaw a dark future. The murder of the ringmaster, the aether storm, the riots and looting in Boston, the laborers involuntarily indentured in Seppanen Town, the many, many deaths—she didn't need a crystal ball to know that bad times were a-coming 'round the bend. When things got this bad, some people hid. Some people tried to carry on as though nothing had changed. Some people reveled in the chaos.

"And some people," Tonya said, finishing her thought out loud, "some people step up."

She'd expected to leave because she was more urgently needed elsewhere, not because of Operation White Rabbit. Still, the result would be the same: no more circus life for her.

She would miss it. She enjoyed playing the flamboyant but mysterious fortune teller. They'd made quite a team: her, Ginger the clown, and the ringmaster. They'd traveled across the country, gathering information in places where an ordinary stranger would have roused attention but the circus was just another spectacle. Their performances gained them access to rich and powerful individuals who wanted private shows. At those shows, the circus provided the distraction, and *they* took away valuable information. The act had taken them all the way to British India and past the gates of the viceroy's mansion.

But times had changed, abruptly and cataclysmically. People with her skills would be needed. Besides, she doubted that the circus would be able to survive in this new world, especially since the regular infusions of cash from the ringmaster's "investors" would surely end.

She schooled her restless thoughts to stillness. Time passed. Morning light filtered in through the curtains. Circus folk began to move around the camp. Outside, a hostler swore as the water he hauled to the animals splashed on the ground. The enticingly acrid scent of coffee seeped into the wagon. It smelt much better than the weak, chicory-cut blend would actually taste.

Horses snorted as they trotted past for their morning exercise, reliable as clockwork. Every morning, the equestrienne took her horses out for a run and made sure they were fed and watered before she sat down to her own breakfast.

"Rule Number 14," Ginger said, quite close to the fortune teller's wagon, "Eat your fill whenever food's available." From the unintelligible grunt that answered, Ginger's protégé—the new ringmaster—was not a morning person. Ginger's voice faded as they continued on their way to the cook fire.

Around the back of the wagon, buttons popped. Tonya's eyes narrowed. The sound of a steady stream of fluid and a contented sigh confirmed her darkest suspicions. Some bum too lazy to walk into the woods was pissing behind *her* wagon.

Tonya's lips tightened. He'd never dare do that again if she stormed out and berated him, perhaps throwing in a dire prediction or two about what might happen to a man who didn't keep his fly properly buttoned. Any other day, she would have done just that. Even today, the idea tempted her sorely. *Her* wagon—but no, she reminded herself. It wasn't hers anymore.

His mission accomplished, the errant pisser left. Tonya gave it another few minutes and then pushed herself up from her bunk and lit a lamp.

The remnants of her former life lay inside a locked cedar box that she kept buried under a mound of shawls. The key hung from a chain that never left her neck. She hesitated for a moment and then unlocked the box and opened the lid. The gray dress, the white gloves, and the black cloak all looked much the same as they had the day she accepted her new job. The clothes were out of fashion, yes, and the white gloves and the bit of lace at the neck of the dress had yellowed, but she would pass. She lifted the dress, shook it out, and winced. A decade's worth of creases couldn't be banished that easily. Well, these days there must be plenty of women who didn't have the time or the starch to iron their dresses properly.

The dress still fit. It hung a little loose around the waist, but most people had lost a little girth since food supplies began to cost more dearly. She tucked the gloves into her pocket, wrapped the cloak around her waist, and then swathed herself in a billowing, eye-shatteringly garish kaftan. Over that went a trio of mismatched shawls. She was accustomed to bundling up, but with her plainclothes dress and cloak underneath, she felt like a toddler swaddled in so much warm clothing that she might topple to one side at any moment.

She accessorized with her usual complement: chunky glass-jeweled rings to mask the youth and deftness of her fingers; heavy, ornate necklaces to draw the eye away from her face; a veil to foil keen eyes; and a pistol. The pistol resided within the cedar chest except when she feared matters might become—interesting. Of late, the pistol rarely left its small holster in her boot. Lastly, she picked up the yellowed envelope lying at the bottom of the cedar chest. She would need a letter of introduction.

Properly accoutered, Tonya faced her veiled reflection. She firmed her lips and saw the shadow of the movement behind her veil. What would it be like to set the veil aside permanently and just be herself again?

She lifted her veil. Yes, she still looked like herself. It was just a face, much like any other. Though kind gentlemen had from time to time told her that her eyes were particularly fine, there was nothing about her to make her stand out in a crowd.

Which was a good thing, she reminded herself firmly. She would still be selling gloves at a ladies' notions shop if she hadn't been unmemorable enough that the same gentleman came back three days in a row and didn't realize she was the same shop girl—or if she hadn't found that little detail vexing enough to point it out to him. To her surprise, he'd been quite pleased, and she soon found herself with a much more interesting line of work.

She hadn't been that shop girl in a long time, because what use would a shop girl be? Plain, ordinary Tonya—what could she do?

Inhaling, she lifted her chin. Enough. She could do enough. But first, breakfast.

~ * ~

Christopher Knall, Ringmaster- and Clown-in-Training
The Loyale Traveling Circus Campground, Some Distance From New York City

"Doom! *Doooom!*"

Christopher nearly spilled his soup when he heard the mournful wail. He hunched protectively over his bowl. He was of no mind to lose his luncheon simply because somebody had finally cracked. Though—what *should* he do? He cast a sideways glance at Ginger the clown, who was spooning his own soup up in undisturbed tranquility. None of Ginger's advice on how to be a good ringmaster and "clown" covered what to do when somebody was wandering through the circus camp proclaiming the End of Times.

"*Doooooom!*"

"What's that?" one of the aerialists asked, her face perplexed. She fiddled with the spangled purple ribbon in her hair. "It sounds like Michael, the animal trainer." Her cheeks pinkened as she said his name.

The other aerialist, the one with an orange ribbon in her hair, finished chewing her bite of cornbread, swallowed, and said crossly, "Then shouldn't he be tending to his animals instead of—instead of whatever it is that he's doing?"

A howl of, "*Doooooooooooooom!*" punctuated her statement

Christopher shot another sideways glance at Ginger. Should they do something? Lunatics could be dangerous, especially when they snapped suddenly. Ginger looked undecided.

As they paused in their meal, Lacey the equestrienne strode up. She ignored the cries of doom floating across the campsite. From the precisely pinned angle of her hat to her smooth blonde chignon, immaculate skirts, and mirror-polished boots, she appeared unruffled.

"Has anybody seen Mr. Ben Doom?" Lacey asked.

The Indian *mahout* looked up from his contemplation of his bowl of soup, his eyebrows rising. "Who's *that*?"

"One of the monkeys," Lacey said briskly. "Black fur, white skin, white fur with a red ruff around his face. Michael's looking for him."

They blinked at her.

"Hmph," said the aerialist with an orange ribbon in her hair.

Christopher still didn't have the aerialists' names straight. When the girls were in makeup and costumes it was impossible to tell them apart; the rest of the time it was merely very difficult. Both were short with the tight-muscled build of a gymnast, their faces an undistinguished—and indistinguishable—sort of pretty.

"He shouldn't go around shouting, 'Doom!' It ain't right!" Orange Ribbon complained. "Who cares if a monkey's gone missing?"

Lacey's eyes widened. "I do. We *all* should. In these dreadful times, we need each part of the circus to keep functioning. Each performer. Each tentman. Each hostler. Each talker. Each animal.

Without all of us working together, there won't be a circus. And without the circus, we'll just be freaks on our own." She met each of their eyes, one at a time. "I think we all know how well freaks do on their own, don't we?"

Christopher sized her up thoughtfully. She didn't look much like a freak. Heck, she looked less like a freak than pretty much everybody else in the circus. Her accent, her clothes, her mannerisms—they all screamed higher class. Her station should have insulated her from ever being seen as an inferior. But that emotion in her voice came from something personal.

"I'll help look for the monkey!" blurted out one of the aerialists—Purple Ribbon, this time. Her ears turned a delicate shell-pink. "We'll *all* help."

A reluctant mutter of agreement rose from the other diners. The phrase, "Once I'm done eating, mind you," figured prominently.

Lacey nodded her head. "I *told* Michael he could count on everybody's help. All he needed was a little faith."

"In humanity?" Ginger asked dryly.

She met his gaze directly. "Don't be ridiculous. In the circus." She looked at the others. "Once you're done eating, start searching the woods. We've checked at least half the campground. It shouldn't take much longer to inspect the rest. I'm off."

"Hold your horses, Miss! You should eat something before you go," Cook scolded. "First you won't sit down for a meal until you've tended to your horses, and now it's the monkeys too? Next thing I know you'll refuse to eat until the ostriches are content, and they're never satisfied!" Cook scowled. "I should know. Lost my best wooden spoon to one when I wasn't looking!"

Lacey smiled, though the smile looked a little startled to find itself there. She picked up a piece of cornbread. "I'll take this for now, and when we finish searching the campground, I'll come back and have a bowl of your fine soup."

"*Before* you start searching the woods!"

One blonde eyebrow rose. "I promise," she said mildly.

"See that you remember!"

Christopher carefully studied his surroundings as he spooned up the dregs of his soup. He wasn't sure if it fell under Rule Number 6, keep track of your numbers, or Rule Number 7, nobody ever looks up, but he knew that Ginger would castigate him if the monkey was nearby and he didn't notice it.

He didn't spot any monkey sign, but he did realize something else. He hadn't seen the fortune teller since she left for a constitutional after breakfast. And whatever else she might be, the woman was usually prompt for mealtimes.

He leaned forward, as if to set his bowl down, and muttered close to Ginger's ear, "Where's the fortune teller? I haven't seen her since breakfast."

Ginger laughed as if Christopher had said something funny, but his eyes sharpened. Smiling, he leaned back and slapped Christopher on the back. A casual observer wouldn't have noticed the way the movement allowed his eyes to roam around the camp.

"Should we ask if anybody's noticed her?" Christopher questioned.

"No," Ginger said firmly, though the easy smile stayed on his face. "We don't ask. We wait to see if somebody else asks. We wait to see who *doesn't* ask. And when somebody *does* ask, we wait to see who chimes in."

"What's going on? Did she take the monkey?"

"If she took the monkey with her, everything's okay—peculiar, but okay. If she left on her own with no warning, we might be looking at White Rabbit." With that cryptic utterance, he leaned back and took another sip of the dreadful chicory-coffee blend. "No, what you're going to do is wait a bit and then go out in the woods as if you needed to shit. Look for a bundle of clothes, maybe concealed. And watch out for monkey-hunters."

"What do her clothes have to do with a rabbit? What kind of clothes?" Christopher asked, totally at sea.

"What was she wearing for breakfast? One of those dreadful bright-colored robes, if I recall. And all her shawls. Look for some sort of marker, above eye level." In a lower voice, he muttered, "That's if she doesn't suspect me."

Discretion being the greater part of valor, Christopher didn't demand an explanation again.

"After that bean chili Cook served us last night, nobody'll be suspicious if you're gone for a good long time," Ginger finished.

"Suspicious?" Christopher made a conscious effort to relax his face and smile a bit, mimicking Ginger's nonchalance.

Ginger's smile gained a bit of genuine wry humor. "Oh, yes. If there's nobody with reason to be suspicious, then a cover story does no harm. If there *is* somebody with reason to be suspicious, it may save your life."

~ * ~

Madame Tonya Wershow, Fortune Teller Extraordinaire

The Outskirts of New York City

Tonya leaned against a barren maple tree and studied the city in front of her without fear of being studied in return. In her grey dress and black cloak, she would blend into the shadow of the tree, even if the guards were looking in her direction. For there *were* guards. Two men in the dark blue tunic and pants of the New York City Police stood guard beside the wall growing around the bridge that connected the mainland to New York.

The wall was why she lingered in the shadows and studied the city. A wall could mean many things. It could mean security, or fear. It could mean war, if there was an enemy to defend against. It could mean peace, if it was a building project designed to give the laborers work and put food on their tables. The wall would not entirely block the road to the bridge. An opening was left—for traders and visitors, she supposed. A good sign.

There were also corpses dangling from the bridge lampposts. Not such a good sign, and it added a certain emphasis to the question of why the wall existed.

In most places the wall was no more than a foot or two high. Men and women carried stones and bricks and timbers from the city, across the bridge, and out to the growing wall. Then they dropped them in a pile, and returned for another load. The slow, steady trickle of stone-carriers put Tonya in mind of ants building an anthill. Other men worked building the wall, setting the stones and mortaring them into place. The builders wore clothes practical for construction work: overalls or canvas trousers spattered with ancient paint and mortar, sturdy boots that would protect their feet from falling bricks, hats to shield their heads from the sun, and heavy gloves. The stone-carriers wore a mismatched collection of clothing. Women in ornate walking dresses labored beside men wearing beggar's rags. Tonya winced when she saw the thin gloves the lucky ones wore. Precious little protection *those* would provide! The unlucky ones went bare-handed.

Had the policemen been herding the workers, or guarding against runaways, Tonya would have faded back into the trees and found another way into the city. But that didn't seem to be the case. They stood with their rifles slung over their shoulders, not paying particularly much attention to the laborers at all. Every line of their bodies was relaxed. They weren't expecting trouble. They were just doing a job.

It was still tempting to ease away and look for an unguarded boat that she could paddle across to the city. There couldn't be enough patrolmen to keep eyes on every foot of the shoreline at all times, not with whatever had gone on inside the city. The close-packed warren of tenement buildings in the Lower East Side and the Five Points Neighborhood ... She shuddered. *It must have been even worse than Boston.*

That last thought, and the corpses dangling from the lampposts, decided her. She needed to know what to expect inside the city.

She pushed herself away from the shelter of the maple tree and walked forward.

A branch snapped behind her. She froze. Her head whipped around and she searched the trees for any sign of what had caused the noise. Nothing moved. Maybe it had been a rabbit diving into its den, or a branch snapping under the weight of snow. She didn't *see* anyone.

She resumed walking forward, though her skin still crawled. It took no effort to adopt the hesitant, nervous stride of a countrywoman coming to the big city for the first time since the world unraveled around her. Her pistol was a reassuring weight in her boot.

She stepped onto the road and walked toward the city. The guards straightened when they saw her coming, but they didn't unshoulder their weapons or shout for her to *stoprightthere!* Another good sign.

When she reached the intersection of road and soon-to-be-wall, the plumper of the two policemen stopped her with an outstretched hand and a smile.

"Just a minute, ma'am. We have questions to ask before you can proceed."

His partner, a rail-thin older man with hard eyes, asked, "Where are you from?"

"I come from the country," Tonya said. It took no effort for her eyes to widen with shock as she stared up at the dangling corpses. "I ain't been to the city since." Since *what* didn't require stating. "What did they do?"

The patrolman spat. "Thought they could do whatever they pleased, that's what. This lot ran down colored people and beat them something terrible, even women and children. They lynched a brave little boy who called them cowards when they knocked his mother down."

"A child? That's awful."

"That's right. The commissioner said the only use they'd be was as an example to the others, so—" he gestured like a man holding a noose and made a *kttth* sound as he stuck his tongue out, imitating a hanged man. "After the first few, the ones hanged for looting or violence or assaulting an officer or causing a public disturbance, the commissioner hangs quick and then buries proper. It's just the ones to be made an example of that get strung up like this." He pinched his nose. "The smell's the worst of it, I tell you!"

Tonya shuddered. "They make a fine example," she agreed, her eyes straying to the laborers. Not a one of the workers looked at the bodies or so much as glanced in the direction of the police, despite the novelty of a stranger's presence. "I certainly don't plan on making trouble."

"A little bit like you?" the policeman said indulgently. "I'm sure not."

His laconic partner spoke up. "In the Draft Riots, the women were the worst."

His dark gaze raked Tonya. She kept her hands open and harmless in plain view.

The friendly policeman rolled his eyes. "I keep telling you, we're not *in* the Draft Riots! Do you see a crowd of thousands trying to tear us into itty-bitty pieces? No?" He turned back to Tonya with an exasperated sigh. "You got any contraband?"

She turned wide eyes up at him. "What's contraband?"

"Any kind of food," the suspicious policeman said. "Gunpowder or ammunition. Weapons. Liquor."

She shook her head. "No, I'm not carrying anything like that. I had my last crust of bread for breakfast," she added.

"Why do you seek to enter New York City?"

"My sister's best friend owns a candy store, Hardy's Candy Confections. I thought she might need a hand. Things are terrible tight in my village. I hoped there might be more food in the city." *Which would be a mighty dumb idea if it were true.* "I'm willing to work for it!"

"Aren't we all," the suspicious policeman said, his eyes on the mixed lot of people hauling stones to the wall. "Have to search you before letting you in. That's orders." He started forward.

Tonya hopped back. "I'm a decent woman, sir! Don't you go putting your hands on me!" *Or you'll find that gun, and certain papers I'm carrying, and I'll have a hard time talking you into letting me go free.*

"Wait." The friendlier policeman put his hand out, frowning. "Did you say Hardy?"

"Yes, sir."

He turned to his compatriot, muttering in an undertone, "That's the candy shop the commissioner's wife is all agog over. Talks about the owner like they're friends. That's why it's in with the allowed shops. Hate for her to complain to the commissioner's wife about us."

His partner grunted a reluctant agreement.

The friendly one turned around. "All right, ma'am. Go on. Keep your head down and don't cause trouble. Steer clear of the special patrolmen. If any of them give you trouble, you tell them I said you were okay. They're not wearing uniforms, but," he tapped his left bicep, "they'll have a blue armband. Once you get to Hardy's Candy Confections, your friend will set you straight. Just get there before curfew. That's dusk."

"Thank you! Thank you so much!" Tonya said, making a mental note to compliment Mrs. Nave, the candy shop owner, on her tradecraft.

Tonya hurried past the wall and onto the bridge before the policemen could change their minds. The Hardy candy store was little more than an hour's brisk walk away. She was in no danger of missing curfew, which she became increasingly grateful for as she took in the changed tone of the town.

The streets were emptier than she remembered. The pedestrians who did venture out walked quickly, their heads down. Special patrolmen were everywhere, with their blue armbands and swagger sticks. They frequently stopped travelers, especially those that might be carrying contraband, and questioned them. Still, they were not—quite—bullies. Tonya passed unmolested, as did most of those she would categorize as hard-working civilians.

Corpses dangled from the lamp-posts about every mile or so. They bore placards around their necks that named their crime: looting, murder, rape, assault on an officer.

Other hastily painted signs reminded everyone of the curfew. Posters in store windows advertised what was on offer at "set prices," reminded shoppers to bring their ration books, and warned that hoarding and offering a bribe for extra food were punishable offenses.

It all combined to make Tonya glad when she saw the sign for Hardy's Candy Confections. The cheerful color of the striped awning and the gleam of warm lamplight inside seemed quite welcoming compared to the rest of the city. Before she crossed the street to the candy shop, she stopped in front of a nearby hardware store to read the list of rationed goods on offer.

As she bent forward, a flicker of movement reflected in the shop window caught her eye. A dark figure followed her. She glanced to the side. Apart from them, the street was empty. The pistol in her boot suddenly seemed inordinately out-of-reach. She leaned down as if to ease a stone from her shoe. Behind her, she heard the sound of running footsteps.

She yanked the pistol out and spun to face her attacker.

The first blow of the lead pipe knocked the pistol from her hand. The second smashed across her skull, sending her reeling into the street. The pipe rose and fell once more, and then there was only darkness.

Chapter 10

~* * *~

What the Watcher Saw

The Indian mahout paid close attention to the footprints every person left in the snow. He tensed like a dog on the scent when the fortune teller walked past him. Shortly after she walked out into the woods for her morning constitutional, so did he. I noticed when she didn't return, even after a time period that would satisfy the demands of the most vigorous constitution. With nothing to do all day but watch, I am quite good at it.

Some hours later, the mahout returned from the woods with a dark red blot on his paper-white sleeve.

I told myself I didn't care if he'd hurt the fortune teller, though she had been kind enough to me—in the way that she was kind enough to everyone. The mahout was more promising. He was not bound by the same conventions and fears as the rest of the circus. He had seen me and not flinched. But he would do nothing unless he benefited from it, and what could I do for him?

~ * ~

Christopher Knall, Ringmaster- and Clown-in-Training
Not Too Far From New York City

Wind whistled through the branches. If that wind hadn't set the fortune teller's veil to flapping, Christopher wouldn't have seen it. It had been tied around a tree branch a good four feet above head level, and the veil blended with the dark gray of the tree bark.

His boots crunched across the snow as he searched around the base of the marked tree. A couple of feet away, he found a depression where the snow and leaves looked like they'd been recently disturbed. He knelt in the snow and dug.

He found the fortune teller's eye-shatteringly bright kaftan, her shawls, a number of her rings and necklaces—and nothing else. Huffing with frustration, he straightened and dusted the snow from his knees. A single line of footprints led up to the clothing cache.

None led away.

That just wasn't *possible*. The fortune teller might, maybe, have some special insight into the future; he would not credit that she could also fly. He glared at the smooth, unbroken snow surrounding him.

Wait. Smooth, yes. Unbroken, no. One swath lacked the crystalline sheen of the rest. He squatted beside it and squinted. Small brush marks rewarded him. She'd swept out her footprints. Grinning, he rose and trotted along beside the path-that-wasn't.

After a few minutes of tracking, a line of small boot prints resumed, heading for New York City.

Out of sight, something clattered against the branches. Christopher jumped. A weird animal cry like the rasp of a saw mocked him.

Christopher looked around but saw nothing.

With a shiver, he retraced his steps. At the marked tree, he bundled up the fortune teller's clothing and tucked it under his coat.

As he approached the circus camp, he heard a wavering cry of, "*Doom!*"

~ * ~

"You found footprints?" Ginger the clown asked, incredulous.

"She'd swept them away with a pine branch, but it left the snow looking disturbed."

Ginger nodded. "After even a light snow, nobody could have followed her trail." Ginger looked at Christopher appraisingly. "Most wouldn't have found it, even now. You'll do."

Christopher fought to keep from grinning, until Ginger spoiled the moment by adding, "Of course, even a halfwit would know that the only place *to* go around here is New York City."

"Ginger, why would she go anywhere? What's going on? What's Operation White Rabbit?"

"Kid, *I'm* not even supposed to know about White Rabbit. I'm just nosy by nature—and trade—so I took the chance to snoop through her orders when she was first sent to join the circus."

"Sent."

Ginger gave an exaggerated shrug and a clownish raise of his eyebrows.

Christopher refused to be distracted. "White Rabbit."

Ginger sobered. "If the fortune teller suspected an enemy among us, she was to disappear into the night and report." He stared in the direction of the city. "Whether there's anyone still alive to report *to* is another question."

"Can we tell everyone she's missing now?"

Ginger visibly weighed his answer.

"No," he said finally. "If the person she's running from doesn't know she's gone, we won't tip her hand. We'll just make sure we're both in the groups sent into New York."

"Sent to New York?" Christopher echoed.

Ginger raised an eyebrow. "What, you thought we came here just to stare at the city and then go away?" He squinted at the sky. "You wait and see, it'll be hashed out around the cook fire tonight. Tomorrow morning, some of us will go in. If we left now, there wouldn't be much daylight left once we reached the city. Not a good idea to go into a strange city after dark without proper reconnaissance. Don't know if it's hostile or not, can't see as well to escape or fight ... just a bad proposition."

~ * ~

That evening, Ginger's prediction proved to be true.

At first, they all ate supper in glum silence. The stew was bland, filled with parsnips and potatoes, with only a smidge of carrot and the faint memory of bacon grease to add flavor. Nobody particularly liked it, but nobody particularly blamed Cook.

One of the hostlers took a bottle of pepper sauce out of his coat pocket and gave it a good shake over his bowl.

"Hey, pass that down!" the roustabout sitting next to him said.

The hostler cuddled the bottle closer to him. "No! Maybe you ain't been paying attention, but grocers are getting kinda scarce on the ground."

"Yeah, so we got to share and share alike. Give it!"

"Like your mama does? Hell, no!"

The roustabout's hands fisted and he took a swing

The hostler, accustomed to dodging hooves, scrambled to his feet and out of the way.

The hostler tucked the hot sauce bottle back into his coat, but when his hand came back out, he held a hoof pick. Its wickedly curved blade gleamed in the firelight. "It's mine," he growled. "You want it, you come and take it."

Lacey the equestrienne was on her feet. "Boys!" she said, with all the sharpness of an irate governess. "Stop that this instant!" Her refined accent cut crisply through the night air.

The hostler fell back, his hoof pick disappearing back inside his coat. The roustabout plopped back down, looking rather shamefaced.

"We are not savages," Lacey reminded them. "And we are not starving." She scowled at the roustabout "A man's hot sauce is his own." The hostler began to grin—until she turned her attention on *him*. "You are quite free to *choose* whether or not to share." Her tone left no doubt as to what she thought the proper outcome would be.

"Sorry, ma'am," the hostler muttered, settling awkwardly back down beside the roustabout. "And sorry about the cussin'." Slowly, as if the movement pained him, he pulled out the hot sauce bottle. He held it in his hand for a moment, weighing it, and then tossed it to the roustabout. "Here, help yourself."

The roustabout gingerly caught the bottle. He sprinkled just enough of the sauce on his stew to be polite before handing the bottle back. "Thanks. You didn't got to share."

Both the men looked up at Lacey. She smiled approvingly back.

When she turned around, she found the eyes of everyone upon her. A blush rose to her cheeks.

"Brings up a good point, though," Cook said. "What we traded for in Seppanen Town will keep us from starving, but there's not a whole lot of variety. I know my limitations. Soon enough I'll be trying fir needle soup just to spice things up. If we could get a few more staples from New York ..."

Lacey nodded. "We do need to go in, but—"

The Indian *mahout* interrupted her. "I am thinking we do not want to be going in big parade. We are not knowing what we will find."

Lacey blinked. "Yes, we should send emissaries to speak with the mayor." She paused, as if she expected someone else to speak. When nobody did, a slight frown pinched her brows. She looked around with, and then continued, "A lady shouldn't put herself forward, but I suppose I would be the best choice, for the same reason that I was asked—" again that searching look, "—to speak to the mayor of Boston."

"A lady needs an escort. I'll accompany you," Ginger volunteered gallantly.

"What about Mr. Doom?" blurted out Michael, the monkey handler. "He likes people. If he got lost, he'd go to the city." He gulped. "I can look around and figure out where he might go while you're talking to the mayor."

"No-one should go alone," Lacey said, her brow creased. "We should travel in groups—at least pairs. Cities aren't safe." Her eyes flicked to Christopher and away. "If they offer us food or drink, not all of us should take it. That way, even if they drug it, they'll still have a fight on their hands. Worst case, there's one person to escape and warn the rest of us."

Christopher grimaced, not in disagreement, but because of what he could have avoided if he'd followed a similar plan when he entered Seppanen Town.

Then he jumped, because Ginger had just elbowed him in the ribs. "I'll go too," he volunteered.

Lacey smiled maternally at him. "Thank you."

The rest of the meal passed in peace. After the crowd broke up, leaving Cook to do the washing-up, Lacey walked over and sat beside Ginger. "The fortune teller isn't here," she said quietly. "I know that you and she talked often. Do you know where she is?"

Ginger shook his head. "I wish I did. New York, maybe."

"Well." Lacey stood, shaking out her skirts. "We have another stray to look for, then."

~ * ~

Lacey Miller, the Fabulous Lady Equestrienne Who Defies the Fiery Rings of Death!
Bronx County, on the outskirts of Manhattan

Lacey frowned at the river that lay between them and the city. Their little group's progress through the Bronx countryside had left her skittish. They'd passed too many abandoned farms stripped of anything of value, including—perhaps especially—the livestock. The few farmfolk remaining had watched them pass from the farmhouse steps, unsmiling, rifles to hand. A couple of farms they'd glimpsed in the distance seemed *overpopulated* by farm hands, a circumstance that reminded them all too closely of Seppanen Town. They'd swung wide to avoid those.

It would have been a quick trip if the railroad through the Bronx countryside to New York City still ran, or if they'd ridden horseback. She would have felt much better if she'd been astride a fast horse, instead of stumbling along on foot, but Ginger had pointed out that horses would be seen as valuable and maybe worth ambushing a small group of travelers for.

In general, it had been an expedition unsettling to Lacey's nerves. The uncanny wheezing and rattling animal noises that trailed them, as if they were being stalked by some predator just out of sight, hadn't helped.

And now they faced the Harlem River and the curved wall grew in an arc around where the bridge connected the mainland to New York. The wall was only a couple of feet high, but the ant hive of activity around it would soon change that. A stream of men and women carried bricks and stones over the bridge and dumped them in a mound. Other laborers worked to mortar the wall's building blocks into place. Even complete, the wall wouldn't entirely block off the outside world; there was a four-foot gap where the wall marched across the road. A blue-clad policeman sat on the edge, his rifle leaning against the wall. He appeared to be eating something. Beyond the wall, a single layer of bricks marked a square that might become the foundation for a new building.

"They're defending the bridge over the river, building—a fort, or something," Lacey said. "That can't be good."

"They're not doing a very good job of it, either," Ginger said. "See there—they're only building the wall to the river edge. Unless they guard the water's edge as well, any attackers could just circle around and attack them from the river. So whoever's doing this doesn't have military advisers. That's very interesting. This is a port town; there are military forts near the harbor. Why isn't Fort Hamilton helping?"

"Maybe because it's slave labor building this fortification," Christopher said grimly.

Ginger cleared his throat. "Could be, but let's not overlook the most important part." He pointed at the bodies dangling from the lampposts on the bridge.

"Are we armed?" Lacey asked, wishing she'd asked before they left the circus camp.

"I have a pistol," Ginger said. "And it's hidden where nobody will find it unless they're very fond of other men."

"Oh!" Michael said. "I didn't even think of—I mean, I don't have a weapon anyway, but ..."

"Should we go back?" Christopher asked.

"I think the nice policeman sitting on the edge of that wall would find that suspicious," Ginger said. "He's looking right at us."

"He hasn't aimed his rifle at us," Lacey said dubiously.

"Maybe because he doesn't want to drop his sandwich. Let's not give him reason to." Ginger strode forward, hands open by his sides and a wide smile on his face.

With a dismayed, "*Hmph!*" Lacey hurried after him. She looked over her shoulder and saw Christopher and Michael still standing there, with identical doubtful looks on their faces. "Come on!" she said. "We're committed."

"Ought to be committed—to *Bedlam*," Christopher muttered as he followed along after her. She pretended she hadn't heard.

"Hello!" Ginger was saying to the policeman when she caught up to him. "You are a sight for sore eyes."

The policeman blinked, clearly unaccustomed to being greeted with such enthusiasm. He cleared his throat. "Welcome to New York City," he said gruffly. He straightened into something approximating attention, though one hand—the one that *had* been holding a sandwich—remained tucked behind his back.

Lacey's nose twitched at the scent of boiled ham, and her mouth salivated involuntarily.

Any bits of meat the circus hunted up got tossed in the stew, making it more nourishing and adding a bit of welcome flavor. The knife thrower was getting better at pegging squirrels, and the girl sharpshooter had bagged a rabbit or two, but they agreed that there was less game in the countryside than there ought to be.

Lacey pushed away the thoughts of food and put on her brightest smile. "We are here to speak with the Mayor. Can you direct us to him?"

One of the policeman's lips twitched up at the corners. "The Mayor? Oh, yes, I know exactly where you can find him."

Sensing something amiss, but not sure what, Lacey changed the subject. "Did you see a woman come in yesterday?"

"What does she look like?"

"Um—ah—" Lacey's mouth flapped like a beached fish.

"An outsider," Ginger put in. "Not someone who'd been in the city before."

The policeman shrugged. "Not during my shift. We rotate, you know."

Lacey's shoulders slumped slightly before she pulled them straight. "Well, we need to speak to the authorities. We'd welcome an escort—"

"Sorry, lady. I'm on duty." He glanced over at the laborers hauling bricks. "Hey, one of you want to guide these strangers? It'll count toward your food ration. I'll square it with your gang boss."

A small woman with sweat running down her forehead and dirt in the creases of her neck scowled in the policeman's direction, but after she dropped her stack of bricks—nearly half as tall as she was—on the pile of building materials, she trotted over to them. "I'll do it, boss," she volunteered. "I know the way to Central." In marked contrast to her slum accent, she wore what had once been a fine dress, before it was dirtied and patched with lower-grade fabric.

"I bet you do," the policeman said. "No tricks, hear? You deal straight with these people, even if they are strangers. The commissioner wants trade." His face soured and his hand tightened on his ham sandwich. "Not like we've got anything to trade, though, unless you're looking to collect bodies."

"No, thank you," Lacey said politely.

"No tricks," their new guide promised. "I don't want to be an example." She turned to Lacey. "Pleased to meet you, ma'am. Name's Deborah Rowan." She stuck out her hand.

Lacey took it, dirty though it was. When they shook, she felt the strength of that small, calloused hand. "Lacey Miller. Charmed, I'm sure, Miss Rowan," she murmured.

"Call me Deb."

Lacey inclined her head.

The policeman grunted. "You lot carrying any contraband? Food, weapons, liquor?"

"No, sir," Ginger assured him.

The policeman seemed to weigh the value of searching them against the inconvenience of having to set his ham sandwich aside. "You look like decent people, so I'll let you go without a search this time. If you *are* carrying contraband, they'll find out soon enough, and you'll regret it." He jerked his head. "Go on."

"Thank you, officer," Ginger and Lacey chorused.

Deb smiled sweetly. "This way, lady and gents!"

She strode ahead, leading them past the fortification-in-progress and out onto the stone bridge that arched over the river. "Welcome to New York City," Deb said. "We call this the High Bridge, because if you look over the edge, you'll see it's mighty high!" She chuckled at her own joke. "Its fancy official name is the

Aqueduct Bridge, but if you call it that when you're trying to find your way back here, nobody'll know what you're talking about."

Lacey froze. "You said aqueduct? We're walking across an aqueduct?"

Deb shrugged. "Yes."

"The water aether could explode at any moment!" Lacey hoisted her skirts. "Run!"

Michael bolted. Ginger peered at the bridge with a thoughtful expression on his face, and Christopher dithered beside Ginger.

"No, no!" Deb caught Lacey's arm. "It's safe. No aether engineering involved. We know all about the exploding water mains. That's in the warnings posters." Deb rolled her eyes. " 'Do not use water taps or pumps. Use only pumps marked as safe by the Sanitary Squad. Do not use mechanical lighting unless the same applies.' I tell you, I'm not fond of coppers, but the guys on the sanitation squad are made of solid brass, if you know what I'm saying." She stomped her foot on the bridge. "This is just water flowing downhill. Good thing, too. Without fresh water, we'd be drinking from the harbor." She made a face. "That's not a good idea if you want your bowels to stay regular."

"Oh." Lacey dropped her skirts, feeling a flush creep across her cheeks. She'd made a fool of herself. She lifted her chin and pasted a perfectly correct smile on her lips. "Well. Thank you."

Michael returned, rather shame-faced. Lacey gave him a charitable smile. "Not your fault," she said. "I was mistaken." Her expression gave no sign that the words tasted like gall on her tongue.

Once they were halfway across the bridge, out of earshot of the officer guarding the wall, Ginger mused, "Police putting up safety warnings and checking the aetheric devices. Police as city guards. It will be interesting to learn if the mayor is a figurehead only, or if he's controlling the police force."

Lacey shot him a quelling look. "Interesting? If we play this wrong, we could all end up hauling bricks like those poor people building the wall."

Ginger refused to quell. "Exactly. Interesting, like I said. The bit where they said they want trade was promising."

"You mean the bit where they said they didn't *have* anything to trade?" Her voice rose incredulously. She glanced ahead of them, but their guide kept walking as if she hadn't heard anything. "Except *bodies*?" She shook her head and stalked away to walk beside their guide.

On the other side of the river, Lacey stopped and looked around. No guard waited for incomers. No pedestrians bustled around on errands. No children played in the street. No hackney cab drivers waited to pick up custom. The only sign of life was a mangy dog pissing against the wall of a jewelry shop. When he saw he had an audience, he slunk away into the shadows.

"Where is everybody?" Christopher asked.

"Going about their lawful business or sitting in the dark in their apartment," Deb answered. "Come on, keep it moving. It ain't good to linger."

As they moved through the deserted streets of Manhattan, Lacey couldn't suppress a crawling feeling, as if a venomous spider were walking over her skin. There was no visible reason for it. Three- and four-story brick buildings rose placidly on either side of the street, staring down on the travelers with darkened windows. A light dusting of snow gilded the wrought iron balconies and fire escapes. No laundry hung out the windows. Colorful shop awnings arched over the sidewalks, but the shops beneath were locked and shut, or boarded shut. She'd seen far worse in Boston. Here, there were few broken windows, and most of those had been boarded up. Only one building showed signs of a serious attempt to set fire to it. But Boston had been filled with life, even though the dead were everywhere. Here, the only sound was their own footsteps. The only company was the dead.

"Did she linger?" Ginger jerked his thumb at a female corpse dangling from a flag pole. Swelling distended her rotting flesh. She wore the dress of a laboring-class woman. The worn fabric had been carefully patched with cloth scraps that almost matched. "Is that what happened to her?"

Deb glanced at the body and away. "She did something. I don't know what. I don't know her. She died a while ago. She doesn't have a sign on her neck, so it was probably during the riots."

"So you *did* have riots!"

"Not for long. Turns out the commissioner was a patrolman during the Draft Riots. He saw his partner torn to pieces by a mob, and he swore he'd never let that happen again. He had a plan to keep riots in check. It worked. We're all peaceful and law-abiding now." Deb's face set in grim lines.

"Surely that's a good thing?" Lacey said.

"Sure. Sure it is." Deb plowed forward through the streets. "Just ask the dead."

They walked in silence for the next couple of miles, passing perhaps a dozen pedestrians along the way. All hurried past with their eyes downcast and their shoulders hunched. They also passed men who seemed to be of a different sort. Those men leaned against doorways or sat on stoops, watching those who passed with hard eyes. They weren't visibly armed except with a short truncheon, but they still struck a certain intimidating note. Each wore a blue band tied around his upper arm.

"If it's so safe," Christopher asked, "why are there no shops open? Why are there so few people in the streets? And who are they?" Christopher jerked his chin slightly at one of the blue-banded, a rough-looking fellow sitting on a stoop smoking a cigarette.

"Most of the shops that are still open moved closer in to the center, so they aren't drawing people out here," Deb answered. "You'll see soon. There's no workers because the corpse gang and the authorized salvagers already moved through here."

"*Authorized* salvagers?" Ginger raised an eyebrow.

Deb jerked her thumb at a bloated and fly-bit corpse hanging from a tree. "Looters get strung up."

"And them?" Christopher began to raise his hand, but Deb grabbed it.

"*Don't* point," she hissed. "They know you're tourists because of the way you're rubbernecking. But you've got a guide—that's me—so they've decided you're not trouble. Don't change that."

"Okay, okay!" Christopher pulled his hand back. "So who are they?"

"Special patrolmen," Deb said quietly, not looking in the man's direction. "Police commissioners have the power to appoint special patrolmen when there might be riots and suchlike. We only have the one commissioner now—" she didn't specify what had happened to the others, "—and he used that power." She shrugged. "They're not so bad, I guess. They know what it is to be poor. Most of them aren't bullies, especially after the commissioner hanged a couple who, ah, 'overstepped their authority.' There's just so *many* of them, all snooping and prying, it makes a body nervous."

Particularly, Lacey thought, a body who hadn't necessarily been on the right side of the law even in regular times. "Where did he get them all?" she asked. "Surely they wouldn't just volunteer."

"It's not a bad choice. I volunteered to carry bricks out to the wall. You think *I'm* the volunteering type? People volunteer real fast when food is on the line. The corpse gang? Volunteers. The authorized salvagers? Volunteers—and I *wish* I could have gotten in that gang. I hear they can slip a little something in their pocket as long as it's not contraband."

Lacey blinked. "Compared to the corpse gang, I suppose the special patrolmen have a pleasant job."

"Yeah, the special patrolmen have it pretty good. Worst they have to deal with is cracking skulls if there's trouble. Most of them come from the street gangs so they've got no trouble with that." She eyed a patrolman enviously. "They wouldn't take the girls, though."

Lacey refrained from comment.

"Anyway," Deb said, "we're almost there."

"There where?"

"There where people moved. Once the corpse gang cleared out the apartments, if they left a zero chalked on the door, well, you could move right in. People feel more comfortable living near each other, instead of in a dead zone. More company, fewer memories. The stores followed. You'll find ones that are actually open here. It feels like the city used to, except most of the neighbors are new. " Deb chuckled harshly. "The new New York!"

"Where are we going?" After the reaction of the policeman at the wall, Lacey didn't want to ask directly about the Mayor.

"The rail-line. The commissioner's got some of the horsecars running again. They only run on a few of the lines they used to, but it's better than walking. You won't find a horse-drawn cab these days, not unless the cabbie's extremely well-armed."

Lacey didn't ask for details. She didn't want to know, not in a city this hungry. Of course, the instant she tried not to think about it, her imagination conjured up all sorts of gruesome images. She was very glad they hadn't ridden into New York.

Seemingly tiring of the question-and-answer routine, Deb strode ahead.

The new New York was a shadow of what the city had been before the aether storm, but it was a shadow cast by a living thing. Everywhere were posters warning about prohibited behavior and allowed consumables. The sound of babies crying penetrated through apartment walls. Laundry flapped from windows overhead. Women swept building stoops. Men hustled past with bags of—well, in these times, best not to think too closely about what might be in the bag. Within two blocks, Lacey saw a grocer, a butcher, and a ladies notions shop that were open for business. The ladies notions shop seemed best stocked and least populated.

"Here we are," Deb said, stopping in front of a jewelry store whose proprietor eyed them with a particularly hungry expression and then turned away with his shoulders slumped when they clustered under a sign that said, "Horsecars stop here." Deb sighed. "Poor bugger. Pardon my language. Wonder how long he'll last? Nobody's buying gewgaws."

"When will the horsecar come?" Michael asked.

Deb shrugged. "When it comes."

"We should split up and go look for Mr. Doom," Michael said to Christopher. "He won't be in a government office." A look of doubt came over his face. "I don't think so, anyhow."

Deb laughed. "Doom's everywhere, Mister. No looking needed."

"No, no!" Michael hurried to explain. "Mr. Ben Doom is a monkey who ran away from the circus. Have you heard anyone talk about seeing a monkey? Have you seen him?"

The girl blinked, and for a moment the mask of cynicism fell from her face. "A monkey, here? Wouldn't *that* be a sight! I'd trade my ration coupons for a week to see something like that!"

"That's rather the idea," Ginger muttered under his breath.

Deb sighed. "No, I haven't seen anything like that. No one else has either. They'd talk about something like that, you can bet on it!"

Michael squared his shoulders. "We'll just have to keep looking, then. Somewhere, somebody has to have seen him!" He strode away.

"We'll turn this place inside-out," Christopher said to Ginger, with what Lacey thought seemed like extra emphasis. "See you back at the camp."

Ginger nodded. "I'll keep an eye out too. Good luck."

"Likewise!" Christopher turned and trotted off after Michael, who was already making inquiries of a young girl holding a basket of flowers for sale. The girl shook her head.

Watching them, Lacey said, "Finding a stray monkey in a city this size—or persuading the powers that be to let us set up the circus and maybe even to resupply us? I think they have the easier task."

Sometime later, the horsecar stopped in front of them. Seeing it did not change her mind. The horse-pulled streetcar was three-quarters full, and every face inside was tight with anxiety. On the front platform, two hawk-eyed policemen with rifles to hand accompanied the driver. "Central Police Department," the conductor announced. "All aboard."

"That's you," Deb said, nudging them.

"You're not accompanying us?" Lacey asked.

"Not me."

Lacey must have looked as adrift as she suddenly felt, because Deb relented and added, "Look. It'll be okay. The commissioner isn't unreasonable. And if you need a guide later, you can usually find me at the Glorious Green Grocer. Spend half my day waiting in line for rations there, I do."

"Thank you." Lacey shook the other woman's grimy hand again, vigorously, before stepping into the horsecar. As the conductor blew his whistle one last time and the driver *giddyap*ed to the horses, she leaned in to Ginger and said quietly, "We asked to see the Mayor, the authority in charge. Why did she take us to the police station?"

"Maybe he's under arrest," Ginger answered whimsically.

The horses sweated as they pulled the car along the rail lines. Inside, the passengers did, too. The air inside the car was sharp with the acrid tang of anxious perspiration.

Lacey's nerves were wound too tight for her to pay much attention to the passing scenery. Still, she noticed that every mile or so, swollen fruit hung from tree or lamppost.

"City's going to smell a lot worse once the thaw sets in," Ginger said after they passed one particularly gruesome specimen. "If the city was more Northern, it wouldn't be this bad. They've had just a few too many warm winter days."

"In the spring, sickness will hit hard, with all the corpses around."

"Dead bodies, in and of themselves, don't spread disease as much as you might think. Ask the doctor."

"Perhaps I will," she said, giving him a sideways look and pointedly *not* asking, *And why do you know so much about dead bodies?*

When the conductor blew his whistle and shouted, "Central Police Department," Lacey and Ginger clambered down obediently. The other passengers pressed past them, swarming up wide stone steps to an imposing brick building. Iron bars guarded the windows. Special patrolmen and uniformed policemen teemed around the doors.

Lacey snagged the sleeve of a passing patrolman. "Excuse me, sir," she said, chin thrust forward. "We were hoping to see the Mayor." This time, she would get a straight answer.

The patrolman looked at her with an expression she couldn't decipher. Surely, she'd done nothing to earn his—distaste?

He jerked his thumb upward. "Look your fill."

Lacey and Ginger followed his gesture up, to the flagpole—and the corpse dangling from it. His features were too distorted to recognize. In life, he'd been a portly man. He wore fine clothes, though his trousers were soiled. Nobody had stripped the corpse's body. His fingers puffed around heavy golden rings, and the mayor's chain of office dangled from his neck like a noose.

The placard hanging around his bloated neck read, "Accepted bribes."

"We will talk to the commissioner, then," Lacey said numbly. "He would seem to be our only choice."

"You saw how he treated the mayor," Ginger said in an undertone, after looking around to be sure nobody was within earshot. "That was a man with power in this town. We sure don't have any. What do you think he's going to do with us?"

Chapter 11

~* * *~

A Hive of Scum and Villainy

Michael Hunter, the Animal Handler
New York City

Michael stared unhappily at the tall brick buildings. One look at those wrought-iron balconies and fire escapes, and Mr. Ben Doom would be up them and across the roofs. Or he might go to ground in one of the thousands of abandoned apartments. Or he might perch in a tree in one of the parks, maybe sharing limb-space with a dangling corpse. Or—

The city was so big, it could swallow him whole and lick its lips afterward.

"We won't *never* find him," Michael lamented. "It's like finding a needle in a haystack—although," he added upon reflection, "monkeys are more active than your average needle."

"I thought you knew where the monkey would go?" asked Christopher.

Michael set his jaw. "I had to say *something*. They weren't going to look for him. And it's *kinda* true, it's just—this is an awfully big city."

"Come on. We've only been looking for a few hours. There must be *some* sign of what happened to her—er, him."

Michael stared at Christopher. "What do you mean, 'her'?"

"Nothing! I just couldn't remember if the monkey was a boy or a girl."

"Because 'Mr. Ben Doom' is such a girl name?" Michael scoffed, happy to have something to take his mind off the impossibility of their search. "Pull the other one; it's got bells on. Go on. Who's the girl?"

"No girl, really!"

"Come on. Who is she? You got a sweetheart in New York City?"

Michael watched as an internal war waged across Christopher's face. Anything to distract him from his own worries.

"You'll find out soon enough, I guess," Christopher finally said. "The fortune teller's gone missing. Ginger thinks she might have come here, and maybe something bad happened to her."

Michael blinked. "Oh. You're looking for her, not really helping me find Mr. Doom at all." He felt his face twist into a glower. He wasn't much good at not showing his first reaction to things. Just another reason he was better off working with animals than people.

Christopher sighed. "No—I mean—yes, I'm looking for her, but I'm also looking for the monkey. Hell, for all I know, she could *be* a monkey under all those shawls and veils!"

Michael chuckled despite himself. He sobered up quickly and guiltily. "We've been asking these city folks for hours, but nobody's seen nothing! We must have talked to a hundred people!"

"That leaves—what? A thousand still to ask?" Christopher said.

Michael looked around. By the nearest apartment building, a lean man with unkempt, white-streaked hair huddled on the steps leading down to the basement. A blanket tent was pitched at the bottom of the stairs, and a small fire smoldered beside it. A skinned animal roasted over the fire on a makeshift spit, its naked pink muscles half-charred and glistening with grease. Michael didn't look too close at the hobo's dinner. Squirrel was one thing, but if it was cat or rat, he didn't want to know. It was too small to be a monkey. That was all that really mattered.

"Maybe before that hell-storm. Not so many, now." Michael headed in the hobo's direction.

Christopher trailed after Michael. "Who camps outside in a city that's filled with empty apartments? In the winter?"

Michael looked over his shoulder at him in surprise. He himself preferred being outside over pretty much any other accommodation. When the weather was fine, he slept on the roof of the monkey wagon. When it was nasty, he bunked with the roustabouts.

"Maybe he likes to see the stars," he said finally.

"With the coal smoke from all the chimneys?"

Michael shrugged. "Ask him yourself." He walked up to the hobo and squatted near the man, rocking back on his heels. Christopher hovered nearby.

The hobo squinted at them. "Ask him what?" he asked.

Michael waited, but Christopher didn't pipe up. "Why you don't squat in an apartment," Michael said. "Ain't it cold outside?"

"I lived in Antarctica, once," the hobo boasted. "Picked up some tricks from the natives. Snow, that's the key." He pointed at his tent. Snow was packed around it on all sides. "It's warmer now. The eskwimoes, they know about snow."

Without much hope, Michael asked, "Did you see a monkey last night?"

"I saw three!"

Michael blinked. "Er, what did they look like?"

"One was green, one was all black except for white fur around his face, and one had a skull for a head." The hobo shuddered. "I ain't never forgetting that skull-monkey."

Michael leaned forward. "Do you know where the black monkey went?"

The hobo screwed up his face. "Now that's an interesting philosophical question. What do monkeys like?"

"Fresh fruit, and being groomed, and climbing on shoulders—" Michael began, when the hobo interrupted him with a snap of his fingers.

"That's it! Tropical islands! Monkeys and parrots and fruit and pretty native girls without any sense of proper decency at all." The hobo sighed. "That's where I'd go if I were a monkey, you bet. Luscious mangoes and massive cantaloupes." He smacked his lips.

"There aren't any isl—" Michael hesitated. "There aren't any *tropical* islands here."

"Sure, sure, but they know how to get there, don't they?"

Behind Michael, Christopher snorted. "Come on, Michael. This is useless," he said.

"Monkeys know how to get to tropical islands? What are you talking about?" Michael asked the hobo.

The hobo touched his nose and winked slyly.

"I don't understand."

Christopher heaved an expressive sigh. *We're wasting time. Let's go*, it said.

Michael jutted out his lip and prepared to wait. He could be plenty stubborn when it was called for. After all, hadn't he managed to teach the ostriches to steal the clown's top hat and cane? There may have been some fuss later when the ostriches practiced their new trick outside the ring, but that wasn't the point. The point was that if Michael could out-stubborn an ostrich, he could *certainly* out-stubborn a hobo. Or an upstart ringmaster-in-training.

The hobo stared at Michael. "Sailors," he explained. "Monkeys and parrots know that sailors will take them aboard. Then the sailors go to tropical islands because of the *wanton* island girls and their long, smooth legs and loose hair and unbound cantaloupes and—"

"Thank you!" Michael said hurriedly. "I get the fruits—er, the picture. I get the picture."

Michael backed away. When he turned around, he found Christopher grinning at him. Not a word needed to be said, but Christopher said it anyway.

"Cantaloupes."

Michael set off at a brisk pace, heading toward a young girl with a basket on her arm.

"Unripe mangoes."

Michael veered aside and addressed an older, pinch-faced woman, touching her arm to persuade her to stop. "Excuse me, ma'am. I am new to New York, and I've lost an animal."

She scowled. "Then you'll never see it again!"

Michael persevered. "He's a monkey with black fur and a white face. His name is Mr. Ben Doom. Really, it's most important. Have you seen or heard anything about a monkey loose in the city?"

Her mouth pursed into a scowl. "With so many people dead, you're worrying about an ungodly animal? Shame on you, sir!" She jerked her arm away and stalked off.

"Pineapples," Christopher pronounced.

It was too much. Michael wheeled on him. He seized Christopher's collar, hauled him into an alley, and pushed him against the wall. "Enough mockery! For all you know, that hobo had a good idea."

"Coco—"

Michael held up a warning finger and fixed him with his best backing-down-a-lion glare. "Don't!"

He waited.

Blessed silence. The only sounds from the street were the clatter of cart wheels and the quick clack of pedestrians' boot heels.

Michael smiled. "Thank you. Now. If you found a monkey, what would you do? *Don't you dare* say nothing about bananas!"

With a sober face, Christopher responded, "In this town? I'd make stew and try to eat it all before a special patrolman came and used the power of his blue armband to take it away from me."

Michael swallowed. "But if you *didn't* eat him, what would you do with him?"

"Turn him over to a special patrolman?" Christopher shrugged. "I don't know. Rationing, a strict curfew, people staying off the streets—it feels like a wartime town under occupation."

Wind whistled a counterpoint down the alley. Tall brick buildings loomed on either side of them. Here and there, a lamp flickered inside, but most of the windows were dark as a dead man's eyes. For just a moment, Michael felt as tiny and insignificant as an ant under an elephant's foot. He fought the feeling off. Even an ant could make a difference, and *this* ant had lived in wartime towns before.

Michael tightened his jaw. "Exactly," he said. "And in wartime, people try to get around rationing."

"A black market?"

Michael shrugged. "Something like that."

Christopher shook his head. "That doesn't help. Your monkey's a nice slab of meat, and food is still the most valuable thing."

Michael flinched at that description, but he stuck to his guns. "Except for things nobody can't get around these parts. There's a big port here, and sailors are real expert at trading contraband on the side."

"And everybody knows sailors like monkeys. *That's* what you meant when you said that maybe the hobo had a good idea."

Feeling like he'd used up all his words for a month, Michael nodded.

Christopher clapped him on the shoulder. "Let's go find some sailors!" Half to himself, he added, "Not a bad idea to get an outsider's view on how the city's running, either."

~ * ~

Lacey Miller, the Fabulous Lady Equestrienne Who Defies the Fiery Rings of Death!

New York City, Central Police Department

"I'm barely keeping this city from devolving as it is," Police Commissioner Andre Guirard growled at Lacey and Ginger. "I allowed for a certain number of immigrating outsiders, but not for a circus! This is neither the time nor the place for frivolity. We can only absorb a limited number of people before our rationing system becomes strained." His bushy eyebrows lowered and his face darkened. "For now, at least. I hope that we will unlock another source of food—soon."

As if I'd want to be 'absorbed' into this dreadful place, Lacey thought. Aloud, she said, "You misunderstand, sir. We are not planning on joining," she paused, "your city. We only want to enter New York and perform for a week or so. Hopefully, we could buy more supplies while we're here. All we need is your permission and a large space to set up our tents."

If she wasn't exerting herself to be charming and persuasive, it was because she was no longer certain the circus *should* enter new New York.

Commissioner Guirard shook his head sharply. "Absolutely not. We don't have the resources or the time to waste on fripperies. You're welcome to trade for non-contraband items, but all food sales are strictly rationed. The penalty for black-market sale of food is—severe."

Lacey suppressed a shudder. "So we have seen," she said, taking refuge in the cold tones of a lady in front of whom an unsuitable subject has been raised.

Ginger was no help. Upon entering the office, he'd sat in the chair the farthest from the commissioner's desk, where he remained silent and motionless. A man less aware of his surroundings than Commissioner Guirard might have forgotten Ginger was there at all. Commissioner Guirard's eyes flicked to him occasionally, but he'd clearly decided that Lacey was in charge.

"If you people choose to stay in New York, you'll be my responsibility," Commissioner Guirard continued. "I cannot turn away any honest individuals who wish to escape the uncertainty of life in a lawless zone."

Had there been extra emphasis on that "honest?" Lacey unsheathed her most polite, high-society-drawing-room smile.

When she didn't say anything but simply sat there looking expectant, Commissioner Guirard cleared his throat and added,

"Ration books will be issued to you for the length of your stay, if you settle here. They're tracked by district."

He leaned back, his conscience apparently satisfied by this concession. "There are a number of vacant apartments available. Look for the ones with a zero chalked on the door."

"We have our own caravan wagons," Lacey informed him. "All we need is a large open space where we can set up our tents and perform."

He was shaking his head as soon as she spoke. "Impossible," he said briskly. "We're barely maintaining order as it is. Groups of more than five people are not allowed to congregate in public except for the purposes of their employment. Without that restriction, a mob could form, especially in the—" he glanced at Lacey, "—ah, *casual* atmosphere a circus would create."

Loose, she translated. It was hardly the first time she'd faced the prejudices of the morally upright. To counter that same negative perception of the circus, the old ringmaster had created little Biblical playlets for the menagerie and the museum of educational novelties. The lion lying down with the lamb, that sort of thing. Such subterfuge might keep preachers from running the circus out of town. It didn't prevent townies from imagining that females in the circus indulged in all sorts of licentious behavior with strange men.

Her lips curved up slightly in a private smile. Little did they imagine exactly how far from the mark they were.

"Why, it would be as bad as those—" Commissioner Guirard stopped talking. "Hmm."

The speculative tone in his voice snapped her attention back to him.

"I can think of one place where your presence wouldn't cause extra problems," he rumbled.

"Yes?" Lacey asked.

"The docks of Rumsey Port would have room for you to set up your circus tents. Lord knows, you won't cause any extra disturbance *there*. It may be rough—"

"That's no obstacle," Lacey said hastily. The rough-and-tumble of a seaport sounded positively endearing compared to the stifled order in new New York.

Commissioner Guirard cleared his throat and continued, "—but the sailors certainly aren't using the space to unload their ships. You're welcome to distract them as much as you wish. I wouldn't count on them being willing to trade for food, however."

"Thank you!" Lacey said. "We are most grateful for your indulgence."

"Er, well." He shifted in his chair. "The docks are not included in our rationing system. You may do better to take apartments in the city. Our reserves are limited," he said gruffly, "but not so limited that I would turn anyone out to starve, whether or not they could contribute. Although ..." He looked thoughtful. "We could use your circus animals. A lot of meat on an elephant!"

"Not on ours, sir." Lacey smiled. "It's an aether-powered elephant."

"Eh?" He looked disappointed. "Still, your menagerie must have other edible livestock. Ostriches, hippos, that sort of thing."

"Hippo meat is entirely unpalatable," Ginger assured Commissioner Guirard. One eyebrow cocked. "Far too gamey for easy consumption."

That eyebrow twitch meant Ginger's peculiar sense of humor was stirring. Lacey hastened to add, "And we have just returned from traveling overseas to India, where they bathed in the rivers. One must be cautious about the risk of catching a foreign disease."

Commissioner Guirard appeared disappointed but not defeated. Ginger's eyebrow remained elevated. Lacey's mind raced as she tried to come up with plausible reasons to classify the entire menagerie as inedible before Ginger said something disastrous.

The door of Commissioner Guirard's office slammed open.

"Andy-poo!" A curvy young lady with a pixie face and an upsweep of dark curls burst into the room. "It is *simply* intolerable! You must—oh!" She blinked doe eyes at Lacey and Ginger. "I'm sorry! I didn't know you had guests!"

For the first time, Lacey saw the commissioner flustered. "My dear—" he began.

Ignoring him, she turned to Lacey. "I am Mrs. Andre Guirard."

Lacey inclined her head. "I am Miss Lacey Miller."

Mrs. Guirard smiled winsomely. "Delighted to meet you!"

"Likewise, I'm sure." Lacey gestured to her companion. "And this is Ginger."

"Just Ginger?"

"Just Ginger."

"How peculiar!" Mrs. Guirard looked at Ginger with interest.

Commissioner Guirard's choler had been rising throughout the polite exchange. Now, he burst out, "My dear, what are you—? You know I've asked you not to come to my office!"

"Well!" she huffed. "As I said, I didn't know you were entertaining!"

"We were just leaving," Lacey assured her. *Entertaining* though this scene certainly was, Lacey would rather exit the stage before the commissioner's mind returned to the edibility of their circus menagerie.

"Nonsense! Why, Andy-poo hasn't offered you any refreshment!" Mrs. Guirard clapped her hands together and called over her shoulder, "Mr. Akrill, bring tea cake and lemonade!"

There was nobody there. Did the lady think that fairies would bring her cakes and lemonade?

With an irritated *moue*, the lady looked behind her. "Oh!" she said with a note of surprise. "Now where did—? He was just there a minute ago." She turned to Commissioner Guirard. "Really, you must tell Mr. Akrill the proper way to receive guests!"

"What have you done with my aide?" Commissioner Guirard asked in a constricted voice.

"Oh, nothing! But he *will* insist on following me when he sees me in the Central Police Department! Quite unnecessary, as I've told him a hundred times!"

"If you would stay home where it's safe—" Commissioner Guirard shook his head. "I suppose the men I assigned are guarding an empty house?"

She gave a dainty shrug. "They weren't paying attention when I slipped away. You can't blame them. It is simply *too* boring."

Commissioner Guirard looked grim. There *would* be blame assigned, Lacey thought.

The thud of rapidly approaching footsteps drew Lacey's attention away. Curious, she leaned forward in her chair so that she could see through the doorway to the source of the commotion. A puffing, red-faced fellow in police blues trotted toward them. When he saw Mrs. Guirard already inside the commissioner's study, he groaned and slowed to a walk.

Mrs. Guirard clapped her hands. "*There* you are! The commissioner has guests. As his aide, *your* responsibility now is to bring refreshment. Tea cake and lemonade, I think."

"I'm sorry, sir," Mr. Akrill told Commissioner Guirard earnestly. "I was coming back from the file room with that casualty list and I saw her out of the corner of my eye as she was going up the stairs. I tried to catch her, really I did!"

Commissioner Guirard massaged his temples. "I know you did, Peter. Thank you. Put the reports there—" he indicated a spot on his desk, "and—"

"—and bring tea cake and lemonade!" Mrs. Guirard finished triumphantly.

"Thank you *so* much for your hospitality, but there's no need for that," Lacey hurried to say.

Mr. Akrill breathed a sigh of relief, mopped his reddening face, and stepped back to wait outside the door.

"We were just leaving," Lacey continued, addressing what was clearly the greatest threat in the room: Mrs. Guirard. "Your husband has kindly offered us a place to stay and perform, but we really *must* go and prepare our colleagues to move tomorrow."

"Perform?" Mrs. Guirard asked.

A light of amusement dancing in his eyes, Ginger explained, "We are the Loyale Traveling Menagerie, Hippodrome, Circus, and Museum of Educational Novelties!"

Mrs. Guirard uttered a squeal of delight. "A circus? How splendid! New York is so dreadfully tedious these days, all rations and rules and no fun at all! Even normal, everyday things are so difficult. Half the shops are just *gone*, and those that remain have such peculiar hours and they're quite reluctant to work on credit the way they used to." She turned to Commissioner Guirard. "That's why I came to your office. The dressmaker is being frustratingly obstinate and I thought if you *explained*—"

Commissioner Guirard shook his head. "I can't, my dear. That would be an abuse of power."

"Oh, poo!" She pouted.

"Perhaps this will cheer you up." He opened a drawer in his desk and pulled out a gaily striped paper bag. Gold foil lettering on the bag read, "Hardy's Candy Confections."

Mrs. Guirard pounced. "Chocolates! You darling!"

"I was able to stop by the confectioner yesterday, but by the time I got home it was so late that I didn't want to wake you."

"You're working too late every day! All responsibility and no reward," she grumbled through a mouthful of chocolate nougat. She swallowed. "Though I suppose that conscientiousness is part of why I adore you so."

Spots of red appeared high on Commissioner Guirard's cheeks. "Don't eat those too fast," he warned her. "The confectioner warned me that New York is out of cacao beans. That's the last chocolate we will see for some time."

"I'm sure you'll fix it," his wife assured him with a sweet, chocolate-smeared smile

"I'm—working on it," he said grimly.

"You know he's a very important person now," Mrs. Guirard confided earnestly to Lacey. "*Do* tell me if there's anything else he can do to help you."

Lacey nodded. She felt her eyes widen helplessly as she tried not to laugh. Once she'd recovered herself, she said, "There *is* one thing."

Commissioner Guirard's bushy eyebrows lowered ominously.

"Nothing onerous," she hastened to add. "One of our circus members came to New York yesterday and hasn't returned. Have any females new to the city been detained or—or found injured?"

Commissioner Guirard leaned back. "Any fresh bodies reported matching that?" he asked Mr. Akrill. "Strange females?"

Lacey was quite relieved that he didn't press for a more complete description.

Mr. Akrill shook his head. "No, Commissioner. Only rotters."

"Fresh injured?"

Mr. Akrill shook his head again.

"There you go," Commissioner Guirard told Lacey. "We don't have her. We're not much for detaining people these days. If she committed a crime, she'd be free to go by now." His eyes skittered to his wife, which Lacey interpreted as him choosing *not* to add, *or dead and hanging from a lamppost.*

"Thank you kindly. And thank you for the suggestion of where we might set up." She rose and nodded her head to Mrs. Guirard. "It was a pleasure to make your acquaintance. I do hope you are able to attend our performance. Come, Ginger."

"Miss—" Some internal struggle showed on Commissioner Guirard's face. Lacey awaited the outcome with interest. "Miss, Rumsey Port is not a good place for—for a lady."

Ah. That one. It was not the first time she'd confused gentlemen by acting as a lady, instead of as the coarse, wanton creature that they expected a female circus performer to be.

"The docks were rough even when our men patrolled them regularly," he continued. "Without us to keep order, it's only gotten worse. A certain criminal element has shifted to that area since the city is no longer friendly to their kind. Why, it's—it's a regular hive of scum and villainy!"

"Oh!" Lacey carefully did not smile. "Thank you for the warning, but I believe we will do well enough."

Later, as they walked down the wide stone steps of the Central Police Department, Lacey said to Ginger, "Didn't there used to be a group of commissioners who ran the police board?"

"You saw the Mayor. Don't ask about the other commissioners. It's pretty clear who's in charge here."

"Except the sailors and the forts aren't letting him boss them around. Did you catch when he said that the criminals had left the city for the docks? He doesn't consider that part of his territory. It will be interesting to see what the sailors have to say about the state of things."

~ * ~

Michael Hunter, the Animal Handler
Port Rumsey, New York City

Stacks of packing crates blocked the street leading to the port. "That's not exactly welcoming," Michael said doubtfully to Christopher.

"As long as we act like we know what we're doing, we'll be fine."

Michael hoped Christopher was right. He felt eyes on them as they wound their way through the maze.

When they emerged on the other side, he stopped short, blinking.

"What the—hell?" Christopher said, almost reverently.

It was as if they'd stepped back in time to before the hell-storm struck. Sailors, merchants, and more dubious characters bustled across the pier. Compared to the devastated population of new New York, Rumsey Port seemed almost overfull. Michael's shoulders unknotted and his stride lengthened.

Colored globes gleamed in the sailing ships' rigging and along the rails of the steamships. And instead of dim lamplight, ships' cabins and the port authority offices were brilliantly illuminated.

"They've got aether lights," Michael exclaimed.

Christopher nodded. "Like us. Ships out to sea when the aether storm struck wouldn't have been as damaged."

It could have been a scene from months ago, except—the port buildings didn't serve functions quite so official anymore. Above the doors, newly painted planks advertised, "Nancy's," "Fair Trade Winds," and "The Soiled Dove."

Sailors carried small parcels or bags into Fair Trade Winds, but the ships rode low in the water and nobody unloaded them. Each laden cargo ship had a contingent of armed sailors pacing the decks. Unlike the portside crowd, they looked quite sober.

Three large steamships had cast anchor farther out in the harbor, instead of docking at the port. Odd, but Michael didn't dwell on it. There was plenty to keep his attention on the ships that *were* docked. Yellow, green, and blue globes dangled from a sailing ship's rigging, waiting to be kindled to light. On the steamship beside it, a man leaned against the chimney stack and peered through a spyglass at new New York. As Michael stared along the long line of docked ships, he saw sailors moving in the rigging, tightening ropes or checking sailcloth, and—

Michael stared hard at a sailing ship with *Beauty's Reward* written along its side. It had a muscular male Triton for a figurehead instead of a buxom mermaid, but that wasn't what had caught his attention. Something *skittered* along the mizzen mast, something too small and too quick to be a human.

"Did you see that? There!" Michael grabbed Christopher's sleeve and pointed to the *Beauty's Reward*.

"What?"

"I saw him. I think. Come on!"

Without waiting for a response, Michael trotted across the dock to where he'd seen—something. When he reached the *Beauty's Reward*, he stopped in front of the lowered gangplank and shouted, "Ahoy, the ship!"

Then he waited.

And waited.

Something moved in the ship's rigging. The sails blocked it from view, but it cast a monstrous and distorted shadow—one in which four legs and a tail were discernable.

"*Doom!*" Michael hollered as he bolted up the gangplank.

"Shit!" Christopher swore.

Michael ignored that, as he ignored the sound of Christopher pursuing him as he galloped onto the ship, across its deck, past the center mast, and—

A lady stepped out from behind the mizzenmast and aimed a revolver at his heart.

Michael froze. Behind him, the thump of Christopher's footsteps also halted abruptly.

She wore a tight pair of men's trousers, a red-and-gold embroidered waistcoat, a red sash at her waist, and a second gun tucked into it. Her sun-streaked brown hair was bound back in a tight, practical braid. Michael hardly knew where to look, but he settled on her face.

Once she had Michael's full attention, she smiled.

Michael revised his first impression from "lady" to "female." He didn't know of *any* ladies who filed their teeth like that!

"If there's doom to be found here today," she said, her tongue slithering a little around the points of her teeth, "it's yours. Now, you have one chance to tell me why you boarded the ship crying my doom."

Michael's world narrowed down to the dark, hungry mouth of the Colt Navy revolver, and the hand that held it.

"Last chance," she said pleasantly. She cocked the hammer on the gun.

Michael's breath rasped loud in his ears. He couldn't move. He couldn't speak. He couldn't do anything but stare down the barrel of that revolver.

"No!" Christopher shouted from behind him.

The noise jerked Michael out of his paralysis. Reflexively, he lurched forward.

A thunderclap split the day, and something hit Michael hard enough to knock him to the deck. Fluffy white clouds floated through the bright blue sky above him. *Where did the thunderbolt come from?* His head spun, but he tried to sit up. He put his arm out to brace himself. It folded under him.

Then he felt the pain burning through him. He collapsed. His cheek crashed to the polished wooden deck. A red slick oozed across the deck in front of him.

Oh, he thought. *She shot me.*

It seemed like the right time to pass out, so he did.

Chapter 12

~* * *~

Monkey Business

Not Far From New York City

*I*t was late afternoon, and nobody had returned yet from New York. The circus sat idle.

Nobody else had noticed that the fortune teller was missing. That excitement was still to come. I could have told everyone that she hadn't returned after her walk into the woods—but I still wanted a way to persuade the Indian mahout to be on my side, even if I didn't know yet how useful he would be. I needed to figure out what he wanted. The fortune teller had walked into the woods. He had followed her. He had returned. She had not. Why? I thought if I could only ask just the right question, I would learn the key to everything. Of course, I would have to be careful, or he might "take me for a walk in the woods."

That afternoon, he never came over to the same side of the circus camp as me, leaving me frustrated. Betty and Roxane were chattering about fashionable dresses or some such tedious subject.

Maybe, *I thought,* I'll make Betty and Roxane go into the woods with me tonight. I might learn what happened to the fortune teller. And that would give them something more interesting to talk about!

In retrospect, I'm very grateful that I did no such thing. If I had, our bones would be moldering in that forest, a freak show curiosity for anyone who found them.

~ * ~

Michael Hunter, the Animal Handler
Port Rumsey, New York City

Michael opened his eyes. It felt like he'd just closed them, but the sky above him was a darkening, cloudless blue and the shadows of the ship's rigging had shifted around him. Why was he lying on his back, anyway? Christopher, the new ringmaster-in-training, sat nearby. Maybe he knew why. Michael tried to speak, but it came out as a harsh croak.

Christopher jumped. "He's awake!" he called.

A woman's head intruded into Michael's field of view. She smiled broadly, showing rows of sharpened teeth that a shark would be proud of. "How are you feeling?"

"*Gah!*" Michael pushed himself upright and backpedaled away from her. Memory returned. "You shot me!" he accused her. Then, "Hey, why doesn't my arm hurt anymore?"

He lifted his arm and moved it back and forth. It wasn't entirely true that it didn't hurt anymore, but the searing pain had muted to a dull ache. He studied himself. A scorched hole decorated the right side of his shirt, just below his collarbone. He poked his finger in the hole.

"*Yowch!*" he yelped, jerking his hand away. His head swam.

"I wouldn't say your arm doesn't hurt anymore," Christopher said dryly, "but you won't die. Captain Angie was kind enough to use some of her store of bone aether to knit you back together."

"Captain—?"

"He's muzzy-headed from blood loss," the woman said. "I've seen it before." She made a mock curtsey. "Angie Endo, Captain of the *Beauty's Reward*."

The movement dizzied Michael. He shut his eyes. Then they sprang open again as what she'd said earlier penetrated. "You wasted bone aether on *me*?"

Even before the storm, if he'd broken a bone or been careless around something with sharp teeth, he'd healed in his own time. Bone aether was too expensive to waste on anything less than a life-threatening wound. He shuddered to think how expensive it must be now, after the storm spoiled most of it.

"You sprang a pretty good leak," Captain Angie said. "I'd rather not kill somebody by *mistake*. Besides," she grinned, "I want to go to the circus."

Michael shook his head. The world didn't spin around him. His head must be clearing. How had he gotten here? He and Christopher had come into New York with the others and then split off to look for Mr. Ben Doom. A booze-addled bum had suggested they look for the monkey with the sailors. They'd gotten to the port—and boy was it different from the subdued, fearful city! He'd been looking at the ships and he'd seen—.

"*Doom!*" he hollered.

Captain Angie buried her face in her hand. "Not this again!"

"At least you know not to shoot him this time," Christopher said. "Hey!" He put his hand on Michael's uninjured shoulder and shook him. "It wasn't your monkey, okay? It wasn't Mr. Ben Doom."

Michael stopped. "It wasn't?"

"No. It was hers." He nodded to Captain Angie. "Go on."

She put her fingers to her mouth—the proximity to all those pointed teeth made Michael wince—and whistled. Something scuttled through the rigging above them. Michael looked up, just as a four-legged *thing* plummeted down to land on the deck.

It had the size and shape of a monkey, but if Michael had seen more than its shadow, he never would have mistaken it for Mr. Ben Doom. Like the circus' aether-powered elephant, this had been made from the bones of a living creature, but it was a far cruder creation than the elephant. Instead of the morbid elegance of bone and brass, a patchwork of dog hide covered it up to the skull. Underneath that loose skin, gears and joints shifted awkwardly.

The monkey-creature ran over to them with a weird, jerky scuttling motion and crouched beside Captain Angie. Naked bone grinned at Michael when it turned its head in his direction.

Michael shuddered and looked away. "No," he said. "That's not Mr. Ben Doom."

Late afternoon sun sparkled on the waves in the harbor. A breeze ruffled the slack sails. Beside the powerful, towering modern steamships, Captain Angie's sailing ship seemed quaintly old-fashioned.

"You don't know where our monkey is, do you?" he said quietly, keeping his eyes on the other ships.

"No." She sounded sorry. "He's not in the port, though. I would have heard. We're all bored silly—word of something new would spread like syphilis."

He had nothing to say to that. Silence stretched.

Eventually, she said, "I'm just glad I'm not captain of a steamship."

Startled, Michael glanced at her. She wasn't looking in his direction. She'd followed his gaze to the modern ships berthed nearby. "What? Why?" he asked.

"Why do you think so many of them are still sitting in port? They don't want to waste their aether catalyst unless they have a damn good reason. Me, I'm free to travel wherever the wind blows."

"So why don't you?"

She smiled wryly. "I have a cargo to sell. Here seems as good a place as anywhere else—at least they haven't stormed the dock. Yet. The military forts are on *our* side, and the commissioner is keeping a tight rein on his people. You might not think it—" she waved her hand at the licentiousness on display, "but this is one of the safest ports around. The dock might get a little rowdy—" on land, a shouted argument was resolved when one of the disputants smashed a bottle over the head of the other, "—and the commissioner might just be waiting for his chance, but there's a lot worse out there."

She stared out over the sun-sparkling water, but she was seeing something else.

"You were out to sea when the storm hit," Christopher said softly. "This wasn't the first port you tried, was it?"

"No. We never sailed in close enough to dock anywhere else, though. I saw—bodies floating in the sea, and the hulks of ships burned down to the waterline. I lost crewmen anyway. A few had family in those ports. I wouldn't dock and I wouldn't give them a boat. They just—dove into the sea. They were pretty good swimmers. They should have made it to shore." She shook herself. "I like New York. Things are holding together here. A girl can disembark to get a drink or a little friendly male company without coming back to find her ship pillaged."

Michael didn't know where to look, but he felt his face growing red at her frankness.

"Did I shock you?" She chuckled. "Maybe I'm too used to sailors. But like I said, it's not so bad here. I miss the old New York, though. The theaters, the restaurants, the dress shops—" She noticed the incredulous looks Michael and Christopher exchanged.

"What?" She grinned. "You should see the expression on those prissy shopgirls' faces when I smile ever so nicely at them and say I want to try on every dress in the shop! Such bargains I get, it's piracy!" She sighed. "And then I wear a pretty new dress and go to a park or the zoo—"

"Wait!" Michael struggled to push himself up into a sitting position. "Did you say the zoo?"

"Yes." She looked quizzically at him. "There's a quite nice little family-run zoo in Manhattan. Planning some sightseeing? Oh—wait. I see. You think your monkey might have gone there."

Rising hope choked any words in his throat. He nodded furiously.

Christopher interrupted. "The monkey might have, but *we* can't. Look at the sky. It would be twilight by the time we got to the zoo. We'd never make it out of New York before curfew. We have to get back to camp and make our report."

"I'm going to the zoo," Michael insisted. "You do what you like!"

"I can't just leave you! Remember? Nobody should go alone."

"Then I guess you're going too."

"An expedition to the zoo!" Captain Angie clapped her hands. "I'm glad you came to my ship. This is *so* much more fun than tedious war games. I got to shoot a man, the circus is coming to town, and now we're going to the zoo. Just like old times!"

"Not—quite," Michael managed. He felt he ought to protest the way she counted shooting him as a fun thing, but she'd also saved his life and he didn't want to be ungrateful.

She sighed. "Maybe not quite like old times. I'd better get a few things to take with us. Wait right here!"

Before he could protest that she really shouldn't risk herself, she was gone.

When she returned, she wore a dark gray shawl and a long drab skirt. Michael suspected that she still wore her scandalous trousers underneath. The skull-monkey skittered beside her, a blanket-wrapped bundle strapped to its back. Behind her loomed a silent, burly man with more tattoos than Michael had seen outside the circus before.

"This is my first mate," she introduced him. "He'll be watching the ship while I'm gone, and he wanted to eyeball you lot before I left. In case anything happened."

Michael gulped and tried to look harmless. He hoped the bullet hole helped.

Christopher eyed the skull-monkey askance. "What's in that pack?"

"Oh, just a few things I thought we might need."

Some of the shapes under the blanket had a distinctly weaponlike profile. Captain Angie might not be wearing her revolvers at her waist, but there were two lumps of about the right size in the package. A suspicious mind might think that long, thin shape resembled a rifle. Michael poked a square shape. Something rattled inside, rather like cartridge shells. And— "Do I smell sausage?"

She smiled. "I'll never tell."

"You're not worried about them catching you with contraband? Or being trapped away from port after curfew?" Christopher asked.

"I never spent the night in a zoo before. Should be entertaining." She shrugged. "Even if the zoo is—inhospitable— we'll be fine. We just have to avoid the special patrolmen."

Michael narrowed his eyes. Not that he would let fear of the patrolmen stop him, but she seemed mighty confident. He looked at the aether-powered monkey's horrible misfitting dog-hide coat and its gleaming bone face. He remembered the hobo saying, *I ain't never forgetting that skull-monkey.*

"You been out in new New York after curfew!" he accused. "You *and* your monkey-thing."

"The captains decided somebody had to scout out the lay of the land," she said. "Somebody small and quick enough to hide, but strong enough to fight their way out of any trouble. Besides, I was bored."

"They sent a woman?" Christopher asked blankly.

"You say 'they' like I'm not a captain! *We* sent *me.*"

"What if they caught you?" Michael exclaimed. "We *saw* what they do to people who break their laws."

"They might catch me, but they can't hold me."

Her hands went to the neck of her shirt. Michael didn't know what she was doing. Then she parted the buttons, and he knew she was opening her shirt but he had no idea why or what to do about it.

When she pulled her shirt open, he saw why. Brass tendrils arched up from her ribcage, curving over startlingly white flesh to flatten against her collarbone. Now that he looked for it, he saw other ridged outlines crisscrossing under her shirt.

"You're wearing a slave harness!" he blurted.

"What once *was* a slave harness," she corrected him swiftly. "I'm no slave and never was! An inventor of my acquaintance modified this harness to remove the master controls and to pull from bottled aether instead of spindling it from my bones. It's not as powerful as a war harness, but I have a strength advantage over any man in this port."

"But that's not—"

"And you should be happy I do," she continued. "How do you think I just happened to have bone aether to spare to heal up some fool who boarded my ship without permission, shouting, '*Doom!*'?"

"But—." He stopped himself. "Thank you."

She nodded. "That's more like it." The motion made her shirt fall open further.

He averted his eyes, feeling heat creep up his cheekbones. "You can—" He waved his hand vaguely in the direction of her shirt.

She chuckled but took mercy on him and buttoned her shirt up again. When Michael felt it was safe to look, he found Christopher staring searchingly at Captain Angie, a frown on his face.

"The captains sent out a scout. Are you expecting trouble? Do you think the commissioner is going to storm the docks?" Christopher asked.

"If he tries it, he'll learn his mistake fast enough. He may have stopped the riots. He may control the city. But he doesn't have the artillery to take the port. The ships at sea when that hell-storm struck? *All* their weapons still work, not just the simple projectile ones. Sure, most ship stores of aether catalyst are low, but low is more than the nothing he has."

Christopher winced. "He's got more men, and whatever weaponry is in the civilian armory. From the sound of it, he's been stockpiling for a while. You might not be able to handle him."

Captain Angie grinned sharply. "You know how the commissioner learned about the disturbances to aether-powered mechanical devices? He'd squirreled away a couple of Striders, those fire-spitting tanks the North used during the War of the Rebellion. He was going to use them against his own civilians to enforce order! Instead, the tanks exploded. If you ask me, it was fitting that the men willing to commit such abomination died in the backfire."

Her voice harsh and low, she continued, "We'll *not* be turning our cargoes over to some tin-pot dictator just because he says so.

We can fight off pirates at sea, and we can fight off pirates on land. You see those steamships out there?" She pointed to the massive cargo ships anchored farther out.

Christopher nodded.

"Those are the ships he wants. Their holds are packed with tasty edibles. But they know it's too risky to dock. So he can't storm them from the land. And the military forts have made it known that they won't tolerate piracy on the sea, no matter what happens in new New York. But!" She clapped her hands. "Enough grim talk! It's time for an outing to the zoo!"

~ * ~

"It don't *say* it's a zoo." Michael frowned at the locked wrought iron gate in front of them. To either side stretched a fifteen-foot-high brick wall whose top bristled with jagged glass shards and pointy spikes. Beyond the gate, trees arched over an overgrown path. Snow caked the thick underbrush.

Captain Angie squinted at the top of the gate. "It used to say 'Zoo' in big fancy letters on top of the gate. Look, you can see where the letters were sawed off."

The fresh cuts to the metalwork on top of the gate gleamed in the rays of the setting sun. Their sharp, jagged edges gave the gate an appearance about as friendly as an alligator's smile.

"Perhaps this isn't the best time to visit," Christopher said. "It's probably a wild goose chase anyway."

Before Michael could round on him, Captain Angie took care of it. "Would you rather be on the streets of new New York after curfew? We don't have enough time to get back to Port Rumsey. It's your choice." She bared her teeth in a gleaming grin. "I'll have fun either way."

Christopher mumbled something to the effect that since they were there anyway ...

"That's what I thought you'd say." She rattled the gates. "Shouldn't be hard to climb the gates as long as you avoid the sheared off bits on top. It's a hell of a lot less risky than climbing up the wall, with all those spikes and that broken glass on top, and hyenas on the other side."

Michael perked up. "They got hyenas?"

Captain Angie gave him a *look*. "It was an expression. I'm just saying that climbing over the main gate is the safest way to get in." She grabbed the bars, braced her feet against the bottom of the gate, and heaved herself upward.

The sound of a rifle being cocked from inside the zoo made her drop down, lift her hands, and take a few steps back. "Or, of course, it could be a trap," she continued. "Make every other way in difficult and dangerous, but leave one spot looking vulnerable. Then you can concentrate on guarding that one spot. It's a good trap. I should have thought of it."

"Sir, we don't intend any harm!" Christopher called to the unknown rifleman. "We're strangers in town. We heard there was a zoo. We'd dearly love to see it, if it's possible to arrange such a thing."

No response.

"I work with animals myself," Michael tried. "At the circus." That exhausted his store of diplomacy. "I really need to see your monkeys! Honest!"

No response.

Captain Angie clicked her tongue to summon her skull-monkey. When it skittered up beside her, she untied the blanket pack it carried and began rummaging around inside.

Fearing she might be planning to start a shootout with the zoo's invisible guard, Michael hissed, "Don't start nothing— please!"

She straightened with a string of sausages in her hand. "Don't fuss," she told him. "I know what I'm doing. I've traded with natives in hostile ports before, you know." Raising her voice, she called, "I'm not from New York. I'm a trader, a sailing ship captain. I thought cacao beans and some sausages might be a fair trade for a visit to the zoo."

The bushes rustled. A young girl on the verge of womanhood poked her head out. "Sausages? And chocolate?"

Captain Angie smiled. "And chocolate. If you need anything in particular, I could maybe arrange a trade for you."

The girl pushed her way out of the bushes. Like the captain, she wore men's trousers. In her case, Michael thought they might be a new addition. The cuffs were rolled up like they were hand-me-downs from an older brother. As a concession to modesty, she wore a knee-length skirt over them, similar to the Bloomer costume some women had tried to adopt twenty years earlier. Her eyes fixed on the length of sausages Captain Angie dangled, but she kept the rifle pointed in their direction.

"I'm Captain Angie Endo," the captain said, as calmly as if gunpoint introductions were an everyday occurrence. For her, they might be! "What's your name?"

The girl thought about it but appeared to find no danger in introductions. "Rosie Sasse."

"That's better." Captain Angie smiled. Waving a hand in their general direction, she added, "This is Michael, the animal handler, and Christopher Knall, who claims to be some sort of clown and ringmaster-in-training."

"Um, pleased to meet you," Rosie mumbled.

Captain Angie beamed like the girl had invited them in for a sit-down family dinner.

"Wait," Rosie said. She braced the rifle against her hip, reached up, and pulled on a cord dangling from the tree branches near the gate. A bell jangled in the distance.

Now that his attention was drawn to it, Michael saw that the cord swooped down between tree branches all the way back along the path.

"I can't let you in," she said apologetically. "Papa has to decide."

"That's fine. Sensible costume you're wearing," Captain Angie approved.

"Er, thank you." For a moment, the rifle wavered in Rosie's hands. She cleared her throat and steadied her stance. When she spoke again, her voice was gruff. "Why were you going to break into our zoo?"

"We're hunting a monkey—" Michael began.

Rosie braced the rifle against her shoulder and looked down the barrel at him. "We're not selling any of our animals, and we're not going to let you take them!"

"No, it ain't like that! You see—"

A short, broad-shouldered man with a bushy beard and mucky Wellingtons charged down the path toward them, an old musket in hand. He skidded to a halt when he saw the gate inviolate and Rosie with her gun. "What's this, then?" he demanded.

The bushes on either side of the path rustled.

"They want to hunt our monkeys, Papa!" Rosie said. She narrowed her eyes and moved her finger to the trigger of her rifle.

Feeling he was close to being shot for the second time that day, Michael hurried to say, "No, no! We're from a traveling circus! I'm looking for one of *our* monkeys who went missing. I'm worried about him."

If anything, Rosie's scowl deepened.

The bushes to the right of the path shook furiously. A massive, majestic yellow-maned head poked out. Michael froze as the lion turned topaz eyes to gaze at him.

After due consideration, the lion pushed his way out of the bushes and paced over to sit in the middle of the path. He yawned widely, incidentally displaying his long, white, wickedly sharp incisors.

Beside Michael, Christopher opened and closed his mouth several times before managing to say, "Um. Lion. Backing away." He suited action to word.

Michael studied the other areas of the underbrush where there had been movement. "He ain't feral, or they wouldn't never let him near the children." Indeed, small faces peered out from around the trees near the entryway. "They're the easiest prey." The little faces popped back into the underbrush. "The lion's comfortable around them, and they're comfortable around him. That means the lion's fed well enough that he won't attack just anything. Besides, it's the females who hunt. They're the ones you got to watch out for."

"Maybe they trained him to attack," Christopher offered from a distance away.

Michael shot him a disparaging glance. "It's *hard* to train a lion. Easier if you start young, but—no. He's a zoo lion. It don't make sense to train him to attack the customers."

As if sensing that his role was over, the lion yawned, flopped onto his side, and stretched.

"You know your lions," Papa Sasse said approvingly. "Maybe you're not one of those barbarians who thinks a zoo is just a farm with funny-looking animals. We had a few of those come around, thinking that we should share the butcher's bounty."

"Oh, no!" Michael gaped, aghast that anyone might think that *he*—. "I'd never! That's worse than eating humans! I'd starve first!"

Behind him, he heard Captain Angie mutter, "Worse?"

"He's here about the monkey, Papa," Rosie said.

Michael rushed forward and seized the bars of the gate with both hands. Rosie jerked a step backwards and raised her rifle.

Captain Angie chuckled. "Your friend, he doesn't learn fast, does he?" she said to Christopher.

Michael ignored that. His eyes fixed on Rosie, he demanded, "*The* monkey? You've seen him? You have him?" He looked past her, searching the the treetops. "Mr. Doom?" he called. "Mr. Ben Doom? Doom! *Dooooom!*"

"Oh, not this again," Captain Angie grumbled.

"You have no idea," Christopher said under his breath. "The first time he did that, at our campsite? We all thought he'd snapped. Or that the world was ending. Again."

"*Doooooooom!*"

"Settle down, son!" Papa Sasse told Michael. "I knew something wasn't right when another monkey just showed up out of nowhere. We'll let you and your friends in to see him. Rosie, unlock the gate."

"You can't!" Rosie whirled on her father. "They're so happy, you just—you just can't! It isn't right!"

"Now, Rosie," her father began, raising his hand placatingly.

Michael stared at the girl. What was she talking about? It couldn't be Mr. Ben Doom. The monkey wouldn't be happy away from the circus. He was a member of *their* monkey troupe. Even if he wasn't particularly close to any of the other monkeys, Michael took really good care of him, making sure he got his share of the food and was groomed properly. He wouldn't just leave him—wouldn't just leave *them*, Michael corrected himself.

"Unlock the gate, Rosie," Papa Sasse said. "They deserve to know what happened to their monkey. Think how you'd feel if it were Marigold."

Scowling, Rosie walked over to the gate and unlocked it. "You can't *make* him go if he doesn't want to," she warned Michael.

He hardly heard her as he hurried inside. Mr. Ben Doom might have run away from the circus, but Michael couldn't imagine anything that would keep him from coming back.

Chapter 13

~* * *~

The Importance of Apples

Michael Hunter, the Animal Handler
The Sasse Family Zoo, Manhattan

At first the reunion was everything Michael could have hoped for. When he stepped into the clearing holding the monkey pen, his heart was hammering fit to burst. Monkeys of all varieties perched on branches or groomed each other as they sat under the trees. Most of them looked healthy and well-cared-for, though a couple huddled against the fence, pressed as far away from the other monkeys as they could get. Now and then, they twitched spasmodically.

"Papa," Rosie muttered, "they're getting worse."

Papa Sasse nodded. "Still can't figure out what in tarnation is wrong with them. At least it hasn't spread to the others, and they're eating well enough—*more* than well enough. As long as an animal keeps eating, it'll usually pull through in the end."

Michael ignored them. As long as whatever-it-was wasn't spreading and *his* monkey wasn't among the afflicted, it didn't matter. "Doom?" he called. "Mr. Ben Doom?"

One monkey broke away from the rest and loped toward the pen gate, uttering the soft, twittering call that was monkey-speak for, "Friend!"

Papa Sasse unlocked the gate and opened it. When Mr. Doom—no. Mr. Ben, Michael corrected himself mentally. He really had to stop calling him 'Doom'; people kept reacting funny to it. When Mr. Ben flowed through the gate and jumped into Michael's arms, all was right with the world again. Michael ran his fingers through Mr. Ben's fur, checking for injuries. The monkey responded by relaxing bonelessly against Michael. He seemed just fine, but Michael kept grooming him.

"Here."

Michael looked up to find Rosie Sasse standing beside him, offering him a couple of apple slices. "For the monkey," she said, jerking her chin at Mr. Ben.

"Thank you," Michael said, accepting the apple slices. Maybe she was reconciling herself to the situation.

She didn't answer and she didn't smile. She just took a step back and watched.

Michael offered the apple slices to Mr. Ben. The monkey stuffed one slice into his mouth, gripped the second in his paw, and hopped down. Before Michael could pick him back up, Mr. Ben lurched away with a lopsided sort of gallop—and ran back into the monkey pen.

Michael's jaw dropped.

Mr. Ben handed the second apple slice to a smaller monkey sitting alone under a tree—a *female* monkey, Michael saw—and sat down beside her. She plucked a leaf from his fur and then settled down to some very attentive grooming. Mr. Ben's eyes drooped, half-lidded with contentment.

"Oh," Michael said, very quietly.

"You see?" Rosie said. "You can't separate them, you just can't!"

Papa Sasse reached out and clapped Michael on the back. "There, there, lad. Don't look so stricken. It's the way of things, that's all."

"Mr. Ben belongs with *us*," Michael said, about as convincingly as a country rube claiming he could out-wrestle a bull gorilla.

Rosie flared up again. "It doesn't matter if he belongs to you! You can't have him."

Papa Sasse patted the air in a calm-down gesture. "You can't take him *now*, that's true." As Michael drew in breath to argue and Rosie stuck out her tongue victoriously, Papa Sasse hurried on. "It's almost dark. Curfew starts soon. You don't want them to catch you on the street after that, believe me! Stay and have dinner with us."

Captain Angie perked up at that, though Michael wasn't sure if it was at the idea of food or if she hoped they'd be able to play leapfrog with the local policemen after all.

"You can stay with us," Papa Sasse continued. "We have space, and Mama Sasse will just have to stretch the soup a little farther."

Michael might not have fancy manners, but he figured that these days it wasn't polite to take food from those who didn't have much. "You don't have to feed us," Michael said.

Christopher looked relieved; he had his own reasons for not trusting local hospitality.

Papa Sasse's beard bristled with affronted family pride. "Nonsense! Mama Sasse wouldn't hear of it! She's probably already preparing for guests."

He led them back through a maze of overgrown paths. By the time Michael found himself standing in front of a large cottage with smoke curling cheerily from the chimney, he *really* hoped the Sasse family's hospitality was genuine. He was all turned about, with no idea which way was out. If he tried to find his way through the zoo in the dark, he could just as easily end up snuggled next to the alligators.

Papa Sasse led them up to the cottage and opened the door. Light spilled across the path, and the aroma of baking fish and apple pie floated out to welcome them. Inside, a woman laughed and was answered by a flurry of childish giggles.

A sharp pang twisted Michael's heart. The sounds reminded him of the family he'd left behind in Virginia, his mother and his brothers and a whole passel of cousins. Used to be, he'd send them a letter now and then and never really worry much about them, since they were a family that did a fine job of looking out for each other. He worried about them a lot these days, but there was nothing he could do. He tried to push the worry aside. He had to concentrate on what he could do in the here and now. He couldn't afford to be sidetracked because this family reminded him of his own.

Rosie Sasse darted into the cottage ahead of them. "Mama, we're home!" she called. "Papa *insisted* on bringing guests!"

A tall, rawboned woman walked into the front room as Michael and the others entered. "Of course he did," she said, drying her hands on her apron. "The little ones told me. And Rosie, for shame! That is not how we talk about our guests."

Rosie flushed. "But Mama—!"

"As things are, we may have to guard our home. But once we've invited somebody into the zoo, they are our guests, and you will treat them appropriately." Mama Sasse regarded her daughter sternly for a minute. Then she relented slightly. "If they behave untowardly, then you may shoot them."

Michael was decidedly discomfited by how comfortable everybody seemed to be with the idea of shooting him, but Rosie perked right up.

"Yes, Mama! Do you need help in the kitchen?"

"No, your aunt and cousin have everything in hand. You go call the family to dinner." Mama Sasse smiled. "And keep your rifle near, in case you need to shoot our fine guests."

Papa Sasse chuckled and elbowed Michael. "Ain't she a pip? She's the one who thought of sawing the Zoo sign off the gate, and using blackout curtains, and rotating a gate guard between us all— even the girls."

Michael disagreed about the wisdom of putting Rosie on guard duty, but he held his peace.

"Come, sit." Mama Sasse led her guests to the table. "You—" pointing to her husband, "—wash up! I know you've been mucking out the elephant pen!"

Michael, Christopher, and Captain Angie sat. Mama Sasse returned to the kitchen. Michael frowned.

The tightness in Christopher's muscles reminded him of a dog who'd been beaten before, waiting for the next blow to fall.

Michael leaned forward and whispered, "I'll eat first. Like the equestrienne suggested we should."

Christopher's shoulders unknotted and he shot Michael a grateful look, but before he could say anything Papa Sasse strode in. Washed up, wearing clean clothes, and with his magnificent beard brushed out, their host appeared almost a gentleman. Mama Sasse followed, carrying a covered platter that steamed most promisingly. Behind her came an older woman with her hair pulled back into a severe bun, bringing out the breadboard.

Other freshly scrubbed members of the Sasse family drifted in. From the range in ages and appearances, Michael reckoned the Sasses had taken in uncles and aunts and cousins out to a few removes, in addition to their own brood.

"Did you release the dingoes?" Mama Sasse asked a tall young man who looked like he was outgrowing his clothes at the rate of an inch a week.

"Yes'm."

"You got dingoes?" Michael asked.

"We have a fine pack. Since all the upset began, we've started letting them out at night. They're nocturnal, you see. They'll give us warning if any strangers break in, and their yips and howls will spook the intruders."

"I'm sure," Christopher said, shooting Michael a look that said, plain as anything, *You got us into this. You get us out!*

Michael chose to ignore him. He saw no reason why they should fuss about how they were leaving until *after* dinner.

Rosie joined them last, her hair brushed up into a twist, wearing a nice dress. She set her rifle in the corner before joining them at the table.

"Shall we eat?" Papa Sasse asked.

Michael's stomach growled in noisy approval. Chuckles rippled around the table. Even Rosie smiled.

After Papa Sasse said a quick but heartfelt grace, they all dug in. When Michael pressed his fork into the baked fish, it flaked into perfect white layers. The bread was as good as only bread fresh from the oven can be. Everything, right down to the pitcher of cold milk, delighted Michael—though he decided not to ask what kind of mammal the milk had come from.

He was so caught up in his meal that he didn't notice the lack of conversation until Mama Sasse demanded, "Don't you like my cooking?"

He looked up to find her frowning at Christopher and Christopher's untouched plate.

"He's got, ah, indigestion," Michael stammered. "It will pass soon."

Enlightenment flashed over her face. "Situational indigestion?" she said approvingly. "I suppose I might have some too, if I were in your shoes. If I thought of it in time."

"How can he have indigestion if he hasn't eaten yet?" Papa Sasse protested.

She patted his hand. "Don't worry about it, dear. Just save the man his portion. I'm sure his indigestion will clear up soon."

Michael smiled weakly. Then, realizing Christopher might take that as a sign of illness, he tried to smile more vigorously. Captain Angie looked at him and her eyes widened. Michael gave up on trying to smile in any particular way and focused on his plate.

Knowing that Mr. Ben Doom was safe—even happy—gave him patience enough to hold back until the dinner plates were taken away. Barely.

Then he launched into his pitch. "I saw how Mr. Ben Doom is with Marigold. I don't want to split them up either."

Rosie narrowed her eyes.

"I'd be happy to take her with us. They could start a family. We've got plenty of room for more monkeys, and ..."

He trailed off as Rosie pinned him with a glare so fulminating he nearly raised his hand to check if it had set his hair afire.

Christopher cleared his throat. "Perhaps we should have this discussion after the ladies retire."

Papa Sasse's eyebrows flew up. "I'm not going to try to persuade them to retire!" he said hastily.

"Huh!" Captain Angie snorted. "You'd better not. I want to see how it all pans out!"

"I'm not needed in the kitchen," Mama Sasse said comfortably. "Besides which, nothing will be agreed upon without Rosie's say-so."

"Nothing?" Michael asked weakly.

"Nothing."

"Then I *don't* agree!" Rosie snapped.

"Now, now, hear them out," Papa Sasse said. "I rather like the idea of more baby monkeys about the place. What else do you have? Zebras? Baboons? A lioness or two?"

"No lionesses or baboons. Plenty of ostriches. A pair of zebras, a crocodile—I don't suppose you have any camels?" Michael asked hopefully. "People might not think them as valuable as horses, but they're mighty tough and they can fend for themselves. I've got three, but they're all female."

"No," Papa Sasse said with a sigh. "Just a couple of months ago, there was a ship in port that offered me a pair of camels. I turned them down. I thought they weren't flashy enough for the New York crowd."

Rosie's face began to redden as her father continued, "Now I wish I had taken them up on it. Camels could have been useful around the place." He shook his head. "We at least have pasturage. I don't know how we'll keep feeding everyone else. Our food supply isn't entirely self-supporting. Some of the animals have special dietary needs, and the big cats—" He shook his head.

"Might be I could see my way to a word with my fellow captains," Captain Angie offered. "You've got something to offer in exchange. Might be that—"

Rosie interrupted, her face as red as a baboon's butt. "We're not trading Marigold!"

"I was thinking visits to the zoo," Captain Angie said mildly.

"*He* wasn't!" Rosie stabbed her finger at Michael. "All he wants is to steal Marigold away!"

"That's not—" Michael stopped. "I just want what's best for them. Have you seen what it's like in the city?"

"On the way here, we hiked through the Bronx countryside," Christopher said quietly, joining the conversation. "The commissioner has already stripped all the farms for miles and miles around. I've seen the ration notices. Food is in mighty short supply, and I'm not talking just for the animals. How long until the commissioner gets around to deciding that your menagerie is an edible resource?"

"That would be a damn shame!" Captain Angie looked up from her skull monkey, which she had been making dance for the entertainment of the youngest children. "What's a sailor in new New York supposed to do for entertainment? The commissioner already shut down the bars and the—" her eyes slid to the children, who had frozen as still as rabbits in hopes of not being noticed, "—and the other establishments, that, er, cater to sailors."

"I'd keep Marigold safe, really I would," Michael said earnestly. "The monkeys have a fine circus wagon with plenty of room, and I make sure they get their exercise and plenty of fresh stuff to eat, and our doctor fixes them up if they get sick, and they're very friendly really, and I'm sure they'd welcome a new female into the troop." He ran down. There wasn't much else to say. *And he's my best friend and I'd miss him* wasn't the kind of argument that would persuade Rosie.

Rosie crossed her arms.

"Rosie," Mama Sasse said.

Rosie jutted her chin out stubbornly and refused to look at her mother.

"Rosie," Mama Sasse coaxed.

A flicker of eyes.

"We won't do anything unless you agree, but you need to think about what would really and truly be best for her in the world we live in now. Or did you think it was all fun and games and being allowed to wear men's trousers?"

"At least in the zoo we have walls," Rosie retorted. She shoved her chair back and stomped out of the room.

Papa Sasse leaned over and rested a hand on Michael's arm. "Rosie needs some time to think. You have to understand, Marigold is like a member of our family."

Michael's throat tightened. He nodded. "I understand," he managed.

"Well!" Captain Angie clapped her hands to her thighs, breaking the moment. "Somebody point me to a bunk. I'm about ready to keel over."

~ * ~

Lacey Miller, the Fabulous Lady Equestrienne Who Defies the Fiery Rings of Death!
The Loyale Traveling Circus Campground, Some Distance From New York City

The horses had been unsettled all day, and Lacey didn't blame them. Since returning from the scouting trip to New York, she'd been unsettled too. Strange sounds came from the trees: huffs, and eerie rasping noises, and rattling like somebody was dragging a stick along the tree trunks. Nobody actually saw anything, but everybody was spooked.

Lacey took extra care to corral the horses in the center of the circus encampment for the night. She also took straw from the lion cage and spread it in a wide ring around them. The horses reacted to the predator scent by flaring their nostrils and shying away. She hoped the whatever-they-weres in the woods wouldn't want to tangle with a lion either.

The night air seemed to carry the creatures' calls particularly well. At one point, the lion roared a challenge, and the night fell silent. Lacey hoped they'd fled, but after a while, the noises resumed, closer. Something scraped high along the side of her wagon, and she froze. She could have peered out the window to see what it was, but she was seized by the superstitious fear that if she did, *it* would see her, and then it would not leave until it had winkled her out of the wagon like an oyster out of its shell.

If one of her horses had screamed in pain or trumpeted a challenge, she still would have gone to them, though the only weapon she had was the brass-and-enamel hoof pick the Indian *mahout* had given her. After the incident in which she was forced to shoot a bandit, she hadn't been able to bring herself to retrieve her derringer. She cursed that squeamishness as she lay rigid in her bunk, though she didn't know if a derringer would have done much good against whatever haunted the night.

Chapter 14

~* * *~

Blood and Bone

Lacey Miller, the Fabulous Lady Equestrienne Who Defies the Fiery Rings of Death!
The Loyale Traveling Circus Campground, Some Distance From New York City

After an eternity or two, dawn broke over the camp. The alien sounds had died away perhaps an hour earlier. Lacey had remained awake, waiting, but when the camp stirred back to life, there were no cries of fear, no sharp crack of firearms.

Lacey rose to her feet and prepared for the day. Her face was calm—but she tucked the hoof pick into the waistband of her riding skirt before leaving her wagon.

Cook had a pot of plain corn mush on the boil. They'd run out of sweetener and pork fat weeks ago. Despite this, Lacey's appetite quickened as she sat beside the motley crew of early-rising circus folk: roustabouts, Ginger the clown, the girl sharpshooter, the Indian *mahout*, and the animal handlers (*not* including the snake charmer, who had no need to rise early to tend to her charges). Lacey was surprised to see the *mahout*; she wouldn't have expected him to have the discipline to rise early.

She said as much to him, though she discreetly omitted the part about lacking discipline.

"It is being very simple," he said cheerfully. "I am finding the morning to be the best time for the practicing of my *asana* and *pranayama*. I am usually eating first thing. I am thinking you are surprised because you are usually being with your horses when I am finishing breakfast."

His *asana*—he must mean the outlandish contortions he employed. She had of course glimpsed his exertions and averted her eyes, as a lady should. It was hardly an appropriate topic of conversation. She smiled noncommittally and dutifully returned her attention to her bowl of mush, which seemed unlikely to do anything improper or even remotely interesting.

The other circus folk ate quickly and without much conversation, but Lacey noticed that their eyes strayed often to the trees. She wasn't the only one whose sleep had been disturbed.

Genevieve Woodward, the girl sharpshooter, ate with hearty appetite. Her rifle leaned against the fallen log she sat on. When she'd scraped her bowl clean, she returned it to Cook and asked, "Any special requests? I'm going hunting."

"Why, yes!" he responded in kind. "Some nice tender lamb would be lovely."

She nodded. "Squirrel it is."

Genevieve came back to camp rather quickly, before Lacey had even finished her corn mush. Cook bustled forward. "You're back so soon! What did you bring me?"

Silently, the girl tossed a dead animal on the ground in front of her.

Judging by its size and long, tattered ears, it had once been a rabbit, but something had savaged it nearly past the point of identification. Blood and fouler liquids matted the patches of brown fur that clung to the carcass. The rabbit's soft underside had been hollowed out. Its ribcage had splintered. Chunks of meat and segments of intestine dangled from the corpse, leftovers of a very messy meal.

"I can't use what's left of this meat!" Cook protested. "It wasn't butchered properly. The meat's contaminated!"

"I didn't bring it to eat," Genevieve said. "But I ain't going back into the woods."

Lacey set aside her porridge—she was no longer hungry—and stared at the mangled creature. "Whatever could have done this?" she asked.

"Can't venture a guess," Genevieve said laconically. She swaggered off to her wagon like it didn't really matter, but Lacey noticed that she kept her hand close by her rifle. She was spooked.

"Perhaps ... perhaps it was butchered by cityfolk hiding in the woods who didn't know what they were doing," Lacey tried.

Cook squinted at the carnage. "A knife didn't do that. There's no cutting marks."

"An animal, then."

"A crazed animal, maybe," one of the animal handlers opined. "That ain't natural."

Lacey thought of how unsettled the horses had been all night, and of how high the scratches on her wagon were. "We need to leave. Today. As soon as possible. Cook, when people come for breakfast could you keep them here? We need to persuade them. It'll be easier to do it in one go."

"You could just tell them we're rolling out," Cook said. "It would save time—and me having to corral them."

"We decide things as a group," she said sharply. "I'm not in charge."

"Aren't you, though?"

She ignored him. She had to. She couldn't be the one to run the circus. It wouldn't be proper.

"Leave that—" she pointed to the mangled corpse, "—right where it is. It should do my arguing for me."

And so it did. Most of the circus folk had slept badly. Those who had not were happy to take the word of the others, particularly after a good look at what was left of that rabbit—though they no longer wanted their breakfast after.

"Good," Lacey said, once they were all in agreement. "It's decided. We'll camp in New York City tonight, in the space on the Rumsey Port dock that the commissioner has so generously offered us."

When he heard the name of the port, the *mahout* snorted a surprised laugh.

Lacey looked at him curiously. "What is it?"

"They named the port after the inventor of the aether-powered steamship," he explained.

"How do you know that?"

The *mahout* appeared to recollect himself. His accent thickened as he spoke. "In India, I am working for an American *sahib* with much interest in such things. A very peculiar man." He shook his head. "I am thinking that now the sailors are cursing *Sahib* Rumsey and saying a *rakshasa* is possessing him to invent such a terrible thing."

"Perhaps. However, the port is our best option now."

"You don't want to scout it out first?" One of the roustabouts looked confused, and she didn't blame him. Before entering New York the first time, she'd lectured them all on safety in numbers and always scouting places out before going in.

She didn't much like it either, but she *really* didn't like the idea of sticking around to find out what the—the *things* from last night were capable of.

"We did scout New York," she said briskly. "The commissioner appears to be very much in control. If we follow his rules, we'll be safe."

"What about the fortune teller's wagon?" the *mahout* asked. "You are not finding her in New York, or there would have been being a hullaballoo when you are returning. Who will be driving her wagon into New York?"

Lacey frowned. "How did you know she was missing? There hasn't been talk of it around camp."

"Oh. I heard it from Michael the animal handler."

"Ah." She smiled tightly. She supposed expecting discretion from a simple animal handler was asking too much, but really! "We'll take her wagon, of course. She may find us in New York. Even if not, we can't afford to lose anything of value."

"What about Michael and Christopher? Where are they?" chimed the aerialist with a purple ribbon in her hair—Pamela Dyer-Bennet, her name was. She clutched the hands of her orange-ribboned partner.

"We will probably meet them on the road to New York, but we should leave them a message just in case." Lacey looked over to where the girl sharpshooter was cleaning her nails with a hunting knife. "A warning carved into a tree?"

She waited. Genevieve kept cleaning her nails.

"Perhaps you could carve it now, if you're not otherwise occupied?"

Genevieve lifted her hand and squinted at her nails. "Done now."

She walked over to a tree near the center of the circus camp, sank her knife into the bark, and carved, "Gon Newe York" into the trunk. She picked up the savaged rabbit carcass and strung it up beside her message. Seeing Lacey's raised eyebrow, she shrugged. "You said a warning. I ain't no hand at writing, but I figure that'll do. Cook said we couldn't use it, so I ain't wasting food."

Lacey glanced at the hanging body and away. Yes, that would do.

~ * ~

Lacey had never seen circus wagons packed so fast. She sat on her white mare and enjoyed a small upwelling of hope. A breeze brushed her cheek. The sun warmed her shoulders. Beneath her, the mare snorted and shifted. Perhaps the fortune teller would be found unharmed. Perhaps the commissioner would cause them no trouble. Perhaps their performance run in new New York would be a fabulous success and they would be able to trade for all the supplies they could ever need. Perhaps—

Something clattered among the trees behind Lacey. An uncanny rasping call mocked her and sent her mare dancing sideways. The hoof pick in her waistband pressed hard against her flesh as she reined the mare back and pulled her into a tight pirouette.

A squirrel jumped from one branch to another. Nothing else moved.

"There's something in the trees," Lacey called out. "Keep an eye on your neighbors and stand ready to help if it attacks!"

"We always do," the snake charmer said lazily from where she lounged on her high driver's seat. A small and—Lacey hoped— non-venomous snake poked its head out of the snake charmer's bosom and flicked its tongue inquiringly. "If somebody hollers, 'Hey, rube!' we'll all come a-runnin'. Promise." Her shockingly low-cut green silk dress shifted to bare even more creamy white flesh as she raised her hand in a mocking vow.

"Of course," Lacey said, feeling heat rise up her neck.

In the end, leaving the warning at the campsite turned out to be an unnecessary precaution. Just as the bridge to New York came into view ahead of them, so did two travelers walking in their direction: Michael the animal handler, and Christopher the ringmaster-in-training.

Pamela squealed happily and darted in the newcomers' direction, the purple ribbon in her hair bouncing as she ran. The aerialist came to an abrupt stop just short of Michael. "What took so long? We were worried! Didn't you find your monkey?"

"I did, sorta, but—" Michael shrugged, "—it's hard to explain. I couldn't bring him back with me just yet."

Pamela reached up and picked something out of his hair. "Where have you been? You got a leaf in your hair!"

He looked rather stunned, as if she'd whacked him over the head instead of just plucking a leaf from his hair. "I didn't even give you an apple slice," he said faintly.

She frowned. "What?"

He shook his head quickly. "Nothin'. I just, um—you need any help unpacking your wagon? Um, like, lifting any chests—uh, heavy boxes?"

Lacey didn't roll her eyes, but *really*! Men were so clumsy. In his place, she would have told Pamela the thrilling tale of their city adventures, but there the boy was, offering to lift her chest!

"Maybe later," Pamela said coyly.

Michael blushed. "Oh, yeah, right. Wouldn't make much sense to unpack now. Since we're not there yet."

Upon hearing that exchange, Christopher winced.

Pamela at least seemed to find Michael's lack of sense pleasing, since her response was to tuck her arm through his.

"Christopher," Lacey rescued him, "why don't you ride with me and tell us what you've learned."

By the haste with which Christopher followed her suggestion, he was happy enough to leave the lovebirds. Ginger the clown also rode up alongside Lacey's wagon to listen to his protégé's story.

Christopher had gotten as far as their adventures on the dock, and the circus procession was halfway to the bridge, when rustling and an unearthly rattling noise in the underbrush interrupted him.

"What was that?" he asked.

The image of the butchered rabbit flashed through Lacey's memory. "Something with a taste for rabbit," she muttered.

"What?"

"Some creature was skulking around our camp last night, and the girl sharpshooter found a dead rabbit this morning. Hopefully it won't bother us in the daylight."

Christopher shrugged. "I'm no rabbit."

"No, but—" Lacey stared hard at the trees and the underbrush, but she couldn't spot anything amiss, "—that rabbit was butchered like nothing I've ever seen. Hya!" She slapped the reins, urging her wagon horse to go faster. Around her, she heard others doing the same.

The protective wall around the bridge might only be half-built, but in that moment, Lacey wanted to be on the other side of it with a longing so intense it felt like homesickness. It would hardly be their usual grand entrance into town. Nobody wanted to stop and gussy up before they were safely onto High Bridge.

It wasn't until they were traveling at speed that she realized how they must look, barreling down on the bridge.

The laborers working on the wall looked up, saw the motley cavalcade approaching, dropped their tools, and scattered. The policeman sitting on the edge of the wall dropped his sandwich, bolted upright, and seized his musket. He aimed it uncertainly in their direction.

"Whoa!" Lacey shouted, reining in her horse as she approached. "My apologies for startling you! We come in peace— our circus has permission from the commissioner to set up in Rumsey Port and perform."

The policeman did not look convinced, even as the rest of the circus straggled to a halt. His gun wavered, but he didn't lower it. Lacey didn't blame him. She counted herself lucky he hadn't fired as soon as they came into range.

"Honestly," she added. "You can check."

"You look peculiar enough to be circus folk," the policeman allowed, "but that don't explain why you came galloping up like an invading army!"

The snake charmer eased forward. "Let me," she murmured as she passed Lacey.

The policeman's eyes widened as the silk-swathed charmer sauntered toward him. Her exotic beauty was undeniably compelling, though Lacey knew it was just as undeniably contrived: when the snake charmer wasn't putting on foreign airs, her accent was as Southern as a magnolia blossom.

"I am pleased to see the bridge so well guarded!" The snake charmer leaned forward and gazed soulfully into the policeman's eyes, managing to expose more cleavage as she did so. "I was so frightened. I feel much safer now."

The policeman stood taller, but Lacey didn't miss the nervous jerk of his eyes as he glanced in the direction the circus had come from. "Of course, Miss, I can protect you, but—. Um. From what?"

"I do not know. We've been followed by something strange that we cannot see. It is terribly unsettling." She shuddered daintily, allowing her neckline to slip a fraction lower.

The policeman's eyes riveted on the tenuous hold her dress was maintaining. He swallowed hard.

The girl sharpshooter guided her horse close to Lacey's and leaned forward to murmur in her ear. "Something moving in the trees back there. More than one something. They're getting closer."

Lacey kneed her horse forward. "We have permission from the commissioner himself to set up our circus. May we pass?"

"Yeah, sure," the policeman mumbled, his gaze still locked on the snake charmer.

The snake charmer smiled sweetly, though her face wasn't where the policeman was looking. "Thank you so much."

The policeman visibly shook himself back to attention. "Hey!" he shouted to the laborers who had fled at the circus' dramatic approach. "Get back here or I'll have your rations cut, see if I don't!"

Some of the workers were too far across the bridge to hear his call, but the closer ones slowed their flight, hesitated, and began returning. They stared at the circus procession as it passed, but nobody, not even the children, smiled.

Tough crowd. Of course, the circus wasn't putting on much of a show. They hadn't taken the mud-spattered canvas covers off the wagons. The gilt and mirrors on the wagons were covered. The animals slumbered in their concealed cages. The signs that advertised miracles and freaks of nature were folded up inside the wagons. None of the circus folk had wanted to stop the caravan until they were on the other side of the river and preferably far into the city, well away from any uncanny creatures that stalked the countryside.

One of the ostriches poked its head from behind the canvas flap and blinked long eyelashes at a little girl walking by. The little girl blinked right back and then giggled and ran ahead to tug on the hand of an older boy. "Jonah, look!"

"We got to get to work, Tracy," he told her, wearily. "Come on." He didn't even glance toward the circus.

Lacey bit her lip. She could at least give the onlookers a little piece of wonder.

"Help me untether my horses," she said to the girl sharpshooter.

"Giving 'em a show?" Genevieve nodded approvingly. "I got some targets in my saddlebag, too. I could toss 'em up and shoot 'em!"

"Ah, no. I don't think we want to risk any misunderstandings." Lacey glanced back at the policeman. "In fact, you should probably keep your guns out of sight except when you're performing. They have strict rules about such things here."

Genevieve cheerfully pantomimed being strung up. "Right. Wouldn't want any 'misunderstandings'." She turned and trotted back toward Lacey's string of horses at the end of the procession.

Lacey dismounted, tightened the girth on her mare, attached her horse's headpiece, and fixed the rather bedraggled plume in place. Hadn't Christopher mentioned something about a zoo? She wondered if she could persuade them to part with a few peacock feathers. She pulled out her trick-riding straps and began attaching them to her saddle.

A musket boomed. Lacey dropped the strap she was holding and whirled to see what had happened. The laborers were staring over the wall. Some—creatures—sprinted toward them.

Deer? she thought. But no. The shape of them was not right, though she was too far away to see precisely what it was that seemed so wrong about their flesh. They moved with a lurching, awkward speed, power replacing nature's grace. No deer had ever grown antlers that huge and twisted. And no deer had ever charged a wall lined with people.

The policeman fired again. Then the screaming started.

Lacey snatched the last strap from the ground and jerked it into place with unnecessary force, startling her mare into crow-hopping sideways. She leapt into the saddle and pulled her mare into a tight caracole turn to face the direction they'd come from.

"Run!" the snake charmer screamed at Lacey, as she followed her own advice and goaded the horses pulling her wagon into an awkward gallop.

The other circus wagons streamed past Lacey, heading for the safety of the city.

At the end of the caravan, Genevieve struggled to re-tether the horses that she had just *un*tethered. Their eyes rolled and their ears were laid back. One of them even reared *without* being commanded to do so. Unthinkable, after all the training Lacey had put into them! If they bolted ... Lacey reined her mare around and galloped back to save her horses.

She executed a flying dismount and seized the tethers from Genevieve.

"Circle up!" she commanded the horses. As soon as they bunched together, she tied all the tethers into a rough knot. "Pursuit!" she said sternly, watching the horses to make sure they'd understood the command. A skittish gray gelding reared his head, his eyes rolling. She seized his bridle and pulled his head back down. "Pursuit," she said, as calmly as she could. "Pursuit." His ears pricked forward. Good. He would focus on the act now. She thanked all her stars that she'd rehearsed it recently with them.

In the ring, Lacey would "flee" on her mare. The other horses pursued her while maintaining a perfect circle. It wasn't her flashiest act, but it was a good solid piece of performance, especially when she threw in some zig-zags and jumps that the unridden horses mirrored perfectly.

Now, they would flee in earnest. She glanced over at the wall.

Laborers streamed away from it, running along the riverbank or bolting onto the bridge in hopes that the creatures wouldn't follow them.

The policeman who'd fired the shots was down. *Not so good at protecting us after all*, the analytic part of Lacey's mind noted. He wouldn't be protecting anyone ever again. He'd been trampled into a bloody mash of shattered bone and torn flesh beneath the hooves of the hell-creatures. The only way she even knew it was him was the useless musket lying nearby and the scraps of blue fabric clinging to the misshapen muzzle of the animal nuzzling the corpse.

The deer-thing jerked its head up and tossed something into the air, then snapped it up like a crocodile. Even from a distance, Lacey saw the blood dripping between its teeth.

Not deer, no. Deer don't attack. Deer don't run people down. Deer don't—. She shuddered and looked away, clapping her heels to her mare's sides and shouting, "Hiya!" to goad the mare to a gallop.

When Lacey heard clattering hooves on the bridge behind her, she risked a glance over her shoulder, rising in the stirrups to see better.

The deer-things stampeded onto the bridge. Those laborers who had fled to the bridge in hopes of safety were diving off the side into the uncertain safety of the river below.

One elderly man was too slow to get out of the way. At first, she thought the deer would race right past where he cowered. He was not so lucky. Two of the deer broke from the pack and lowered their heads. The old man screamed. They charged. The old man's scream turned into a wail of mortal anguish as both deer skewered him on their unnaturally long and twisted antlers.

The deer tried to back up, but their antlers were stuck, trapped by their own viciousness. One of the deer tossed his head. The motion jerked the old man up, pulling the other deer along. The old man howled and blood trickled from his mouth as something vital ruptured inside him. The deer tossed their heads and jerked and tugged, trying to free themselves. Every movement wrung another scream from the old man until he fell silent. Dead or passed out, either was a mercy.

Thanks be to God everyone else fled. Even as Lacey had the thought, the girl sharpshooter galloped back past her, unlimbering her rifle.

At first, Lacey thought Genevieve had run mad—and then she saw the small figure in the center of the bridge, huddled against the railing. It was Tracy, the little girl who had giggled at the ostrich. She was alone and frozen in place.

At a gallop, Genevieve aimed and fired. A blossom of red sprang from the chest of one of the creatures, but it didn't even slow its pace. Again she fired, and again, to no effect.

The child was doomed.

"Not if I can help it," Lacey said through gritted teeth. She shouted a command to keep her string of horses racing across the bridge, and then she wheeled her mare around to face the horror.

Chapter 15

~* * *~

Hail the Heroes

Lacey Miller, the Fabulous Lady Equestrienne Who Defies the Fiery Rings of Death!
New York City

Lacey clapped her heels to her mare's flanks, urging the horse to a flat-out gallop. Her breath thundered in her ears as she galloped toward the child trapped on the bridge.

Ahead of her, the girl sharpshooter aimed and fired at the monsters. One jerked its head to the side as its jaw exploded. Lacey could have cheered. Then she saw lumpy flesh crawl over the shattered bone. Within seconds, it was as the beast had never been injured.

Genevieve dismounted and sank to one knee to steady her rifle as she aimed and fired. One of the monsters collapsed to its knees and then pushed itself up and rose again. She was aiming for the joints, Lacey realized. It wouldn't stop them, but it might slow them down long enough.

The little girl huddled against the railing, easy prey for the monsters unless Lacey could get there first. The angles flashed through her mind. The only way to rescue the girl at a gallop would be to perform a modified Cossack drag. Lacey needed to circle in front of them and grab the child on the way back.

"I'm coming for the girl!" Lacey shouted, hoping her voice carried over the thunder of hooves. "Don't shoot!"

Genevieve aimed, fired. Reloaded, aimed, fired. Her horse bolted back across the bridge. Genevieve could have fled then, but she didn't. She stayed by the little girl and kept firing as Lacey galloped past them.

"Don't shoot!" Lacey shouted, as she raced between them and the deer-things.

The monsters were so close. Too close. She saw every detail of the creatures as she wheeled in front of them: the bloodshot eyes, the foam at nostrils and mouth, the bone spurs erupting from their flesh, and the blood smeared across their muzzles. It was a relief to swing herself over the mare's side and hang down from the saddle.

Lacey focused on the small girl huddled beside the bridge railing. She had only one chance. The girl shrank back as the horse bore down on her. Lacey had expected that. She seized the child's wrist with one hand and wrapped her other arm around the girl's waist, sweeping her up as they galloped past.

Lacey's arms burned like fire. She couldn't haul herself and the girl back into the saddle, but all she had to do was hold on to the child.

Upside down and half under the horse's belly, Lacey saw what happened next.

Genevieve should have run, but she didn't. She kept firing, aiming for the deer-things' legs. Giving Lacey time to widen her lead and escape.

The monsters were a scant yard away when Genevieve tossed her rifle aside.

For a second, Lacey thought she'd make it. Genevieve climbed onto the railing and was about to dive into the river below. Then a deer-monster stretched its neck out, sank its teeth into her shoulder, and wrenched her back onto the bridge. It jerked its head, sending her tumbling through the air like a rag doll. She landed headfirst on the hard stone of the bridge and did not move again. It was a mercy. Lacey looked away from what happened next.

The sound of Lacey's horse's hooves changed timbre, but it took her a minute to realize what that meant. They were off the bridge, in New York City. She caught glimpses of buildings, lamp poles, sidewalks, wagons. *Wagons?* She'd caught up to the rest of the circus.

"Whoa," she croaked. "Whoa!"

Her mare slowed to a canter and then to a trot. They passed the roustabouts, the doctor's wagon, and the animal cages.

"Whoa!"

The mare came to a stop beside two massive columns of bone and brass: the aether elephant's legs. The *mahout* had stopped, even as the rest of the circus continued to flee farther into the city. Lacey released the little girl. She'd been gripping the child so hard that straightening her fingers sent throbbing pain through them. The girl fell to the ground and began to cry.

Lacey summoned her last reserves of strength and hauled herself up to the saddle. The world righted itself. She cast a quick look around.

The mahout hunched over the neck of his elephant, feverishly pushing buttons and pulling levers. The elephant's giant, hammered brass ears rotated straight up. Its ribcage heaved and parted, ribs rippling open. Brass tubes inside slotted into new locations. And yet it did not move. *What a terrible time for a malfunction*, Lacey thought.

As the doctor's wagon approached, Lacey shouted, "Doctor! Take the child!"

He nodded in response, pulling on the reins to slow his wagon. Seeing the promise of safety, the little girl bolted to him. He leaned over, lifted her up onto the seat beside him, and slapped his reins to get his wagon moving again.

Lacey wondered if the best chance for survival might be to abandon the wagons and seek shelter inside the buildings nearby. Deer couldn't handle doors and stairs. Neither could her horses, though. Without her horses, she would be nothing.

Beside her, the bone and brass elephant lurched into movement—*toward* the attacking deer-creatures. Lacey gasped. Her eyes were drawn to the *mahout* sitting atop the elephant. She expected to see terror in his face. After all, he was trapped aboard a malfunctioning aether elephant, and it was carrying him to certain death.

He was grinning.

As the elephant strode onto the bridge, the *mahout* reached into the long brass canister by his seat—the canister that held a ceremonial flag—and pulled out a large bore gun. Lacey gasped as he mounted it onto a "flag holder" that fit it perfectly.

A veil lifted from her eyes. The elephant had never malfunctioned. Those upright brass ears acted as shields on either side of the *mahout*'s seat. The pointed ends of the splayed ribs would be as effective as a field of bayonets. And how had she not noticed that the protective brass caps on the elephant's tusks had vanished, baring its wickedly sharp war ivory?

The *mahout* sighted his gun on a deer and fired. Half its head disappeared, and it tumbled to the stones and lay there, thrashing. He fired again, gouging a chunk out of another monster's chest. Then he was among them.

Lacey felt sick, thinking of how casually they had treated the *mahout* and his war machine. If he was capable of this, what else could he do? What else did he know? The hoof pick in her waistband, a present from the *mahout*, seemed to grow heavier.

The monstrous bone elephant was as unstoppable as an avalanche in monsoon season. It speared the deer-things on its tusks and tossed them in the air. It crushed them beneath its hooves. It swung its side against them, stabbing them in a dozen places with bayonet-sharp ribs. The *mahout* aimed and fired from his protected seat on the elephant's back. Flesh spattered against the stone.

Yet it wasn't enough. The monsters kept getting back up again. The elephant inflicted horrendous wounds—and the deer healed them. Even that first head shot hadn't been fatal. The deer staggered to its feet. Half its head was lumpy and misshapen, like a bag of rocks. Its eye had regrown halfway back on its skull, where it stared blankly at the sky. The beast should have been dead, but it shambled forward.

The *mahout* must have reached the same conclusion. Instead of continuing his attack, he stopped and did something complicated with the elephant's control apparatus. The elephant's ornamental collar unlatched and rotated counterclockwise. He seized the end, fed it through the elephant's skull, and hooked it to the opening of the elephant's trunk.

The elephant wheeled around and stampeded through the deer pack, mashing them to the ground. It kicked left and right, shattering their ribs and pulverizing their legs.

As soon as the deer were down, the elephant charged to the end of the bridge. The deer began to struggle to their feet. The bone and brass elephant raised its trunk as if to trumpet defiance. Instead, it expelled a shining golden sphere that flew from the elephant's trunk and shattered among the deer.

For a heartbeat, nothing happened.

Then flames roared to life, wrapping around the monsters' flesh. The deer screamed as pain finally penetrated their maddened minds. They reared and fell and reared again. Some managed to run, though fire wreathed them.

Lacey stared in shock. He had fire aether bombs? Those shining golden balls decorating the elephant's collar were more armament than ornament.

The *mahout* steered his elephant back into the fray. It waded through fire and crushed the deer until they moved no more. Lacey expected it to catch fire, but it didn't. When the last deer lay still, the elephant emerged unburnt, though soot streaked the bones of its legs.

She heard a roaring in her ears. Then she realized the sound was cheering. She looked back at new New York. The townies hung out of building windows, shaking their fists and shouting approval.

Only one thing to do.

Though her muscles screamed in protest, Lacey leapt to stand on her saddle. "You've seen Rajesh, the Hindoo mystic, and his fearsome aether-powered bone-and-brass elephant!" she shouted. "We are the Loyale Traveling Menagerie, Hippodrome, Circus, and Museum of Educational Novelties! See us perform tonight on the dock at Port Rumsey! Tell your neighbors, tell your friends—heck, tell your enemies! Come, see our performance tonight at Port Rumsey!"

She signaled her horse. The mare reared, the momentum catapulting Lacey up in the air. She executed a neat flip before landing on her feet and bowing. People clapped, so she assumed they couldn't tell how close she came to falling over.

The circus doctor hurried over, trailed by the little girl Lacey had rescued. "I saw that. You nearly toppled over there at the end. How are you?"

"I'll be fine," she assured him. "I strained my muscles a bit, that's all. You needn't worry. I'm sure you have your own business to attend to."

He nodded. "I need to go and see if what I suspect about those creatures is true." He frowned at the carnage on the bridge. "Assuming that mad Indian left me enough to examine! But first, Miss Tracy LaChance wants to tell you something." He nudged the little girl forward.

Tracy stared at Lacey with big eyes and sucked bashfully on her thumb for a minute. Then, mustering her courage, she removed that appendage and said, "Thank you, lady. I was scared." Having covered the matter to her satisfaction, she popped her thumb back in her mouth.

Lacey reached out and swept Tracy into a hug, feeling a pang in her heart. There had been a moment, when she hung off the side of the horse and reached for the child, that she had been sure she would miss, that the child would die. A wave of gratitude for her well-trained horses washed over Lacey. Without them, she would be nothing but another useless female—and Tracy would be dead.

"Tracy!" Lacey released her grasp on the little girl as the girl's brother ran up to them. He was soaking wet from his head to his toes. "You shouldn't have pulled away, Tracy! You scared me! Next time you jump with me, you hear!" He blinked, looking past them to the charred corpses on the bridge. "What happened?"

"Something to be scared of," Lacey said dryly. "See that you take better care of her in future."

"Yes'm!" he said earnestly.

Relenting, she added, "And come see the circus. We'll be performing at Rumsey Port tonight. I'll leave word with the ticket-taker that you and your sister are to be allowed in for free."

"The circus? Yes, ma'am!" And there it was, the grin that she'd been hoping for back when she first tied the trick-riding straps to her saddle.

The doctor was examining the corpses of the dead deer-monsters on the bridge. Lacey rode up to him. The smell of charred meat made her stomach grumble.

"Can we eat them?" she asked.

The doctor frowned. "Bone aether is usually administered by injection into the flesh, but taking your nourishment from this thing, having it spread throughout your body ... no, I wouldn't eat it."

"What does bone aether have to do with it?"

The doctor scowled and didn't answer the question. "Shouldn't we be moving along?"

"Excellent point," she allowed. "You should return to your wagon and hang up your posters, Dr. Panjandrum. Best we be off soon, but we can put on our finery and give this city a proper grand procession."

"I need the bodies—"

She held up her hand to stop him. "Quickly. Get the strong man to help you. And leave plenty for the police to inspect. One thing we learned while scouting the city is that we do *not* want to interfere with what they consider proper legal procedure. Tell the others to gussy up while I consult with our Indian warrior."

"Our ...? Oh." He nodded.

Lacey approached the mahout. She planned to say something carefully roundabout. Polite, but firm. Demanding answers, but respectful. Instead, she heard herself say, "The elephant is a weapon."

He looked levelly at her. "Anything can be a weapon. We are all having hidden depths. But as you yourself were saying, we must stick together."

She found her mouth opening and closing without a word coming out, so she spun on her heel and stalked back to the caravan to prepare for the grand processional.

It took less time than she would have expected. Everyone was eager to get away from the bridge. Meanwhile, however, word of what had happened had spread. People came out on the street to watch the circus parade. At first, they pretended to be on some errand that just happened to bring them near the circus. Now and then a scowling policeman would stalk toward the gaudy circus procession, but one of his brethren would intercept him and whisper in his ear and he'd fade back without pestering them. Seeing that tacit approval, the spectators became brave. First, they stopped and stared openly. Then they smiled. Then they waved and cheered. Even the corpses dangling from the lampposts seemed to take on a festive, ornamental air.

At Rumsey Port dock, an unruly crowd of sailors awaited them. They welcomed the circus with shouts that included several crude suggestions Lacey pretended not to hear. No wonder the commissioner had trouble with this bunch! The hastily pulled aside barricades did not escape her notice either. She smiled and waved, glad that the animal trainer and ringmaster-in-training had made some friends while they were here.

One member of the crowd separated itself from the others and came forward with arms outstretched. "Welcome!"

Hearing a woman's voice emanating from the mannishly dressed figure shocked Lacey. It must be that female captain that Christopher had mentioned meeting.

Michael and Christopher hastened forward. After they greeted her and introduced her to the rest of the circus, Captain Angie showed them where they could circle their wagons and set up their circus tents for the performance tonight. Then she invited them all to the tavern to tell her all about how, as she put it, "demons from hell chased you onto High Bridge, where you battled them with a dozen trained war-elephants."

Lacey winced at that description but found herself being swept along with a dozen others into the dark, beer-smelling interior of Nancy's Harbor Cafe. They were greeted by an older barmaid who looked like she'd seen everything, done most of it, and regretted none of it. Despite this, she still managed a blowsy kind of beauty, like a past-its-prime rose.

Lacey found herself sitting beside Michael the animal handler. Nobody was paying attention to them. Lacey seized the opportunity. Her father had taught her that servants should be reprimanded in private, to allow them to preserve their dignity. Michael was no servant of hers, but she supposed the same principle applied.

"Michael, the *mahout* told me that you let it slip the fortune teller was missing." She smiled, trying to be reassuring. "We don't know why she vanished. A little discretion might be in order."

"What?" Michael set down his beer. "But—I didn't say a word."

"It's okay," Lacey hurried to say. "Just think a little before talking about other circus members, even amongst ourselves, if you don't know what's going on. We all need to stick together."

"No, really, I didn't! I don't talk to the *mahout* hardly at all."

"It's fine. That's all I wanted to tell you," she said, with exasperated patience. "You don't have to pretend you avoid him!"

Michael lowered his head. "I do. I know it ain't right to treat him like that, but his bone elephant gives me the shivers. It ain't natural. The animals get nervy when it's around." He met her eyes. "I'll take their judgment above most people I know."

"Oh!" His obvious sincerity took Lacey aback. "I'm sorry. I must have misunderstood."

"I didn't even *know* the fortune teller was missing until we were in New York and Christopher let it slip he was looking for her."

"Ah." Lacey glared toward the bar where the *mahout* stood. He seemed in danger of being drowned by the free drinks being thrust upon him.

"Even if I had known, I don't know why you thought I'd spread it about," Michael continued, aggrieved. "I'm not a fool, you know!"

"Of course not. I—I'll just go over—." Lacey fled.

Her attempt to retreat to a more solitary corner backfired when she found herself wedged in between the lady ship captain and the snake charmer.

The snake charmer heaved a sigh of relief. "Thank goodness, a corner for just us girls! I declare, dealing with some males' idea of chivalry is positively exhausting!" She extended her hand to the captain. "I'm Alis Gray. Delighted to meet another sensible female."

"Captain Angie Endo," the captain said, with a crocodilian grin. "And I find one warning is enough to make them back off."

"With teeth like those, I bet it is! Now *that's* an idea that would keep the punters coming back for more," Alis said admiringly, as she assessed the captain's sharpened teeth. "And I daresay it would come in quite handy for scaring off unwanted suitors. Did it hurt?"

Captain Angie flashed a very pointed smile. "It hurts plenty if some bastard pisses me off enough to make me bite!"

Both women laughed. If they heard the harsh edge to the sound, it just made them laugh the more. Lacey smiled politely, wishing she could make her escape.

"No, but really," Alis persisted. "Did it hurt?"

The lady captain shrugged. "Not so's you'd notice. You can only file the edges. Be careful to avoid the core of the tooth—if you go too deep, it hurts like bloody hell. I did that a couple of times, but a drop of bone aether put it right again."

"That's not so easy to come by these days."

"No."

The topic of conversation turned to other matters and Lacey relaxed. Prematurely, as it happened.

Captain Angie paused in the middle of telling a story involving a peacock, a priest, a madam, and a saint's relic. "My glass is empty," she said sadly.

"Let me," Alis volunteered. She rolled her shoulders in a way that drew attention to her feminine assets. "I know sailors, and this lot have been away from women for too long. They'll fight each other to provide us with liquid refreshment."

"Wait!" Lacey put out her hand. "What if one of the sailors decides to press his attentions—forcefully?"

Alis laughed huskily. "Then he'll find that I have a bite like one of my snakes. After me, he'll never press his attentions on any poor girl again."

Alis sashayed away from the table. When she returned, she was followed by a clutch of sailors who insisted on gifting the ladies with drinks. Captain Angie's grin and the snake inquisitively poking its head out from behind Alis' fichu sent them on their way, but the drinks remained. As the level of liquor lowered, so did the tone of the conversation. Lacey was hardly a blushing prude, but she found herself controlling her expression with great difficulty.

"Ah! There's the doctor!" she finally said hastily. "I must speak with him. Do excuse me."

Alis' raised eyebrows warned her that she was not entirely believed, but it was a polite enough pretext for her to escape graciously.

"Doctor!" she called, hurrying over to the bar where he sat.

He identified the source of the call, gave her a quick once-over, and then picked up the shot glass in front of him and slammed the liquor, signaling the barmaid for more. His face was pale and taut with strain.

"Is that wise?" Lacey asked, instead of the more polite opening she'd planned.

"You're not injured," he said. "I checked." The barmaid put a second shot in front of him. He drank it down and gestured for another one. "Do you remember the Grey Steel Regiment?"

"I wanted to talk to you about whatever happened to those deer-creatures," Lacey said.

"Do. You. Remember?"

Lacey nodded slowly. "The monsters of the South. They slaughtered our soldiers. Hell, they *ate* our soldiers. The surviving members are still being held for war crimes, though people can't quite figure out how best to put them on trial without hanging every farm boy who used to fight for the Confederates."

"Sure, they were monsters," the doctor agreed. "By the end of the war. In the beginning they were just boys. The brass put them in those war harnesses, and the aether pumped into their bones made them nigh invincible."

"Uh-huh."

"When defeat approached, the generals stopped listening to their doctors. Those boys should have been pulled back from the front lines and treated. The aether overdose did horrible things to them. It twisted and pulled them and made them into monsters. It burned through their bodies' resources so fast that they were swept away by a mad, ravenous hunger. That's when they started to hunt the battlefields and to eat what they killed." The doctor paused. "Mostly after they'd killed it."

"Oh," Lacey said, taken aback. "That's horrible. But I wanted to—"

"Need to tell the 'thorities," he interrupted. "Need to make plans. First," he gulped down the liquor, "need a drink."

"Er, you might want to slow down," Lacey suggested. "You'll be needing your own patent remedy in the morning, else."

"Hrm?" He squinted at her.

"The Great Doctor Panjandrum's miracle remedy?" she prompted. "Excellent for toothache, neuralgia, and sore chests? A sure-fire cure for muscle aches and tremors?"

"Tremors," the doctor repeated moodily. "'Splains why business has been so good. Do you know what my remedy does?"

"No," Lacey said carefully. "You always said it wouldn't cause any harm at the recommended dosage—"

"Nothing!" he bellowed, slapping his hand down on the bar. "It does nothing! All those poor, doomed people—nothing!"

Heads were starting to turn. Lacey leaned forward. In an undertone, she said, "Doctor, you shouldn't say such things here."

"Eh?" He squinted at her. "Oh, right. Barmaid!" He waved his hand.

Lacey wished she could melt into the floor. There were enough sticky patches and puddles; one more wouldn't be noticed.

An older fellow eased his way through the crowd and grabbed her elbow in a very forward way. Lacey straightened and pulled away. She ought to be offended. In truth, she welcomed the distraction.

"I beg your pardon, sir!" she said frostily.

"Ma'am." His hand raised, as if to tug the brim of a cap that wasn't there. Recalling himself, he coughed and tucked his hands into his belt. "The commissioner sent me. He wanted to talk to your lot right promptly. You and the other fella who came to see him the first time."

"Oh!" Now that the man had declared his allegiance, she noticed the straight-shouldered way he carried himself, like a man accustomed to a uniform. He'd wisely removed his jacket and cap to get by on the dock, but his pants were the dark blue of the New York policeman's uniform, and his boots likewise bore the police force's imprimatur.

She dismounted from the bar stool and found Ginger the clown. Somehow, the strongman, the snake charmer, the snake charmer's baby boa, and the rather drunken doctor also ended up trailing along. Their motley appearance dismayed Lacey, but she tried to console herself that they were a good advertisement for the circus.

~ * ~

Their guide abandoned them inside the Central Police Department with a muttered, "His aide will come for you when he's ready."

Several dozen policeman and special patrolmen stared at the little group of circus folk. Lacey fidgeted. She wished she was back in Nancy's Harbor Cafe.

Then—"Hey! It's them! With the elephant and the fire and—tonight! The circus!"

The doctor gave a tipsy little bow and murmured, "Obliged, I'm sure."

With that, all the policemen relaxed. Chicory coffee was pressed upon them, and a couple of slices of stale pound cake. It turned into an impromptu sort of celebration of the Battle of High Bridge. Before they were entirely drowned in the rather terrible coffee, Lacey threw the snake charmer a desperate glance.

With winsome charm, Alis made their excuses, saying that they really, truly needed to pay their respects to the commissioner and return to Rumsey Port to prepare for their performance tonight—which all the policemen would surely be attending, yes?

An awkward silence fell. "The commissioner's not in a real good mood," one of the younger patrolmen ventured. "You should maybe stay out here until he's ready for you."

"Hate to see him take his temper out on such a fine lady," another seconded, attempting chivalry.

"Nonsense!" the doctor proclaimed, lurching upright with the peculiar energy of a man who has had much alcohol topped with far more coffee than is good for him. "He wishes to congratulate us on the Battle of High Bridge." He managed a wink. "Details he needs to know, don't you see. Hush-hush. Now, his office is off this way?" He turned and began to stride toward a door clearly labeled "Holding Cells."

One of Alis' would-be swains leapt forward. "No, no—this way, sirs and madams." He blushed. "Ladies, I mean."

They followed his guidance until they were in front of Commissioner Guirard's door. "I don't know if you—"

Lacey ignored his dithering. She pushed open the door, walked in, and found herself amidst a heated discussion between Commissioner Guirard and his aide.

"—all the ration-hoarders?" Commissioner Guirard demanded.

"As many as we could, sir," Mr. Akrill responded. "Making an example of some so early put a stop to most of it. And the rewards have brought out the rest."

Commissioner Guirard paced back and forth. "Perhaps in the dead zone? You could search those houses that are unclaimed."

"The men don't like it, sir. They say they're haunted. Besides, we rounded up the food supplies right after we cleared the corpses out."

"I don't care if you get it by digging up graves and robbing the bodies!" Commissioner Guirard said furiously. "If that dratted female causes any more civilians to besiege me with complaints about her impossible expectations ..."

"The men will ask why, sir."

Commissioner Guirard sighed and rubbed his face, his anger evaporating. "And I can't take special privileges. It wouldn't be right, especially after I made such a big fuss about how important it was to share and share alike. But my darling wife needs something 'civilized' to calm her down. It's damn hard to find civilization right now. Chocolate did the trick for a while, but now I can't find any of the precious stuff. I'm afraid that once she realizes the situation we're in, she'll single-handedly try to re-create civilization in her own inimitable style. Probably hold costume balls for orphans, insist on a hundred patrolmen to re-open the park promenades, and chivy the seamstresses into sewing the latest Paris fashions instead of turning out the basics we need."

"Yes, sir," Mr. Akrill said.

Commissioner Guirard grimaced. "It's enough to drive me to declare war on the ports. I know those ships are brimming with supplies we need."

Lacey stepped forward. "Ahem," she said delicately. "Your messenger indicated you wished to speak with us?"

He blinked. "Right. Come in then, all of you." He nodded to his aide. "You may go."

"Yessir."

After the assorted circus members crowded into his office, he lowered his brows and glared at them. "What madness have you lot stirred up in my city?" he growled.

Lacey gaped. "What?" After the cheers of the cityfolk, the jubilant greeting of the sailors, and the warm welcome of Commissioner Guirard's own policemen, his greeting was a dash of cold water to the face.

"I've heard all kinds of crazy stories about what happened on the bridge," he said. "The *facts* are as follows: one of my policemen is dead; work on the defensive wall is interrupted; a mound of burned animals is clogging up the bridge; and it all happened when *you* came to my city. What can you bring to the city to make up for this? I want an inventory."

Lacey blinked, unable to come up with a response. Ginger the clown seemed to be likewise stricken, and the doctor was intently studying a spot on the ceiling.

"We saved your city," rumbled the strong man. A frown broke through his normally impassive expression, twisting the thick tattoos on his face.

"That's as may be, boy," Commissioner Guirard said dismissively. "We'll see what my coroner has to say about that once he's taken a look at those deer."

The doctor pulled his attention back to the here-and-now. "We didn't save the city," he agreed.

Lacey spun to look at him. "What?!" she gasped.

"I knew that 'monster' business was just a wild story," Commissioner Guirard said, in a grimly satisfied tone. "Now if we can get down to discussing what I summoned you here for—"

"The city's doomed. We're all doomed. You think you've gathered the survivors here, but you haven't. You've just got people that haven't finished dying yet."

"What?"

"Do you remember the Grey Steel Regiment?"

"That's past history," Commissioner Guirard said gruffly. "A gruesome campfire tale. It's got nothing to do with the here and now."

The doctor laughed, a bit hysterically. "How I wish you were right, sir! But the storm that laid us all low and killed so many, that was an aether storm. Since then, I've seen people complaining of excess energy, muscle tremors, strange growths. Tumors. Bone spurs. Some have a milder case, some have it worse. It depends on where they were, if they were higher up, or behind walls, or near water, or just in a place where the aether currents were particularly agitated."

Commissioner Guirard frowned. "This isn't—"

The doctor interrupted him. "They're turning into monsters. At different rates, depending on the excitation of their bone aether. Do you understand? Not just people, either. Those things on the bridge? Those were deer. Harmless deer. What do you think a bear is going to be like? Or a wild boar?" His shoulders slumped, and he slowed to a mutter. "I figure a third of your 'survivors' are turning. They'll slaughter the rest of you."

Commissioner Guirard shook his head. "No. I've secured the city. My doctors have seen no signs of this—this coming plague. I'll take their word above that of a snake oil salesman! No doubt you've some *cure* you'd like to peddle to me at a very dear price."

"I wish I did. What I need is live specimens. If I could examine—"

"No," Commissioner Guirard interrupted. "I will not discuss this further. I *will not* borrow trouble because of some circus sideshow." He rubbed his face. "Today's problems are more than enough." He turned his attention to Lacey. "You said you were an equestrienne?"

"Yes," Lacey said faintly, still stunned by the doctor's revelation.

"How many horses do you have?"

Lacey frowned. "You want to know about my horses?"

Commissioner Guirard nodded shortly. "They're wasted with you. Resource like that should serve the population. Trained horses—hell, *any* horses—will be invaluable for riot control and defense of the city."

Lacey paled. "We're not part of your city, sir," she choked out. "I note that you currently lack both riots and external enemies."

"And as long as I'm in command, we won't be threatened by either," he growled.

"I'm sorry, the horses are not for sale." Lacey fought to keep her voice calm as panic began to rise. Without her horses, she was nothing.

"Who said anything about sale?" He lowered his brows. "They're being requisitioned."

Chapter 16

~* * *~

The Equestrienne's Worst Fear

Ginger, the Whitefaced Clown
Police Headquarters, New York City

"I'm requisitioning your horses for the good of the city," Commissioner Guirard said gruffly. "What other animals do you have that are edible or capable of being trained to work?"

Shocked silence swamped the room. Ginger glanced sideways at Lacey Miller, the lady equestrienne. He had observed that in every situation, her first thought was for her horses. They were who she *was*. What threatened them, threatened her.

A rim of white showed around her eyes as she stared straight ahead. Her hand clenched and unclenched. Ginger wouldn't have been surprised if she pulled a knife and attacked the commissioner.

If they let Commissioner Guirard take the horses, the circus would be trapped in a city that didn't have much use for them. If they tried to stop him, they would lose more than their horses.

Someone had to untangle this mess. If he were still in the military, Ginger would have dumped it all on the captain's lap and been glad to be rid of it. But here he was, in a company without a captain. Ginger missed the old ringmaster. He had been good at sorting out messes before they threatened his profits, even if his solutions tended to resemble Alexander the Great's answer to the

Gordian Knot. He'd always put the profitability of the circus first, the effectiveness of its spies second, and the welfare of its members a distant third.

These thoughts flew through Ginger's mind in the minute of dead silence that followed Commissioner Guirard's demand. No sign of them showed on Ginger's face. Rule Number 11 of being a clown: Your face is a canvas. Keep it blank when you're not using it.

Lacey's hand was straying toward the hoof pick tucked into her waistband.

Ginger reached out and caught it. She looked at him with wide eyes and then blinked down at her hand, as if she had been unaware of its slow drift.

"I'll write up an inventory for you, sir," Ginger told Commissioner Guirard. "We'll be going now. Don't want to take up any more of your valuable time." He ducked his head respectfully, took Lacey's arm in a grip more vicelike than it appeared, and swept them out of the commissioner's office before she recovered enough to do anything truly unfortunate.

She tried to tug her arm away. "I have to explain," she said. "I have to explain to him why he can't take my horses."

"Later." Ginger continued to tow her along.

She dug in her heels. "You don't understand. *He* doesn't understand. I have to explain to him." She spoke in the same tone that a hysterical person would use to insist that they were perfectly calm, *thankyouverymuch.*

"Not now." He leaned in close and kept his voice low. "I'm working on something. You have to stay calm. You're no good to your horses if you don't stay calm."

She focused on him. "They don't like it when their handler is agitated."

"That's right."

Once they were on the stone steps in front of Central Police Headquarters, Ginger stopped and patted his pockets. He painted a look of mild distress across his face. "I dropped something. I'll be right back. Stay here." He met the strong man's eyes as he said the last words, and was rewarded by a fraction of a nod. The strong man understood, and he wouldn't let Lacey do anything foolish.

When Ginger eased open the door, Commissioner Guirard looked up and frowned. "I thought I made myself clear," Commissioner Guirard said. "No special exemptions will be made for you people. Simply by offering to allow you to stay, I'm stretching our resources to the limit."

Ginger nodded. "Yes, sir. About the circus ..." He pulled a pair of tickets from his pocket. "I hope you and your wife might enjoy our performance tonight."

Commissioner Guirard's eyes hardened at the mention of his wife. Perhaps it was a warning, perhaps it was an involuntary response. "The circus will get no special treatment."

"You may find it a pleasant diversion, sir." Ginger waited.

After a moment, Commissioner Guirard swept up the tickets and gave a curt nod of dismissal.

It seemed more ominous that he didn't feel the need to say, "Don't try to leave town." The corpses dangling from the lampposts made that message clear.

~ * ~

Ginger didn't need much preparation for his clown act. As the rest of the circus bustled about the docks getting ready for the evening performance, he tackled the next part of the mess.

Three rough-looking sailors were sitting on packing crates watching the circus. Ginger ambled amiably up to them. "Afternoon, gentlemen," he said.

The biggest of the sailors grunted an acknowledgment, the oldest raised an eyebrow, and the youngest and friendliest of the three said, "How-do!"

"You like watching the circus set up?" Ginger leaned back against one of the packing crates.

"Not much else to do," the older sailor said noncommittally.

The big sailor roused enough to grump, "You trying to run us off? 'Cause the last time somebody—"

"No, no," Ginger soothed. "I'm in need of distraction myself, you see. I've watched this a million times." He waved his hand in the direction of the roustabouts hoisting up the king pole for the main tent. "I'm thinking of going to the zoo that my compadre was so fired-up about, but I don't want to go on my own. One man, alone, if those special patrolmen get to feeling their oats ..." He manufactured a grimace.

"A zoo?" The young sailor perked up. "We're stuck on this pox-rotted dock, and New York's got a zoo? Think they'd sell me a monkey? I've always wanted a one."

"I'm pretty sure all their monkeys are spoken for," Ginger said hastily.

The young sailor looked downcast for barely a moment before he brightened. "What are we waiting for? Let's go!"

The older sailor put out his hand. "Hold on, young buck." He squinted at Ginger. "What's your angle?"

Ginger intentionally relaxed his body. *No tension here, not hiding an ulterior motive, no sirree.* "My pal said the zoo owners would be grateful if I put a little business their way, if you know what I mean."

The young sailor nodded, but the older one wasn't so easily convinced. "Why don't you want us to go to your circus instead?"

"I don't figure it's a competition. Besides, whatever the circus takes in goes to keep it running. I won't see hardly any of it." Ginger shrugged. "Take some nice trade goods down with you. The zoo gets customers, you get entertained, and I get a cut. If you like what you see, tell your friends. I'd be happy to guide them there, too."

As Ginger had hoped, the explanation was close enough to the truth to satisfy them. Of course, once one group of sailors knew where the zoo was, there'd be no need for a guide. As long as they believed he hadn't figured that out, they'd think they had one up on him. That tended to put people in a good mood.

The older sailor shrugged. "Fair enough. Trade goods, huh? I've got a few things they might be happy to see."

"Delighted to hear it." Ginger smiled and leaned back to wait. When the sailors returned with the goods they were willing to barter, he made a few delicate suggestions that he thought might help them get through the city without drawing the attention of any of the special patrolmen.

Following Ginger's example of "how to walk like a landlubber," they made it to the Sasse family zoo unaccosted. The big sailor grinned when a trousered young woman challenged them at the gate. "Scrappy," he said.

The girl scowled and raised her rifle, which only made the big sailor grin more. "Who are you, and what are you doing here?" she demanded.

Ginger stepped forward, hands raised pacifically. "I'm from the circus. My friends said such wonderful things about your zoo that I just had to visit it myself."

The girl scowled. "Uh-huh."

"Look, I brought sailors!" Ginger said brightly, in the same tone he might have said, *Look, I brought flowers!* "And trade goods!"

"Oh?" The girl edged a bit closer to the gate.

Ginger tugged the young sailor's bag out of his hands and pulled out a bolt of shining silver cloth. "Hey!" the sailor protested.

Ginger ignored him. "See?"

"Oh, that's pretty," the girl admitted.

"And there's more. Why don't you go get your father? We'll wait right here. We don't want any trouble, just a tour."

After another longing look at the silver cloth, she nodded and trotted away.

Once she was out of sight, the younger sailor hissed, "She was wearing trousers! It ain't proper."

"Practical," the big sailor rumbled. "You've seen sailor females wearing trousers."

"That's different. Proper women don't."

The big sailor grunted. "These days, proper's only good so long as it helps you survive. I reckon she'll survive."

"She looks like she's no better than—"

The big sailor cut him off. "Don't."

"Sure, but—"

The big sailor growled, a low, menacing sound that silenced everyone until the girl returned with her father.

"Here they are, Papa," she said.

"Hello, gentlemen," her father said. "I'm Mr. Sasse, and this is our family zoo. What's this about the circus and sailors and trade goods?"

Ginger stepped forward. "I'm from the circus, sir. Some of my colleagues visited you last night, and they said very good things about your menagerie."

"Oh, did they now?"

Ginger smiled and hoped it didn't look pained. "Absolutely. These fine gentlemen are sailors from Port Rumsey. They hoped to tour your zoo, and they brought trade goods to pay for the privilege."

"Huh."

"I'd consider it a favor," Ginger tried.

"Would you now? That's mighty interesting." Mr. Sasse took a long, slow look at Ginger. "Mighty interesting. All right. Rosie, you run and warn the family we've got visitors."

Papa Sasse waited to open the gate until Rosie returned with her taller, bigger brother. Then he waved Ginger and the sailors inside. He led them past the peacock enclosure, where the males strutted and fanned their plumage. He walked them past an alligator pit, which inspired the older sailor to tell a story about seeing a gator down South tear a cow apart in under a minute. And he ushered them over to the monkey cage, where the younger sailor's fumbling attempts to buy a monkey were politely rebuffed.

Ginger noted that a couple of the monkeys didn't seem to be feeling well. Muscle twitches, odd bumps on their limbs ... He shivered and looked away.

Rosie Sasse and her brother led the sailors on to the next part of the tour, but Papa Sasse stayed back.

Ginger waited.

"You're here about that runaway circus monkey, aren't you?" Papa Sasse said. "Here to try and take him and Marigold away? I tell you, like I told the other fellow, Rosie's the one you have to convince!"

"Yes and no," Ginger answered. "I don't want Michael pining away for the monkey he left behind. I don't think he's convinced your zoo will be here in a year. There might be something I can do about that."

Papa Sasse snorted a bitter laugh. "You'll be lucky if you can get *your* menagerie out of this town intact. You think you can persuade the commissioner to see us as something better than exotic meat on the hoof once he remembers we're here?"

Ginger raised his eyebrows and smiled slightly.

"Oh. You do, do you?" Papa Sasse leaned forward. "Tell me more."

"In a minute. First, though, can you explain why Michael didn't just take his monkey? I don't understand it." Ginger allowed a plaintive note to creep into his voice.

"Ah, that. It comes down to love. It so happens that ..."

As they walked through the zoo, Papa Sasse told Ginger the tale of two monkeys in love. When he was finished, Ginger told Papa Sasse the tale of how one powerful man really loved his flighty wife. Though they stayed behind the sailors, Papa Sasse took Ginger along a slightly different route. There was at least one stop on Ginger's tour that he figured the sailors didn't get.

After they strolled past an ornery pair of ostriches, Papa Sasse led Ginger into a small clearing. Birds sang in the trees nearby. Two handmade wooden crosses were planted in the ground. As soon as Ginger realized what he was looking at, he took his hat off to show respect.

"That small cross is for Rosie's littlest sister," Papa Sasse said. "She got real sick after the storm, and she just kept getting weaker and weaker. I risked my life to get a doctor in and everything, but there was nothing the doc could do. He said the storm had pulled bone aether right out of her flesh and hadn't left enough to keep her going. He would have given her a transfusion, but his bone aether was all spoilt." Papa Sasse's tone was so matter-of-fact that it hurt to hear.

"I'm sorry—" Ginger began.

Papa Sasse held up his hand to stop him. "My second-oldest son went out to look for bone aether that was still good. My little girl died a week after he left. My son never came home again, and so I added a cross for him. " He met Ginger's eyes. "My wife lay in her bed and cried for a week. I'd never seen her cry before, you understand? Once she picked herself back up, we sawed off the zoo sign, put up blackout curtains, and set a guard. We haven't lost another baby since. Now you ask me to open the zoo back up. The commissioner has ignored us so far, but you want to bring him into my home and show him everything that he could take away from us. Why would we do that? We're safe here."

Ginger met Papa Sasse's eyes levelly. "No, you're not. You'll need the commissioner's help to survive. You *want* him to see you as a unique and precious resource."

Papa Sasse's bushy beard bristled indignantly. "And why is that, pray tell?"

"Is anybody in your household sick?" Ginger asked. "Irritable? Over-energetic? Given to muscle twitches and spasms?"

"One of the cousins," Papa Sasse said slowly. "Miss Brenda Anderson. Brenda's muscles spasm so much she can't hardly move. She complains of terrible pain in her joints. She stays abed most of the day. My wife has muscle problems herself. It started in her right hand, but it's spread up past her elbow now. She still manages. I think it's a lingering ailment caused by that aether storm. Half my zoo animals have it, too. Their appetite is healthy, though. That's a good sign in a sick animal. It means they'll recover on their own, given time." His eyes pleaded with Ginger not to contradict him.

"No. It isn't. And they won't," Ginger said, with a brutality that was its own sort of kindness. "Did you hear about the battle on High Bridge?"

"One of the women we barter eggs to had some ridiculous story about monsters and an Indian war elephant. Without the newspapers, nobody knows what's really going on. The craziest rumors get started." Papa Sasse shrugged, but his eyes remained worried.

"The story was true. When our circus was crossing High Bridge, monsters that used to be deer attacked us."

"Used to be—? I don't understand."

"The aether sickness drove them mad with hunger and changed them into monsters. Their bodies warped until they were almost impossible to kill. It was like the Grey Steel Regiment during the war. You remember that."

Papa Sasse was shaking his head. "No. It can't be."

"I'm sorry."

"You're wrong. My wife isn't like that. She isn't a monster. She just has a little nervous problem with her arm. That's all. It will go away on its own."

"It might," Ginger allowed. He was no doctor. For all he knew, it might be true. "But there are worse cases. In the next few weeks, they'll get hungrier. From what I remember during the war, they'll be super-strong. And they'll be able to jump really high."

"I can cage the sick animals separately from the healthy ones. I have a deep pit I'd planned on using for a pair of elephants. And there's plenty of extra fencing—strong enough to withstand a bull gorilla, so it ought to do." Papa Sasse managed a smile. "Never get rid of anything that might be of use, that's what I say."

"Might want to use some of that fencing to reinforce the wall around your zoo," Ginger suggested.

Papa Sasse's smile wavered and vanished. "Yes. Right. Against those poor souls who are so much worse off than we." It sounded like a prayer.

"You need all the help you can get to protect your family," Ginger pressed. He hated himself a little for the next thing he said, but he didn't allow that to affect his tone or expression. "You don't want to add more crosses." He gestured to the children's graveyard with a sweep of his arm.

"No," Papa Sasse said hoarsely. "No. What's your plan?"

"The sailors should be finishing their tour soon, right? Take all the trade goods they offer. Save them for me."

"All right." Papa Sasse stumbled into motion.

"If everything works out the way I hope, I'll send you a message tomorrow morning. You need to prepare for the most important tour you've ever given. Pleasing this visitor is the key to saving your zoo."

"We'll be ready."

"One last thing. I noticed that a few of your monkeys suffer from the aether sickness. Might you let us take them? Our doctor needs subjects to study."

Papa Sasse fixed his eyes on Ginger. "You think there could be a cure?"

"Everything is cured eventually," Ginger assured him. He didn't add that that was because death cured all ills.

They found everyone by the gate: the sailors, Rosie, Rosie's brother, and what must have been the whole Sasse clan. A tall, rawboned woman surveyed glass jars of spices with all the delight of a kitten in a yarn basket. The other females oohed and aahed over the bolt of silver fabric. Children held up glass beads and cats-eye marbles to see the sun shine through them. An older gent blissfully inhaled the aroma from an open tobacco pouch.

"Remember," Ginger said, "keep all the trade goods in one place for now. Don't use them or barter them away."

Papa Sasse huffed a laugh. "That may be trickier than I thought!"

As the two of them approached, the tall woman waved her hand in welcome. Her arm shook slightly with palsy, though it was nothing Ginger would have noticed if he hadn't known to look for it. This was Mama Sasse, then.

"They have cinnamon!" she told Papa Sasse happily. "I'll be able to make your favorite apple pie the way it's meant to be." She laughed. "I may have to have one of the girls roll out the pie dough, though, if this arm of mine doesn't behave!"

Love and fear flashed across Papa Sasse's face. Ginger looked away.

"What is it?" Mama Sasse asked, in an altered tone. "What's wrong?"

"Not now," Papa Sasse told her. His words sounded choked. He cleared his throat. "I'll tell you later. What do we have here?"

Mama Sasse gave him a sharp look, but she went along. "These boys brought a choice of things to pay their way. The younger girls fancy that silver cloth, and I admit it would be terribly becoming on Rosie, but I think spices are a better investment, and—hey!" She pointed a steady finger at the old man with the tobacco pouch. "Don't *think* I didn't see you inching that toward your pocket. Put it back in the pile! We don't have an agreement yet."

Ginger circled around the trade goods. Could it be—yes! He pounced, pulling out a brown paper bag with *Cacao Beans* hand-printed on the outside. He allowed himself a triumphant grin. "I'll take this," he said.

"I beg your—" Mama Sasse began.

Papa Sasse rested his hand on her arm. She gave him a quizzical look. "Later," he repeated.

~ * ~

By the time Ginger returned to Rumsey Port, circus tents billowed in the breeze. Talkers strutted in front of their pitches, practicing the spiels that would lure marks into giving up their hard-earned coin—or, in this case, food. Posters announced the wonders and marvels to be found within the tents. A pair of ostriches strutted along the dock, ostensibly being "exercised," but really serving as a walking advertisement for the menagerie. A handful of costumed circus folk roamed nearby. Now and then, as if on the spur of the moment, they did rolls or flips, to the assembling crowd's delight.

Judging by the size of the gathering, word had spread that there was something new in town. The ticket wagon blocked the main road entering the port, and the line of customers stretched up the street and around the corner. As Ginger approached, the wizened old ticket taker ended an argument with a customer by leaning out of his window and pointing to a hand-lettered sign pinned up between a poster advertising *The Daring Miss Dyer-Bennet, Who Dives Into Thin Air!* and another that boasted of *The Conjoined Murray Sisters, a Medical Miracle Alive Only By God's Grace!* In large letters, the handwritten sign admonished, "No Cash Money! No Ration Coupons! Barter ONLY!" followed by a list of suggested barter items. Even the man brandishing a handful of useless paper currency must not have been surprised; after a heated back-and-forth with the ticket taker, he shrugged and reached into his coat to produce a jar of peaches.

Ginger made a mental note to have someone keep watch for the commissioner and his wife, so that they could be kept away from the ticket wagon. Many of the cityfolk had begun comparing trade goods while they waited, and the line was beginning to resemble a black market.

Although—Ginger glimpsed a familiar face—it might already be too late. The commissioner's aide wasn't wearing his police blues, but Ginger recognized him by his reddened face. This time the red was caused by the cold instead of the exertion of chasing down Commissioner Guirard's wife, but the effect was distinctive. Commissioner Guirard already had the tickets Ginger had given him. Had he sent Mr. Akrill here to spy?

Then Mr. Akrill sneaked a look around him, opened his coat, and revealed a small jar of molasses to the old woman standing next to him. Not very long on common sense, Ginger mused. If Mr. Akrill wasn't the police spy, then he should have expected that someone else in the crowd was. Ginger shook his head sadly. Rule Number 10 of being a clown: Know who your audience is.

After waiting long enough to allow Mr. Akrill to finish his illegal black market transaction and long enough again to let the man relax, Ginger sauntered up to him. "Sir!" he said, as if seeing him for the first time. "Whatever are you doing waiting in line? There's no need for this! Come along with me. Here, this ticket is yours." He placed a ticket in Mr. Akrill's palm and closed his fingers around it.

"Er, well, I don't want any special favors," Mr. Akrill protested feebly. "I'm not an important man like the commissioner, you see, and I don't want anyone thinking—"

"Ah!" Ginger threw his arm over the man's shoulders and guided him away from the rest of the crowd. "Think of it as a trade, then. I was hoping you could do something for me. For the commissioner, really," he amended hastily, when the aide began to look stubborn.

Chapter 17

~* * *~

A Small Favor

Ginger, the Whitefaced Clown
Port Rumsey, New York City

Mr. Akrill frowned. "For the commissioner?"

"Exactly. But he mustn't know about it."

Mr. Akrill pulled back. "Hold up there. I won't do anything that might—"

"Oh, it's nothing to worry about!" Ginger hastened to assure him. "I was hoping for the name of that candymaker his wife favors so much. It's a surprise, you see. Entirely harmless."

Mr. Akrill's brow furrowed. "Hmm."

Ginger smiled amiably. As he waited, he thought of a half-dozen ways that the information could be used against Commissioner Guirard. Apparently, Mr. Akrill did not. His frown faded. "No harm in that, I suppose," he agreed. "She adores Hardy's Candy Confections. The proprietress is a Mrs. Nave. I don't think you'll find any chocolates there, though. Commissioner's been grumbling about it."

Ginger heaved a sigh and put on a resigned face. "It was worth a try. I'd hoped a gift would sweeten his temper."

"Everyone tries," Mr. Akrill commiserated. "Just abide by his rules and you'll be fine."

"Absolutely. Thank you for trying to help," Ginger said, reinforcing the idea that Mr. Akrill's answer had been useless because the candy shop could no longer supply the desired candy. And if his answer had been useless, there was clearly no reason to bother telling the commissioner about this conversation, now was there? "I have to prepare for my performance. Enjoy the show!"

"Good luck!" Mr. Akrill said. Ginger tried not to wince.

As Ginger headed for his wagon, he walked by a couple gawking at the poster for *Rajesh, the Hindoo Mystic, and His Fearsome Aether-Powered Bone-and-Brass Elephant!* "That's him!" the man was saying excitedly to the woman. "I tell you, I've never seen anything like it in my life. That elephant was unstoppable! Even in the war I didn't see anything to match it. I think it could have taken out an aether tank all by itself."

Ginger stopped, caught by the man's assertion. He'd been in the war too, and he hadn't seen anything to match the aether-powered elephant either. The thought nagged at him.

"Ginger!" One of the roustabouts ran up and caught his arm. The thought dissipated. "We're setting up the sideshows, but Doc Panjandrum says he ain't playing. Claims he's too busy dissecting those things that attacked us on the bridge. Says that's more important than lying to a crowd of sick folks."

Ginger shrugged. "Why ask me what to do?"

"You're good with people. The fortune teller's missing. The new ringmaster's just a kid. We tried to get Lacey to talk to him, but she went all stiff and said it weren't proper and she couldn't boss the circus."

"Hmm." Ginger took a second to consider this. It seemed another mess had fallen to him to clean up. "If the doc wants to cut up monsters, let him do it in front of a paying audience. Put up a table in the tent, get lots of lights, and move all the deer-things onto tarps inside. Take all Doc's tools and knives, and any extras you can scrounge up. Polish them up all shiny and put them on display too. Get a rope ring around him to keep the crowd at a distance, and let him cut to his heart's content."

The roustabout seemed much struck by this idea. "Hell, I bet the rubes will pay double to see that! Thanks, Ginger."

"You bet. Say, could you do a favor for me?"

"Name it."

"I gave the commissioner and his wife a pair of tickets to tonight's performance. I want him to be happy with what he sees, and that means keeping him well away from the ticket wagon."

"Why's that?"

Ginger bent an exasperated look on him. "Have you seen what these rubes are bringing to barter? We might as well be running an Indian trading post."

Understanding dawned. "Oh! Sure, I'll ask the boys to keep their eyes open and snag the commissioner before he sees anything that might upset his digestion."

"Appreciate it." With a nod of thanks, Ginger continued on to his wagon, where he stretched out and took a quick snooze until he heard the trumpet that announced the imminent start of the main show. He found himself humming as he pulled on his costume. When he took this role, he hadn't expected to enjoy being a clown so much, but he did. It was relaxing to be able to perform so openly, to wear expressions that everyone knew were false.

His happiness lingered as he gathered up his props and trotted over to the backstage tent where the performers waited for their entrances. A wrangler gave him the reins for Zahra the Zebra. Ginger pulled himself up to sit facing backwards in the saddle and arranged his props. He nodded to a circus hand, who opened the curtain to the main ring.

The zebra trotted forward, and Ginger entered the circus ring ass-first. His brilliant yellow hat was tucked under his arm, his boldly striped suit coat was draped over the zebra's neck, his right shoe was on his left foot, and his left shoe was on his right foot. He held a mirror in one hand and a gigantic, fluffy powder puff in the other. He was the very image of a clown entirely unready for an audience. As he entered the ring, he powdered his nose so vigorously that a huge cloud of chalk powder poofed up into the air. He surveyed the results in the mirror, turning his head this way and that. Then he brought the very edge of the powder puff closer and daintily dabbed his nose.

The crowd laughed.

Ginger jumped a little and peered around him, as if he'd only just realized that he had an audience. Quickly, he shook the powder puff out and used a little sleight of hand to transform it into a large orange flower while the cloud of glittering chalk dust settled. He tucked the flower into his lapel.

Then he pulled his hat out from under his arm and brandished it. The audience hushed. He put it on his head and pulled it down over his wig ... and his ears ... and his eyes ... and his nose ... and his mouth ... and his neck. The crowd began to laugh. By the time the top of his hat popped open and he peered indignantly over it, they were rolling in the aisles. He pulled his hat back off, pantomimed giving it a stern talking-to, and put it back on. This time, it stayed in its proper place. He continued to ride around the ring.

"Mama, he's riding the painted horse backwards!" a child in the crowd exclaimed.

Bless children. Ginger couldn't have asked for a better cue. He turned around and stared at the zebra's head as if he'd never seen it before. Then he pulled his feet out of the stirrups, pushed himself up to a precarious stand on top of the saddle—and toppled off into a splendid pratfall in the dust. The zebra kept on going without him.

Ginger remained motionless for just long enough to start the crowd murmuring, before he pushed up off the ground into a rising handspring that landed him on his feet. He removed his hat and dusted it off. He dusted off his legs. He dusted off his chest. He dusted off his arms. Then he did a comic double take and swung around to stare at the zebra, who was walking away—with his coat still slung over its neck.

He began to chase the zebra. And his trousers fell down, revealing bright red long underwear. He hiked his trousers back up and resumed the chase. His trousers fell down again. He stopped, pulled them up, squinted suspiciously at them, and took a step. Nothing happened. He took another step. Still nothing. He took a third step, and his trousers fell down yet again. The crowd roared. Ginger pulled his trousers back up, gripped them firmly, and carefully inspected them for defects. He twisted this way and that. He bent over and looked between his legs as if the answer could be found there. Then he pantomimed a sudden, astonishing realization. The crowd hushed and then burst out laughing as he proudly fastened his suspenders.

Ginger resumed the chase, but this time he kept tripping over his shoes. By the time he figured out that his shoes were on backwards, switched them to the proper feet, caught the zebra, put on his jacket, mounted the zebra the right way around, and finally finished "preparing" for his performance, the crowd was laughing and in an excellent mood to enjoy the rest of the show.

When the ringmaster came out, Ginger pantomimed furious protests but allowed himself to be shooed back behind the curtain, where he waited with giggling aerialists, a snake charmer who was cooing to her giant boa, and a dyspeptic camel being groomed for its appearance. Ginger settled back to wait for his next cue.

Lacey rode through to perform her equestrian act. Then the crowd roared, deafeningly loud. Ginger jerked the curtain aside, expecting to see he knew not what.

Lacey was performing the Cossack drag, hanging from the side of her horse as it galloped around the ring, but that trick alone would not have roused the crowd so very much. Word of the rescue she'd performed on the High Bridge must have spread. Ginger hoped it would help his case with Commissioner Guirard.

When Lacey trotted backstage, roses bloomed in her cheeks and her eyes sparkled. "Did you see how much they loved me?" she asked Ginger, as she dismounted. "It's because of what they're calling the High Bridge Battle. We could make a play out of it, with monster costumes for a few of the horses. They could be trained to fake attack, and I could swoop down and rescue one of the aerialists."

"A longer equestrian performance would help fill the show," Ginger said neutrally, "since we no longer have a sharpshooter act."

The joy faded from her face. "I'm sorry. You must think me devoid of any proper feeling, turning her death into an entertainment. It's only that after the first time you see someone die in front of you, it becomes harder to feel as deeply as one ought."

Ginger nodded. He'd observed the same thing in the War. Confront a man with enough corpses, and eventually when he looks around, all he sees is dead men walking.

"I do honor her courage and her sacrifice," Lacey continued, "but I need to do whatever I can to make my equestrian act a success. The circus must not fail now."

"And you hope that by reminding the populace of how you rescued the little girl, you'll make Commissioner Guirard less likely to seize your horses," Ginger finished.

She whitened and then flushed an ugly red. Her hands clenched and unclenched. "I can't let him," she said. The words tumbled out too fast as she lost her composure. "The horses are all I have. I've talked to the ship captains. None of the aether ships will carry us anywhere. Not even the Indian *mahout* could persuade them."

"What's this about the *mahout*?"

"He was trying to persuade one of the ship captains to take him back to India. None of them would. I don't think they even could. Captain Angie said she couldn't make it all the way to India, but she could take us somewhere closer. It would have to be in one trip, and her hold is too small for the horses. I'd have to drug them. Some of them would still injure themselves so badly I'd have to cut their throats, but I'll do it if it's the only way to keep them from being taken. I can't bear it that they might—"

"Whoa, whoa!" Ginger patted her shoulder. "No need for that yet. I tell you, I have a plan to get us all out of here."

"Really?"

"Really and truly."

She straightened her back and made a watery attempt at a polite smile. "What you must think of me!"

He smiled kindly at her and made no comment on what he thought of her, which was that if *he* ever wanted to take her horses away, he was going to make damn sure he was out of her reach at the time. Fortunately, he had no such plans. The circus really did need her and her horses.

Locating Commissioner Guirard and his wife after the performance was easy; Ginger simply had to watch the currents of the crowd. Everyone gave Commissioner Guirard a wide berth, which created an odd island of peace amidst the bustle.

"Commissioner Guirard," Ginger said as he approached. He bowed courteously. "I hope you and your lady wife enjoyed our humble performance?"

Commissioner Guirard's face hardened a bit, but words tumbled from Mrs. Guirard in an effervescent cascade. "It was delightful! The lady horse rider—I *heard* there were monsters! And flying through the air! I could never—. So funny you were! The bone elephant made me shiver, but the lion was so adorable! Just like a giant kitty! I wonder, might you have a lion cub? If it was raised in a home, I'm sure—"

Commissioner Guirard's eyes glazed a bit. Ginger felt his do the same, as he imagined the result of raising a lion in a fine home. He cleared his throat. "Lions do get a bit too large for a city home, ma'am," he managed.

"Oh. I daresay." She pouted. "I suppose we'll have to keep the circus instead, so I can visit the cuddly lion whenever I like!"

Ginger blinked. He knew his face was blank. He simply could not think what expression to put on it.

Her pixie face grew stubborn. She turned to her husband. "But you *must* do something about where the circus performs, dearest! These sailors can be quite crude. I assure you that my hearing is excellent, and their language really isn't fit for a lady to be around. I didn't say anything at the time because I know how it distresses you. And the port is so untidy! You will need to clean up the docks and teach the sailors gentlemanly manners." She touched a slim finger to her lips in thought. "Or perhaps you could clean up

Central Park and move the circus there! I attempted to go for a promenade the other day, and the park was absolutely *littered* with squatters. Why, it was nearly as bad as when I was a child, before they cleared out the squalid little shacks and the pig farms!"

"You would like me to clear out the refugees from the park?" Commissioner Guirard asked. "The poor people who have nowhere else to go? At least Central Park—" He stopped. "You *went* to Central Park?"

Those are the choices his wife gives him? Ginger thought. *Start a war over who controls the docks, or terrorize the survivors with nothing to lose? No wonder he looks like he swallowed a centipede!*

Mrs. Guirard gazed up at her husband with wide doe eyes. "I'm sorry, darling. I know you don't like it when I leave home, but I simply couldn't stand being shut inside that giant house for one more minute! And the city is deadly dull. Once the circus moves on, there will be absolutely nothing to do."

"My dear," Commissioner Guirard said, "I'm afraid that at the moment, the city isn't—isn't able to match the expectations of a lady of breeding. Society can't recover until—until certain other matters are dealt with."

It was the gentlest way that Ginger had ever heard anyone say, *Until I've hanged the troublemakers, buried the corpses, and fed the survivors.*

Mrs. Guirard's mouth firmed. "I'm aware of the difficulties! I know you don't think my upbringing suited me for anything practical, but I can be resourceful. I shall simply have to create my own diversions." She clapped her hands. "I know! We will have a costume ball. And since all the seamstresses claim to be busy sewing such boring clothes, I shall take a dozen of those refugee women and set them to making costumes! I am sure they would be grateful for such an enjoyable occupation. I shall need to find a source of inspiration for them, of course. We can get started tomorrow!"

Ginger couldn't let that opening pass. He jumped in before Commissioner Guirard could promise that his wife would never need to come up with her own diversions because the circus couldn't leave after he requisitioned all their horses. Better to volunteer than be conscripted.

"Perhaps you could postpone that, ma'am? I have a different suggestion," Ginger said.

"Oh?" she asked.

"Oh?" Commissioner Guirard echoed, his tone much darker than his wife's.

"Yes, ma'am. I would be delighted to offer you a chaperoned, behind-the-curtain visit of our circus. Our performers will answer all your questions."

She perked up. "All of them?"

Commissioner Guirard winced.

Ginger didn't, since he had no intention of actually introducing her to any circusfolk. "Absolutely," he said smoothly.

"That could take a while," she warned him.

"It would be our pleasure," Ginger assured her. To Commissioner Guirard, he added, "I can also arrange for your wife's escort to have a tour of our menagerie and working animals while your wife chats with the ladies of our circus." He gave him a conspiratorial between-us-men smile. "After all, men of action may find women's fripperies rather tedious."

As Ginger had hoped, his suggestion sparked a flicker of avarice in Commissioner Guirard's eyes. The commissioner wouldn't pass up an opportunity to have his men take an accurate, unforced inventory of those assets he planned to requisition.

"That would be acceptable," Commissioner Guirard said, in a measured tone of voice that Ginger diagnosed as an attempt to conceal his anticipation. "If you wish it, my dear?"

"Oh, yes!"

"Marvelous," Ginger said honestly. "Shall we say tomorrow at an hour past noon?"

Chapter 18

~* * *~

The Price of Chocolate

Ginger, the Whitefaced Clown
New York City

The first gray light of winter's dawn crept through the streets as Ginger walked into the city. It would take him about an hour to reach Hardy's Candy Confections, the candy shop favored by Commissioner Guirard's wife. While he walked, the city came alive around him. Yawning special patrolmen headed home after the night shift, transforming from curfew-enforcing bogeymen into ordinary tired men. Candlelight flickered briefly in the windows of reclaimed houses as their new inhabitants prepared for the day. A scattering of storekeepers opened their doors, lit their lanterns, swept their stoops, and generally faced the new day with a desperate kind of optimism.

When Ginger reached Glorious Green Grocery, a long line snaked away from it even though the grocer hadn't opened yet. Deborah Rowan was among the sleepy-eyed men and women who waited with ration cards in hand.

Ginger stopped and tapped her shoulder. "Deb."

She jumped, surprise widening her eyes and bringing her fully alert. "You!" she said. "The man from the circus!"

He took it as a compliment that his erstwhile guide to the city couldn't remember his name. "Yes. How long will this," he jerked his chin at the line, "take?"

"Grocer opens in less than an hour. I'll be done in two, back hauling stone at the bridge in three. Why? Did you get a ration card? If you're planning on getting food, you won't find a better time for it. Lines are worse later in the day."

"I'm not trying to steal a place in line," Ginger assured her, "just passing by. I saw you and wondered if you'd deliver a message for me. You can buy groceries first; the message will wait two hours, though not much longer."

"Payment?"

"Tell them to give you a little something from the sailors' trade."

She cocked her head. "Them? Sailors? Where do you want this message to go?"

"Do you know where the old Manhattan Zoo was?"

"Sure. Been a long time since I thought of it, though. Not sure what's there now."

"With any luck, the new Manhattan Zoo. And I make my own luck."

She snorted a laugh. "What's the message?"

"Half past one, today. They'll know what I mean."

"I reckon nobody ever knows *all* of what you mean," Deb said shrewdly, "but I'll give them your message, sure enough."

"Appreciate it." Ginger tipped his hat to her and continued on his walk.

When he saw Hardy's Candy Confections, Ginger stopped to loiter across the street. He pretended to read a hardware store's list of rationed goods as he assessed the candy shop. Inside it, a comfortably middle-aged woman bustled around. She swept the floor. She slid trays mounded with colorful candies into a glass display case. She lit the lamps and did not spare the lamp oil. Warm light spilled out onto the gray street. The shop's gaily striped awning propped up the illusion of happy warmth and comfort.

Workers ignored it as they trudged past, on their way to earn their ration coupons. They kept their heads down, like they hoped trouble wouldn't see them if they didn't see it.

As if that would work, Ginger thought. Trouble had found someone here, and not too long ago. Frozen horse manure and less readily identifiable filth coated the street. The dark brownish-red stain left by spilled blood still distinguished itself.

Fortified by this evidence of the wickedness of mankind, Ginger approached Hardy's Candy Confections. A large poster pinned to the door advertised that it was an "Approved Seller of Non-Rationed Food Items." As Ginger pushed open the door, a bell jingled. The woman behind the counter looked up with a smile. The long counter stretched along one side of the room. Chalkboards hung on the wall behind the counter. At the back of the store, a curtained doorway led to less public areas of the shop. Dustcloths covered two display cases. The third sparkled in the lamplight, and the candies inside glowed. In the far corner, two chairs sat beside a small table.

"Welcome to Hardy's Candy Confections," the woman said. "I am Mrs. Nave, the proprietress." She gestured to the large chalkboards hanging on the wall behind the counter. "There's the list of the trade goods I accept, and I'm willing to consider other offers. I'm afraid that right now I have a very limited selection of candies available. Caramels—" she indicated a neat pyramid of wax paper-wrapped squares, "—and sugar drops in ginger, sarsaparilla, cinnamon, lemon, beet, and tea flavors." She winked conspiratorially. "If I were you, I'd purchase cinnamon drops and lemon drops while I still have them."

"Actually, I'm looking for something special," Ginger began.

She froze. It was only for a fraction of an instant, but Ginger noticed it. "I can also make custom cakes, cookies, or candies, but I'm afraid you must provide any rationed ingredients," she told him.

"Something more special than that," Ginger said, just to see what she would do.

She shot him a quick, assessing glance. "You're not one of Commissioner Guirard's patrolmen."

"No, ma'am. Just a traveler passing through."

She nodded briskly, walked over to the shop windows, and pulled the curtains shut. Then she uncovered one of the unused display cases, revealing a wide assortment of items: silver tea sets, pistols, jewelry, knives, pocket watches, small musical instruments, bullets, music boxes, canned fruit and vegetables, and other small but valuable things.

"Aren't weapons considered contraband?" Ginger asked.

She tensed. "If that's not what you want, what are you here for?"

A plain young woman came through the curtained doorway at the back of the store and joined Mrs. Nave behind the counter. She wore an old gray dress. A heavy bandage was wrapped around her head. She kept her right hand hidden in her skirt. "Yes, what *are* you here for?" the young woman asked, in a voice so quiet it was almost a whisper.

Ginger reached into his coat and pulled out the paper bag of cacao beans he'd taken from the zoo. "I understand that chocolate is nearly impossible to get in New York these days, but I happened to acquire these cacao beans. I was hoping that Mrs. Nave could make some of the chocolates that Commissioner Guirard's wife favors."

"That's all you came for?" the young woman said, speaking normally.

Something about her rang a distant bell. He frowned. "Well, yes."

"Don't you recognize my voice, Ginger?"

He didn't. And then he did. His mouth dropped open.

He knew he was gaping like a yokel, but mastery of his expression had deserted him. "Madame Wershow! You're alive! I thought ...! We all thought ...!" Hearing himself, he stopped. He inhaled deeply. He smoothed his expression to calmness. "Report, please. What happened?" He glanced at the candy shop proprietress. "Or perhaps we should wait to discuss this until we're back with the circus."

Tonya Wershow laughed and then winced a little, as if it hurt. "Mrs. Nave is our contact here. We can talk in front of her. She's one of the few people I'm sure *didn't* try to kill me, since I was watching her when it happened." Tonya lifted her hand to reveal the pistol that she'd been hiding in the folds of her skirt. "Whoever it was saw my face. Nobody else in the circus knows what I look like underneath the fortune teller's veil. I was ready to shoot you if you recognized me."

Ginger cleared his throat. "Start from the beginning, please."

"Do you remember when we found the ringmaster's list of our contacts in different cities? He had other classified documents hidden in his wagon. The skeleton man found them. He decided to keep them. I doubt he's a player; he just likes secrets. I was passing by the skeleton man's wagon, and I overheard a man with a British accent interrogating him about these papers. When I tried to see who it was, my foot slipped. The noise alerted them to my presence. I had to flee. I followed protocol: I left the circus and headed toward our nearest contact to report that our mission was compromised by an unknown agent." She snorted. "What's left of our mission, anyway. How can we identify threats to our country if our country no longer exists?"

"There are still threats," Ginger said quietly. "Right now, we have more resources to deal with them than most. Keep going. You fled to New York. What happened next?"

"I found my way to Hardy's Candy Confections. I was across the street, scouting the shop, when I heard something behind me. I tried to reach my pistol, but—" she sighed, "—I must not have made it. I don't remember much else. A blur of movement. Pain. Darkness. I woke up here. The pain was overwhelming until Mrs. Nave gave me a spoonful of syrup that took the pain away. Then I was warm and happy and nothing hurt. I was swaddled in feather comforters. The air smelled like caramel. I thought I'd died and gone to heaven."

Mrs. Nave sniffed. "Perhaps I gave you too strong a dose of poppy syrup. You called me an angel and asked why the clouds you were floating on were full of chicken feathers!"

Tonya chuckled.

"She may look better now," Mrs. Nave continued, speaking to Ginger, "but this is the first time she's stood on her own. She was unconscious for a full day, and I've had to help her manage the chamber pot. She's not recovered."

"No," Tonya agreed. "And I think I need to sit down now."

Ginger hurried around the counter to take her arm. He guided her to one of the chairs in the corner. Tonya sat with a sigh of relief. "Who have you reported to?" Ginger asked Mrs. Nave.

Mrs. Nave laughed. "There's nobody *to* report to. My nearby contacts are gone. Dead, most likely. I have no way to reach my superiors. I'll help you however I can, but what you see is what you get. I'm nothing more than a candy shop owner and small-time black marketeer now. At that, I only survive because I had the favor of the commissioner's wife before everything fell apart."

"Good tradecraft."

Mrs. Nave shrugged. "I always tried to cultivate clients who might be useful. I sent them samples to draw them to the shop. If they came, I memorized their names and their birthdays. I always sent them a small present on special days. I asked after their families. I did my best to make them feel special. The wealthy and the powerful, politicians, even the gang leaders or their girls— them I made feel high-class. Worked like a charm." Mrs. Nave chuckled. "The commissioner's wife was low on the list. Could have knocked me over with a feather when she turned out to be the most important of the lot!"

"She certainly did. She brought me here, too," Ginger said. "For my plan to succeed, she must be pleased. Can you make the chocolates now? I'll wait."

"If you need them that much," Mrs. Nave said. "It won't take more than an hour for me to cook up her favorite recipe. You may—"

"Wait," Tonya interrupted. "Ginger, this is hardly the time for candy. Didn't you hear me? There's a traitor in the circus. We're cut off from all support. He tried to kill me. He probably *did* kill the ringmaster, before we docked in Boston. Certainly, survival has been our priority since we saw what the aether storm had done. But if the traitor is willing to kill again, now, we have to stop him! What could be more important than that?"

"Don't forget the skeleton man. I bet he's gone missing, too. We can assume this traitor has the papers and either terrorized the skeleton man into running off or killed him. It doesn't much make a difference which." Ginger smiled tightly. "As for what could be more important, you do remember that I said we had more resources than most? I'm not the only one who thinks so. The Commissioner of New York wants to requisition our horses and anything else that he might find of use. His charming *wife* would like to keep us here to entertain her forever. Unless we do something, the circus will be broken apart, and we'll be trapped. Besides," Ginger continued, working it out as he spoke, "it should be simple enough to flush out your would-be murderer."

"How?"

"You said it yourself. He's the only person in the circus who knows what you look like. He'll react when he sees you. If he believes you dead, his reaction will be even stronger. But before we save the circus from this traitor, we have to make sure there's still a circus left to save."

~ * ~

Ginger, the Whitefaced Clown
Rumsey Port, New York

Ginger smiled as he introduced Mrs. Guirard's police escort to the wrangler who would show them around. He smiled wide and did not grit his teeth. A professional would not grit his teeth. Had he *not* been a professional, he would have been grinding his teeth loudly enough to be heard back in Boston.

Although the officer in charge acted professional enough, the five special patrolmen he was in charge of did not. They were practically licking their lips as they looked around. No doubt they saw this meeting as a reconnaissance before they returned in force to seize whatever took their fancy. The wrangler Ginger had foisted them off on kept looking back over his shoulder as he led them away, as if to ask, "Are you sure you want me to show these yahoos everything? Really?"

Ginger kept smiling. *Remember that this is all a grand trick,* he told himself. *What they see doesn't matter. What she sees does.*

With that in mind, he offered a polite smile to Mrs. Guirard, the *she* in question. "Welcome, ma'am. I hope to provide you with a delightful afternoon full of surprises!"

"That's not quite how you put it yesterday," she observed in a tone as mild as milk.

"Well, you've already seen most of what our humble circus has to offer. I thought you might enjoy something more novel."

"Oh?" she asked, one eyebrow raised. Her eyes were sharper than Ginger would have expected from the featherheaded way she acted.

"In truth, I didn't bring you here to show you the circus," Ginger said, carefully doling out the necessary amount of honesty. "I hope to persuade you to my cause."

She held up her hand to stop him. "I can't keep my husband from requisitioning your animals. I do not interfere in city business. Consider yourself lucky that you were able to give one last performance."

"I would never expect a lady such as yourself to interfere in her husband's business! I have something else in mind."

"And what is that?"

Rather than answer, Ginger smiled and crooked his elbow for her to slip her hand through. "If you will allow me to surprise you?"

She simpered and batted her eyes at him. Just like that, the featherhead was back, though Ginger was no longer convinced by her performance. "That sounds delightful, sir. As long as it is not hazardous. My husband worries, you know."

If anything bad happened to Commissioner Guirard's wife, Ginger would worry, too—about his own skin. Out of self-preservation, Ginger had asked the strong man and a couple of roustabouts to come along. In the case of Michael, Ginger hadn't had much choice. As soon as Michael had heard that there was another zoo trip in the offing, he'd found Ginger and insisted that he be allowed to go along. That made four men from the circus, plus Ginger, who would be accompanying Mrs. Guirard. Barring an all-out war or another attack by monstrously twisted deer-things, Ginger reckoned they had enough muscle to protect her.

"You will be perfectly safe, I promise," he assured her. "Nothing terrible will happen to you today."

Chapter 19

~* * *~

A Winning Argument

Ginger, the Whitefaced Clown
The Sasse Family Zoo, Manhattan

Massive jaws clamped shut around the flailing body. The victim's blood spurted, staining rows of serrated teeth. One gulp and only shreds of silver skin remained.

Mrs. Guirard applauded. "Oh, fabulous! Do it again!"

At the sound of her voice, the alligator jackknifed around to face them. Mrs. Guirard squeaked and seized Papa Sasse's arm.

Papa Sasse grinned. "There, there, little lady." He pulled another flopping fish out of his bucket and tossed it into the alligator pit, with gratifyingly gory results.

So far, the tour of the zoo was a rousing success. Every animal had displayed itself to advantage. Mrs. Guirard had been appropriately charmed, awed, impressed, and shocked. She clutched a lovely fan made from peacock feathers, which Papa Sasse had given her as a souvenir. To his own surprise, Ginger found himself genuinely enjoying the visit. It took effort to keep his mind on the business at hand.

"This way to our aviary," Papa Sasse said. He guided them up the path to a large barn whose roof glittered in the sun. Tar and shingles had been replaced by thick panes of glass set in a cast-iron framework. Ginger squinted at it. He suspected Papa Sasse of saving the best for last.

Ginger followed Papa Sasse into the barn and stepped forward through the seasons into summer. The panes of glass arched overhead, letting in the winter sunlight but keeping out the cold. In the corners, four furnaces radiated a tropical heat. Potted trees towered above their little group, the green of the leaves a shocking sight in the dead of winter. Birdsong cascaded over them. Golden orioles, parrots, blue buntings, cockatiels, yellow-headed blackbirds, and a rainbow of finches swirled through the aviary.

"Oh!" gasped Mrs. Guirard. She fluttered the peacock fan excitedly as Papa Sasse led them through the aviary.

When Mrs. Guirard passed one of the potted trees, a parrot perched on a branch cocked its head and said, "Pretty lady! Pretty lady!"

A faint tinge of pink stained Mrs. Guirard's cheeks. "How charming!" she exclaimed.

How clever, Ginger thought. A thin chain stretched from a cuff on the parrot's leg to the branch it perched on, making sure that if they walked by that particular tree, the parrot would be on display for Mrs. Guirard, and vice versa. Also, the parrot had cocked its head and studied Mrs. Guirard's brand-new peacock fan before it uttered its compliment. Ginger wasn't an animal wrangler, but he'd seen enough of their trade to recognize a trained response.

"This way, please." Papa Sasse ushered them toward a courtyard in the center of the aviary, where a marble fountain burbled a merry counterpoint to the birdsong.

The strong man, the roustabouts, and Michael the animal handler moved to sit on wrought-iron benches at the edge of the courtyard, making themselves as unobtrusive as possible.

Ginger and Mrs. Guirard sat on benches beside the fountain. Ginger leaned back for a few moments, enjoying the warmth, the sun on his face, and the birdsong. *Rule Number 15 of being a clown: Enjoy life. How else can you know what will move your audience?*

A chattering sound near at hand made him sit upright. A small monkey tugged at the hem of Mrs. Guirard's skirt. It wore a diaper, because the Sasses were taking no chances.

"What a darling creature," Mrs. Guirard said, extending her hand to the monkey. It climbed up onto her palm and wrapped its arms around her wrist, staring up at her with large, trusting eyes.

She lifted it up. It curled up in her lap and began to play with its tail, now and then reaching out to pat her hand.

The time was perfect. Ginger made a little hand signal. Papa Sasse nodded.

"Allow me to offer refreshments," he said. A plain-faced young woman in an old gray dress emerged from behind a row of potted rose trees. She carried a silver tray with a plate of Mrs. Nave's finest chocolates and three glasses of cold pomegranate shrub.

When performing a juggling routine, Ginger avoided watching the path of any one ball, the better to track the gestalt. In the same way, he now fastened his gaze on a point above and slightly to the left of the four men he'd asked to be Mrs. Guirard's escort. As he observed them, he slid his hand to his pocket and the weapon he'd concealed there. His plan to have Tonya show her face in controlled surroundings could misfire badly. If it worked, however, it would give him four tough men—well, three tough men and Michael—whom he knew were innocent of the attack on her. He had to start somewhere.

None of them gave a second look to the young woman bringing the refreshments. Tonya set the tray on the wrought-iron table in front of Mrs. Guirard, curtsied awkwardly, and retreated. Ginger relaxed. These men, at least, were cleared.

Mrs. Guirard gasped. "It can't be!" Her hand darted out and seized one of the chocolates. She brought it to her mouth and sank her teeth into it. Her eyes half-closed. A blissful expression spread across her face. "Oh, it is!" The chocolate disappeared in short order, and she leaned forward and took another one. "However you managed it, these are *wonderful*!"

Papa Sasse bowed. "Glad you think so, ma'am. You might wonder how we acquired the cacao beans for your chocolates and the pomegranate syrup for your drink. Well, we got them from sailors, in trade for entry to the zoo! If more sailors visit us, we will use some of their trade goods to offer an even wider selection of refreshments. The rest, we will sell in the city."

"In trade," Mrs. Guirard said, as if she were trying out how the words tasted on her tongue. "How marvelous." She looked around her at the tropical forest and the birds darting through the trees. "And to think that my husband so carefully explained to me that there was no way he could peacefully persuade the sailors to give up their cargo."

"We've been setting aside a portion to pay the trading tax, ma'am," Papa Sasse said. "We thought maybe half? These are difficult times. We all have to make sacrifices and pull together.

We wouldn't want your husband to think we were trying to skip out on our responsibility."

"Trading tax," she mused.

"If the zoo remains open—" his voice faltered, and he paused to compose himself, "—it would be a regular payment."

"I wonder what other diversions the sailors would enjoy?" Mrs. Guirard said, half to herself.

"All the city can offer, I imagine," Ginger cut in smoothly. "Life aboard ship becomes extremely tedious. Given the right incentive, I'm certain that a trade could be arranged. Why, they might even agree to a trading schedule that ensures a regular flow of needed goods. In return, of course, New York would need to provide the diversions and civilized comforts that are sorely lacking at sea."

Mrs. Guirard's lips curved up and her dark eyes sparkled. "What a delightful notion."

~ * ~

Michael Hunter, the Animal Handler
The Sasse Family Zoo, Manhattan

Michael didn't pay much heed to the fancy aviary or to Mrs. Guirard's reaction, although he reckoned that a lot of careful thought had gone into creating both. He'd only come along to the zoo to visit Mr. Ben. Saving the circus by charming the commissioner's wife was all well and good, but it wasn't really Michael's job. His monkey was.

So when Ginger made his excuses and motioned at Michael to come along with him, Michael bounded out of his seat like a dog who'd scented sausage nearby. He knew it wasn't polite to look so eager to leave, but he couldn't help himself. He kept quiet, though, at least until they were outside the building.

"Can I go see—"

"There's something I'd like your opinion on first," Ginger interrupted.

"What do you need me for? Mr. Sasse knows his business. He don't need my help."

"Good thing it's not for him, I suppose." As Ginger spoke, Rosie Sasse walked up the path to join them.

"What's this about, then?" Michael demanded. "If you brought me here just to yammer at me until I change my mind—!"

"No, no," Ginger reassured him. "Rosie knows a lot about handling animals, since she grew up in a zoo. She's particularly good at training, um," he paused, "birds! She asked me if she could join the circus, but she's worried about her safety. She heard about the monster attack on High Bridge. As you've seen, I'm making arrangements for the Sasse family to be under the protection of the commissioner. What do you think would be safest for her?"

"Uh, we'd have been dead if the monsters attacked us earlier, or if the elephant wasn't around," Michael said awkwardly. He wondered why Rosie wanted *his* opinion. They didn't exactly see eye-to-eye. "It ain't what most folks would call safe out there. Circus folk got to roam, but she ain't got circus in her blood, not yet. I guess she should stay here. She's got family. Family's important. And if the commissioner's looking out for them special, I don't figure she could be any safer." Michael had seen Ginger's "arrangements" often enough that he didn't question whether they'd work. He thought of the corpses left dangling from lampposts. "Nobody in their right mind's going to do anything to piss him off." He flushed. "Begging your pardon for my language, miss."

She nodded.

"I think you're right," Ginger said. "So the situation with your monkey and the zoo is settled, then?"

"What? No, I didn't say—"

"Because I'm absolutely certain that Commissioner Guirard will extend his special protection to the zoo, once his wife has a word with him. Like you said, you can't get safer than that, can you?"

"No, but—"

"And your main concern is for the safety of your monkey, right?"

"Yes, but the circus needs—"

"Oh, don't worry about us. The zoo has traded us a couple of other monkeys that should make an interesting addition to our menagerie, though they'll have to be kept separately."

"Separately?" Michael asked. Then he shook his head, pushing away the distraction. "Wait, I didn't agree that—"

"You said it was safer here." Ginger leaned forward, his eyes merciless. "You said it was important to stay with family—loved ones. Your monkey's got a sweetheart, and your monkey's sweetheart has a family, and they're all safer here, so by your own logic, your monkey should stay in the zoo. You'll see him again.

You understand how important it is for sweethearts to stay together, don't you?"

Unaccountably, Michael found himself thinking of Pamela the aerialist and the way the purple ribbons in her hair bounced as she walked. He flushed. "Yes, but—"

"No buts. You've persuaded me. It's the best thing for the circus, and it's the best thing for the monkeys. Go say your goodbyes. Then take those new monkeys back to the circus."

Michael opened his mouth and closed it again. He couldn't really argue because it was all his own opinions. That was the worst part.

"Good," Ginger said briskly. "I have to get back to Mrs. Guirard. Rosie will help you get the new monkeys ready to take back to the zoo. Mr. Sasse said he had an old cage we could use that's plenty strong enough. Once you get back, let Doc Panjandrum see the new monkeys before you do anything else."

Michael waited until Ginger was out of sight before he dared look at Rosie Sasse. To his surprise, she didn't gloat. "We'll take good care of Mr. Ben," she said.

He nodded. Her sympathy reassured him and made him feel worse at the same time. After an awkward silence, she set off toward the monkey enclosure. He trailed along behind her with his emotions all in a tangle. When they reached the monkeys, she drew back far enough to be out of earshot unless he shouted.

And so he found himself saying goodbye to his monkey without ever making the decision to leave him behind.

When Mr. Ben saw Michael, the monkey strolled over to sit beside him. Michael crouched to talk to him. He told him that it was safer in the zoo right now. The monkey played with Michael's bootlaces. Michael explained that the circus would have to go on without him. The monkey hopped onto Michael's back and draped his arms around his neck in a loose hug. Michael said he'd miss him. The monkey ran his fingers through Michael's hair, grooming him. Michael said it was for the best. The monkey snaked his paw into Michael's shirt pocket, stole the dried apple slices that Michael kept there for treats, and bolted away with his prize.

"I'll visit," Michael promised Mr. Ben's retreating back. "I will. Somehow." He stayed crouched for another couple of minutes, watching Mr. Ben and the other monkeys. When he straightened and walked over to where Rosie waited, he felt a painful sort of lightness.

"I'll take special care of him." Rosie's eyes were serious. "I promise."

Michael nodded. "I know. Thank you." He added, "I'll take real good care of your monkeys, too."

Rosie looked away, like something about his promise pained her. "Come on. Papa loaded the monkeys into their cage before you arrived. The wagon is waiting by the gate. We moved it out of the way for the tour, but as soon as you'd passed by, we moved it back. One of my brothers will go fetch the wagon and the donkey back tomorrow. You can keep the cage. You'll need it." Judiciously, she continued, "Whenever he handled these monkeys, Papa wore the really heavy gloves and kept my brother standing by with a musket. You might want to do the same when you unload them."

"You make it sound like they're baboons or something," Michael said, following her.

"Or something," she agreed.

Michael let the conversation lapse into silence until they reached the main gate. An old cage sat on a wagon in front of the gate. At Michael and Rosie's approach, the donkey hitched to the wagon brayed loudly.

Rosie buffeted the animal on the shoulder affectionately. "Quiet down, you! It's risky enough sending meat on the hoof out there without you announcing it to everyone."

The donkey gave her an evil glare, quite as if it understood exactly what she'd called it.

Michael turned his attention to his new charges. The cage holding them was old but strong, with bars nearly twice as thick as the ones at the circus, and it seemed in good repair. He couldn't say as much for the monkeys. Two of them twitched in the corner, one chattered and jerked ferociously on the bars, and a fourth kept picking at its arm. "They look sick."

Rosie gave him an odd look. "The sick ones are what Ginger wanted. That's why we're giving you a separate cage for them."

"Oh." It was true, Ginger *had* said to take the monkeys to see the doctor first. Adding sick animals to the circus didn't make much sense to Michael, but he had no desire to get into another brain-twisting argument with Ginger. "All right then. Ginger usually knows what he's doing."

~ * ~

Michael Hunter, the Animal Handler
Port Rumsey, New York City

Back on the docks, Michael quickly spotted the circus tent whose painted canvas walls advertised, "The Great Doctor Panjandrum and His Amazing Panacea That Cures All Ills!"

"Doc?" Michael asked, pulling back the tent flap.

A scene from hell greeted him. Doc Janzen stooped over a table mounded with offal and gobbets of flesh. Gore splattered his apron. A stack of disjointed limbs rose beside him. Shining metal torture instruments gleamed on a bench nearby. Aether lamps burned brightly inside the perimeter of the tent, adding ghastly illumination to what should have been dark and secret.

Michael's gut rebelled. He dropped the flap and staggered around the side of the tent. Strings of sour vomit splattered on the dirt. Once he'd mastered himself, he returned.

Doc Janzen looked up, scowling. Light glittered off his blood-speckled glasses. "You again. Close that flap. You'll let the flies in."

Michael stayed in the doorway, holding the tent flap open and breathing shallowly through his mouth. He gulped. "Can't breathe. The smell—"

"What?" Doc Janzen sniffed the air. "I suppose. You get used to it after a while. Why are you here, then, if not to watch me work?"

"Ginger said I should see you about the new monkeys?" Michael blurted. "They're sick?"

"Hm, yes." Doc Janzen removed his glasses, absentmindedly rubbed them on his filthy apron, and then frowned when that only moved the smears around. "You have a strong cage for them?"

"Sure."

"How strong?"

"Strong enough for a bull gorilla, I guess," Michael said.

Doc Janzen nodded. "That should do it. Never let them out of the cage unless you've got them on a collar with a pole to keep them away. An elephant pole." He thought for a minute. "They might not eat fruits and vegetables. They'll need lots of meat."

"Monkeys don't eat meat!" Michael protested. "Oh, a few grasshoppers or a lizard now and then, but not *lots* of meat."

"These ones will," Doc Janzen said grimly. "Plan for what you'd need to feed one of the big cats."

"I know how to take care of monkeys," Michael said. "What you're telling me doesn't make any kind of sense!"

"You don't know how to take care of *these* monkeys." Doc Janzen sighed. Suddenly, he looked like a very tired man instead of a demon out of hell. "They've got the aether sickness. Ginger arranged for us to take them because I need test subjects."

"What?" Michael said. "You're not going to dissect them, are you?" His horror must have shown on his face, because Doc Janzen frowned.

"Certainly not," he said sharply.

Michael exhaled, relieved.

Doc Janzen took away that relief by adding, "They must be alive to study the progression of the disease." He walked to the tent opening, stared at the monkeys for a moment, and then pointed to the one plucking at its arm. "I'll start with that one."

"Start what?" Michael demanded.

Doc Janzen raised his eyebrows. "Amputation, of course. This one appears to be primarily affected in one limb, which makes him an excellent candidate." He lifted a wicked-looking saw. "Tie him to the table, if you would. Make sure the straps are tight. I have neither chloroform nor laudanum to spare."

"Wait! I promised—" Michael began, when another interruption saved the monkey, if only temporarily.

The snake charmer ran up and seized his arm. "Michael!" she exclaimed, out of breath. "Where are Ginger and the others?"

"Why?" Michael asked.

"Something strange is going on. I was sunbathing with my snakes when I saw two special patrolmen crawl out from behind the bags of horse fodder. Strangers, not the men that have been poking around all afternoon. I went looking for Ginger, since he's been dealing with the commissioner. While I was looking, I saw at least a dozen other special patrolmen coming out of hiding. I don't think it'll be safe here for much longer. Ginger needs to know. Maybe he can do something."

"Um, he's not here," Michael said numbly, as he struggled to figure out what he should do.

The snake charmer huffed in exasperation. "So go find him! Fast!"

Chapter 20

~* * *~

Hostages to Fortune

Michael Hunter, the Animal Handler
Port Rumsey, New York City

"**W**e need Ginger. Right. Right!" Given an order, Michael's mind began to work. To get to Ginger in time, he needed a fast horse.

He ducked out of the doctor's tent, took a deep breath of fresh air, and walked briskly toward where Lacey kept her horses corralled. He wanted to run, but there were policemen everywhere. More emerged every minute. Years of being a disreputable outsider in every small town the circus passed through had taught Michael that policemen were like big cats: either running or freezing in place would provoke an attack. The best plan was to keep moving normally.

As he passed one pair of patrolmen, he overheard, "Find the commissioner's wife and get her out of here."

Make that two fast horses he needed, Michael thought. Ginger and Mrs. Guirard both needed to be here to keep things from going bad, if it wasn't already too late.

~ * ~

Ginger, the Whitefaced Clown
The Sasse Family Zoo, Manhattan

In Ginger's experience, nothing important went smoothly. Mrs. Guirard's zoo visit was going so well that when catastrophe interrupted, it seemed inevitable.

In this case, catastrophe came as they were bidding the Sasse family farewell. It arrived in the form of Michael and two lathered horses.

"For you and the commissioner's wife," Michael explained to Ginger, as he slid off his horse. "You got to get back. The police are taking over the port. They ain't going to wave us on our way, 'specially not if they think we got the commissioner's missus. Hope your plan works."

"What?" Papa Sasse exclaimed.

The circusfolk looked to Ginger, shock writ sharply on their faces.

Ginger bit back the curse that tried to rise to his lips. "I thought we had more time. Mrs. Guirard, if I can come up with a way for your husband to change his mind without seeming to back down, do you think you can sweet-talk him into it?"

"Perhaps, but I don't understand," Mrs. Guirard protested. "My husband thinks I'm there. He'd never attack if I were at risk."

"He expected to get you out first, ma'am," Michael said. "They were looking for you."

Ginger nodded. "Everybody knows how much he cares for you, ma'am. If the sailors know you're visiting Port Rumsey, they won't expect him to attack. They have their guard down. It's the perfect time to attack. I expect that Commissioner Guirard used the circus as a pretext to sneak his men into hiding on the docks last night. Lots of strangers were coming and going."

Mrs. Guirard nodded slowly. "He's always been one to take any opportunity he sees. It's what saved us, after ... after." She met Ginger's eyes. "If he sees this scheme of yours as a way to get what he wants without risking any of his men, he'll want to try it. Get me to him, and I'll persuade him. But what *is* your idea? What do you want me to say? Chocolates won't persuade him to back down, no matter how delicious they are."

"I'll figure that out on the way. The rest of you," Ginger looked at Michael and the other circusfolk, "stay here with the Sasse family. Wait until it's safe to return to the circus."

"I'm not certain that's a good plan," Papa Sasse said slowly. "Do you really think you can make him listen to you now, after he's committed his forces?"

"What other choice do we have?" Ginger asked him. "If Commissioner Guirard is willing to take on the sailors, he won't stop there. He'll strip our circus bare. I don't think keeping quiet will save the zoo anymore, either. Sure as shooting, he'll come for you too."

Mrs. Guirard regained her customary spirit. "You men, always fussing! It won't come to that. I've talked him down from worse." She laughed, a bubbling, infectious laugh that invited them in on the joke. "Not that he thinks I knew what I was doing, of course."

Ginger chose not to think of what "worse" might mean when it described the intentions of a man who left bodies dangling from the lamp posts of his city. Instead, he offered Mrs. Guirard a small, respectful bow. "Of course. We must get you to him as soon as possible."

Michael held out the reins of the two horses he'd brought. "Here you go."

"Hold up there!" Papa Sasse interrupted. "You're right, Ginger. The way things are going, there's no point anymore in us sitting on our hands and hoping that the commissioner forgets we exist. We've already thrown our lot in with yours. If things don't go according to your plan, could be that a few more men on your side would make a difference."

Ginger knew that he should act appreciative and inspired, to seal the bond between them, but he just felt irritated. These people and their good intentions were *slowing him down*. He barely managed to keep the irritation off his face as he said, "Could be. I'll always welcome your help, but Mrs. Guirard and I need to go *now*."

Papa Sasse gave him a sharp nod. "We'll follow behind as close as we can. Excuse me. I need to get everybody ready to ride." Without waiting for a response, he strode off to do just that.

Ginger took the reins from Michael. "Listen to me," he told him. "This is very important. Have they sealed off the port?"

"Yeah, I reckon so."

"How did you get out, then?"

"I rode right past 'em." Michael gulped. "I thought they were going to shoot me, but I heard one of them order the others to let me go. Said the commissioner told them to let the small fry swim away, and that they'd sweep me up in the net later."

Ginger nodded. "That's what I'd do. Commissioner Guirard controls the city. If people stay, he can pick them up any time he likes. If they flee to the countryside, that means there are fewer mouths for him to feed. It's good for us, too. If they don't care much whether people leave, I'll wager that they didn't bother to block all the entrances either."

~ * ~

Ginger, the Whitefaced Clown
Rumsey Port, New York

On any occasion that he found himself in new surroundings, Ginger made a habit of taking long walks at two o'clock in the morning. As he would freely tell any and all official-looking persons, he suffered from terrible insomnia whenever he was sleeping in a new town. Simply terrible.

As a result of the wakefulness that could be achieved by drinking four large glasses of water immediately before bed, he knew of three entrances to the docks that were more alley than street and were, accordingly, more likely to be overlooked.

Ginger and Mrs. Guirard rode to within eyeshot of the first entrance before dismounting and walking their horses into the front parlor of an abandoned boarding house. Hopefully, nobody would think it a likely place to find valuable livestock. Ginger shifted his weight as they walked out of the house, feeling the reassuring press of his bowie knife against the small of his back.

Mrs. Guirard gathered up her skirts and darted into the shadows. Ginger mentally rolled his eyes. He'd found that no matter how tense the situation, a man casually walking into it was much less likely to be shot than a man—or woman—sneaking through the underbrush or climbing over a fence. He walked after Mrs. Guirard at a brisk but not overly hurried pace. He caught her arm before she could attempt to sneak up on the unsuspecting alley. No doubt she would have dashed from shadow to shadow and attempted to hide behind street lights and other entirely inadequate objects.

"No hiding," he said in a quiet voice that avoided the attention-catching sibilance of a whisper. "Pretend that you have every right to be here and that you don't know anything unusual is going on. Stand here, in the sunlight, and look at the ground as if you're searching for something you've lost. Keep your head down. Move a little, but not too much. Let me check the alley."

A flush burned her cheeks, but she nodded. That was good enough for him. He chose a path perpendicular to the alley mouth, one that would allow him to see down the alley while still clearly heading somewhere else.

Two alert-looking special patrolmen stood guard at the other end of the alley. Their attention was on the docks, where they expected any trouble to come from. As soon as he saw them, Ginger averted his gaze. It made no logical sense, but sometimes people really could tell when they were being watched. He did not allow his footsteps to speed up as he passed the alley and circled around to return to Mrs. Guirard's side.

"Not that way," he said shortly. "No—try not to look anxious."

Her face instantly smoothed into a charming smile.

"That might catch too much attention too," he said dryly, "but it's better than looking worried. Come on. It's a bit of a walk to the next possibility."

The next likely-to-be-overlooked entrance couldn't even be dignified by calling it an alley. Years of drunken sailors staggering back to their berths had worn a footpath between two buildings. No patrolmen guarded it. Ginger sauntered down the footpath, knowing that he was heading for trouble. Mrs. Guirard followed him before he could tell her not to.

When they emerged onto the docks, Ginger saw that he'd arrived too late to prevent hostilities. Or perhaps he'd arrived just in time, since Lacey had yet to use the sharp point of the hoof pick dimpling the skin of Commissioner Guirard's throat.

On the city's side of the docks, ranks of regular policemen stood shoulder-to-shoulder with special patrolmen marked by their blue armbands. If he were a gambling man, Ginger would have said that the police force's disciplined and uniformly armed troops, experienced leadership, and sheer numerical advantage made them the odds-on favorite. If Lacey hadn't taken Commissioner Guirard hostage, it seemed likely that they would have already overrun the sailors' defenses.

Ship-side, the sailors formed a ragged brigade armed with everything from crowbars and knives to muskets and rifles. They scowled fiercely at the policemen, as if they could be outfaced like bullies picking a barroom fight. Those still aboard ship must be scrambling to prepare for battle. Despite the menacing scowls of the sailors on the docks, the real threat came from the ships behind them.

Ship cannon boosted by aether catalyst could strike deep into the heart of the city. Shatter bombs would unfurl into a lethal ivory mist of bone aether darts. And although their use was banned by every maritime accord, some of these ships might even have fire aether splashers, which burned unstoppably through ship hulls and human flesh alike. Of course, that was if the aether armament onboard the ships still worked. It might, if the ships were at sea when the murderous storm struck. Or it might not. Anyone who used aether-powered devices took their own life in their hands. Ginger shuddered as he remembered the horrific accidents they'd seen when they first docked in Boston.

Lacey and her hostage stood midway between the ships and the main road to the port, near the circus tents. The open space between the two forces gave Lacey an empty arena. She might have been a ringmaster at the center of his ring, if she weren't so obviously failing to control the situation. Commissioner Guirard's weapon lay at his feet. She had a hoof pick to his throat. And she *still* didn't look like she was in command.

A hoof pick made a poor weapon, so Lacey hadn't planned this ahead of time. Something had pushed her to this state. It was pretty easy to guess what. Commissioner Guirard must have seen the circus, given an order—and Lacey overheard it. Now she held a weapon to the throat that had issued that order.

"I won't let you take them!" she yelled. "My horses are my life! All I want is to be left in peace. Why does nobody understand that?!"

Ginger winced inwardly. That was not the sound of a person who could be reasoned into lowering her weapon. Experienced policemen would hear the same pushed-past-the-breaking-point desperation in her voice that he did. Indeed, when he looked for the officer in charge, he spotted Commissioner Guirard's deputy standing beside a man holding a sharpshooter's rifle. The sharpshooter had a calm, distant look on his face.

Ginger wracked his wits. He needed a distraction to buy time. It must be something that they wouldn't perceive as a threat. He couldn't afford to make this mess worse. He needed something unexpected but nonthreatening, something that would make them lower their guard. He needed, he realized, to make them laugh. He had just begun to concoct a plan when an indignant voice shouted, "Halt or I'll shoot!"

The policemen tensed, readying themselves for action. The sailors surged forward and then stopped when they realized that nobody was threatening them. Lacey's hand jerked. A thin ribbon of blood unspooled down Commissioner Guirard's throat.

It was in this delicate moment that the Sasse family and company made their entrance. The source of the shouting turned out to be a storklike young special patrolman guarding the alley the Sasse family emerged from. "Stop right there!" he ordered again. His Adam's apple bobbed convulsively as he swallowed.

Papa Sasse looked determined. Mama Sasse looked embarrassed at being so easily caught. The rest of the Sasse family wore expressions that were elaborations on the theme—and indeed, they had brought almost their whole family, from children barely old enough to be trusted to point their guns in the right direction, to oldsters who had avoided fighting in the War Between the States because they were already considered too elderly. Even Miss Anderson, the aether-sick cousin, had roused herself to join them. She'd been abed when Ginger visited the zoo, but he recognized her by the signs of her sickness. Her body shook like a leaf in a high gale, and thin strands of saliva dripped untended down her chin.

For once, Ginger thought wryly, it would have been nice if the circus members *hadn't* made a grand entrance. Alas, they had all trailed along behind the Sasse family. Their reactions to being caught varied. Michael's eyes were wide and scared. The strong man's dark face was as impassive as a lifetime of hard experiences could make it. The roustabouts wore surly expressions, like they'd just been given a nasty job of work. Madame Tonya Wershow looked meek and scared, as if she were a Sasse family member dragged along against her will. She'd even thought to move closer to the family, separating herself from the rest of the circusfolk. Ginger approved. Under the circumstances, she was doing everything she could to avoid drawing further attention to herself. Nobody should be looking at her, except—

Except one person among the small cluster of performers that had gathered by the circus tents. At the edge of the group, Rajesh stared at Madame Wershow as if he'd seen a ghost. Taken by surprise, the Indian *mahout*'s unguarded expression was as good as a confession. Ginger took it as such. In order for them all to live long enough for him to pass sentence on the guilty party, however, Ginger had to do something that went very much against his nature.

"Excuse me!" Ginger said, stepping forward with his empty hands spread wide.

Everyone stared at him.

"This is all a terrible misunderstanding," he babbled, as he approached Lacey and her hostage. "Nobody needs to do anything unfortunate." He waved his hand toward the ranks of armed policemen. "A very natural reaction to your wife going missing, Commissioner," he said, blithely papering over the timing of Commissioner Guirard's offensive and what Ginger knew to be his true motives. Ginger phrased his next sentence carefully, emphasizing the words he wanted to linger in Commissioner Guirard's mind. "Now that *your wife* is here and unharmed, as you *can see*, you decide *what happens next*."

Your wife can see what happens next.

Men who loved their wives wanted to appear worthy in their eyes. Ginger gambled everything on that simple truth. Loving husbands didn't want to be seen as despots willing to slaughter everyone who opposed them. They wanted to protect their wives' delicate sensibilities, assuming that they believed their wives had such things.

"Lacey, set down the hoof pick," Ginger continued, switching targets. "There's no need for that now. Let's not do anything rash before the commissioner has had a chance to talk to his wife. Let him go."

"If I let him go, there's nothing to stop him from taking whatever he wants. The only leverage we have is *what we hold*. If I let him go, we have nothing."

She'd stopped shouting. She sounded calm and she made a logical argument, but her eyes were wide and staring. He might have talked her back from the ledge, Ginger thought, but she was still on the rooftop.

"The commissioner is a man of the law," Ginger told her, feeling his way toward an argument that might work. "I am certain that we can trust him to abide by any agreement he makes, particularly with his own men as witnesses."

Lacey scowled at him, but she eased the hoof pick away from Commissioner Guirard's neck. Just a fraction, just enough that the point no longer dimpled his skin, but enough to give Ginger hope. After all, he didn't particularly care what Commissioner Guirard agreed to, or whether he planned to honor that agreement. Ginger's aim was to keep Commissioner Guirard unharmed— mostly unharmed, he amended—until Mrs. Guirard could bring gentler methods of persuasion to bear on her husband.

"Sir," Ginger said, "surely you wish to *speak with your wife* and reassure yourself as to her well-being! I understand how much you must have feared for her safety, once you realized she was missing. This is all an unfortunate misunderstanding. Lacey was also in fear when she seized you." Ginger continued talking, painting a picture of fragile, terrified womanhood, as he eased toward the not-at-all-fragile and increasingly angry-looking woman holding Commissioner Guirard hostage. "You know how impetuous women can be when their protective instincts are aroused. I'm sure she realizes that it was a terrible mistake. If you reassure her, Lacey will put down the hoof pick. Perhaps if you give her assurances that her horses will remain untouched and that the circus can depart your jurisdiction as soon as—"

Commissioner Guirard and Lacey both responded angrily and at the same time, their sentences stepping on top of each other.

"You can't—" "I will *not*—" "—trust a man who—" "—bend to a threat simply—" "—hangs his own civilians!" "—to protect myself!"

Lacey jammed her weapon back against Commissioner Guirard's throat with such force that a fresh trickle of blood ran down his neck. Commissioner Guirard's face was red with rage and his hands were fisted tight by his legs. They both glared at Ginger. The air thickened with the promise of violence. Ginger saw Commissioner Guirard's gloved right hand twitch, beginning to signal his troops.

Ginger had gambled everything, and he'd lost. Soon, the silence would shatter. Nothing he could do would change what was about to happen.

That knowledge felt like freedom. Because it would make no difference, he broke the final and most important rule of how to be a clown, Rule Number 20: Look only at what you wish to draw attention to, because your audience's eyes will follow yours. For those in a more dangerous line of work, that translated to, "If you don't want your enemy to see what is precious to you, ignore it."

Ginger looked at the circus. He looked at the patched tents and the bravely gaudy circus wagons, at the painted canvas posters with their cheerfully outrageous lies. He looked at the men and women who put everything they had into making those lies real. With hand-sewn sequins and endless practice, they transformed cheap canvas tents into an enchanted wonderland, if only for the length of a show. He feared not all of them would survive what was coming.

Chapter 21

~* * *~

The Killing Ground

Ginger, the Whitefaced Clown
Port Rumsey, New York City

Because he was already looking in that direction, Ginger noticed clown-in-training (and probationary ringmaster) Christopher Knall peer around the corner of the fat lady's tent. The tent used to belong to the fat lady and the skeleton man, but now—. Ginger cut off that line of thought.

A moment after Christopher pulled his head back, a beak poked around the edge of the tent.

Ginger grinned so widely that his cheeks hurt from the unaccustomed strain. Training Christopher had been a good use of his time after all. The young man had seized on the same idea that had crossed Ginger's mind earlier, but *he* had been in the right place to execute it.

One ... two ... three ... four ostriches stampeded away from the circus tents, their feet thudding against the ground, their plumes bouncing, hissing like a sack full of angry cats. As a distraction, it worked. Commissioner Guirard froze mid-signal. The policemen fell silent, their attention arrested. The seamen's weapons sagged along with their jaws. The Sasse family halted their approach and the storklike guard paused in his attempts to arrest them. Everyone stared, from the most battle-scarred sailor right down to

Miss Anderson, the Sasse family's sickly cousin. The spectacle seized her attention so firmly that she ignored everything else, including the shining trail of saliva that dribbled down her chin.

Even Lacey lost her focus for a moment, gawking at the ostrich stampede and letting her hand drop slightly. In that moment, Ginger moved. As smoothly as he could, he covered the last few steps to Lacey and her hostage. He lifted the hoof pick out of her grasp as casually as if she'd passed him the table salt.

She snapped back to awareness too late. Her grab after the hoof pick would have ended with its point embedded in her palm, if Ginger hadn't reversed the blade as he pulled it away. "Nooo!" she cried.

Commissioner Guirard reacted immediately, striking Lacey with a hard elbow to her solar plexus. It knocked the breath out of her and sent her stumbling backwards several feet. Ginger tucked the hoof pick into the back of his waistband, beside his bowie knife, and spread his open hands in front of him peaceably.

The ostriches hissed as they bolted past. Their closest escape route happened to be the alley chosen by the Sasse family. The family stared with dawning apprehension at the three-hundred-pound birds headed their way.

The storklike patrolman reached out and grabbed the arm of the nearest member of the Sasse family, who happened to be Miss Anderson. Miss Anderson responded by grabbing the patrolman and sneering—no, *snarling*. Comprehension hit Ginger hard.

"Watch out!" he shouted.

Miss Anderson whipped her head around and growled at Ginger. Strings of drool dangled, swaying, from her mouth. Her hand tightened possessively on the patrolman's arm, clawlike fingernails digging deep enough to make the patrolman cry out and attempt to pull back. Ginger held her gaze without blinking. Showing weakness seemed ill-advised.

Miss Anderson's stare shifted to Commissioner Guirard. Her nostrils flared, as if she were scenting the air. She bared her teeth. Ginger remembered the trickle of blood on Commissioner Guirard's neck. With the memory came a wave of bowel-loosening apprehension. The clarity granted on a battlefield before the combatants engage descended upon Ginger. It would last for only a few moments, but in those moments, he knew precisely what must be done.

"Mrs. Guirard!" he shouted. "Hide behind the—" he quickly measured the distance between her, the seamen, and the policemen, "—sailors. Do it *now!*"

Confirming his estimation of the steel she kept hidden behind fluff and nonsense, she reacted instantly. Without hesitation, she dashed toward the sailors. Not just any sailors, Ginger saw; she chose an exceptionally well-armed, nasty-looking crew.

With his most important asset safe, Ginger moved on to his secondary goal: keeping the rest of them alive.

"Seamen!" he shouted. "Fire to port *only*! 'Ware cross-fire!" They stared at him like he was sunstruck crazy, but that was all right. They'd figure it out soon enough. Time to warn the other side. "Police officers! Keep your aim to the right!"

Commissioner Guirard's eyes widened as he put the pieces together. Miss Anderson released the storklike patrolman and loped toward the commissioner. He had time enough to either direct his men or retrieve his weapon from where it lay at his feet, but not both. "Fire at target—*only* if you have have a clear field!" Commissioner Guirard bellowed, pointing at Miss Anderson. Then she was upon him. Her skirts wrapped around his legs as if they were embracing, and she leaned in for a kiss that would rip his lips off.

Before that could happen, he threw a haymaker that crushed her nose and snapped her head back. Blood fountained from her nose as she reeled back, her hair flying up in a parody of a young girl's flirtatious hair toss. Despite all that had happened, most of the men present winced to see a member of the fair sex treated so brutally. Commissioner Guirard didn't even pause to shake the sting from his hand. He stooped, seized his revolver, and fired.

Ginger guessed that Commissioner Guirard was aiming for Miss Anderson's head, but the punch must have affected his hand after all. He missed. His shot blew out her throat. A bloody red mist sprayed in all directions as she curled forward and clutched her neck. For a moment, Ginger allowed himself to believe that it was over. That they'd won with a single shot. That the aether sickness hadn't granted her the same kind of freakish abilities as they'd seen in the deer-monsters during the battle on High Bridge.

Then the spray of blood sputtered and stopped. She didn't fall. Her hands dropped to her sides. Blood coated her arms from her fingertips up past her elbows, as if she wore sanguinary opera gloves. She lifted her head. Worms of scar tissue squirmed across her throat and crudely knitted it back together.

Everyone stared, enemy and ally alike. Angry, hungry madness stared back at them. Once those eyes might have looked affectionately upon a child or a suitor, but the hunger had burned out gentler emotions and left nothing but coals. They should have opened fire on her immediately. Instead, they froze like mice in front of a corn snake.

Should be wharf rats, not mice, Ginger thought irreverently. A clown always looked at all the angles in a situation to find the funniest one; this time, that was enough to shake him free from his mesmerized state.

The thing that had once been Miss Anderson sniffed the air and snarled. Ginger guessed that she found Commissioner Guirard's blood to be an irresistible lure. If she attacked him again, the policemen wouldn't fire for fear of killing their commander. If the sailors also held their fire, Miss Anderson would devour Commissioner Guirard before their eyes. The circus would either escape in the resultant turmoil or be trapped in New York in the midst of a new civil war as various factions fought for power and resources. If the sailors did bring their heavy armament to bear, they'd destroy Miss Anderson and most likely Commissioner Guirard as well. In that case, those outcomes still held true, except that first the circus would have to survive the looming battle between the policemen and the sailors. The docks would be awash in blood. The only way Ginger could see to prevent that was with a little blood of his own.

Ginger pulled out his bowie knife and sprinted toward his target. He spared a brief prayer that nobody would shoot him out of sheer confusion.

The ostriches were running in panicked circles when he intersected them. Their leader uttered a booming territorial call to warn Ginger off. Ginger darted to the side and slashed, opening a deep, bleeding gash down half the length of the ostrich's leg. The ostrich hissed. It whirled to face Ginger and tried to kick him with its good leg. When the ostrich's weight shifted, its injured leg crumpled beneath it. It plummeted to the ground in a flurry of blood-splattered feathers.

A rasping growl behind him raised the little hairs on the back of Ginger's neck. Without even looking, he dove out of the way. Years of practice at rolling back up out of a pratfall and strolling away helped him; in seconds, he was back on his feet and running. He expected at any moment to hear a snarl next to his ear and feel teeth sinking into the meat of his shoulder.

He didn't.

He made it back to the relative safety of his corner of the docks just as a fusillade of gunfire hammered the air and was answered by a howl of rage. Sailors and policemen temporarily united in unloading their weaponry on this new threat. Ginger could only be grateful that they heeded his warning and kept their fire aimed diagonally at the killing ground, so there were none of the cross fire casualties that he'd feared.

Bullets struck Miss Anderson, jerking her back and forth like a rag doll. Blood spurted and stopped abruptly as lumpen scar tissue plugged her wounds. Scars seethed across her body, rapidly deforming her into a monstrosity more terrifying than any freak show. She snarled and screamed when she was hit, but she ignored the people shooting her. Each time bullets knocked her down, she doggedly launched herself back at the dying ostrich. After it bled out, she savaged its corpse. She ripped up gobbets of meat and gulped them down without chewing, stripping the ostrich down to the bone at an incredible rate. It wouldn't hold her much longer.

Bullets weren't going to be enough to stop her. The rate of fire slowed as that truth sank home. Commissioner Guirard signaled his men to cease fire and bellowed something about bringing up the heavy cannon. The boom of the guns had partially deafened Ginger, and so he only heard bits and pieces. The sailors scurried around their ships, hauling what weaponry they could up from belowdecks. Heavy ship weaponry would be mounted and bolted in place, meant to fire to port and starboard at enemy ships, useless when docked. Even if the sailors cannibalized what they could, it would not be the equivalent of an at-sea bombardment. That was good, because a true bombardment would reduce the entire dock to splinters, along with most of the people standing on it. As it was, Ginger hoped to hell that if any of these ships had shatter bombs, their crews were smart enough not to use them. Projectile weapons had little effect on Miss Anderson, and those things had a nasty habit of going off-target and maiming innocent bystanders like himself.

He saw weaponry with the distinctive shape of aether armament being pulled up to the deck rail on several of the ships. He was pretty sure that yes, among them was a shatter bomb hurler. He began to back slowly toward the footpath that he'd used to reach the docks. Calm, slow, and steady, that was the ticket. He didn't want to attract attention from anybody or any*thing*.

A golden ball flew overhead, shining brightly enough to be mistaken for a second sun. Ginger dropped all pretense of calm and bolted to safety. Behind him, he heard a deceptively innocuous *crash-tinkle* as the blown glass ball broke. Anything nearby would be showered by a detonation of sparks, along with small droplets of fire aether that would keep those sparks burning long past the point where they ought to turn to ash. They would melt stone. They would burn under water. Sinew and bone posed no challenge at all.

Miss Anderson howled in anguish as she finally suffered an injury agonizing enough to break through the haze of animalistic hunger that drove her. Ginger dove into the narrow opening between two buildings and pressed his back to the wall until Miss Anderson's screams died to whimpered moans. The sounds of weapon fire had long since ceased. When Ginger was as sure as he could be that no more fire aether splashers would be launched, he stepped away from the wall and went to see what had happened.

The policemen and the sailors still aimed their weapons at the burning wreck of flesh that shuddered and twitched in the center of the dock, but they held their fire. Miss Anderson was dead. Her body just hadn't realized it yet. Bubbles of scar tissue rose and fell, trying and failing to regenerate cauterized tissue. Charred pits pockmarked the planks around her, marking where aether-fueled sparks had tunneled into the wood and on through to whatever lay beneath. Flames sputtered around the edges of the holes.

A huge wave of relief washed through Ginger. They might yet be saved. He opened his mouth and—

"Execute clean sweep!" bellowed Commissioner Guirard. In unison, the policemen brought their firearms up and swiveled to point them at the sailors.

The sailors were caught with their weapons aimed at the ground or at the spectacle in the center of the docks. When they were not immediately slaughtered, hands started shifting and gun barrels began to lift. On the decks of ships, seamen scrambled to redirect their armament.

"Halt or we will fire!" Commissioner Guirard ordered them. The sailors froze, but the tension in their muscles still promised violence. "Do not move! My patrolmen will disarm each of you individually. We *will* shoot the first person who so much as blinks in the wrong direction!"

Not, Ginger noticed, "Don't move or we'll shoot," but, "We will shoot." It rather sounded as if Commissioner Guirard had decided that making an example would be useful. Ginger relaxed into an immobility that would prevent him from betraying any physical response to loud noises, or surprises, or whatever else Commissioner Guirard might have up his sleeve to provoke an "example" should one not be provided for him.

A burly sailor moved a bit too slow when ordered to drop his Arkansas toothpick. Commissioner Guirard strode across the dock, seized a revolver from one of his men, and sighted down the barrel. Ginger didn't react. Not everybody had his control. A commotion started nearby—and was stilled by a gunshot.

When a woman's scream of pain broke the sudden silence, Commissioner Guirard's satisfaction peeled away. His face a mask of horror, Commissioner Guirard bolted toward the screaming woman with no care for his own safety. He charged at the knot of sailors gathering around her. They parted at his approach, revealing Mrs. Guirard on the ground.

Ginger ran after Commissioner Guirard. Mrs. Guirard's screams died to whimpering moans. She lay with her arms wrapped around her waist as if she could hold herself together despite the gut wound draining her life away. Red soaked her bodice and streaked her skirts.

Commissioner Guirard raised his revolver and pointed it behind him without even looking where he was aiming. Ginger dodged sideways. Commissioner Guirard pulled the trigger, sending a bullet flying back to strike one of his own men in the center of his chest. The policeman staggered and dropped his weapon, staring dumbly at the wound that killed him before his eyes rolled up and he crumpled to the dock.

Commissioner Guirard never even looked back to see if the man he'd executed were the one who'd fired the fatal shot. He knelt beside his wife. He reached toward her and then pulled back as if he were afraid his touch would hurt her. Under other circumstances, it would have been humorous to see such a big, tough man wringing his hands.

It hurt to watch.

"Don't die, sweetheart," Commissioner Guirard begged. "Please. I'll do anything."

Chapter 22

~* * *~

The Final Reckoning

Ginger, the Whitefaced Clown
Port Rumsey, New York City

"**D**on't die, sweetheart," Commissioner Guirard begged. "Please. I'll do anything."

Mrs. Guirard tried to smile, but pain pulled her lips so tight that it was almost a grimace. "Nothing you can do," she gasped. "Not even you. Nothing anybody can do. Sorry."

"There must be something. I can't lose you. Tell me! What should I do?"

The answer revealed itself to Ginger in a flash so bright that he might have been struck by lightning. His vision refocused slowly. Once he could see again, he stared at the ships, looking for one distinctive silhouette in particular.

He found the creature he sought staring back at him over the bow of a nearby ship. Gears jolted into motion as the aether-powered dog-monkey scuttled jerkily along the deck of the ship, keeping watch. Its loose patchwork coat of dog hide bunched and stretched as it moved. Only one ship could have such a grotesquely misshapen mascot. *Beauty's Reward* was painted on the side of the hull. Seeing it, Ginger remembered Captain Angie saying that that was the name of her ship.

He pointed. "There!"

Everyone ignored him.

He seized Commissioner Guirard's shoulder. "We have to—"

Commissioner Guirard shrugged him off and rose with a violence that set Ginger back a fortunate step. Fortunate, because as Commissioner Guirard surged to his feet, he lashed out with the butt of his revolver. He missed. Before he had a chance to correct his aim, Ginger spoke.

"I can save her," he said quickly. When Commissioner Guirard didn't immediately strike him down, Ginger took it as permission to keep talking. "The captain of *Beauty's Reward* has a small supply of bone aether. If we act immediately, it is possible to heal your wife."

Commissioner Guirard's eyes sharpened. Then he shook his head. "Not enough time. Yes, we could probably kill the ship's crew and take the ship. We would have to fight off attempts to retake it, though. My wife would die before we could slaughter enough sailors to discourage them."

He said this without any attempt to prevent the seamen surrounding them from hearing him. The sailors looked at each other with *Did he just say what I thought he said?* expressions on their faces. "Now see here," a short, burly fellow said as he hefted his fire ax. "What's to keep us from—"

"I was thinking we might ask politely," Ginger interrupted. "The captain's a friend of mine," he said, adding some shine to their relationship, "and likely to listen to reason. A merchant sailor, you understand?"

"Traders." Commissioner Guirard muttered it like a curse.

"Yes, and you should be glad—" Ginger began, but Commissioner Guirard had ceased to listen.

"Take her shoulders," Commissioner Guirard barked at Ginger. He hunkered down beside his wife and looped his arms around her knees. "We need to keep her as level as possible. Hop to, man!"

Ginger did as he was ordered.

"I'll help you," a young man said as he pushed his way through the gathering crowd. He had the kind of cheerful, open face that Ginger instinctively distrusted. "I'm Pablo Virgo, crew on the *Beauty's Reward*. Let me lead the way."

Commissioner Guirard nodded brusquely. "Hurry."

"Yes, sir," Pablo said. As he passed Ginger, he added in an undertone, "This I have to see."

Mrs. Guirard screamed when they lifted her, but she fell unconscious before they reached the *Beauty's Reward*. Above them, the aether-golemed monkey had been joined by its mistress, Captain Angie Endo. She watched them from the bow, unmoving, a forbidding figure with her arms crossed under her breasts. Still, she hadn't ordered the gangplank pulled up. Ginger considered that a promising sign.

The boards of the gangplank creaked underfoot as they carried Mrs. Guirard onto the deck of the ship.

"I don't recall ordering a fresh corpse," Captain Angie said, raising her eyebrows and smiling a smile that showed her sharply pointed teeth to advantage.

Ginger winced. "Captain, I know that you can heal this woman if you choose."

"Why should I?"

Commissioner Guirard's face flushed red. "If you don't, my men will burn this boat to the waterline and use it as a pyre for your—"

Ginger jerked his chin in a warning movement. Commissioner Guirard managed to bottle the rest of the threat, although the effort empurpled his already colorful cheeks.

"It's a devil of a risk," Ginger told her, keeping his face and tone sober but letting a gleam enter his eye. "You'd be betting that the brutal, bloodthirsty autocrat who would have used Strider tanks against his own civilians is also a man of honor who acknowledges his debts."

"I like a gamble, at times," Captain Angie drawled.

Ginger smiled internally. He'd hooked her. Beside him, Commissioner Guirard practically radiated tension. Ginger suspected that he held on to his self-control by a rapidly thinning thread.

"The stake for that bet is enough bone aether to heal the lady," Ginger said to Captain Angie. He shrugged. "Of course, you could also play it safe and shoot him now. Without their commander, the police might lose the heart to fight."

Commissioner Guirard could take it no more. "Shoot me if you must," he burst out, "but save my wife! She is innocent." He looked down at his unconscious wife. She hung limp in his grasp. His choler fading, he added quietly, "Enough innocents have died."

Ginger nodded. "There's that, too."

Captain Angie shook her head in wry self-mockery. "I always was a sucker for long odds. I guess I'm all in." She gave a shrill two-fingered whistle that summoned a matronly woman with silver-salted hair who wore trousers under her skirts, a combination of propriety and practicality that Ginger thought spoke well of her. "Mrs. Hobbes will see to it. She patches us up around here."

"And I'm a dab hand with sailcloth, too," Mrs. Hobbes said dryly. "Lay her out here on the deck where I can see what's what."

~ * ~

Ginger, the Whitefaced Clown
Beauty's Reward, Port Rumsey, New York City

Ginger shifted in his chair and attempted to nap. Whenever he found himself in a safe place with nothing else to do, he tried to sleep. That wasn't one of the rules for how to be a clown; it was plain common sense. He wasn't having much luck. He shifted his weight again and leaned a little more to the left. The chair, being bolted to the floor of the cabin, couldn't be moved to accommodate him, so he was having to do all the moving for both of them.

In the bunk beside him, Mrs. Guirard slept untroubled. She breathed deeply and evenly. Mrs. Hobbes had aligned Mrs. Guirard's innards and administered the bone aether. After the healing took hold, she'd sponged the blood off, dressed her in a billowy white nightgown, and tucked her into a bunk. She'd shooed the menfolk away during the latter duties, even Commissioner Guirard.

He would have returned to sit by his wife's side, but Captain Angie had pointed out that his men were likely to get nervous if he disappeared for too long, and she wasn't *that* much of a gambler. Commissioner Guirard had grudgingly agreed. That didn't stop him from coming belowdecks "to see how she was doing" every quarter-hour. Mrs. Hobbes popped in even more frequently, listening to Mrs. Guirard's breathing and laying a hand against her cheek to check for fever. And Ginger sat vigil, still awake despite his best efforts.

As he closed his eyes again, he heard two sets of footsteps in the corridor. "Commissioner," Ginger heard Mrs. Hobbes say, "there's hardly room for the both of us in there. I promise that I will tell you if there are any changes in her condition. Won't you wait on deck?"

The cabin door creaked open. "After you, ma'am," Commissioner Guirard said, his tone polite but inflexible.

With a put-upon sigh, Mrs. Hobbes walked across to the bunk where Mrs. Guirard lay. "Her breathing is fine." Pause. "No sign of fever." Pause. "Her stomach is not unusually swollen."

"She will recover," Commissioner Guirard stated firmly.

"How could she not, with you here to give her her marching orders?" Mrs. Hobbes asked.

"Don't fight," murmured a drowsy female voice.

Ginger cracked his eyes open a sliver, enough to see but not enough to draw attention to himself. He had a hunch that this scene would play out better without his interference.

"Oh, my dear!" Commissioner Guirard collapsed to his knees beside his wife's bunk and seized her hand.

"There, there. I'm sure everything will be all right." Her eyes opened wider. "I feel so peculiar, as if I could sleep for days. Yet my skin is fizzing with energy! And I'm so hungry!"

"That would be the effect of the bone aether treatment, Mrs. Guirard," Mrs. Hobbes said.

"Who are you?"

"I am Mrs. Barbara Hobbes, crew onboard the *Beauty's Reward*. I was a battlefield nurse during the War Between the States, and now I patch up whatever needs patching on this ship. Sometimes it's the sails, sometimes it's the people." She smiled. "You're lucky I wasn't away visiting friends on *The Lamprey's Grin*, as I was the last time somebody needed healing. The captain can manage in a pinch, but her technique lacks delicacy and some find her bedside manner distressing."

Mrs. Guirard blinked. Ginger wondered how much of that she'd followed. "Thank you, Mrs. Hobbes. I am much obliged to you for your care."

"Yes," Commissioner Guirard agreed, holding his wife's hand. "Mrs. Hobbes, I'm in your debt." He stated it as a self-evident truth, with no hint of a grudge in his tone. He spoke as if it didn't cost him anything at all to bow his neck in gratitude to one of the enemies that he'd been within minutes of defeating utterly. Perhaps, in comparison to the cost of losing his wife, it didn't.

Mrs. Hobbes demurred. "You should thank the captain, not me. I'm just doing my job."

"I'm in her debt as well. But tell me, Mrs. Hobbes, what would *you* ask of me? Name it. If it's within my power, you shall have it. Free passage into the city? A good position in a prosperous household?"

She looked down at her hands for a moment, and then she looked up and met his eyes. "Peace."

"Peace?" he repeated, taken aback.

"Peace," she said firmly. "During the War Between the States, I saw enough of neighbors killing neighbors. A couple of years earlier, they would have been helping each other with the haying, but there they were, trying to rip each other's guts out. I don't want to see that again. The young man who led you aboard? He's my nephew. Pablo was too young to serve in the last war. I don't want him caught up in a new one. I want peace."

"Peace."

"Find a way for us to live together without another war."

"That may be difficult." Commissioner Guirard rose and paced. Ginger continued his pretense of sleeping, even when Commissioner Guirard bumped his leg. In the cramped confines of the cabin, it was like being trapped inside a tiger's cage with the tiger still in it. "We need those cargoes to survive, and your captains have shown no willingness to sell them for what we can afford to pay."

Mrs. Guirard had remained quiet while Commissioner Guirard and Mrs. Hobbes talked. Now she feathered a wink at Ginger and lifted her hand. "Andre?" she said.

Caught by her use of his first name, Commissioner Guirard took her hand and knelt beside her again. "Yes, my dear?"

She smiled. "I may be able to help with the captains. I think you've been overlooking some of our resources, darling. There's more to life than simple survival. I met quite the most amazing people ..."

Epilogue

Ginger, the Whitefaced Clown
Port Rumsey, New York City

Later that night, after the policemen left the docks and the sailors returned to their ships, and after the circus put on a performance that was thankfully less exciting than earlier events, Ginger went looking for Rajesh. He found the Indian *mahout* sitting at the end of a pier, looking out over the bay. The inky blackness of the water was relieved only by sparkles of reflected moonlight. It was pretty enough, Ginger admitted, but the breeze blowing in off the bay reeked of raw sewage. Rajesh didn't seem to notice.

"I saw you talking to the captain of *The Dancing* Mongoose before the show," Ginger said, stopping just behind him. "Are you thinking of leaving us?"

"Don't worry," Rajesh said bitterly. "I am not going anywhere."

"No aether ships going to India just now?"

"No ships going to India for a very, very long time. Maybe not until you and I are old men. No ships carry enough aether to fuel them all the way there, you see, and there is no more untainted aether to be had. The engines would explode, they say, or the ship would be left adrift in the middle of the ocean. Or both."

Ginger slid out his bowie knife and held it beside his leg, tip slightly tilted forward, poised to strike. "How long have you been planning on sailing away from New York?"

"As soon as the storm hit, I wanted to return—"

"—to your employers?" Ginger interrupted sharply. "Did you need the ringmaster's hidden papers so that you would have something to offer them?"

Rajesh flinched. He looked over his shoulder and froze when he saw the knife Ginger held.

"Who are they, anyway?" Ginger continued. "Indian or British? Your accent is slipping."

"Indian," Rajesh gritted out. "I attended a British boarding school, but my loyalty is to the princely state of Udaipur. Do you plan on killing me, then?"

"Perhaps. I suggest avoiding sudden movements. I appreciate your willingness to answer my questions, though I admit I'm a little surprised by it."

"My answers no longer make a difference, do they?" Rajesh asked fatalistically. He faced forward again, staring into the night. Ginger wondered if he saw the bay at all.

Ginger shifted slightly to the side so that he could see Rajesh's face. "Perhaps. Perhaps not. Why take the papers before you knew you could escape? What was your mission?"

"I was to come to the United States and find allies to help us in our struggle for independence. I suspected that the ringmaster had figured out that I was more than a simple elephant *mahout*. I needed to know what he had guessed, what he had written down."

Silence could be a threat, when properly used. Ginger let it linger as he appreciated the view. Moonlight glistened on the dark water like silver lace, and the smell of the bay was not so bad once you got used to it.

"I may never see the Udaipur again," Rajesh said. "I wonder. Is the Maharana of Udaipur taking advantage of this catastrophe to secure his power, or is he already dead? Does my mother still make *chapatis* for the neighborhood children? Do my sisters still consult the astrological charts of their suitors? Do they even still have suitors? My mother may be dead. Anything could have happened to my sisters."

Ginger had not come to offer false comfort. "Yes. You may never learn what has happened to them. I don't know if it makes it easier or harder to have remembrances of the home you lost, but I suggest you treasure them. Your oleander plant, for instance. It must take a lot of care. It's lovely. And quite poisonous, of course, as our late ringmaster found out."

"I was waiting for you to get to that. Yes, I tried poisoning him while we were still at sea. He did not die, though he was ill for several days. You recall his 'seasickness'? I suspect he kept atropine nearby as a counteragent in case of just such an occurrence." A wry smile crossed Rajesh's face. "First the ringmaster, then the fortune teller. I seem to be a most incompetent murderer."

"You succeeded well enough later," Ginger said blandly. "After both your attempts to poison the ringmaster failed, you stabbed him with a hoof pick and gifted the murder weapon to Lacey."

"No, you don't understand, I—"

"And I doubt that the skeleton man will return to the circus anytime soon. Or ever. Will he?"

Rajesh stopped protesting. Ginger saw his eyes narrow slightly in calculation.

"Would you give the fortune teller my apologies?" Rajesh asked. "Despite the differences between us, she was never anything but kind, and I—"

"—saved her home," Ginger finished.

"I beg your pardon?"

"On the bridge into New York, when we were attacked, you saved the circus from being destroyed. You saved my life too, incidentally."

"Yes, but—"

"The circus is our only home, now. The world has changed, and we changed with it. Before, we were different people. What those people did does not have to be part of who we are now. It just took some of us longer to realize that."

Rajesh stared at him with stunned eyes.

"We cannot afford to lose any more circus members," Ginger said.

Rajesh held still, listening.

"Surviving what is coming will take all of us." Ginger let the silence expand, waiting for Rajesh to fill it.

For the first time, Rajesh turned away from the darkness in front of them. He looked at Ginger. "So, am I one of you now?"

Ginger returned his stare. "I'd say that depends on you. Can you be one of us in truth?"

"It sounds better than being stabbed in the back and dropped into the bay, which is my other choice."

Ginger didn't deny it.

"What's the catch?"

"I'll be wanting the ringmaster's papers back. They could prove useful to us."

"Of course. What else?"

"You will teach one of us how to operate your aether-powered war elephant, so that we can defend ourselves even if you die."

Rajesh hesitated for a moment. Then he said, "Yes." No doubt he wondered what his life expectancy would be after he was no longer needed, but he'd correctly decided it was longer than it would be if he gave the wrong answer now.

"Rajesh—or whatever your name really is—will you travel with the circus, but this time truly be one of us? Will you promise to put the interests of the circus first and to keep no other secrets from us?"

"Yes, of course."

"That was too easy," Ginger said. "Will you swear it on the lives of your mother and your sisters?"

This time, there was a long pause before Rajesh spoke. "I swear on their lives," he said.

Ginger tucked his bowie knife back in his waistband. "That's all right then," he said, his tone casually matter-of-fact. He sat down beside Rajesh and dangled his feet off the edge of the pier. "Pretty night," he commented, "if you can ignore the smell."

"I hadn't noticed." Rajesh sounded stunned. "That's it? I say I'll live my life as a different man, and we're done? I just ... start again? It's that easy?"

"It's not that easy, but it is that simple. People do it all the time." Ginger allowed himself a small smile. "I'll grant you, usually it's not at knife-point. Though that happens more often than you might think."

"Ah." Rajesh stared out over the bay as if he were seeing it for the first time. "So where *will* we be traveling to next?"

"I asked around. There are rumors that Fort Augusta in Pennsylvania has been treating those afflicted by the aether sickness."

"You think they have a cure?"

"The only way to know is for someone to go find out, and we're the best ones for the job."

"A rumor is a slender thread to pin your hopes on."

"I have to pin them to something. Maybe if we have enough strands of hope, we can braid them into a rope strong enough to lift us all."

Rajesh snorted. "Now *that* sounds like a circus trick."

Ginger smiled and watched the moonlight dance over the waves. "That it does."

~* * *~

~ * ~

Also by Abra SW

To enjoy other stories by this author, writing as Abra Staffin-Wiebe, visit her website at http://www.aswiebe.com.

~ * ~

Thank you for reading my book! If you enjoyed it, won't you please take a moment to leave me a review at your favorite retailer or book review site? I'll wait right here.

...Done? Great. Turn the page to find other extras, including a special bonus story that takes place after the events of *A Circus of Brass and Bone*!

~ * ~

Extras

Bonus Story
What Happens Next
Cast of Characters
Glossary
The Story Behind the Story
Essay: You Might Not Have to Die
(With Discussion Questions)
Acknowledgments

Bonus Story
(Rough Cut)

Bradley Roberts, the Negro So Strong He Can Carry a Mule Under Each Arm!
Approaching Fredrickston, Pennsylvania

"**V**ultures!" called the conjoined sisters riding the elephant with Rajesh, the Indian *mahout*.

"Halt!" shouted Rajesh. "Stop!"

Vultures? Bradley's stomach tightened and he found himself running forward even as the implications filtered into his consciousness. Lacey galloped past him to speak with the Indian *mahout* at the head of the procession.

Rajesh leaned down from the elephant's back to talk to Lacey. "The girls saw the birds," he was saying when Bradley caught up with them. "Vultures circling, they say."

"Turkey vultures," the girls said in unison.

"When I looked through the spyglass, I saw crows boiling up into the air and then settling back down," Rajesh continued.

"That's bad," Lacey agreed.

"If there's only a few vultures—" Bradley interrupted.

The *mahout* and the equestrienne both looked at him with pity on their faces. He stopped.

"The rest are most likely on the ground," Rajesh said. "I doubt there are many survivors, if the carrion birds are feeding freely."

Bradley shook his head.

"You have my condolences," Lacey said. The words were stiff, but a terrible pity burned in her eyes.

"No. No, you're wrong. You don't see that's not possible." He couldn't seem to stop shaking his head. "We're survivors, my family."

"We need to scout to see if the danger's gone," Rajesh said to Lacey. "We need supplies, weapons, but we may need to swing wide around the town if the aether-sick monsters are feeding." He ignored Bradley, as if they weren't discussing impossible things right in front of him. It wasn't possible that his family was gone. It wasn't.

"I'm fastest on a horse," Lacey said. "I'll go."

Rajesh nodded. He straightened and reached down to pluck a narrow brass tube from beside his seat. "Telescope." He tossed it to her. "Keep your distance."

She nodded grimly. Then she clapped her heels to her mare and galloped away toward Fredrickston, the small town of free blacks that held all the family Bradley knew. Toward the carrion birds.

"She doesn't need to scout," Bradley said to Rajesh. It was difficult to talk; his lips felt numb. "They're fine. I'm sure they're mostly fine. They could fight off an attack. I'm sure it's safe now. I'll go look." Yes, that was a good idea, he decided. Lacey might think there was nobody there. A well-bred white girl couldn't understand how well successful escaped slaves could hide. They could have fought off monsters and then hid. That would make sense. He nodded. "I have to look. They're probably hiding. They won't know it's safe."

"*We* don't know it's safe," Rajesh told him. "Wait until Lacey gets back."

"They might need me." Bradley stared around with blind eyes. Everything blurred together. Horse. He needed a horse. He stumbled over to the closest wagon hitch.

"Hey! That's my horse!" protested Leah, the aerialist.

He ignored her. His fingers fumbled over the buckles. His world narrowed down to the worn leather straps. One buckle came undone, and he moved on to the next.

The horse was almost free when the thud of hoofbeats signaled Lacey's return. He didn't look up. Whatever she might say didn't matter, he told himself, because she didn't know where to look. He heard her sigh.

"Dead," she said flatly. "They're all dead. The doors are all caved in. There are bodies lying out in the main street. They've been there some time. The vultures are feeding undisturbed. There's nothing alive in that town, not even a dog."

The last fastening resisted him. It. Just. Wouldn't. Go. His hand tightened. His muscles flexed. Pain radiated through his hand, leather creaked, and the buckle ripped free. He dropped it and hauled himself up on the back of the horse, ignoring the burning ache in his hand where the leather strap had cut into his palm. Blood dripped down his fingers and stained the snow. He bent low over the back of the horse, wrapped his hands in its mane, and kicked it into a gallop. He plunged forward along the winding dirt road that led to Fredrickston. Behind him, the aerialist shouted a protest and the *mahout* called out, "Wait!"

Bradley smelled the town before he saw it. His stomach churned at the stench, like raw pork left too long in the sun. The horse tried to turn away, but he jerked its head back and goaded it on. It went reluctantly, dancing sideways at the slightest rustle in the trees.

Then they rounded the last bend in the road, and he saw home. Except it wasn't home. Couldn't be. Home had hardworking families and well-maintained houses. Home had children playing in the street. Home didn't have broken doors half-hanging on their hinges, or snow drifting across abandoned thresholds. Home didn't have gnawed corpses sprawled across doorsteps, or a carpet of carrion birds glutting themselves on the dead.

"Go!" he bellowed, waving his arms at the birds. "Fly away, you horrible—agh!"

Tested beyond endurance, his horse reared. He tumbled off, landing on the ground with an impact that knocked the breath out of him. He lay there, struggling to breathe, listening to the horse's hoofbeats recede as it bolted back up the road. A crow hopped closer to him and tilted its head inquiringly.

Bradley gritted his teeth. He pushed himself up from the ground. He stood, swaying. He bent over to brace himself against his knees. In front of him, he saw white snow marred only by the bloody handprint he'd left beside a fallen branch. He stared at that handprint until his head cleared and his breathing evened out, and then he looked up.

The vultures and crows had gone back to their feeding. They ignored him entirely. Bradley's jaw tightened. The birds thought humans had no power to stop them. Anger bloomed in him. He grabbed the fallen branch in front of him and ran forward, shouting something unintelligible even to himself. Crows exploded into the sky in a startled cloud. He swung at the fleeing crows and missed. The vultures raised their heads, staring at him with beady eyes. He charged them. They flapped their wings and took to the air.

He stopped in the middle of main street, panting. Vultures wheeled above. Crows huddled in the trees, watching him. Waiting.

Bradley remembered shooting marbles in the street in front of the dry goods store with the other boys. They always started playing under the giant pine tree that grew in the center of Main Street, but their game always expanded until they took up half the street. They'd kneel in the dust and play for swirlies and aggies and milky cat's eyes until somebody chased them out of the road.

A crow perched on the railing in front of the dry goods store now, a pale white marble in its beak. A pink thread of flesh dangled from it. Bradley turned from the sight and stumbled away from the main street, trying not to look at the corpses sprawled through the town.

Behind his Aunt Hattie's house, laundry was hanging out to dry, though half the clothes had been blown down. When he was thirteen or so, Aunt Hattie had always sent him out to hang up the laundry, despite his protests that laundry was women's work. Sheets blew in his face as he walked between the laundry lines. A lost half-smile bent Bradley's lips.

He almost tripped over the body. He put his hand out to catch himself against the laundry line. The cord cut into his injured palm, but he didn't notice the pain. A young mulatto girl lay swathed in fallen drifts of linen. Blood and other liquids had soaked through the sheets and crusted them to her body. Hollows where there should have been curves promised horrors unseen.

Her face was untouched, and that was the worst thing. Bradley had never met her, but she bore a strong resemblance to his Aunt Hattie. Recognizing a new member of his family this way created a tangled-up knot of grief and wistfulness in his heart. He should have come back to visit earlier. Now it was too late.

They can't all be dead. He called out and no-one answered, but they were probably all hiding. His family hadn't survived slavery to end like this. He just had to find the survivors, that was all.

He pushed back the village well cover and squinted into the darkness. Something pale bobbed in the water far below, but nothing answered his call.

He went to the little hollow covered by bushes where he'd always hidden when his older sister was on a cleaning rampage, or if his Papa found out he'd done something bad. He squatted down and pushed the bushes aside.

Movement. Bradley tensed.

A mouse popped its head up out of a nest of leaves and squinted at the invader of its home. Bradley let the bushes fall closed again and stepped back. Life went on, after all.

Then he saw the furrows in the dirt. Four crooked lines dug deep near the roots of the bushes and then faded away, as if somebody had scrabbled at the dirt as they were being pulled out by the ankles. It would have taken a small hand to leave marks with that narrow of spacing between them: a woman's hand, or a child's.

Bradley was barely old enough to remember when his family fled slavery, but he found his memory of their hiding places coming back to him as he searched Fredrickston for survivors. He investigated root cellars and ransacked closets. He poked his head into dusty attics and belly-crawled under porches. He held his breath and lowered a lantern into latrines. He tapped walls and stomped on floors, listening for the telltale hollow sound of a hidden passage. He peered inside chicken coops and tossed aside hay bales in case there was room for a person between them.

He found only gnawed corpses and the remnants of their struggle for life: bloodstains, smashed furniture, and weapons twisted into scrap metal and tossed away.

Only one of the aether-maddened monsters had been killed, and that by his own hand. Bradley found the body inside a small, whitewashed house. A woman's mauled body sprawled across the bedroom threshold. Her soft innards had been devoured, and large chunks of flesh had been chewed off. Half her face was gone; the half that remained bore a peaceful expression, as if death had erased some unendurable knowledge. A hand-carved wooden cradle sat beside the blood-splattered family bed. The aether-sick man lay on the bed, clutching two rifles pointing at where his face had been. He must have rigged both of them to fire at the same time to be sure his brain was completely destroyed. It would have taken great willpower to clear his head long enough to follow that plan. He had been deep in the grasp of the aether sickness. His clothing was torn at the seams where muscles bulged through. Bone spurs erupted from his shoulders. The hands that gripped the rifle barrels were twisted into clawed monstrosities. Only something truly terrible could have shaken him loose from the madness long enough to kill himself.

Bradley turned away and left the room.

~ * ~

Dainty Miss Eads, Who Flies Through the Air Like a Bird of Paradise!
Fredrickston, Pennsylvania

Leah tugged nervously on her orange hair ribbon as the circus wagons rolled into Fredrickston. Bodies sprawled everywhere. It was worse than Boston. Here, nobody was left to bury the dead.

"They're all dead," murmured Pamela, her fellow aerialist.

Before Leah could answer her, Michael echoed her unspoken thought. "There ain't even anyone to bury them."

Left without anything meaningful to say, Leah shot a sideways scowl at the interloper in her wagon. *She* should have been the one with the profound answer to Pamela's comment. This was the aerialists' wagon, after all. Michael should have been with his precious monkeys.

Her irritation grew when she realized that neither Pamela nor Michael noticed her displeasure. Pamela stared adoringly up at Michael, and Michael gazed down at her with an idiotic smile that was quite inappropriate for their surroundings.

The circus was trapped among the dead. The equestrienne may have scouted ahead to check for danger, but nobody really knew if it was safe. One of those monsters could be lying in wait. Ahead of them, there was a loud bang like the slam of a door. Leah's muscles tensed, just as they always did before she dove off the trapeze platform, but there was nowhere for her to fly to.

A horrible howl echoed through the town. Leah flinched and curled into a protective ball.

The howl broke apart into ragged sobs. Leah uncurled enough to peek over her knees.

The strongman staggered out of a small whitewashed house farther down the main street. He clutched his hands to his chest, as if he were trying to cover some terrible wound. Leah held her breath, waiting for the monster to burst out of the house and attack them.

A long minute passed. She couldn't bear to look. She closed her eyes and turned to bury her face against her sister aerialist's shoulder, but there was no shoulder there for her to rest against. She leaned forward more. Still no shoulder. She cracked one eye open.

Pamela had leaned *away* from her! Her dearest friend, closer to her than any sister, had chosen to nestle up against that—that *animal handler*. Why, he was hardly better than a roustabout!

The instant she had that thought, Leah felt ashamed, but it didn't take away the hollow of hurt that Pamela's desertion left.

At the head of the circus caravan, the Indian mahout threw the lever that transformed his curious brass-and-bone elephant into a fearsome war machine. He reined the beast in front of the wagons and waited for the attack. Leah wrapped her arms around herself. She wished she had a rifle, and that she knew how to use it.

The other circus members readied their weapons and waited. The only sounds were the impatient stamping of the horses and the disjointed sobs of the strongman. In the distance, a crow cawed.

"If there were monsters here, they would have attacked by now," the Indian *mahout* said eventually. He moved the elephant out of its guard position, but Leah noticed that he didn't transform it back into its peaceful configuration. "Causing a false alarm is highly irresponsible!"

The veiled fortune teller stepped down from her wagon and walked toward the strongman, who had collapsed to sit slumped in the center of the street. "Let me," she said to the *mahout*. "He must have seen something terrible. The poor man."

In the aerialists' wagon, Pamela shivered and quietly asked, "Do you think we're safe?"

"You heard the *mahout*," Michael said. "They ain't here. They moved on. Like wolves looking for new prey."

"New prey—that's us!" Pamela shuddered and leaned closer to Michael.

Leah felt a spurt of irritation. "So what you're saying is that nobody knows if they are here or not, and nobody knows where they might have gone. That's terribly useful!"

"You think you can do better?" Michael demanded.

"Maybe I can!" Leah ignored the hurt look that Pamela gave her and jumped down from the wagon. She stalked down the main street, past the strongman and the fortune teller, to a kind of island in the middle of the street where a giant of a pine tree towered above a bench and a hitching post.

Leah hopped onto the bench. She launched herself from it and alighted on the hitching post. Her landing was picture-perfect, her balance as perfect as a tightrope-walker's. She glanced over her shoulder.

Pamela wasn't even looking in her direction. She was already paying attention to Michael instead. Leah gritted her teeth and reached up to a branch above her head. A good upward pull with her arms and a swing of her legs, and she sat astride the branch. Her skirt was a hindrance, but she could manage it. She pushed herself up to stand on the branch, hiked her skirt, and tied it up above her knees. Then she reached up for the next branch.

In that way, she swung herself up the pine tree like a monkey, until she attained a height above any of the surrounding houses and trees. She could see all the way to the horizon. The world seemed very large, and she felt very small.

The circusfolk gathered below the tree. "Do you see any sign of where the monsters may have gone?" Ginger called up to Leah.

"I can't see any other towns nearby," she said. The words came out so quietly, they were almost a whisper. Annoyed with herself, she cleared her throat. If there were monsters nearby, they would have heard the ruckus raised by the strongman. There was no reason for her to be quiet. Still, she had to force herself to raise her voice enough to be heard by the circusfolk below.

"I can't see any other towns nearby that the monsters might have gone to attack. No rooftops. I don't see any smoke in the distance. No other carrion birds, either." She felt rather flat as she admitted, "I suppose the monsters really are all gone, after all. Oh, wait—" She squinted. "Is that—? I think I see smoke in the South. Wait. No. It looks like there was a rockslide. I think I'm just seeing dust in the air. That's all. I'm coming down now—you all better move out of the way if you don't want pine needles in your face."

"Wait!" Leah heard a note of hope in the strongman's tear-ravaged voice. "What rockslide? Where?"

"South," Leah said. "There's an old run-down shack with a chute coming out of it and some kind of tower collapsed behind it. A granary, maybe? The rockslide is right beside it."

Leah heard a scuffle below her.

"Wait!" shouted the fortune teller.

"If you're going to be a damned fool, at least take this!" the Indian *mahout* said.

Something thumped against the ground, and then footsteps thudded into the distance. Leah clung to her branch. "Um, what just happened?" she called down.

When the fortune teller responded, she sounded sad. "The strongman muttered something about finding their hiding place and bolted for the trees. Heading South. He's not thinking clearly.

It's hardly safe out there. A few monsters could still be lurking nearby."

Lacey the equestrienne spoke for the first time. "Should we go after him?"

"The man needs to be alone. He'll come back," said the fortune teller.

"What if the monsters are in the woods?"

"Then maybe he won't come back. Doesn't matter. Right now, he needs to be alone more than he needs to be safe."

"If he runs into a monster, he's got a fighting chance," the *mahout* said. He continued to speak, but Leah stopped listening.

Something much larger than a squirrel had rustled the branches above her. She wasn't alone.

~ * ~

Gloria Brehm
Near Fredrickston, Pennsylvania

Darkness.

"I haven't heard him in a long while," Gloria ventured. "Maybe he's gone and left us."

"Maybe."

Most times, Gloria found her common-law husband's silent strength reassuring. She appreciated that Bosley didn't natter on about unimportant things. Buried in a cold, dark hole under the ground, however, she would have welcomed the distraction.

"Why didn't he give up and leave with the rest of them?"

A long silence. "Don't know."

Gloria thought back to what now seemed like an idyllic life, despite growing hardship and her oldest remaining son's illness.

"Every time you went up to the mine, you always promised you'd come back," Gloria said softly. "Maybe some part of him remembers."

Bosley didn't answer.

She wished she hadn't said it. She wished she hadn't thought it. It was easier to think of her son as gone. She'd had three of her six children sold away. She understood the pain of losing a child. This was worse.

A little voice piped up. "Mama, I'm thirsty."

Gloria wrapped her arm around her youngest son. "I know." She gingerly explored the floor until she found their water pitcher. It weighed almost nothing. "Here, child. Open your mouth."

She didn't want to risk spilling even a drop in the transfer between pitcher and cup, so she placed the pitcher spout against her son's lips and tilted the pitcher for him to drink. After he pushed it away, she upended the pitcher above her own mouth to catch the last precious drops of water.

Her parched throat made it hard to speak, but she managed. "Bosley, this mine is mighty damp. Is there water down here somewhere?"

"Mine water ain't good for drinking."

"It's all we've got. There's no more water in the pitcher."

A long silence. Then, "Tear up your petticoat. I'll put rags against the dampest spots. We can wring 'em out to get a little bit."

She rustled about in the dark, untying her muslin petticoat and slipping it off. Tearing the thin material was pitifully easy. "It's ready."

A lucifer match rasped against sandpaper and hissed to life, a sound Gloria cherished after the long dark days of their confinement underground. She shielded her eyes against the bright little light and squinted until she could make sense of the illumination.

Bosley lifted his lantern's glass, lit the wick, and then turned it down to preserve precious lamp oil.

Gloria's daughter blinked at her from the other side of the mining chamber they'd settled in. Coal dust coated Louisa's already dark skin, but it didn't hide the gauntness of her cheeks or her cracked and bleeding lips.

Gloria gasped. Her thoughts churned as she tried to remember when her daughter had last asked for the water. "Louisa! Why didn't you say you were thirsty?"

Louisa gazed back at her with steady dark eyes. "The baby needs it more. I know you and Daddy weren't drinking."

"Yes, but—oh!" Gloria pressed her fingers against her eyes to stop the tears. Moisture was too precious to lose. Once the threat receded, she picked up the pile of torn petticoat rags and handed them to Bosley. "We need any bit of water you can find," she told him.

He nodded and took the rags. In that moment, she hated him a little for not offering false reassurances.

"I have to stoke the ventilation fire, too. I'll be back in a while." He hunched forward and pushed himself to stand.

The rustle of his clothes as he moved almost covered the other sound. Gloria put out her hand and caught his arm. "Wait. What's that?"

The scraping sound came again. Bosley's shoulders slumped. "He's back."

"I don't think so. Listen."

Dislodged pebbles rattled. Something metal clanged against the rock blocking the mine's entrance.

"Is he able to think well enough to use a shovel? He couldn't earlier."

Thud. Clang. Thump. Rattle. Thunk-ka-thump-bump. *Thud!*

Gloria wrapped her arms around her waist and hugged herself.

Bosley reached out and patted her shoulder. She caught his hand and held it.

"Don't fret yourself," he said. "A shovel alone won't do it. The rocks will just tumble down to fill the gap. You need to brace it."

"With timbers?"

He nodded.

"Like the ones lying beside the mine?"

He nodded.

"But you'd have to be thinking clearly to use those," she said. "Our boy would have to be himself again."

The scrape of something heavy being dragged carried clearly into the mine, as did the thump and creak of it being wedged into place.

Bosley nodded again. "Timbers."

Gloria tightened her grip on his hand and reached out with her other arm to embrace her daughter. Her little son buried his face in her skirts. At the mine entrance, the sounds of heavy labor continued. The shovel clanged against stone. Rocks thudded into the ground. Timbers groaned as they were wedged into place. As the digging sounds grew louder and nearer, the sound of harsh panting echoed through the mine. Gloria pulled her children closer. Part of her wanted to call out to their rescuer, to hope that her son had returned to his senses and come back to help his family. The larger part of her feared what might answer her call.

They huddled silently in the dark, quiet as church mice. Without a word, Bosley turned up the lamp wick to its full brightness. There was no need to save lamp oil now. They all stared at the blocked-up entrance to the mine, as the sounds grew closer and closer.

When the first chink of light appeared, Gloria flinched as if from a blow. She'd spent the last few dark days longing for sunlight, but now she feared what it would reveal.

Another seam of light joined the first, and another, as fallen rock was cleared away. Sunlight shone through a hole in the stones. A large, callused hand reached through and began clearing the last layer of rocks away.

Gloria swayed. Her son had inherited his grandmother's narrow, delicate hands. Their rescuer's hands were large and blunt-fingered, calloused and scarred from fieldwork.

"Hello?" she called. "Hello? We're in here!"

Those large hands cleared out more stones. Rock fell and timbers groaned, but their rescuer's pace didn't slow. Finally there was enough of an opening for a man to fit his head and shoulders through—even a man as large and bulky as their rescuer.

He thrust his head through and looked at them. Despite the sunlight seeping in and the brilliance of the oil lamp turned up to its full strength, he squinted as if he couldn't quite make out their faces. The mine shaft must seem shadowed and dim to him, Gloria thought. After days in pitch-dark, she felt like she was being flooded by light.

"Who's there?" he asked, his voice as ragged as if he were the one who had gone without water.

"Gloria Brehm and my man, Bosley Gravel, and our children, except for—"

"And the others?" he interrupted.

"I'm sorry?"

"The others! The others who are with you. I know some of my family must have gotten away. I'm Bradley Roberts. You must know the Roberts family. Surely some of them are with you? They know how to run, you see, and how to hide. They must have gotten away."

"I'm very sorry." Gloria felt a sinking sensation in her chest, as if she'd swallowed an anchor that was pulling her down. "We're all there is. Is the town—?" She couldn't bring herself to say it. She knew the answer anyway. If anyone had been left alive, they would have come up to clear away the rockslide days ago.

"No. No." Bradley turned his head from side to side and squinted into the shadows, as if he could conjure his family up through force of will alone.

"I'm very sorry," Gloria repeated.

Bradley pulled back, sending a shower of pebbles rattling down. Gloria stepped closer to the hole. Fresh air swept past her, sweet and cold. The light blinded her, and tears streamed from her eyes as she peered out.

Bradley stood about ten feet away from the mine entrance, his back to them, his shoulders heaving. He muttered something that Gloria couldn't hear.

"What?"

"I didn't come back in time," he repeated. "I didn't come back." He collapsed to sit on the ground, his head buried in his arms. "I didn't come back."

"I knew your family," Gloria called through the hole in the rock. "They were so proud of you, for going out and making something of yourself."

He shook his head.

Her mouth tightened. They had all lost family. They had all known pain. Even before the killing storm had swept down on Fredrickston, Gloria's life had held more loss and sorrow than any person should bear. You went on, that was all. You gritted your teeth and you took it.

"Bradley Roberts!" she said sharply. "You can't lie down and give up when something bad happens! If your family had done that, they would have died slaves. We've all lost family. I bet every single person still alive in this country has lost people! My own son—"

A chill seized her. In the relief of rescue, she'd forgotten something crucial. If her son wasn't the one digging at the mine entrance, *where was he?*

She pressed herself against the opening. "Listen!" she shouted. "Bradley! Bradley, you have to listen to me! Our son has the madness. He's been hanging around the mine entrance for days. You're in danger! Do you hear me?"

The big man straightened his shoulders. He turned around to look at her. He opened his mouth, as if to finally answer—and a growling fury struck him from the side and bowled him over.

Gloria backed away from the hole in the rock-slide, the back of her hand pressed against her mouth. The tears in her eyes were no longer from the bright sunlight. Her boy had come back.

Gideon growled through a mouth twisted into a perpetual snarl. Overgrown teeth sprouted from his mouth like the petals of an exotic flower. He moved awkwardly, without the grace that Gloria remembered her older son possessing. He had been tall and slim, a good-looking young man who sauntered on his way. Now, overgrowths of bone locked him into a lopsided hunch. Knots of muscle made his movements jerky, though inhumanly strong and fast. His clothes were torn. His hair was matted. His ribs showed through the holes in his shirt. He was so emaciated and dirty that Gloria's heart went out to him even as she backed away.

Bosley ran forward and began pulling at the rocks around the entrance. "Got to help him!"

Gloria couldn't bring herself to ask which *him.*

Outside the mine, Bradley rolled and heaved himself up. He'd barely gotten to his feet when Gideon snarled and lunged forward, sinking his teeth in the big man's shoulder. Bradley yelled with pain. He raised one massive fist and slammed it against Gideon's ear. Gideon howled and let go.

Inside the mine, Gloria collapsed to the ground and covered her eyes with her hands. She heard the clang of metal and then the *thud-crunch* of the shovel hitting something soft. She shuddered as if she'd been the one struck.

Gideon wailed.

Another thud.

A low growl.

Bradley yelled, "Get down!"

Gloria heard her son yelp in surprise, and then her husband's arm was around her shoulders, bearing her to the ground. Her hands were knocked away from her face. Her eyes flew open.

Whompf! The day outside exploded into fire.

~ * ~

Dainty Leah Eads, Who Flies Through the Air Like a Bird of Paradise!
Fredrickston, Pennsylvania

Pine needles rustled. Leah froze. She stared up. The hairs on the back of her neck prickled.

The branches above her parted to reveal a small face staring down at her. Leah's breath gusted out in a sigh of relief. The little boy clinging to the tree above her couldn't have been more than three years old.

"Oh, little one," Leah cooed. "It's a miracle you're still alive!" *Never mind how you got this high up a tree to begin with!* "Come here. Let Leah take care of you." She wrapped her legs around the tree trunk to anchor herself and stretched her arms out to the boy.

He launched himself at Leah so quickly that she barely caught him in time. She pulled him into an embrace, her heart pounding. "Hold on tight, little one," Leah told him, shifting his weight to her hip so that she could carry him with one arm. "We'll climb down very slowly. Then you'll meet the circus! You'll like us. All children like the circus. Our strongman will be so happy to—agh!"

The child sank his teeth into Leah's arm and worried at it like a dog at a bone. Leah screamed again. Tears of pain rolled down her cheeks. She grabbed at the boy's face, trying to pry him loose. He growled. She jammed her fingers into the side of his mouth to force him to open up.

The child opened his mouth and let go so suddenly that he was falling before Leah knew what was happening. She grabbed for him too late. He struck a branch below her, rolled off, and kept falling. His eyes widened. He wailed in terror. Her last glimpse was of little, flailing hands reaching for something to cling to.

Leah clung to the tree trunk, weeping, as she listened to the child's fall. Below her, branches rustled and snapped until finally there was a decisive, sickening thud.

"Out of my way!" Doc Janzen shouted.

Leah leaned her forehead against the trunk. No child could survive a fall from that height. Her body shook with sobs. Her mind insisted on revisiting the moment when she'd tried and failed to save the boy, over and over again. She was deaf and blind to all else.

When her tears had run dry and she'd stopped shaking, she wiped the back of her hand against her nose and used her skirts to blot her tears. Her shoulder ached. Though she dreaded seeing the boy's crumpled body, she had to climb down before it became so inflamed that she couldn't support her weight with her arm.

She climbed slowly down the pine tree, wincing every time she saw snapped branches or blood on the bark.

Nobody looked at her when she jumped the last few feet out of the tree. Everyone had gathered into a huddle around Doc Janzen, who knelt beside the child's still body. She must have made a sound—a groan, perhaps—because Pamela looked over and saw her.

"Leah!" Pamela cried, abandoning Michael's side and running over to fling her arms around her.

Leah winced, bringing her hand up to protect her wounded arm, but it felt good to have proof that her sister aerialist still cared.

Pamela pulled back. "Oh, you're hurt! We'll have to make sure Doc sees you once he's done with the boy!"

"Done with?" Leah repeated numbly.

"Oh, yes! Doc says he'll live. It's a miracle! Whatever happened to your arm, anyway?"

"The boy bit me. I was holding him and—" Leah stopped talking when Doc Janzen leaned back and stared at her.

"What was that?" he demanded.

"I said that the boy bit me when I was holding him. "

"Hellfire and damnation! I was afraid of that. His injuries are healing before my eyes." Doc Janzen gestured at the crowd. "Everyone, get back! This boy has the aether sickness."

A gasp went up. "Kill it!" shouted the midget. "Kill it now!"

For once, the midget's wife was not on his side. She thumped her fist into his arm, not gently. "He's not an *it*! He's just a child, hardly more than a baby. And the poor thing has no parents."

"Probably ate his parents," the midget grumbled, rubbing his arm.

"No," a strange woman's voice said, speaking with the slow molasses accent of Southern blacks. "Both his parents had the sickness. If they left their baby behind, it was because he couldn't keep up with the pack."

Leah circled around the cluster of circusfolk so that she could see the stranger. Pamela didn't move to stay by her side. For a second, Leah felt like she'd left something precious behind, but the feeling was eclipsed by curiosity.

The woman who had spoken carried a young boy on her hip and clasped the hand of a girl leaning against her. A wiry man with an old whip-scar on his arm stood protectively near. Memory haunted their eyes as they looked around the remains of the town. Coal dust coated them, but it didn't hide their gaunt cheeks or their cracked and split lips.

Despite that, they still looked better than the strongman. Leah wondered if another rockslide had come down on top of him. That would explain the bruises rising under his skin and his new collection of cuts and scrapes. It didn't explain his sudden lack of eyebrows, though, or the foul perfume of singed hair that accompanied him.

Pamela gasped. Leah thought it was because of the strongman's appearance, but Pamela's next words disproved her theory. "They left their own baby behind? That's terrible!"

Leah would have comforted her, but Michael was faster. Two steps, and he had his arms around Pamela. "Some animals abandon their children after they're old enough to fend for themselves," he offered. "The boy is aether-sick. He's fast and strong and able to hunt his own food. That fall would have killed any of us."

Pamela sniffed and managed a watery smile. "You know just what to say," she whispered.

Leah snorted and didn't bother to keep it quiet. Pamela must be the only one who found it comforting that the boy could "hunt his own food." Upon hearing Michael's theory, everyone else stared at the boy uneasily.

Lacey the equestrienne pushed herself out of the crowd. "He's a threat to us—to the circus," she said. Her face could have been carved from stone. "Without the circus, what are we? If we lose our acts and our animals, we'd become refugees, dependent on the mercy of others."

"With or without the circus, we are still human beings!" the fortune teller answered sharply.

"Shouldn't you let his family decide?" the strange woman said. "And use the boy's name when you're deciding whether or not you're going to kill him."

Silence fell. "What is his name?" Lacey asked.

"Paul Fischer."

"Fischer ..." the strongman said slowly.

"That's the name of the man your sister Minerva married," the strange woman said. "The boy is your nephew."

The strongman swayed and fell to his knees. "Still alive," he said brokenly. "One is still alive."

~ * ~

After that, we could hardly kill the child in front of him. The strongman swept the child into his arms and carried him off to his wagon. He never let go, even when the child sank his teeth into his hand. The doctor followed them, muttering about restraints and sedatives.

We stayed in Fredrickston to help the Brehm family bury the dead and reinforce the most defensible houses. We offered to let them travel with us, but they refused.

"What would we do?" Gloria asked. "Beg to stay in the fort that abandoned us to die? Offer to be house servants? Field workers? Slaves? No."

The strongman halfheartedly attempted to change their minds, but the child took up most of his time. It was all he thought about.

It was all most of the rest of us thought about too. Every meal ended in an argument over what to do with the child. Every conversation was really about the child, even if it wasn't. By our *last evening in Fredrickston, half the circus wasn't speaking to the other half.*

In the end, the debate didn't matter. The child disappeared the night before we began the journey to Fort Augusta.

I owe everything I now am to that child. Because of him, the Indian mahout made his bargain with me. The child traveled with us, you see, though none of us knew it at the time. We didn't see him again until much later, when he almost got us all killed at a guard post outside of the only city still free of aether-plagued madmen.

What Happens Next

Author's Note: A few characters from *A Circus of Brass and Bone* have seen fit to reveal the ends of their stories to me. When they don't contain major spoilers, I am sharing them with you.

The Circus

Michael the animal handler does in fact return to New York to see his monkey, Mr. Ben Doom. By that time, Mr. Ben is the proud papa of a noisy, chattering troupe of baby monkeys, and Michael is starting a family of his own. His first son shows signs of becoming an excellent contortionist.

Adele Murray, the unnamed-in-this-book third sibling of the conjoined Murray sisters, uses her leverage with Rajesh to persuade him that they should be the first ones to be taught to use his war elephant, thus increasing (though not guaranteeing) their safety.

Boston

Patrick persuades **Dr. Fallon** to marry him. She claims she agreed because "he was the only man with sense enough to bring me dead bodies to examine instead of flowers."

Valentine regularly visits **William** and his mam. After a little while in her presence, he looks less like a hard man.

Mayor Padgett's aching arm was unfortunately a sign that he was to be among the third wave casualties of the aether storm.

Seppanen Town

Francis and **Clara** are happily married. She only sometimes threatens to get the shotgun.

Mrs. Della Rocca is still famous for her buttermilk biscuits, though these days strangers are likely to remain conscious long enough to ask for seconds.

New York

Rosie Sasse is being courted by the big sailor that Ginger introduced her to. Neither she nor most of her family know quite what to make of him, but she's begun to look forward to his visits, even if she doesn't realize it herself yet.

Mama Sasse did lose her arm, but she insists that it is easier to get things done with one arm, because everybody else has stopped arguing when she tells them to do something. Her only real regret is that it will make it difficult to scoop up and cuddle any future grandbabies. She knows exactly what to make of that big sailor who's courting Rosie.

Cast of Characters

The Loyale Traveling Menagerie, Hippodrome, Circus, and Museum of Educational Novelties

Mr. Ben Doom, a douc langur monkey.

Pamela Dyer-Bennet, an aerialist, The Daring Miss Dyer-Bennet, Who Dives Into Thin Air!*

Leah Eads, an aerialist, The Dainty Miss Eads, Who Flies Through the Air Like a Bird of Paradise!*

Ginger, the whitefaced clown

Alis Gray, the snake charmer

Michael Hunter, an animal handler*

Dr. Christopher Janzen, the doctor, The Great Doctor Panjandrum and His Amazing Panacea That Cures All Ills!

Christopher Knall, the ringmaster- and clown-in-training

Mr. Loyale, the ringmaster and owner of the circus

Jonathan Matzke, the skeleton man, The Man So Thin He Wears a Wedding Ring As a Belt!

Lacey Moeller, an equestrian, The Fabulous Lady Equestrienne Who Defies the Fiery Rings of Death!*

Adele, Betty, and Roxane Murray, conjoined sisters, A Medical Miracle Alive Only by God's Grace!

Rajesh, The Hindoo Mystic and His Fearsome Aether-Powered Bone-and-Brass Elephant!

Bradley Roberts, the strongman, The Negro So Strong He Can Carry a Mule Under Each Arm!*

Ms. Selena, the fat lady, The Fabulous 600-Pound Fat Lady Who Dances the Five-Step Waltz!*

Madame Tonya Wershow, fortune teller extraordinaire

Genevieve Woodward, The Girl Sharpshooter With the Eyes of an Eagle!

Introductory Scenes

The Culhanes

Mrs. Du Voix (born Marcella Simmons)

Jacob

The Johansens

Mina

Gerhardt Yoder

Johan Yoder

Wilhelm Yoder

Boston

Dr. Elizabeth Fallon

Mrs. MacDougal

Mrs. McCormack

William McCormack

Mayor Arthur Padgett

Mr. Roger

Patrick Sullivan*

Mrs. Tienken

Robert Tienken

Chad Valentine

Roderick White

Seppanen Town

Clara

Margaret Della Rocca

Francis

Lindsay Kleinman

Cathy Williamson*

New York

Peter Akrill

Brenda Anderson

Captain Angie Endo

Commissioner Andre Guirard

Mrs. Andre Guirard

Barbara Hobbes

Mrs. Nave

Deborah Rowan

Mama Sasse

Papa Sasse

Rosie Sasse

Pablo Virgo

Fredrickston

Gideon Brehm

Gloria Brehm*

Louisa Brehm

Paul Fischer*

Bosley Gravel*

* *Tuckerized names changed or not revealed previous to this edition.*

Glossary

Arkansas toothpick, a heavy dagger with a long blade balanced for throwing but also useful for thrusting and slashing. Up through the late 1830s, this blade was also used for dueling in what are now the Southern United States.

asana, yoga positions originally used in the seated position for meditation.

barker, referred to as a "talker" by circus folk, the carnies who talk up the attractions to lure customers in. *Circus slang*.

batman, a soldier assigned to an officer to act as a servant, usually a combination valet, messenger, and cook. Also known as a dog-robber.

butcher, a refreshments vendor who walks around the circus. *Circus slang*.

chapati, Indian flatbread, served with practically every meal. *Hindi*.

colleen, an Irish girl. *Irish slang*.

coppers, policemen.

corn pone, a very traditional, very simple fried cornbread eaten all over the United States (where it goes by many names). Probably early settlers learned how to make it from the Pawtuxet. The basic recipe is cornmeal, water, a pinch of salt, and some grease to fry the cakes in. If you were lucky enough to have them, buttermilk and eggs might be used as well.

Cossack drag, a horseback riding trick where the rider hangs upside-down off the side of the horse, held on only because her feet are hooked through special straps.

fakir, a Muslim or Hindu ascetic. Usually they beg or perform "miracles" to support themselves.

fractional currency, small cent notes. Coin hoarding was so common during the Civil War that by the end of it there was almost no coin left in circulation. During the war, and for a bit after it, the Northern government issued small cent notes for amounts between three and fifty cents (the higher denominations were frequently counterfeited). These were inspired by the original practice of using postage stamps as change.

golem v., to use aether to constrain/control/power a creature or person.

Hic locus est ubi mors gaudet succurrere vitae, Latin for, *"This is the place where death delights to help the living."* Signage frequently found in autopsy rooms. The quote comes from Giovanni Morgagni, a physician from the 18th century who originated the anatomical concept of human disease. The full quote is, *"Let Conversation Cease. Let Laughter Flee. This is the Place Where Death Delights To Help the Living."*

horsecars, trolley cars pulled by horses along railroad track, used in larger cities. They were an intermediate step between stagecoaches and trolleys.

howdah, the covered pavilion on the back of an elephant or camel, in which passengers may ride.

jeff, a rope. *Circus slang.*

king pole, the center pole of a circus tent, the pole which is put up first.

league, an archaic English unit of measurement, usually about three miles. A league was intended to be the amount of distance a person could walk in an hour.

lucifer, a match. Early friction matches caught fire explosively and smelled terrible, leading to them being called lucifers. Even after the process was improved, the slang term persisted.

lumina, plural of lumens, a unit of luminous flux equal to one candle's intensity.

Maharana of Udaipur, a title given to an Indian prince, like Maharajah. During the colonial period in India's history, Udaipur was one of the more powerful princely states.

mahout, Elephant driver and caretaker. *Hindi.*

moue, an irritated grimace or pout. From the French.

noblesse oblige, A French phrase that means a person of higher position must act honorably for the good of those s/he has a responsibility to.

paddy, derogatory slang for an Irishman, used because so many were named after Saint Patrick.

panjandrum, a powerful personage or pretentious official. See *The Great Panjandrum* by Samuel Foote.

pip, in this context, "one extraordinary of its kind." Short for 'pippin'. First used in 1797.

pranayama, yoga breathing practices.

pratfall, a humorous fall on the buttocks, from *prat* (buttocks) + *fall*.

pukka, authentic, first-class. From Hindi *pakka*, for cooked, ripe. Became British slang during the occupation of India.

queer the pitch, to interfere with or spoil the business of a tradesman or showman. Traveling showmen call the place they set out their stall a 'pitch'.

railer, advance scout for the circus. His job is to ride ahead and find the best road for them to take. When the road forks, he finds the roads that lead away from their destination or dead-end in a muddy bog, and he takes a rail from a farmer's fence and uses it to block off those paths.

rakshasas, Hindu demons, prone to typically demonic behavior like consuming flesh or blood, desecrating religious ceremonies, and possessing people.

retiring, a practice up through World War II in which women were expected to retire after dinner, to a retiring room, and leave the men to their port and cigars and purportedly more intelligent conversation.

shanghaiing, the practice of using trickery, alcohol, drugs, or violence to get a sailor working on a ship against his will. So named because this technique was frequently used to secure sailors for voyages to eastern Asia. The use of unfree labor aboard merchant ships was common up until 1915.

shillelagh, a long stick with a weighted head, usable as a walking stick and as a weapon. *Gaelic*.

shrub, a refreshing fruit drink made with vinegar to give it extra zing.

sky grifter, a tent-revival preacher who's out for what he can get. *Circus slang*.

spark, to woo or court. *Slang*.

Striders, the fire aether tanks used in the Civil War. Fire-spitting tanks that walked across battlefields on their "giant mechanical chicken legs." Term original to *A Circus of Brass and Bone*.

talker, also known (pejoratively) as a barker, a carny who talks up the attractions to lure customers in. *Circus slang*.

thunder mug, a chamber pot, specifically a large china mug with a lid that fits under the bed so a person does not have to get up and walk to an outhouse in the middle of the night.

tiffin carrier, an Indian 3-tier stacking metal meal container.

tintype photography, also known as ferrotype photography, very popular for a few decades after daguerreotypes. The photograph was printed on a metal plate (not tin!), making it more durable and able to be shipped through the mail. The quality was not as good as in other photographic processes, but the cost was cheap, making portraits affordable to the lower classes. Itinerant photographers in the late 1800s used this technique.

townies, non-circus people. *Circus slang*

ventilating furnace, a furnace in the bottom of a ventilation shaft, used in the time before the electric fans became widespread. The heated air rose, causing a draft that pulled in fresh air. Without ventilation, the miners would be breathing bad air. Of course, the ventilation furnace was a terrible fire hazard, as was demonstrated by the Avondale disaster of 1869.

War of the Rebellion, a term used to refer to the Civil War, widely in use in the North in the immediate aftermath of the Civil War. Also called "The Great Rebellion." By contrast, Southerners called it "The War Between the States" or "The War for Southern Independence."

water closet, a bathroom. Victorian-era bathrooms in wealthy houses were the size of any other room, and they were decorated in a similar style, with wallpaper and paintings and carpet and couches and chairs. The toilet itself was kept in a small closet inside this room, hence the term "water closet."

wouldna, would not. *Irish dialect.*

The Story Behind the Story

The original working title of this story was *The Circus of Brass and Bone*. It began as a serial story after my mother, Cookie Wiebe, was diagnosed with advanced (Stage 3c) ovarian and endometrial cancer. When my parents found out, they were working at a school in India. That complicated things.

Because they were working in India, they didn't have health insurance. My mother's first plan was to get treated in India, where the costs are lower, but when the first attempted surgery didn't go well, the decision was made to come home to America for surgery and treatment. This meant leaving behind both of their jobs.

Because my parents spent much of their adult life helping others—working with farmers in Africa, teaching in India—they didn't have much in the way of savings that could help with the costs.

No health insurance.

No jobs.

No savings cushion.

Desperate need of treatment for a serious diagnosis.

Eventually, my mother was able to get medical insurance despite having a preexisting condition, but the cost of her care was still quite high. Writing and sharing *The Circus of Brass and Bone* helped to raise funds to contribute toward her expenses, and it also allowed news of her situation to reach friends (old and new) who were able to help.

She survived about 15 months after being diagnosed with ovarian and endometrial cancer. I don't say she struggled or battled or fought, because she didn't like using violent imagery to describe it. She endured it with remarkable grace, and it seemed to leave her outwardly untouched for a very long time, even as it spread through her body. Up until the very end, she would run—and then walk—along the Sand Creek bike path, taking photographs that were displayed in a gallery exhibit after her death.

In the last year of her life, she was able to do much. She saw her photographs from India exhibited in an art gallery. She held her first grandchild. She rejoiced in hearing from many of the people whose lives she had touched over the years. She told me how much it mattered to her that she got so much support from friends, family, and even total strangers who knew of her only from news articles or from *The Circus of Brass and Bone*. During the darkest days of her treatment, my mother found inspiration and comfort in the kindness of strangers.

One of the last things she did was to celebrate her 33 1/3 wedding anniversary. People came from all over the world to see her, to honor her life, and to say goodbye.

She died because breathing became just too difficult. When my aunt, a nurse, told my mother that she thought my mother would probably die that night, my mother's response was to give her two thumbs up. She was ready to go. And when she stopped breathing, she smiled before she died.

Her last coherent words were to my dad: "I love you."

She lived a rewarding and adventurous life, though we all wish she could have stayed with us longer. Mom, this one is for you.

"You might not have to die ..."
An Essay by Cookie Wiebe

When hiking in the Himalayas in the '90s, I categorized the drop-offs at the edge of the trail according to the probable end result:

They might not have to carry you (i.e., you might not even get injured).

You might not have to die (your injuries might not be fatal)

They might not find you (self-explanatory)

This summer vacation I've been thinking somebody's definitely going to have to carry me and I might, in fact, have to die. I've not been well for several months and have been chasing doctors and lab tests trying to figure out what the problem is. Most of my symptoms are consistent with ovarian cancer. However, most symptoms of ovarian cancer are not specific to that and can occur for other reasons—which is why it is often not diagnosed until stage three or four, when it has already spread. Suffice it to say I've been "uncomfortable" in the entire abdominal (did I almost say "abominable"?) region. While tests are ongoing (some of which are inconclusive/non-diagnostic) and while an ovarian cyst has been detected, we are waiting for an endometrial biopsy report to be followed by removal of an ovary, lab tests, etc.

'Nuff said about the medical side. What I wanted to say, is that I've been thinking about dying. Scary things will do that to you. It is heartening to discover that my philosophy about end-of-life and bad things happening to good people (assuming that includes me :-), are already fairly well thought out and intact, due to previous "bad things" happening. Here are the main conclusions I have arrived at since age 27 when the first really bad thing happened.

1. God will not allow anything to happen to me that will not further his kingdom.

That's the only ""guarantee" I can count on and it is predicated on my being willing to be used for the good of the Kingdom of God. Knowing God loves me, cares for me, and is actively involved in my life is no guarantee of a happy life, a healthy life or life at all. I arrived at this conclusion following two critical incidents. The first was the premature birth and death of our second child, Bethany Ann, as a result of multiple, congenital birth defects. She died on her due date after spending her entire short life in a neonatal intensive care unit in another state. After Bethany died, I became somewhat obsessive compulsive about safety: checking the pilot light on the gas cook stove multiple times (including during the night), checking if the doors were locked, etc. I prayed every night for safety, imagining the house burning down and other disasters happening, but had a hard time believing that God would intervene, thus the need to look after ourselves. I remember thinking about other tragedies that God had not averted. There was a toddler who slipped down a well and could not be rescued in France, there were dissidents murdered in Guatemala. Surely, there were Christians suffering as well as non-Christians. How could I hold on to a theology that presumed special protection for some, yet, if I followed that line of thought to its inevitable conclusion, implied a judgment even on the most unfortunate of God's faithful? I had to let go of the "promise" of protection and hope it's loss did not mean a greater loss of faith.

This pattern of fear-based prayer continued in spite of a relatively strong Christian faith otherwise. In 1989, we went as Mennonite Central Committee (MCC) volunteers to Chad, Africa for a three-year term as agricultural and community development workers. While I hope to put my entire journal online eventually, the most exciting part is when we were robbed by deserting soldiers during the coup d'etat that brought current president Idriss Debi to power. Overlooked by the French embassy in their evacuations and unable to drive out due to the number of deserting soldiers on the road, we were sitting ducks. It was only a matter of time before a jeep pulled up and five guys with four machine guns got out. Dave and I looked at each other and said, "We're going to be robbed". It is our most exciting story from

Chad, but I won't tell it all here, other than to say that we emerged unscathed, though significantly poorer. We were each (Dave, myself, and 10-yr. old Abra) taken into the house one by one, and at the end—one of the deserters wanted to take me with them. Through the entire time, we believe that God guided our actions and our words in such a way that it set the tone for what was essentially a very polite robbery without injury to anyone and which, in the end, made the leader tell the other guys to "leave her".

This event, together with Bethany's death, led me to the conclusion that God's protection is for God's purposes alone. It is not a promise of a long, happy, or healthy life—or—life at all.

2. It's okay to die.

Between 2006 and 2008, both of my parents died. My father died of Alzheimer's and my mother most probably from congestive heart failure and other issues. My father went into his "long good-bye" as gracefully and gently as I had known him to be throughout his life: With humor, with humility, and with a sense of overall peacefulness that I think, came from a life well-lived and a heart that assumed the best of everyone and forgave, to the best of his ability, those who had hurt him. My mother had grown up in a much less emotionally healthy environment and had gone through life always fearful that she would anger someone (like her doctor—by asking questions) and get less good care. She spent her life focused on providing for the future, acquiring a huge collection of fabric and art supplies for that day when she would be finally "organized" enough to have time to do all of the artistic things she wanted to do. (Her biggest donation to charity was probably the pickup load of fabric and the boxes of art supplies given to The Et Cetera Shop, the MCC thrift store, after her death). My father died peacefully in his sleep. My mother died after two days of physical reactions that made her struggle to sit up in bed, often with a grimace on her face. In spite of her Christian faith and expressed readiness to die (when she was still able to talk about it), the end of life was a difficult path to walk with her. Watching their ability to care for themselves and, ultimately, to interact with others, desert them over the last year or so, the end did not seem such a loss. It seemed appropriate and the time had come to say "good-bye". With the help of hospice and the care of the nursing home staff, their last days were as painless and comfortable as possible.

They both died in their own room, in their own bed, surrounded by all of their children.

The last thing I would want to do is linger on in some half-life, unable to act and interact with Dave and Abra, family, and friends. Death is not such a fearful thing that I must avoid it by clinging to a life that is difficult for me and for those who love and care for me. I do not want years of anyone's life to be focused on prolonging mine! I want my family to LIVE, rather than to have their lives constrained by stringing out my dying. It's okay to die.

3. A long life and a full life are not necessarily the same thing.

If, indeed, I do have some dread disease that will shorten my life, boy, am I ever glad we didn't just sit in Newton, KS! We did, as one friend suggested, "what the rest of us wish we could do" in going to Africa as volunteers and now twice to Woodstock School in India. We didn't do these things after getting all of our affairs in order (retirement provided for, daughter's college saved for, etc.) We did them in spite of some rather dramatic financial effects—if you consider lost income/savings. So many people, it seems, think they can wait until some perfect time (like retirement) before spending years as a volunteer in another part of the world. Tell me, what guarantee do they have that when they retire, they will a.) think they can finally "afford" to be a volunteer, b.) have the desire to go through culture shock and acclimate to different country/culture, and c.) have the good health and good marriage (if married) that will allow them to do so? Given the obesity rate in America and the increase in lifestyle-related health concerns, who can count on being healthy enough to do anything more exciting than walk the dog and click the remote by the time they retire?

I may not have a long life, but I've had a wonderfully full one. And yes, some of that fullness has been extremely difficult and painful. Yet, I wouldn't trade even those experiences (and the growth gained) to be younger again. I've a wonderful husband for over 32 years; we've walked together through raising Abra, losing Bethany, hosting Sophia, two extremely difficult job situations which devastated my sense of calling/mission for years, and all of those adventures in Chad and India: scorpions and a baby cobra in the living room, observing the entire fast of Ramadan one year, driving "lost" for hours following a trail of bent grass, telling students "you're not going to die, but you're going to get really, really cold" when lost at sundown while hiking in the Himalayas, being advisers to a group of 14 students from 7 countries, making friends across cultures and religions. Not to mention all the animals we've had: dogs & cats (of course), a calf (in town), chickens, ducks, rabbits, owls, goats, donkey and even a baby monkey.

I have not waited for some other time to do and go and experience. And now, I'm really, really glad! As Bill Hybel says in his book, Holy Discontent, "In what other life are you going to go all out?" Amen.

4. My life isn't any shorter today than it was yesterday (before possible dread disease)

If I believe my life is in God's hands (and believe me, every time I've ridden in a taxi or bus down the mountain from Mussoorie to Dehradun, I KNOW it's not in my hands!), then my life—in total—hasn't changed. My life expectancy isn't any different today than it was a year ago. I may know more, in a few days, of what to expect and when, but I'm not sure the actual timing for Cookie, in God's eternal plan, has changed at all. It's the same as my philosophy about the "end of the world": It shouldn't change the way I live my life. I should always be living in the light of an eternal awareness, willing to be used by God, not just when the end is in sight.

5. My goal is to empower my loved ones to move on.

Good relationships are a lot easier to grieve, and then to be able to move forward. I want my husband, my family, and friends, to be able to grieve (yes, I hope they mourn me!), but then to walk forward without anger or hurt or guilt that keeps them from enjoying life and allowing other relationships to fulfill the needs that I filled. So, if life is shorter than I knew, I will focus on what I need to do to help those who will miss me—but who have a life left to live!

6. To-do list:

I ALWAYS have a list of things to do. ...If life is shorter than expected (or maybe, even if not), I'd like to:

Put a lot more on my website www.charitableliving.net that reflects the things I've thought about, as well as my journal from Chad, speeches, etc.

Write a lot more letters/respond to emails and be a lot better about keeping in touch. Maybe even make some phone calls.

Have an exhibition of photos, primarily portraits. It would be great to do it at a Final Friday gallery in Wichita since we went regularly for so many years.

Go home in time to have the house arranged like it will stay for the next five years after I'm gone. Dave does not like change, and if the house is not "homey" when I go, it won't be for a very long time after!

For several years, Dave and I were part of a team of four couples who shared deeply about their marriages with participating couples during Marriage Encounter weekends. The older couple on our team shared on the very difficult topic of death, thinking of their own death and its effect on their spouse. Oliver and Elizabeth's talk brought tears to many an eye and modeled a way to share, even about the prospect of dying, with one's spouse. While we shared other difficult topics, we did not present that one. While it's a topic no one wants to think might actually happen (me included), no matter what the diagnosis is, the process of thinking "what if I'm going to die?" has been good.

Peace,
Cookie

What do you think about your own death?

"You might not have to die ..."
Discussion Questions

In July 2010, while waiting for test results, I wrote the following essay. In October 2010, I added discussion questions for each point for use in our Sunday School class. Below are the shortened points and some questions.

When hiking in the Himalayas in the '90s, I categorized the drop-offs at the edge of the trail according to the probable end result:

They might not have to carry you (i.e., you might not even get injured).

You might not have to die (your injuries might not be fatal)

They might not find you (self-explanatory)

This summer vacation I've been thinking somebody's definitely going to have to carry me and I might, in fact, have to die.

It is heartening to discover that my philosophy about end-of-life and bad things happening to good people, assuming that includes me :-), are already fairly well thought out and intact, due to previous "bad things" happening. Here are the main conclusions I have arrived at since age 27 when the first really bad thing happened.

1. God will not allow anything to happen to me that will not further his kingdom.

That's the only "guarantee" I can count on and it is predicated on my being willing to be used for the good of the Kingdom of God. Knowing God loves me, cares for me, and is actively involved in my life is no guarantee of a happy life, a healthy life or life at all.

What in your life confirms/questions this conclusion?
What conclusions have you come to?

2. It's okay to die.

Between 2006 and 2008, both of my parents died. My father died of Alzheimer's and my mother most probably from congestive heart failure and other issues.

Watching their ability to care for themselves and, ultimately, to interact with others, desert them over the last year or so, the end did not seem such a loss. It seemed appropriate and the time had come to say "good-bye."

The last thing I would want to do is linger on in some half-life, unable to act and interact with Dave and Abra, family, and friends. Death is not such a fearful thing that I must avoid it by clinging to a life that is difficult for me and for those who love and care for me. I do not want years of anyone's life to be focused on prolonging mine! I want my family to LIVE, rather than to have their lives constrained by stringing out my dying. It's okay to die.

Whom have you watched die?
What makes it an "okay" time to die?
What is a "good" death?

3. A long life and a full life are not necessarily the same thing.

I may not have a long life, but I've had a wonderfully full one. And yes, some of that fullness has been extremely difficult and painful. Yet, I wouldn't trade even those experiences (and the growth gained) to be younger again.

I have not waited for some other time to do and go and experience. And now, I'm really, really glad! As Bill Hybel says in his book, Holy Discontent, "In what other life are you going to go all out?" Amen.

What's on your "bucket list"?

4. My life isn't any shorter today than it was yesterday (before possible dread disease)

If I believe my life is in God's hands, then my life—in total—hasn't changed. My life expectancy isn't any different today than it was a year ago. I may know more, in a few days, of what to expect and when, but I'm not sure the actual timing for Cookie, in God's eternal plan, has changed at all. I should always be living in the light of an eternal awareness, willing to be used by God, not just when the end is in sight.

How does your sense of eternal timing affect how you live your life on a daily basis?

If you knew you only had six months to live, what would you do differently?

5. *My goal is to empower my loved ones to move on.*

Good relationships are a lot easier to grieve, and then to be able to move forward. I want my husband, my family, and friends, to be able to grieve (yes, I hope they mourn me!), but then to walk forward without anger or hurt or guilt that keeps them from enjoying life and allowing other relationships to fulfill the needs that I filled. So, if life is shorter than I knew, I will focus on what I need to do to help those who will miss me—but who have a life left to live!

Do you have "unfinished business"?

What can you do about it now?

Conclusion:

For several years, Dave and I were part of a team of four couples who shared deeply about their marriages with participating couples during Marriage Encounter weekends. The older couple on our team shared on the very difficult topic of death, thinking of their own death and its effect on their spouse. Oliver and Elizabeth's talk brought tears to many an eye and modeled a way to share, even about the prospect of dying, with one's spouse. While we shared other difficult topics, we did not present that one. While it's a topic no one wants to think might actually happen (me included), no matter what the diagnosis is, the process of thinking "what if I'm going to die?" has been good.

What do you think about your own death?

Acknowledgments

To my supporters:
Without readers like you, this story would never have existed. It's been a privilege to travel with you.

Peter Akrill * Brenda Anderson * Hannah Barnett * John Bennett * Marisa Brandt * Gloria Brehm * J. Buell * Ben Cragg * Ben Doom * Margaret Della Rocca * Pamela Dyer-Bennet * Leah Eads * Chad Elstad * Angie Endo * Elizabeth Fallon * Paul Fischer * Bosley Gravel * Andre Guirard * Barbara Hobbes * Michael Hunter * Betty Janzen * Christopher Janzen * Lindsay Kleinman * Christopher Knall * Tracy LaChance * Lynna Landstreet * Christine Lloyd * Alice Marks * Cali Mastny * Jonathan Matzke * Jessica Miller * Adele Murray * Roxane Murray * Katie Nave * John Nickerson * Renee Perry * Jessica Reisman * Brad Roberts * Deborah Rowan * Rosemary Sasse (and family!) * Tesla Seppanen * Vaughan Stanger * Charles Stevens * Patrick Sullivan * Margaret Taylor * Robert Tienken * Pablo Virgo * Chad Valentine * Richard Walters * Cathy Williamson * Tonya Wershow * Genevieve Woodward * Conrad Zero